The Second Coming

A NOVEL

Tariq Mehmood

Daraja Press

Published by
Daraja Press
https://darajapress.com

© 2024 Tariq Mehmood

ISBN: 978-1-998309-27-6

Library and Archives Canada Cataloguing in Publication

Title: The second coming : a novel / Tariq Mehmood.
Names: Mehmood, Tariq, author
Identifiers: Canadiana 20240504526 | ISBN 9781998309276 (softcover)
Subjects: LCGFT: Novels.
Classification: LCC PR6063.E46 S43 2024 | DDC 823/.914—dc23

A dystopian, desi mash-up of *The Handmaid's Tale, Clockwork Orange*, and *V for Vendetta. The Second Coming* warns of the dangers of right-wing nationalism and white supremacy and imagines where such hate could take England if it is not, somehow, nipped in the bud.

> – **Paul Cochrane**, journalist, *Middle East Eye*

A must-read dystopian fantasy about race, religion, and love. Unmissable

> – **Melvin Burgess**, novelist, winner of the Carnegie Medal and the LA prize for Teenage Fiction

An unforgettable novel, both vivid and nightmarishly plausible.

> – **Peter Kalu**, novelist, storyteller, playwright and poet

A story of resilience and hope told against the brutal realities of patriarchy and colonial violence.

> – **Amrit Wilson**, activist, feminist, and author of *Finding a Voice: Asian Women in Britain* (Daraja Press)

PART 1 – BEFORE CONCEPTION

PART 2 – AFTER CONCEPTION

ACKNOWLEDGEMENTS

Thank you, Nuvpreet Kalra and Anandi Ramamurthy, for critical insights; students from the American University of Beirut for commenting on earlier drafts, especially Alaa Al Hajjar for reading over the manuscript in the midst of the Israeli onslaught on Lebanon; and particularly Colin Smith for scientific support on genetic mutations; Tima El Jamil for advice on trauma; and Firoze Manji of Daraja Press for tirelessly transforming my writing into a book worthy of publication. Special thanks to Phil Griffin for correcting so many of my errors.

This book is part of a triptych of novels: three separate stories all taking place in the same imagined world. *Three Bullets* by Melvin Burgess, *One Drop* by Peter Kalu, as well as my own, all take place in the UK as it might be in the near future.

BEFORE CONCEPTION

THE PROPHECY

On my way to and from college, I stopped counting how many Muslim houses and shops had been boarded up with 'Pakis Out' scrawled across them. Some were nothing but burnt-out shells, others marked with crucifixes.

I was on the 266 bus coming back from college, thinking about how I was going to make it to med school when Muslims might be chased out of London. Ash, next to me, was completely absorbed in his phone. His eyebrows dipped and rose in quick succession as he scrolled, the curls of his shoulder-length hair bouncing with the rhythm of the bus. I couldn't help but steal glances at him. Suddenly, his head popped up, and he shouted, 'Scotland's declared Independence!'

The breaking news here was that this first-year engineering student found any news interesting.

'We're stuck in traffic, who cares?' I said, pushing him away with my bum.

At least the Scotland news had jerked Ash to life. He began talking about centrifuges and gimbals.

I was enjoying his presence next to me in this overcrowded bus filled with teenage sweat. Leena, my cousin and best friend, sat next to the cheeky little Zainab Ali at the rear of the bus. Leena is 22, and me and Zainab will be 18 this year. Me first by two days, but I still make her call me Baji, elder sister.

I could feel the glare of their eyes on the back of my neck and was waiting for one of them to come out with some cheesy comment or other to wind me up. I didn't have to wait long. Leena must have noticed me, and Ash all cushy together, let out a loud, 'Aah, butterflies!'

I look back at them disapprovingly. Leena elbowed Zainab and then whispered something to her. Zainab winked at me with one of her big green eyes. Her pursed lips told me she had mischief in her mind. I frowned at her. She placed an index finger on her lips and went into a thoughtful silence. Usually, when she did this, she was searching for a couplet from her favourite Urdu poets, and would throw the words at me, not caring I didn't understand much of the language.

But sometimes I did, and then I loved the places they took the two of us, especially when she explained what she thought the poet meant. But today, the last thing I wanted was some romantic poetry thrown at me on a crowded bus. I turned away from her, hoping against hope for what might come.

Zainab raised her voice, pointed her open hand at me, and said a couplet she had often said, 'Maen Kiya Kahoon Kay Mujhey Saber Kiyoon Nahin Aata, Maen Kiya kahoon kay Tujhey Dekhney ki Aadat hai.'

Before I could say anything, Leena loudly translated bits of Zainab's words and added a bit of spice of her own, 'What can I say why I am so eager for it? What can I say when I can't remember what Zainab said?'

I was so embarrassed; I could have killed her. I frowned big style this time. Zainab adjusted her dark blue hijab. I would have loved to swipe that smile off her face if she had been closer to me. Leena wore a black niqab and even a pair of black gloves. She'd been doing this ever since being dumped by her boyfriend. I shifted a bit and gave her the two-fingered "I'm keeping an eye on you" sign.

'Ya Allah, save Leena,' Zainab said.

The girls laughed loudly, and a white man in between us suddenly turned around and shouted, 'Speak English!'

'It's Willesden,' I said.

'Vah Marah Vah!' Zainab roared as though she was praising a poet.

The girls giggled loudly. What a stupid reply you gave, Marah, I thought; you should have called him a racist pig, I thought, looking at the man.

He must have been around 50, my dad's age. He had short brown hair and a thick pink neck with an England flag tattooed on it. He glared at me. He had a twitchy, stubby nose.

'You're one of them, Fucking Muslim, aren't you?' he said, nodding to Zainab and Leena.

'She's an atheist,' Leena shouted from the back.

'All the fucking same,' the man said.

I didn't know what upset me more, the man or Leena, but I went to the back of the bus and asked, 'Anyone got a spare hijab?'

Zainab pulled one out of her bag and gave it to me. I put it over my head and went back to the man. Ash filmed me on his mobile.

When the man saw me coming, he stood up. He stank of tobacco and beer.

Leena and Zainab ran up the bus. They must have thought he was going for me.

'Don't you dare touch her,' Zainab shouted.

I straightened up to the man and said, 'Yeh, so what you going to do?'

Zainab was already next to me, Leena beside her.

The bus stopped. The doors opened. A gust of cold air rushed in.

The man pushed past me and got off the bus.

Leena and me watched him disappear as the bus pulled away.

'What a snake,' Zainab said.

'Yeh, but who put the poison in him?' I asked, repeating one of Mum's phrases.

'That's so poetic, Marah,' Zainab said, putting an arm around me.

I turned to Ash, 'What's with you and filming?'

'I've never seen you wearing a hijab before,' Ash said, and then added sheepishly, 'But I forgot to press the record button.'

I elbowed him in the ribs.

'You know, Baj, it's been a week since I came across a pig like that gora – last one threw acid at me, Shukhar Alhamdolillah, thanks be to God, I jumped out of the way,' Zainab said.

'I would have socked this one if he'd touched you!' I said.

'And I would have sent him to hell without his balls,' Leena added, holding her hand up in the shape of a claw.

We laughed and then Zainab grabbed Leena's claw hand, then took mine by the wrist and stopped mid-sentence, 'You know girls.'

'What?' Leena and I asked in unison.

'Fancy getting these done?' Zainab asked, placing her nails next to ours. She turned to me and said, 'Stop biting yours.'

Hers were near perfect, with a bit of growth beyond the light green nail varnish, and Leena's were covered in a fading black.

'Let's,' Leena replied.

I wasn't bothered and kept quiet.

'And then mendhi, henna, my present!' Zainab said.

We all got off at the next stop, and I asked Zainab, 'Mendhi?

'Yeh, like pretty patterns on hands, arms and feet,' she replied, waving, showing me her hand and then one of her feet. She bit her lips and looked at me strangely. She's trying to play a practical joke on me. I thought.

'I'm really serious,' Zainab said, walking next to me, 'It's for an engagement.'

'Whose?' I asked.

'Mine?'

'Yours?' I asked.

'His name is Saleem, but you've not met him. He's as tall as Ash, his hair is as long as his, but he is, thank God, not an engineer, and has a soft voice, just like a poet,' she laughed. It was the happiest I had ever seen her, but she still glinted with mischief in her eyes.

'Where did you meet him?' I asked.

'Lucky bag job, as you would say,' she laughed.

'Arranged?' I asked.

'Mum introduced us, and we met a few times.'

'Are you really going for the lucky bag job?'

'Well, Mum and Dad had one, and they been together for 30 years, so how bad can it be?'

'Aren't you worried about anything?' I asked.

'Yeh, he lives in Scotland, and I have to move there.' Before I could reply, she added, 'I'm coming to your house on Friday night, and me and you will do our own mendhi and then have the girls done for the Engagement Hen Night in two weeks from then.'

'When's the wedding?' I asked.

'Oh, that won't be before I graduate,' she laughed.

Like Zainab, Leena too had a mischievous look on her face, and the way they were looking at each other, they clearly had a secret between them, and I was not privy to it. Maybe this marriage thing is some bullshit, I thought.

'What's cooking between you two?' Leena asked, nodding at Zainab.

'She's getting married,' I said.

'That's great news, nothing like a wedding to get laid quickly,' Leena said.

'You are so bad, Leena,' Zainab said, nudging her with a shoulder, 'maybe that's why I love you.'

I nodded, trying to figure out what they were up to, as Zainab left us with a wave in the air.

Ash trolled a little ahead. Leena held my hand. She lit a spliff and took big drags as she walked along.

'So,' she said. 'when's it going to be?'

'When's what?' I asked.

'You two get it together?' she replied, raising her voice so Ash would hear. He turned. His eyes looked guilty. 'Me and Marah?' he said, all fake astonishment.

'Ugh, with him?' I said to Leena. 'Never.' But I kept my eyes on Ash. He had stopped walking now and was leant up against a railing with his phone out.

'Look, he's waiting for you,' Leena said.

'Probably texting his girlfriend,' I said.

My mobile buzzed. It was a text from Ash: Can I walk you home?

'So he is,' laughed Leena.

Ash came towards us. 'Can I walk you home?' he said out loud this time.

'No!'

''Ya Allah, I can't take this, I'm leaving,' Leena said.

'You walk me home, Leena,' I pleaded.

She dismissed my request with a flick of her eyebrows and left us, laughing to herself. Ash and I stood silently close to each other for a short while. A gentle wind pushed his hair across his face.

'You can walk me halfway if you like,' I said and put my arm through his. We walked all the way home.

The main window to our house was boarded up – all the Muslim houses on our street had had windows smashed recently. Ours had been like this for over a week. The rock that had been lobbed through it had a red cross painted neatly on it. Dad insisted on getting the insurance company to pay for a repair, but they were dragging their feet as this was the third incident. Mum wanted him to fix it, and so this became another front in the war between Mum and Dad.

'End of days in my house,' I said to Ash, 'unless you like the mottling effect of cheap plywood.'

Ash squeezed my hand.

'Want to come in for a coffee?' I asked.

'I'd love to, but I'd better be going. Got to be up for the field trip tomorrow.'

THE DIVISIONS

Mum saw me through the window as I got to the drive, and she put her hand in front of her mouth in shock. What was that about? I frowned back at her, stepped into the driveway and opened the door.

Inside, both Mum and Dad were playing statues in the hallway, staring at me, eyes wide. Chilli barked and came running from the kitchen but screeched to a halt by the stairs. Chilli was our German shepherd. He got his name from the fact that he loved spicy food. He was my best family friend and always came to me for a pat and a hug, ears erect, tail wagging. Not now, though. He crouched down and whined.

'What?' I asked, dropping my bag on the floor.

Mum's gob had switched to a grin, but Dad still glared.

They kept up their stare-a-thon. Tats, my younger brother emerged from his bedroom, sat on the top stair and looked down.

I thought quickly – what could the issue be? Maybe I forgot to wash up this morning before going out, as it was my day. Maybe Tats had stolen money and had blamed it on me? But neither of those could explain Chilli. Chilli would still have bowled into me.

'Alright, so you're getting divorced?' I said. 'Come on, then, say it!'

'You are utterly shameless, Marah,' Dad blurted.

'Oh, it's not that bad,' Mum said.

'How can you do this, Marah?' Dad asked. His voice was a bit shaky like he was about to cry, something he rarely did.

Had he seen me with Ash? OK, he didn't like Ash, but I'd invited him home enough times. Surely, that couldn't be it. Maybe I smelled of weed? But they both knew I hated the idea of smoking anything, and besides, they couldn't have smelt that through the window. But how to explain Chilli?

'She doesn't look that bad,' Mum repeated.

It seemed her hand had got stuck in front of her face.

Suddenly, it all made sense. I was wearing hot pants. Dad was angry with me for going to college in my hot pants.

'Get over it, Dad. It's really none of your business if I wear hot pants, and if you think it is, then why the heck did you marry someone like Mum?'

'I don't care how you dress,' he said.

'Well, what's your problem then?' I asked

'Just because we don't believe in God doesn't mean we insult our religion,' Dad said.

'She looks rather cute, if you ask me.' Mum dropped her hand. Finally. She had a proud motherly smile.

I stepped forward, looked at myself in the hallway mirror and could have died. I was still wearing the hijab. Hot pants and the hijab! No! I grabbed my bag and ran upstairs, red with embarrassment. Chilli barked and ran past me. He was already on the end of my bed by the time I got there.

I felt sick to the stomach. Everyone must have been laughing at me on the bus.

My bedroom was on the first floor at the front of our house. It was a large room with bay windows. I kept my tiny dolls, rabbits, pandas and my wobbly woodpecker neatly arranged according to which birthday I got them. Above them was a copy of my very first published poem. It made it into the annual school magazine, and Mum had the page framed for me.

The thing I kept organised was my bookshelf and my desk, which was at the opposite end of my king-size bed. My bookshelf was divided into two sections: *School* and *Mine*. My clothes were scattered artistically around the room, so the room had suffered no Mum Invasion. Mum liked to say I was ADHD and wanted me to undergo a test, but I kept telling her she was the one who needed one for OCD because she was always tidying things that didn't need tidying.

Every inch of wall space had posters up. The centre stage above my bed was taken by Ariana Grande – a black and white poster of her, with the words *Dangerous Woman* written in large letters at the bottom. I bought it when I went to see her live. When I was really cross with my brother, I would blast her song, God is a woman, because he hated it, and Mum loved it. Next to it was a smaller poster of two male figures urinating in graffitied toilets. One of these was the half-naked green-bodied Hulk and a sort of weedy little Spider-Man. I had initially put this up to wind Dad up, but over time had come to really like it as it reminded me of my dad's lovable, annoyed face.

I flung the hijab on the floor, jumped onto my bed, sank my head into the pillow and tried to disappear until Tats, the brother, came into my room without even knocking and said, 'Hijabi Hotpants!'

I threw a pillow at him. He slammed the door. The pillow hit the back of the door.

Chilli stood up on my bed and looked at me.

'I am such an idiot, I am, Chilli,' I said, stroking him. 'And you're sooo lucky because you can never make a fool of yourself, can you? Are you fed up with me as well, Chilli, are you?'

Chilli barked in agreement. I patted him on the back. He jumped off the bed. I opened the door for him, and he left. Then I texted Leena:

Me: You're such a cow.

Leena:?

Me: Why didn't you tell me?

Leena: Tell you what?

Me: Tats just called me Hijabi Hotpants.

Leena: Moo

I got angry and rang her.

'How can you find it so funny?'

'Do you fancy a drink?' Leena asked.

'I hate you,' I replied.

'I got some vodka.'

She knew I didn't drink and loathed even the smell of it. It was always on the breath of Mum and Dad every night.

'I thought you were a Muslim again,' I said.

'I need a drink. Shall I come round to yours?'

'No.'

THE NIGHT OF THE SWINE

3

My cousin Leena has a habit of popping in and out of my life. She is back now, and it's like she never left, but a few months ago, she was a student up in the north in Bradford, West Yorkshire, studying Peace Studies at the university there. Then she was a cliché of a pacifist, complete with a rainbow-coloured headband, brown tasselled khaki jacket, wore purple striped pyjama bottoms she claimed were trousers, and loved all things living, and hence became a vegetarian. Of course, she still claims to love animals and can't resist spicy lamb chops.

From what she told me about her life in Bradford, I don't know if she ever went to class because she was forever on demonstrations, or banging a new lover, and then she joined some socialist militia but left it when it started calling for an Independent Yorkshire. Miraculously she managed to graduate, and she said she hated London and was going to live in Bradford, but then came back to London when the Bloods began their attack on the city. She never tired of telling me how much money the Bloods were getting from the US. Sometimes, she would end by saying, 'And Amreeka is giving them the new drone-fired cruise missile,' or 'And they now have a new Amreekan dog drone.'

Before going on the Peace Studies course, she used to disappear to the 'Safety Training' courses in Barnet. As time went on, I learnt that she had joined the Territorial Army, and one day she told me, in the strictest of confidence, that she was going to sign up to join the British Army with the aim of getting into the Parachute regiment. She'd kept it a secret from everyone but me, and I told Mum, who told Dad, who laughed, this pissed Mum.

'Well, is it true you've joined the British Army?' Mum asked when Leen next came to visit.

We were having home-made kebabs.

'I've only joined the TA, Aunty. Honestly,' she said. She looked at me. I looked away. 'And it was you who got me to join the ERSP-YF (that's shorthand for the English Republican Socialist Party – Youth Front).

'But I didn't ask you to join the TA, did I?'

'ERSP did. They said the Bloods were getting too strong, and we had to have trained youth.'

Leena looked across at me. I wished the kebab in my hand could change to a magic wand, and I could just disappear. It didn't, and I cried.

'What are you crying for?' Mum asked.

'You're horrible,' I snapped and ran upstairs to my bedroom, dived on my bed and buried my head in the pillow, as I do in moments like this.

Sometime later, Leena came to my room. She stood in the doorway for a bit. I didn't lift my head. What was the point? No amount of apologies could make up for betraying her.

'I don't hate you,' Leena said.

'Why not? I'd hate me, and I do hate me.'

'You are a silly little girl and my only cousin sister,' Leena said.

I didn't know whether to laugh or cry and looked at Leena. She had brought me a plate of food. She held it out for me. As I took it off her, she grabbed a lamb chop, rubbed it on the floor, dropped it on my plate and said, 'This is for being a dirty little snitch.'

A knock on the door chased Leena's memory away. She turned up in person with a half-bottle of vodka and a can of coke. As soon as she walked into my room, she tossed her hijab and black purdah on my bed. She was wearing a low-cut black top and a blue, mid-length skirt.

'I hate the male species and will never let another one get near me again,' she announced as she plonked herself on my bed, and then she laughed.

Leena was nearly six feet tall. She had beautiful dark eyes, which looked even prettier when she dolled up her face. We made an odd couple. Maybe two of me could fit into one of her.

She picked up a tea mug from my side table.

'I'll get you a clean glass, hang on,' I said, getting off the bed.

'No need.' Before my feet touched the floor, she'd swilled some coke around the cup and lobbed the dregs out of the window.

After knocking back a large shot of vodka and coke, she told me about the new love of her life. She talked so fast; it was hard keeping up with her. I tried to imagine what her new man looked like from what she said. He was a little shorter than her; he had helicopter pilot hair all blowing in the wind; eyes so dreamy deep you could go scuba-diving in them; a kissable button nose; eternally moist lips from which only soft words spilt, and hands that could pick the petals off daisies and pull a sword out of a stone. He didn't drink or smoke, and every girl and some boys fancied him, mostly because he rode a motorbike.

He sounded exactly like Ash, I thought, with jealousy gnawing at my insides.

'If I looked like you, I'd have floored him by now,' Leena said.

'You're really not bad looking, you know, especially now that we can see you without that tent of yours and that hijab,' I said.

'Men will do anything for a woman they can't see,' Leena said. 'I'd be a virgin still if I didn't dress like that. Anyway – I think this one likes your type.'

'What's his name?'

'Can't you guess?' she replied, 'He whose smile could melt...'

' ... not just butter but a mountain,' I joined in saying one of Leena's favourite phrases.

I thought she was winding me up, but I couldn't be sure. She wouldn't cheat on me, not Leena. But I was filled with self-doubt now. Did she fancy Ash too? I went to look out the window. Chilli looked back up at me from the garden.

'So, is a dog's wagging tail more important than me?' Leena asked, leaning over me.

'He's more than a dog. He's Chilli,' I said.

'What would Chilli say?' Leena asked.

'About what?'

'About my beautiful new boyfriend,' Leena replied.

'You mean, can dogs sniff out love?' I laughed.

'No, just the lover,' Leena said.

'That's poetic," I said.

'Drinking vodka with you, what else would I say? So, do you want me to tell you who I fancy now?' Leena asked.

She smiled at me wickedly. Despite myself, my stomach knotted.

'He's coming to pick me up from here in a bit,' Leena said, picking my notebook up from the table.

I tried to snatch it back from her, but she held it out of my reach, flicked her eyebrows and asked, 'Any secrets in here, or just poems?'

'Just ideas for a poem,' I said, leaping to try to get my notebook from her. She easily fended me off. 'So, who is this new man, then?' I asked.

She opened my notebook and asked, 'Can I read your latest?'

'No.'

She flicked through the book, stopped at a page and showed it to me. There was only one sentence on the page.

She read it out. 'Which God strolls the shadows, dragging a chain of bones, on the broken path of this long night?'

'Did you really write this?'

I nodded.

'Very Goth. Where's the rest?' Leena asked.

'Don't know, it didn't want to come, so I left it,' I replied.

She turned to another page and read. 'Should I hold on to love when the world is falling apart with hate?' She stopped and looked at me and said, 'A bit Card Factory, this line.'

'True.'

She went to my page marker, looked at the page and read it aloud in a slow voice.

'Out of the ruins of a story she was writing,

she found the bones of a wounded poem.'

Leena paused, pulled my chair out from under my desk and sat on it. She held the book close to her chest, 'I wish I could write like this. Can I read the rest?'

'No!'

I thought she would ignore me, as was usual for her, but thankfully, she shut my notebook and placed it carefully on the table. But she opened the book again, took a deep breath, and began singing the words she had just read. She started each line with "Ya Allah." When she got to the word *Allah*, sometimes, she repeated it three times and the sentence twice.

Listening to her singing, no one could tell it was Leena. She had a deep, earthy voice, one that was distilled clear water. She could scale so far down that you could feel her voice inside you and then reach such a high pitch that it hurt your ears.

Unlike my godless Dad, my uncle had sent Leena to the mosque, where her singing talents had been picked up, and she had been trained to sing *hmd*s, praises to Allah, and my God, did she do these well. Now, she made my dry words come alive. In between each word, she moved her voice up and down the vocal scale so the words sounded as if they were Arabic, not English. Who would believe that my piss-head cousin Leena could sing like a Vatican choir girl but Muslim style? Really, her voice could melt a diamond. When she stopped singing, she hugged me and whispered, 'I didn't think a poem would make me cry, especially yours.'

'You really become a different person when you sing,' I said, wiping her tears with my forefinger.

She shrugged and pulled herself away.

'Singing is like acting,' she said. 'You've got to get into the character's feelings.'

'You sound like a teacher,' I said. 'But the words weren't meant to make you cry. They were meant to be a cascade of joy.'

'You can't help the poetry, can you?' she said, sitting back down next to me. She put her heavy arm around my shoulders and asked, 'Poetry just drops out of your mouth like shit out of cow's arse, doesn't it?'

'I'm painting pictures with emotions and resting them on a bed of words, that's all.'

'For fuck's sake! Can't you just talk normal for once?' she snapped.

'You daft cow, Leena!'

A motorbike revved madly on the road below my bedroom window. Leena took her arm off me and stood up.

'My man's here,' she said. She raised her eyebrows at me. I smiled back falsely, pretending my heart was not pounding in my chest.

'Don't worry,' she said, putting her gear back on. 'I'm not going to pinch lover-boy off you.'

'I don't care!'

'Ah, you're such an idiot! She got up to go, shook the vodka bottle at me and said, 'Shall I leave this for you?'

'Nah,' I replied, 'Mum and Dad drink enough for the family.'

As soon as she'd gone, I rushed to the window and sighed with relief. It wasn't Ash, of course. Leena was such a wind-up! She was with a bald, bearded man, a type she said she hated. As the motorbiker raced his engine outside, I got a text from Leena:

I've told him what to say to you.

Me:?

Outside, the motorbike roared off. Leena tossed back her head and waved goodbye. I was so annoyed with myself for letting her wind me up like that. I blushed, thinking, did I love Ash? I didn't want to love him. I didn't want to love anyone in this crazy, dangerous world.

I heard mum screaming downstairs and jumped off the bed and ran down. She was on the front doorstep, looking up and down on the street. She heard me, turned around and came back. She had a piece of paper in her hand. She gave it to me. It had upside-down red crucifixes in the corners and a graphic of a pig's head on it and the words: *The night of the pig, Cometh. LEAVE. By Order of the Blood of Christ Crusaders.*

I wasn't bothered by the image, but the words made me shiver all over. I imagined a terrifying night being chased by wild pigs.

I gave the paper back to Mum and shook my head, trying to shake the images out. She ripped it up, kissed me on the head and whispered, 'Don't worry, sweetheart, the night will pass.'

I went to the bathroom to brush my teeth, and when I came back, there was a text from Zainab:

Make sure your Mum knows re mendhi

I replied: OK.

In the coming week, our mosque fenced itself behind tall spikes and CCTV cameras, and then people started putting them outside their houses.

Mum was over the moon about Zainab coming over to do the mendhi. She spread out her old designs across the kitchen table, reminiscing about each one. Zainab arrived with the usual mischief in her eyes, carrying not only pouches of henna but also a tray full of sweetmeats. She looked stunning in her blue-laced short-sleeved top and black trousers. Her hijab was neatly wrapped, with a thin cloth holding the bun of her hair at the back. Small golden earrings dangled by her cheeks, and she wore just a hint of red lipstick that lifted her smile off her face. Her sharp eyes seemed to take in everything, but she laughed a little too loud when Mum mentioned Saleem.

As we scoffed a few laddoos, one of her favourite sweets, Zainab shared a story about her parents, something about how her father used to sell cloth door-to-door while working in a factory and how her mum once sewed a pair of trousers without a hole for the feet to go through.

Mum started singing a Punjabi song filled with sexual innuendos about bitter gourds growing long and hard. I was mortified, never expecting Mum to sing something so risqué, but Zainab loved it, especially when Mum translated it, adding even more spice.

Mum eventually pulled out a design, held it against our arms, and shook her head. After a moment of contemplation, she pushed all the designs aside and began creating something entirely new. Zainab watched intently as Mum made tiny circles on the back of our fingers, followed by small dots around them. When Mum spread the henna on our hands, it looked like a smudge to me, but Zainab just smiled, trusting Mum. When she finished on our hands, she moved to our ankles and upper feet.

As Mum worked, Zainab recited a few lines of poetry, something from Rumi, about how we were not a dot in the ocean but the ocean in the dot. Once the henna was finished, we were told to wait in the garden, holding our arms and hands still for thirty minutes or so. We sat there, talking about Saleem and the move to Scotland and laughing throughout the time.

When Mum finally allowed us to clean the henna off, our arms were adorned with the most beautiful red patterns, like intricate jewellery. The geometric designs on our arms looked like bangles, and the sunflower on our palms was the most beautiful I had ever seen. Zainab admired it quietly, her laughter replaced by a serene smile. Looking at the henna on her, she whispered to herself, 'It's like a poem written by the ghost of henna.'

This got her a great big hug from Mum.

Zainab stayed until around midnight. After Mum gave her a lift, I fell asleep thinking about Ash and woke up thinking about him. In between the two, he lost his clothes.

THE BELOVED

Ash was gone. For two months. 61 days. Here I was, falling in love with a man who had been trying to go out with me for more than a year, and now he was away on a two-month-long field trip. Which was eight weekends lost. Of course, those two months chose to become the craziest two months ever. Every one of the sixty-one days brought with it a new storm. Among the highlights were the Blood of Christ Crusaders, the Bloods as they were called, who took over London. Yes, that's right – the Bloods. The lunatic fringe of British politics had linked up with a mad new American government and proclaimed the Second Coming was nigh, and the new Jesus was on his way; Islam, Catholicism and the Church of England were declared heretic and banned, and Muslims were ordered to clear out of all English churches that had been converted to mosques. You couldn't make it up, right?

When this happened, Dad laughed at his own obscure joke. He slapped his thighs and snorted, 'Henry VIII was playing a practical joke.'

After three attempts at decoding, I figured out that Dad meant that when the sexually frustrated King Henry VIII couldn't get what he wanted owing to some religious frost somewhere deciding it was not cool, our Henry simply set up a new religion. This is exactly what the Bloods were doing. Sort of.

Mum said, 'Come back Guy Fawkes and finish these donkeys.'

This, decoded, meant Mum wished Guy Fawkes would come back and finish off what he had tried to do donkeys' of his time: blow up the Houses of Parliament, with them in it.

That's how Mum and Dad talked.

I put my head on Dad's shoulder – in our family, siding with Dad was a sure way of avoiding Mum dragging me to another protest. I believed Dad when he said, 'This is just a passing whim. This is England. People will come to their senses.'

'Pigs might fly before England defeats Englishness,' Mum said, dismissively waving her hand in the air, and continued, 'We are living through the death pangs of White Supremacy, which is fighting with its last breath to hang on to its global dominance. And here, they will unleash the monster of English nationalism. It will rise out of the embers of dying white supremacy.'

Who in their right mind would want a Mum like this if they wanted to keep their mind?

I always loved taking Chilli for a walk; no man tried anything with me then. I was on my way back, with Chilli's leash in hand, when suddenly, two police vans screeched to a halt on the corner of Olive Road and Oaklands Road. One of the vans blocked the road, and masked police in black uniforms rushed out, placing spiked metal barriers across the junction. It didn't take long for a line of cars to build up.

Whoever they're after must be seriously dangerous, I thought, as I watched the officers bark orders at the drivers. A few men, Muslim types, who protested were dragged from their cars and shoved into a van. I felt a pang of sympathy for them, but maybe they should have kept their mouths shut, I thought. I just wanted to go home.

Chilli and I waited on the side of the road for what felt like an eternity. His tail wagged nervously, sensing the unease in the air. When my turn finally came, I tried to stay calm as a policewoman approached.

'What's going on, Officer?' I asked as she began to frisk me.

'Leave!' she ordered, her tone leaving no room for questions.

This is London's new norm.

Chilli tugged at his leash, eager to get home. When I finally stepped through the door, Mum and Dad were sitting quietly, their eyes glued to a news report showing houses on fire. For a moment, I thought it was London, but then I realised from the headline that it was Ramallah, Palestine.

'You're late,' Mum said without looking up.

Unleashing Chilli, I replied, 'I had to wait to be searched at a roadblock...'

He ran off to the kitchen.

'I was worried about you,' Mum interrupted, her voice flat, still not turning to look at me.

'Did you hear what I said?' I asked, a bit louder.

'Yes, dear, Chilli must be hungry,' Mum replied.

'I put food out for him,' Dad added, not taking his eyes off the screen.

I stomped into the room, blocking their view of the TV and said, 'I was held up at a roadblock…'

'Where?' Mum finally asked, turning the TV off.

'Oh no,' Dad added, his attention momentarily diverted.

I told them, and Mum immediately launched into one of her rants, which had nothing to do with what I had said.

'To maintain its dominance, the West needs to support the Jewish supremacist entity of Israel, which at its heart is just another face of white supremacy. And all of this is tied to the need to save the US dollar, but its collapse is inevitable. I always said this would happen, but you wouldn't listen, would you?' Mum said, directing the last part at Dad.

'What difference does me listening to your doomsday predictions make?' Dad responded wryly.

I stepped out of the room. As I walked away, the TV came back to life, and they went silent.

Two months finally passed, and Ash rang me. We met on the steps of Willesden Library, where Mum worked. It was eight weeks and thirty-five minutes since we had last hugged. His chestnut brown slim leather jacket smelt funky-new, and his patchy blue jeans had an additional, faded ketchup stain on them.

I kept back a smile.

'What's up?'

'No, I like it,' I replied, referring to the new look. He had tied his hair into a small ponytail at the back of his head. He looked like a Japanese Samurai. He hugged me again, and this time all the trees shivered. Even the traffic sounded musical. The light was fading. We were in the embers of Autumn.

He thrust a box of chocolates at me. I took it, and he said fast, 'Marah, your lips are like onions. They make my eyes water.'

Oh, you bitch, I thought, and then asked, 'Leena asked you to say this, didn't she?'

He stepped back, put his hands in his pockets, and looked down, all shy and boyish. 'How pathetic can you be?' I asked.

He blushed, turned around and walked away. I followed him, and he sped up and then started running, and I followed. Yep, you got it:

there I was, playing hard to get while at the same time chasing him up Willesden High Road. When I caught up with him, I grabbed his hand, forced him to stop and said, 'I don't like onions either.'

'But I don't mind them in curry,' he laughed.

'Me too.'

'I just don't like them in salads,' he said.

'Me too."

'And I like you,' he whispered.

'Me too,' I was melting.

'You mean, you like yourself?' he asked.

'I mean, you, stupid.'

I held his hand, and this was the second time I witnessed him blush. Only this time, he didn't take to his toes. In fact, his hand stayed in mine, and we had the longest hug ever. Then, in a doorway, those eternally moist lips of his met mine, and I may have passed out for a moment. I couldn't get enough of him.

Later that evening, we went back to his parents, and the dream I'd had, the one where he'd lost his clothes, came true. We made love on a soft purple quilt filled with the scent of lavender.

Ash's ensuite room was in an annexe to the side of his double-fronted semi-detached house. He had a king-sized bed with a large carved headboard. On either side of the bed were two small tables with identical lamps, both perfectly centred.

I was thinking how messy his room looked. Ash put his underpants back on, got out of bed, picked up our discarded clothes, placed them neatly on a chair and turned around. His frown was almost as big as his headboard.

'Well, at least you know I'm not a virgin, and I'll take the morning-after pill, but you could have thought and taken precautions!' I mumbled without thinking.

'I just love you,' he stepped back, put his knee on the bed and said running his fingers through my hair.

'You're such a softy, aren't you?' I said.

He kissed me on my stomach, took his undies off, and got under the quilt again. I found my eyes closing, and I was drifting away from the noise of the world of words and the pain they paint.

I was half asleep when a bell above his door rang. Ash jumped out of bed and ran to the door.

'Who's that?' I asked.

'Mum, I told you I was busy,' he protested.

'She calls you like this?' I asked. He looked at me apologetically.

I felt all embarrassed at my nakedness seeing Ash wearing his undies. I had no idea when he put them on.

The bell jingled again.

I felt Ash tense.

'Go, if you must,' I said hesitantly.

He stepped towards the door and paused, 'Do you want to come and say hello?'

'She's used to seeing your conquests?' Even as I said this, I thought, ouch.

'You're the first,' he smiled.

'Liar,'

'I've been chasing you for three years.'

'I thought it was one,' I whispered.

The bell rang longer this time.

He left the house door ajar after him.

I could hear Ash's mum, but her voice was too muffled to make any sense. I got off the bed, dressed and tiptoed barefoot into the hallway. It had a tall, cream ceiling with a small chandelier dangling there. The side windows had royal red drapes, and halfway up the stairs, there was a large painting of drooping flowers in a Ming-like jar.

'You took so long, it really is not good enough, you know,' Ash's mum was saying. 'Today of all days is not the best day for you to be inviting anyone home, is it?'

Best you leave, girl, I thought. I turned to fetch my shoes. A small brown corgi dog ran up, stopped a jaw's length from my shins and yapped.

'Is that you, Marah?' Ash called out. A moment later, he stepped out and said, 'Come and meet the family.'

'Doesn't sound like a good idea,' I whispered.

'You heard, Mum?'

'A bit.'

'She gets like that if she doesn't get her meds on time,' Ash said, holding my hand. 'She's not that bad, really, just come and say hi.'

'OK, why not,' I said. Who was I to pass judgment on Ash's parents, given my own cartoons?

As soon as I walked into the living room, Ash's mum turned her wheelchair towards me and said, 'So you are the famous Marah.'

If there was a hole nearby, I would have dived into it.

She was a frail woman with thinning white hair. A pair of diamante-blinged glasses dangled off a gold chain around her neck. She put them on and smiled at me.

Ash's father sat in a high-back hospital chair facing a mock flame under a large wooden mantelpiece. He had a red and white plaid blanket over his knees. He had a slither of a mustache under his thin, long nose and heavily wrinkled face. He looked much older than Ash's mother. He looked at me warmly, adjusted his thick spectacles and asked, 'What would you like to drink, my dear? I have some great cognac.'

'She doesn't drink, Dad,' Ash said.

'I suppose it's against your religion. Of course, I should have known. I'm sorry to have insulted you,' his dad replied with an apologetic flail of a hand.

'It's good that Muslims don't drink, dear,' Ash's mum added.

I cringed.

'He'll ask you the same question the next time he sees you,' Ash whispered.

I smiled and looked around the room. One side was like a library. 'It's all dad's,' Ash said. I thought we had a lot of books in the house, but this was a mini-British library, with walls stacked with neatly organised books. In a central column amidst the books was a row of certificates and awards. Ash tugged my hand and showed me his favourite. Inside a carved wood frame, a scroll proclaimed its possessor was hereby given the Freedom of the Kingdom of Tavolara for Engineer of the Year.

'Where's Tavolara?' I asked Ash.

'Just past the land of fairies,' Ash's father shouted across to me.

'Everyone asks that, dear,' Ash's mother said, wheeling her chair towards me, 'and he says the same thing every time. That's engineers for you, not a scrap of imagination.'

I looked over to Ash's father, expecting a riposte. If my mum had said something about my dad, he would have thrown one of his corny lines back by now.

I must have looked expectant because Ash's mum said, 'Oh, he is just a one-sentence wonder nowadays. He's probably forgotten he said anything.' Then she turned to Ash. 'Where are your manners, young man? Get the young lady a drink.'

''What would you like to drink, my dear?' said the old man. 'I have some great cognac.'

Ash went to make a cup of tea for me, and his mum took me to what she called her study. It was in the next room, and it, too, was stacked with books. Along the way, she told me that a car accident put her in a wheelchair and ended her career as a teacher. She showed me the family photographs: of Ash as a baby in a hotel towel, Ash at nursery in a wet sandpit, Ash at Primary screaming with joy in a three-legged race, and then at Secondary, grinning in braces as he held out a football and a medal, and then at university, looking like a bonged-out suspect in a police line-up. Every time she turned to a new set of photographs, she sighed and said how she wished Ash had a brother or a sister.

It was just after midnight when Ash brought me back home on his motorbike and parked it up on the kerb outside our house. The side curtain stirred. Mum was looking down at me. Our front door had a white cross painted on it. The paint was still fresh. I glanced about. Two figures were walking away from us. One of them had a paint tin in his hand.

'Oi, you bastards!' Ash shouted.

The two broke out into a run, chucking the paint tin. Ash started the bike and went after them.

'Marah?' Mum called from the front doorstep. I waved to her to stay inside and ran after Ash.

As Mum came stomping out onto the pavement, Ash sped past the men, turned his motorbike around, jumped it up the pavement and rode directly at them. They turned and ran back towards me and Mum. They had Guy Fawkes masks on their faces. She pushed me out of the way and slapped the first one across the face as he passed. He stumbled and tripped the other man, and both of them fell.

Ash jumped off his motorbike. He stood over one of them, fist clenched and was about to hit the man. I shouted, 'Ash, stop. I hate violence. You know that.'

Ash's hand unfurled. He ripped the masks off them. They weren't men. They were white lads, about 14, my brother's age. One of them had a broken front tooth, and the other a scarred chin. The boys stared at Ash for a moment, who swore, 'Scumbags!'

'I'm sorry,' burbled the lad with the broken tooth. Ash stood on his leg.

'We want our country back,' Scarface hissed, 'but what's it to you?'

'You racist shits,' Mum cursed, stepping close to me.

Brokentooth tried to free his leg, but Ash pressed down on it. The boy cried out in pain.

'We're not racists, miss, honest,' Brokentooth said, taking a piece of paper out of his pocket, 'Here, look, we were given this with the numbers on it. I swear on my mom's life, we have no idea who lives here.'

'It's not personal, you know,' Scarface answered, 'and we got lots of Muslim mates.'

Ash took pictures of their faces with his mobile and said, 'If I see you around here again, I'll break your legs. Both of you. Understood?'

They nodded.

Ash stepped back, and they shuffled up and ran off.

'Come in for a drink, Ash,' Mum said.

Curtains were twitching everywhere. People emerge onto steps. Ash looked shattered. It's been a long day,' he said. 'Maybe next time.'

'Yeh, ring me,' I said to him.

He took my helmet, clipped it to the back of the motorbike, lowered his visor and rode off. Part of me didn't want him to go, and the other part of me was glad he had gone.

The street looked different suddenly. It was not the place I had been born in. Not the one I had played on. It was now full of shadows and had a strange silence about it. A silence that shouted, You don't belong here any more.

Walking back inside, I noticed Mum was wearing a dark T-shirt and blue jeans. Her neatly tied hair was behind her. Her face was all taut and looked like an angry ghost. I realised I had stopped noticing Mum.

'The night of the long knives has come, my child, but now with new daggers, cutting into a thousand old wounds,' Mum said.

She had never called me 'my child' like this before. It was like I wasn't next to her, and she was talking to some child somewhere else. I don't know what frightened me more, the horror of the words or the terror in her voice.

When we got inside the house, Mum put her hand around my shoulders and said, 'We must be ready for tomorrow.'

Her voice was heavier than I had ever heard it, and her dark brown eyes seemed lost.

'Tomorrow? Mum?' I asked.

'This night is going to be long,' she said, holding my face in her hands. This was Mum-speak, saying it was going to get worse.

I needed Ash more than ever. The more I saw Ash, the more I wanted to see him. I even missed him when I was sitting next to him. I went everywhere in London with him and realised that the city was not one city, but many towns and villages all rolled into one. You moved from bhangra to grime to folk to techno to thrash in the space of a tube stop, in the drop of an earbud, in the blink of a surfed screen. All these sound waves were saw-toothed, jagged as hell's cur, yet when Ash held me or pressed his thigh into mine, or rolled his eyes or did a slight pout, it was all I needed to forget the world around me.

I was about to go out with Ash when Mum came and opened our front door before me. She had a look of fear in her eyes, and her face had lost its colour.

'I'm just going out with Ash, Mum,' I said.

She nodded, took a deep breath and said, 'They burnt Brick Lane, East London.'

'We won't go near the place, Mum, promise.'

'Muslims are being forced out of their homes in Newham,' she said in a breaking voice.

'I told you, we're not going that way at all.'

Ash pulled up outside our house, parked his bike, took off his helmet, placed it on the handlebar, and came towards us. When he got close, Mum said to him, 'Please don't be late back tonight.'

'We won't, I promise,' he replied.

Getting on the back of Ash's bike, I stole a look at Mum as I put the helmet on. She stood in the doorway looking at us like it might be the last time.

There was a heady Autumn chill in the air, filled with decaying leaves.

'Name a place?' Ash asked.

I closed my eyes and took a deep breath. His aftershave invaded my nostrils, and I saw a purple sun sinking, a barge floating along a canal towards an arched tunnel.

'Never mind,' he said, 'Get on the bike, I know a great place.'

Ash rode fast through side streets. I closed my eyes. I didn't care where we went. Our path was blocked by a Bloods parade – men and women all dressed in black, carrying their strange upside-down crucifixes. Ash quickly found another route, and I closed my eyes as he zoomed away. The Bloods were just a nightmare. I lived in the music of my dreams, where hearts beat to the same rhythm.

He rode to Regents Canal. With my arms around him, I listened to him going on about his new university assignment, which was based on old Punjabi architecture. I was about to counter-bore him with the life cycle of nematodes. When he asked me to close my eyes, I did. He blindfolded me with his scarf, held my hand, and led the way. When I opened my eyes, my jaw dropped, and my tongue popped. I was staring at as close a replica of the tunnel I'd dreamed of as was possible in this world.

'What?' he said, as we dismounted.

'Did I talk to you about something like this, maybe in my sleep?'

He laughed. 'You like it?'

'I like hungry kisses.'

We sat down on a bench set back from the pavement, and I devoured him with my eyes as he returned to his architecture theme.

Maybe it was because he kept mentioning the Punjab that a thought about Mum rose and how she would translate Punjabi poetry to me. I remembered the name of Shiv Kumar Batalvi, one of the poets whose picture hung in our living room. As I stared and dreamed, I realised how the shape of the poet's nose resembled Ash's. I couldn't recall the words of the poem in Punjabi, but some of Mum's translations into English stirred. As Ash gabbled, I wrote them in my notebook:

Oh, mother,
the eyes of my songs
are aching with the grains of separation.
I have made strips of moonlight.
soaked them in scent.
Tied them around my head
But still, the pain won't go away.

I shut my notebook and put it away in my bag, and we sat watching life go by. Then, just as a barge was disappearing into the darkness of the tunnel, Ash asked, 'Inspiration?'

'You triggered a memory of something Mum had once said.'

'What?'

'A Punjabi song.'

'Can you sing it?'

'I can hear it in my head even now. She was forever playing the same songs over and over again.'

'Say the words?'

'I can't speak the language that well. Wish I could.'

'Read me what you've written.'

I did.

'That's so cool,' he said, 'Let's listen to the song!'

'OK. But swear you won't tell my Mum.'

'Why?'

'I've always said to her she should stop listening to songs written by dead men.'

'Ouch.'

We listened to the song and watched the translation scroll on the screen of my mobile. To my shame, I had remembered the words wrong.

When it finished, Ash said, 'I like your translation.'

But that was Ash. He knew how to lift me when I started feeling glum. Then he moved up a gear in the break-Marah's-heart-with-gentleness game.

He stretched out on the bench, put his head on my lap and closed his eyes. I stroked his hair and watched leaves float like ugly duckling snowflakes towards the tunnel on the soft waters of the canal. A breeze sang gently through the twirling leaves of overhanging trees. A flock of parrots landed on a tree opposite me. They squawked for a while and then sang. I closed my eyes and listened to their songs and imagined the colours of their green feathered bodies and their red beaks floating around me. Maybe I dozed off because suddenly I dreamt I saw decaying leaves trapped inside a golden beam of sunlight floating in the canal waters, disappearing into the arched tunnel.

The birds went silent. I opened my eyes. Trying not to wake Ash, I eased up and looked around.

A greenish log was floating in the water. It had two outstretched branches and a big dark patch in the middle. I trembled, realising that the branches were a woman's arms. The dark patch was her hijab, stuck to her face. As the corpse moved in the water, the green I had seen was her dress. Maybe she was my age, or maybe she was my mum's.

I nudged Ash. He woke fast. I pointed at the corpse and vomited.

'Dear God,' he said, getting up.

A bird dropped onto the body and started pecking. I retched a bit more.

THE PREPARATION 5

When I got home, Mum told me that the Bloods had decreed that all Muslims either convert to the Bloods or be expelled from London. It was the night before my 18th birthday.

She was ironing one of her favourite tops – a long maroon kameez shirt with beautiful black, blue, green and white squares. Some of the squares had stars inside them, and others were suns. They were stitched together with golden thread.

'What we going to do, Mum?' I asked, expecting magical words from her that would solve everything.

'We will do what needs to be done,' she replied.

'What's that, Mum?'

'We will celebrate my special daughter's special birthday like it was just a normal birthday.'

'I am your only daughter, Mum,' I said.

'My very special number one!'

'I don't feel in a partying mood,' I lied.

'That's all the more reason,' she said. 'Tomorrow belongs to us.'

That's my mum, I thought, she just can't say a sentence without it sounding like a proverb.

'Your present is on your bed, but wait till the morning before you open it,' Mum said.

'I will,' I said and went to my bedroom.

It was a top just like the one Mum was ironing. I held it up and looked at myself in the mirror. It really was beautiful, but I knew the next day when I wore it, I would look nothing like my glamorous mother.

I'd made my happy birthday phone calls, eaten Mum's carrot cake and opened the presents, and I felt shit. Leena was away with her biker, but that was Leena. She wouldn't miss out on a good romp, not even for my 18th birthday, but Ash going cold, that really hurt.

Mum came into my bedroom and said, 'Come on dear, come and join the party.'

I pulled the quilt over my head, rolled over on my bed and buried my face into my pillow. 'How could he do this to me, Mum?' I said. 'Not even send me a card.' I threw the quilt off me, turned around and asked Mum, 'No message of any sort?'

'These things happen...'

'It's not a thing, Mum. It's my birthday,' I interrupted her. 'What's so hard about sending a text?' I asked.

'These are strange times,' Mum said, looking away from me. 'It's good to learn a lesson when someone lets you down.'

I sat up and asked, 'Shall I ring him?'

'Oh, how beautiful that top looks on you,' Mum said, 'Just like a princess.'

'I thought you didn't like princesses and princes, Mum,' I protested.

'Well that's true, but now and then, it would be lovely to have a Prince Charming whisk you away on horseback,' Mum said, shrugging her shoulders, and then she added, 'but, alas, I'm stuck with your dad, but still it's nice to do something for yourself now and then.' She lifted her head when she said this. Clearly, I hadn't seen something she wanted me to see and comment on.

'So, you're wearing your gold earrings again,' I replied.

She cleared her throat in protest.

'OK, Mum, so you got your eyebrows done as well,' I said, and then I asked her, 'But tell me Mum. Shall I phone Ash or not?'

'Are you going to join us?' Mum asked, looking away from me, and left.

You could have said, *yes, phone him, Mum*, I cursed inside my head.

I waited a few moments and rang Ash. He rejected my call. I cursed him and stomped downstairs to my 'party.' Dad and his best friend, Uncle Melvin from Birmingham, along with a woman, were at the furthest end of the garden, beer bottles in hand. When I got closer to them, Dad pointed to the woman and said, 'Helen came here straight after delivering a baby.'

I guessed Helen was Uncle Melvin's new girlfriend. I looked her up and down. She was wearing a striped jacket, striped skirt, and dark blue top. She looked like someone who was attending a job interview, not a party, and certainly didn't look like a woman who had just given birth.

'She's a midwife,' Dad said.

Helen laughed. I guessed she had read my thoughts.

Uncle Melvin was immaculately dressed in a green striped suit, with a long blue scarf that dangled down towards his knees. He had a thick mat of greying hair, unlike Dad, who was almost bald, with his black tee shirt and pot belly hanging over his black trousers. Helen was as tall as Uncle Melvin and had a plastic smile that seemed to be stuck to her lips.

I'd had enough already and was about to go back inside when Mum turned up with a plate of steaming samosas. Uncle Melvin picked one up, dipped it into the coriander chutney and said, 'No, Peter, it's not just a rumour. They're serious about kicking Muslims out – some have already fled. They were told to convert or leave and look at this. It's had over four million views.'

Peter is what Dad calls himself, but it's not his real name.

Uncle Melvin pulled his phone out, scrolled on the screen, and played a post, holding it up for Helen and Dad. I could hear it clearly. A man said passionately, 'England is angry. Really fucking angry. It's fucking boiling, going to explode. Look how Hamas has taken over London. There are Palestinian flags everywhere. It's the same all over this country. No one's bringing fucking Sharia law here. What the fuck has England got to do with Arabs? They want a fucking jihad here. They insult our King, rape our girls, and the police arrest us, us fucking patriots. We want our fucking country back. To the Muslims: we are coming for you, you jihadist bastards. England for the English.'

'Why the hell are you spreading this fascist shit around in my house?' Mum said.

'Not all who talk like this are fascists,' Helen answered. 'But one thing is clear: England doesn't belong to them.'

'Innit, Helen,' Dad said, then turned to Melvin, 'Get real, Mel, how on earth can Muslims be expelled from London? And if we go by rumours, I heard the Bloods don't think much of Catholics either.'

'They call them heathens,' Helen said. Her voice was as cold as her eyes.

'Do they think we're Muslims?' I asked, thinking maybe this is what Ash now thought as well and wanted to keep away from me. Well, if that's what he thinks, then he can go to hell. I never want to see him again.

'Us! Muslims?' Dad laughed. 'We are a proud atheist household!'

'This won't stop them,' said Mum. 'They don't care what we think of ourselves.'

'I don't think they really care about your beliefs, they only care about themselves,' said Melvin. 'Haven't you heard what else they're doing? They call it re-writing – erasing people's memories. Making black people think they are white, I heard.'

'Can they really do that?' Mum asked, and then added thoughtfully, 'Mind you, they've been doing it for centuries.'

Uncle Melvin shrugged. 'They've been able to track thoughts in the brain for a while now. Who knows what else they can do?'

'They can try, anyway,' said Helen. 'And if it goes wrong, and someone's brain gets fried,' She shrugged. 'The Bloods aren't going to worry about it, are they?'

'I'd say get out while you can,' Melvin said, shaking his head. 'I was scared coming here today, so many roadblocks, one every mile. But I couldn't miss your eighteenth from fear of Blood bullshit, Marah.'

I didn't know what to say to Uncle Melvin. I was vexed realising what Ash had done. So, Ash, I thought, you got scared of coming here now that Muslims are dirt.

'You talk too much like my wife, Melvin, always seeing the darker side of things. The Bloods are just a flash in the pan. ' Dad said. 'It's England. Too much God and the English don't go together.'

I really believed in you, Ash, I thought. You dumped me for a rumour, you coward. I felt unclean inside. Violated. I was so angry my ears burnt. I should have run inside and left the adults to sort out this fucked up world, but instead, I just stood there frozen.

'The Gods of England are changing, Peter, I tell you. Go out of London into England proper, and you'll see it written all over the walls: *we will get England back*,' Uncle Melvin said. 'Who would have believed a few years back that we would have some nutters, led by a mad-dog American preacher who goes on about the Second Coming, taking over London?'

Mum added, 'Sometimes you really have to read the writing on the wall, you know.'

Suddenly, I desperately wanted a hug. Chilli came and rubbed against my leg. I stroked him. It helped calm me down.

'Peter does have a point,' Helen said. 'There is a deeper issue which the Bloods have been able to exploit.' She paused, bit into a samosa and added, 'It's because English rights have been ignored that the country is going to the dogs.'

'England screwed the world and deserves to be screwed.' Mum said, stroking my head. 'The English ruling class needs the Royal family,' said Mum. 'They will resurrect them even from the dead if they have to, they've done that before, and throw in a Messiah here and there if they have to.'

'We're not in the dark ages now, you know. The Royal family now are not like the old ones, now they even marry black women...'

'The royal family has been fucking black people for hundreds of years, so what's new?' Mum interrupted Dad.

That's my mum, I thought, can't say anything without going back to the origin of classes and ending it with a punch on the nose.

Suddenly, I thought maybe Ash texted me. I ran back into the kitchen to check my mobile. Chilli followed me. My mobile wasn't where I'd left it, and I shouted out to Mum, 'Mum, that brat of yours has taken my phone.'

'Stop blaming me for everything,' Tats said.

I didn't see him coming. He opened the fridge and took out a carton of orange juice. As he was leaving, I asked, 'Ring my phone, Tats.'

'No,' he replied, stepping away.

'It's my birthday,' I said indignantly.

'So?'

'Mum, can you ring my mobile,' I called out to her.

She did, and it rang. It was near the microwave – exactly where I'd left it. There was no text.

'Can you bring a bottle of wine from the fridge, dear?' Mum asked.

When I got back to the garden, Mum was showing Helen her plants and trees while Uncle Melvin and Dad were busy solving the world's problems.

'Muslims are all going to Birmingham. At least the Bloods aren't in control there,' Uncle Melvin was saying. 'I was looking into buying a rental there, rental market going through the roof.'

He turned to me and said, 'How big you've grown?'

He said this every birthday.

'You were only a wee little kitten not long ago.'

He said this every birthday as well.

He put his hand into the inside pocket of his jacket and looked at me with one of his special birthday smiles and a look that said, *Here comes the surprise*. He then always gave me a card with £10 in it.

He took out a card and held it in front of me. I was about to take it when he snatched his hand back and said, 'No hug for Uncle Melvin.'

I held my breath and hugged him, took the card, thanked him, and opened it. It had a £50 note in it.

'You're only eighteen once,' Uncle Melvin said.

It was so generous of him, but all I could feel was miserable because of what Ash had done to me. I said thank you, kissed Uncle Melvin on the cheek, and went up to my room to weep.

It was 8.30 pm when our landline rang.

Usually, only Tats answered the landline, but I beat him to it in case it was Ash. As soon as I heard the voice, I wished I hadn't. It was an "aunty" from our street. I thanked her and slammed the phone down. She reminded me of my aunt Manjit Kaur. She's Leena's Mum. The story of her marriage and life with my uncle was a legend in our family. She'd married Uncle Rashad back in the days when, like my dad, he was a devout atheist, but when she got pregnant they had non-stop rows. My uncle wanted their baby to have a Muslim name, and my aunty said he could give the child any name as long as it ended with *deep*, *preet*, or *der*. Of course, this implied the name being Sikh.

My aunty died giving birth to Leena. My uncle became all religious and started praying five times a day, and all but raised Leena in the mosque.

My brother stood in front of me with his hands on his hips. He had one of those sibling's taunted looks which made me feel I should scratch his eyes out. That nana-na-na-na-naaah grin, so I gave him an I'm-going-to-kill-you stare, and ended up in a staring fight, and being a stupid little boy, he will put his life on the line in a blink. I was looking for the moment when Mum and Dad had their backs to us. It came. I blinked, and just when the victorious smile flashed across my brother's lips, I stepped forward and pinched him on his chin. He yelled loudly, as though I had axed him.

'Mum, Marah punched me,' Tats cried.

He stepped towards me, and suddenly, I realised I used to look down at him during our stare-a-thons, and now he was as tall as me.

'Marah!' Mum reprimanded without even turning around.

'You always side with him, Mum,' I protested. 'I didn't punch him, I swear.' Turning to Tats, I added the best kind elder sister voice I could manage. 'You know I didn't punch you, Tats,'

'You did too.'

Dad came into the kitchen with Uncle Melvin behind, staring at us in bemusement, puffing on his glowing cigar. Dad put his arm around his son's shoulders and said to me, 'I've told you a hundred times that you need to set an example for your younger brother.'

I'd had enough, stomped out of the kitchen, and ran back upstairs to my bedroom. Chilli followed me. I sat on my bed, crossed-legged. Chilli looked up at me with sad eyes.

'It's my birthday, Chilli, and he doesn't care,' I said.

Chilli wagged his tail.

'Do dogs love, Chilli?' I asked.

He moved closer and put his head on my lap. I stroked him.

'I mean, I love you, and I know you love me, but do dogs love other dogs? I mean, do you have a girl dog you love?' I asked. 'I know it's a stupid thing to want to know, but you are so lucky, you don't have to put up with all this human shit. I mean, if dogs don't need to worry about religion, why do we? And if you don't care about birthdays, why do I?'

Chilli trembled.

'I know what you mean, Chilli, if someone doesn't care for you, why should you care for them? He can go to hell, and I'll never see him again, I promise.'

I got into bed and covered my face with my quilt.

Chilli whined.

Mum came into my room sometime later, sat on the bed next to me, and said, 'Let's make a deal, baby.' This was one of Mum's favourite lines to get me to agree to something.

'If you stop being cross and open your eyes, everything will be fine,' Mum said, adding, ' Here, Marah, take this.'

'I don't want a tissue,' I said without lifting the quilt off my head.

'It's not a tissue,' Mum said.

'I don't want any birthday cake,' I said.

'It's not a birthday cake.'

I lifted the quilt off my face, looked at Mum, and waited for her to tell me what she was smiling about. Chilli jumped off the bed and stared in great expectation at Mum, wagging his tail.

She held a card out towards me. I snatched it from her and ripped it out of the envelope. It was from Ash. He'd written, *9.55 pm, end of your road. XXX*

'It's 9.50 now,' Mum said.

I shot out of bed, ran to the bathroom, threw some water on my face, put some lipstick on, brushed my hair, checked if my breath smelt, and bolted out of the front door.

THE CONVERSATION

Ash was at the end of the road, next to a horse-drawn carriage. Yes, an actual horse-drawn carriage! And did he look gorgeous or what in his cream-coloured shirt, black waistcoat and black trousers! When I got close to him, Tats popped up from behind the carriage and asked, 'Can I come as well?'

'Piss off,' I said, shoving him away.

'Happy birthday, Marah!' Ash said. I swear I thought I saw his teeth glint when he said that, and if someone that day had said there was an angelic halo above his head, I would have believed that as well.

'Please!' Tats pleaded. I pushed him away with the back of my foot as I hugged Ash.

The carriage had two beautiful white horses in front. A bowler-hatted, smartly dressed man, reins in hand, sat in front of the carriage. He nodded to me. I smiled back at him. Ash held the door open for me to step in.

'How much did this cost you?' I asked.

'You're worth it,' he replied.

Okay, so it's corny, but I loved it.

Tats tried to sneak into the carriage before me. Just as well Mum turned up and pulled him away. I was beginning to lose my cool and could have made mincemeat of the little brat. I ran up to Mum, gave her a big hug, and then stepped into the carriage.

I put my head on Ash's shoulder, closed my eyes and listened to the hooves of the horses as the carriage went down our street. We'd only just turned the corner when Ash moved on to a seat facing me.

'Why did you do that?' I protested.

'So, I can look at you,' he replied.

He whispered my name, leaned over, and kissed me.

I don't know where we went. I didn't care. I took deep breaths of his lavender aftershave, and the ride felt like it was a dream where there was just me, my lover and me.

When I got back later that night, Uncle Melvin was snoring so loudly upstairs you could feel the vibrations in the living room downstairs. Mum and Dad were in the kitchen, and you could cut the atmosphere with a knife. It was no longer a rumour. The Bloods had issued a new decree: Muslims must convert or be expelled from London.

'The English will revolt,' Dad said.

'The English herd will happily eat the grass in its own field, then it will eat the grass out of the king's arse and, if it's pickled in hate, that's fine as well,' my Mum said. She must have had more than a bottle, I thought.

Dad scratched his chin, trying to figure out what Mum meant. I had no idea what she was going on about. I made a move to escape, but just as I moved, Mum pressed on my arm.

'This concerns you too, Marah,' she said.

'Didn't I say the American dollar would collapse and with it America? Didn't I say that American soldiers were joining militias all over the world, and they would do the same thing here? No one believes they are going to be hit by lightning until they are,' Mum said.

'England won't put up with this,' insisted Dad.

'The England we were born in is no more,' Mum rebutted.

'You'll tell me the English will accept the banning of beer and bacon next!' Dad said.

'We can just bury our heads in the English sands,' Mum said, pointing a finger at him. 'You can. I will not.'

Usually, by this time, he was in bed, dead drunk. He looked at me with tired, bloodshot eyes. His bald head had become more wrinkled than just earlier today. He chewed his teeth, a sure sign that what was coming was not anything nice. He picked up a stainless steel glass in which he took water to his bedroom. He gulped the water down and went to the kitchen.

I expected Mum to say something whilst Dad was away, but she just looked at me once and then stared ahead to where Dad had sat.

'What are we going to do, Mum?' I asked.

She didn't answer me.

Dad came back with a tray containing three large mugs of sleepy-time tea, each containing a teaspoon. He put the tray down on the coffee table, picked up his cup, stirred the teabag with the spoon, and kept on stirring it. He seemed to be in a trance, almost.

Mum started to cry. Every part of her trembled. I'd never seen her like this. I hugged her, kissed her on the forehead, and before I could tell her everything would be OK, Dad said, 'It doesn't really matter, does it?' He continued stirring his tea and said, 'The way I see it, the new decree is not going to be around for long, the English just won't take this sort of religious bigotry....'

'Oh please, Pervaiz,' Mum interrupted. 'For once, just let go of this English bullshit. You're fourth bloody generation Punjabi, who's dreaming of going back to Punjab, a place you've never been to, and somehow pretends to be English.'

'You've got a real way with words, Mum, when it comes to putting Dad down,' I said. But today the tone in Mum's voice was not the one she used when fighting him, but one of tired resignation.

'It's okay, sweetheart,' Dad said, still staring into the tea. I tried to recall when he had last called me sweetheart and couldn't. Dad continued, 'I may have made many mistakes in my life, but at least I made sure my family had a roof over their heads. All we have is this house, and I will never leave it...'

'What your dad is trying to say...'

'Mum, let him say it,' I interrupted her.

Dad glanced at me and then went back to staring into his cup. After a few moments, he said, 'A family got burned to death today in East Ham. Three kids, Mum and Dad. The father had been interviewed on television yesterday about the conversion decree rumours. He said he would never convert.'

Chilli lifted his head and looked nervously around. Dad continued, 'Me and your mum have been talking about this thing even before this new ruling was issued. We're not a religious family and we've raised you like that. I don't believe in this God thing, as you know, and as far as I am concerned, a label is just a label, it doesn't mean anything.'

'You know, Marah, for once, me and your dad are on the same page. We just have to ride the storm,' Mum said without looking at me.

I got up, walked over to the window and looked out. The oak tree opposite our house was shedding its leaves, which fell in swirling fog.

'So, you want us to convert,' I asked, turning around.

My parents had changed. Dad looked nothing like the beautiful, strong man he once was. He seemed to have shrunk to a frightened child. My fearless Mum looked terrified too. She avoided eye contact with me.

'Right. So, what are we going to convert to then?' I asked, getting all vexed up inside. 'We going to become Catholics then?'

Mum rocked her head from side to side like an old woman.

'Well, we can't do that, can we, they're heathens, according to the Bloods,' she muttered.

'And so are the C of E, and the Methodists and the Jehovah's Witnesses. So, we have to become Bloods-type Christians, right?' I asked Dad.

Turning to Mum, I said, 'Remember you used to say, "We must never settle for crumbs, not even the biscuit, for the bakery belongs to us." So, this is standing up to that brave new world of your poets, is it? That one where all would be fair?'

Tears began to swell in my eyes. I felt really bad for talking to my parents like I had.

I went to sit next to her and held her hand to say sorry. Even Uncle Melvin momentarily stopped snoring. Police sirens wailed somewhere in the empty streets. Maybe they're right, I thought. If we don't do what they are asking, how on earth would I manage to get into med school?

How can you be so selfish, Marah? I cursed myself inside my head. How can you think about yourself all the time? And besides, if we do what Dad says, what difference does it make? It's just a label someone puts on you, especially if you don't believe in any label. But, Marah, I argued with myself inside my head, who would you be?

'You might be right. At least we would live in our house, but that wouldn't be us, even if it was in our house,' I said. 'And could we live in our house if they burnt the ones next door?' I asked Mum, 'If I have to live in a nightmare, then at least it should be mine.'

Dad looked at Mum and then at me and asked, 'So you don't want to convert then?'

We didn't reply.

'I can't convert on my own?' Dad mumbled to himself, 'No point in that, Peter, is there?'

'Looks like Peter's left, and there is only Pervaiz!' Mum said.

I yawned. Mum stood up.

'Goodness, it's nearly 2 am. You must be exhausted, Marah.'

She held my hand and led me out of the room. Chilli stood up to follow. I pointed at him and said, 'Stay with Dad.'

He stayed.

That night, I couldn't sleep. I threw back my curtains and gazed at the shapes forming and dispersing in the play of fog in the street. I kept thinking about what Dad had said. Deep down, I didn't believe in any God. That much was true. The only Muslim bit in our house was that we never cooked non-halal meat, though I knew Dad loved his grilled bacon, which he and Uncle Melvin would have for breakfast in a cafe whenever they had a meetup.

Maybe Dad has got a point, I thought. Who the hell cared if I 'converted'? Buddhism seemed OK. I thought of going to church, having my head dipped in water by some over-dressed dude in dark clothes. Then I remembered that this was a Catholic thing, not Buddhist.

'You nutcase Marah,' I said aloud, 'how the heck would the Bloods be allowing Buddhists? All that Eastern philosophy? All that "peace-out" and "do-no-harm"? They'd push them into sacks and drown them like kittens in the River Thames.'

Mum popped her head into my room. 'I heard voices and thought you were talking to someone.'

'I was,' I laughed.

She stepped in, sat down close to me, and stroked my head.

'What about?' Mum asked.

I sat up and did the Bloods' version of the crucifix, starting from my stomach, up to the forehead and then crossing my shoulders from left to right.

'That's wrong,' Mum said and then showed me how she thought it was supposed to be done.

'You are so yesterday, Mum,' I teased. 'That's the old Jesus Christ. Haven't you heard: the Second Coming is Nigh! This is the Bloods' new Cross sign.'

'Oh Lord,' Mum sighed. Which made us both laugh. Then Mum sang to me like she used to do when I was little, and I drifted off to sleep with her soft fingers stroking my forehead.

The following week was one of the strangest of my life. Dad wandered about the house, talking to himself and cleaning the cooker over and over again. Mum decided to slow-pack for Doomsday. She had a suitcase full of lentils and rice, one for each of our clothes and even one full of food for Chilli. She ensured the books in our house were perfectly stacked.

Mum's study was in our back living room. Every inch of her wall was covered with posters of her favourite poets with quotes from them she had written out in her handwriting. There was Mahmoud Darwish, the Palestinian: *I opened my door and windows and watched a petrified moon.* Faiz Ahmed Faiz, from Pakistan, *We Shall See,* and Fahmida Raiz got a special place above the others: *women, like men, are complete human beings with limitless possibilities.* Mazisi Kunene from South Africa was also given a prime spot: *There is a place, where the dream is dreaming us.* And there was a great big poster of Malcolm X, with a rifle in his hand, looking out of a window: *By any means necessary.* But she also loved William Blake's *Jerusalem*, which she had had framed.

Mum cried when she took the posters off the wall. She stroked each one like she used to stroke my face. When she packed her notes on the book she had been writing ever since I turned up, she asked me to sit next to her on the floor. I did. It was covered in paper. 'It will be called *Lines of Fire – Poetry of The Afro-Asian Writers Movement,* and I will finish it, I will,' she said.

'I know you will, Mum.'

'Do you know why?' she asked. Before I could reply she said, 'Because in the dream of a poem is held the sigh of hope.'

I hugged her, and we rocked to and fro for a little while, her words going round and round in my head.

When she wasn't packing, she was in her bedroom on her exercise bike, listening to poems on her headphones. All the while, Tats ran around trying to figure out what was happening, but no one told him. Chilli went from room to room, trying to cheer everyone up, before coming to mine and sitting next to me.

Each night, I made sure every door and window was locked. I listened for the sound of running feet, sloshing paint, and burning doors. I only slept if Chilli was in my room.

Just when I thought things couldn't get worse, that time of the month started for me. Terrible period pains. The worst cramps I'd ever had. I was in the living room, curled up on the sofa.

Tats was in the hallway, slamming doors like a door-testing robot. Mum had asked him to go to the shop and get sanitary pads for me.

'It's so unfair,' the brat brother of mine said, bursting into the living room.

I could see his point, but how could I feel sympathy for him at a time like this?

'It's not her fault, and I have a deadline to meet, so I can't go,' Mum said.

This wasn't true, Mum just wanted to cuddle up next to me.

'She's always on her periods,' Tats said.

'Only once a month, and sometimes she gets this bad, sweetheart,' Mum said.

'She's just a moaning bitch,' he cussed.

'That's no way to talk about your sister,' Mum said. 'I won't have such language in my house.'

'I'm sorry for being racist, Mum,' he said. 'But she is a cow.'

'Sexist, you stupid numbskull, not racist!' I shouted out. I loved it when he got everything all wrong.

'Racist is when people go on about your race or colour, or like they do about Muslims,' Mum laughed.

'Why can't she go herself?' Tats said.

'She's not feeling well, dear,' Mum said.

If I behaved as he does, I would lose my pocket money or worse, but when it comes to him, Mum's feminism goes down the toilet.

'No, Mum,' the brat protested.

'Why dear?'

'I'm a boy.'

'She's your sister.'

'She's horrible.'

'I'll give you some extra money,' Mum tutted. 'You can get yourself a lolly.'

'I'm not a baby, Mum.'

'I'll give you an extra pound.'

'Three!' he demanded.

'Two,' Mum said.

'This is the last time,' he said.

'Alright, dear,' make sure you phone me as soon as you get to the shop.'

As he went past, I called him, 'Tats!'

'What?'

'Make sure they're the ones with wings.'

'Stuff you,' he said to me.

'Do as your sister asks, else you're in trouble,' Mum shouted after him as he opened and slammed the front door shut.

He called me on my mobile when he got to the shop.

'Do you want the blue ones?' he asked.

'No, they're purple,' I replied.

He ended the call but rang back again.

'There's only pink ones and blue ones here,' he said.

'They always have them. Just make sure they have wings,' I replied, 'I've often got them from there.'

He phoned back again and said, 'I can't see any wings.'

'Well, look closer.'

'There are no bloody wings here,' he said slowly and then added, 'You come yourself then.'

I'd had enough and got up, slipped my shoes on, and Mum said, 'Where are you going, Marah?'

'That brat of a son of yours is so thick,' I said. 'He's bloody hopeless.'

'He tries, the poor little lamb.'

All the way to shop, I cursed this poor little lamb who could do no wrong. Besides, I'd get two pounds for myself – a simple little job and even that he couldn't get right.

When I got to the chemist, he was still standing in front of the shelf with the rows of sanitary towels, staring at the packs.

The chemist, a big fat man, was cleaning a red cross off from the shop front. He was one of the types who had a proverb for every occasion. They rarely made sense. I tried to sneak past him because I was in no mood for bits of wisdom. He saw my reflection in the glass, stopped, smiled at me with his shiny new dentures, and said, 'I heard they marked your house as well, Marah.'

'That was some time back, Uncle Taj,' I replied.

'How's your father, have not seen him in a long, long time.'

'He's fine, Uncle Taj.'

'As they say, don't get a bride to catch a thief,' he said. 'Boys don't understand these things.'

I went into the shop, stomped over to Tats, picked up a purple pack, and said, 'These!'

'You wanted them with wings,' he said.

I pointed at the picture of wings and said, 'There they are. Not airplane wings, you idiot.'

Tats laughed.

'Give me the money.'

He kept two pounds and gave me the rest.

'And the two pounds,' I insisted.

'Why?'

'Because I had to come here.'

He laughed again, walked out of the shop and waited for me outside. When I came out, he spread his arms and pretended to be an airplane. I swung the bag with the sanitary pads at him but missed. He ran off with his arms stretched out, turned, and then began to dive-bomb me. All the way back, he buzzed me like an angry mosquito. I was livid.

'Where is he?' I asked when I got home.

Mum blocked me, arms across her chest.

Tats was in the kitchen, hiding behind the kitchen door and Mum.

'Why are you two fighting?'

'Did you see the way he came back?' I said.

Mum looked puzzled. Suddenly, Chilli ran in from the garden, barked and ran towards the front door. I followed him. He was barking furiously at some people outside our door. Even through the coloured glass panels, they clearly looked like they were in uniform.

Holding Chilli by the collar, I opened the door. A stiff wind rushed into the house. Chilli snarled. The two men on our doorstep were in dark blue uniforms. They wore helmets with black visors that reflected an image of myself. The shorter of the two had a writing tablet in his hand.

'Is this the house of Mr. Sultan?' the tall one asked.

'Who's asking?' I tightened my grip on Chilli which got him snarling even more.

'We're from the Redeemed Christian Church of the Second Coming of England. We're just here to gather data and sort out some dos and don'ts.'

'What do the police want?' Mum called out, coming towards me.

'They're not police,' I said, and then shouted at the top of my voice, 'Dad! Come here.'

The tall man stepped back from the doorstep and placed his hand on something dangling off his hip.

Dad came down, mumbling unintelligibly.

'You have requested a family conversion slot, and we need to discuss some logistics face to face,' the tall one called out to Dad.

Mum held my arm. Her hand was sweaty.

'What's up, Marah?' Tats asked, walking down the stairs.

'I am a Muslim,' I told them. 'Put that in your tablet. I was born one, and that's that.'

The words shot out of my mouth, I don't know where they came from, but in that moment, I became my words.

Chilli barked furiously. I held him even tighter.

'Silence the dog,' the tall man warned. He stepped back a little.

'No one from this household will be silenced,' I replied. 'Not even the dog.'

Maybe it wasn't the most diplomatic thing to say. Next thing you know, the tall one had done a pure cowboy move for his hip, and Chilli was howling. He'd sprayed him. Chilli bucked and bucked as I held onto his collar.

'Why did you do that?' I yelled, dragging Chilli back for their own sake. 'He's just a dog, and I'm holding him. If I let him go, you'd be in hospital.'

Mum shut the door and sat down next to Chilli.

'Get some water,' she told Tats. Tats ran to the kitchen.

Dad wandered off upstairs, muttering to himself.

'I'm so sorry for getting you hurt, Chilli,' I said, stroking him.

'You are not to blame, Marah darling,' Mum said, taking a jar of water from my brother. She tried washing Chilli's eyes, but Chilli was having none of it. She gave up and said to me, 'I am so proud of you, my girl. So, so proud. You stood up for us all. I wish I had your strength.'

'You are my strength, Mum,' I said.

'Nice one, big sister,' said Tats. And then he kissed me. Both Mum and I were gobsmacked.

Suddenly, my atheist dad changed. He started praying five times a day, every day, and at night got pissed on homemade cider.

THE NIGHT OF THE LOUDSPEAKERS

Just before midnight a few days later, all the lights in our house suddenly went out. Chilli ran around barking madly. I looked out of my bedroom window. It was dark as far as I could see.

I ran into Dad's room and shouted, 'There are no lights anywhere.' Chilli followed me.

'It's just a power cut, it happens in Pakistan all the time,' Dad said sleepily.

'We're in London, Dad,' I said.

Chilli turned around and ran past me, barking furiously.

'Dad, something's seriously wrong,' I said.

He snored.

I ran after Chilli. By the time I found him, he was next to mum. She was on our landline.

Her mobile torch's light bounced off the hallway mirror.

'Southern Electric say there is no power cut,' Mum said, ending the call. Then she put her index finger to her lips and said, 'Shh.'

An announcement was being made through a loudspeaker outside, but it was too far away to make any sense.

I followed Mum to the front door. Chilli followed me. All our neighbours were out, mobile phones lights in hand, looking in the same direction.

Aunty Evette White, our neighbour to the left, shone a powerful torch on us and asked in her Jamaican accent, 'And the electric people say there is power.'

'They said that to me too,' Mum replied.

'Don't tell me that father of yours is asleep through all this, Marah?' Aunty Evette asked.

'He thinks it's normal in Pakistan, Aunty,' I replied.

'Oh Lord, go tell the man we here live in Cricklewood,' Aunty Evette said.

'How's Marcus, Evette? Not seen him for a long time,' Mum said.

Marcus is Aunt Evette's 23-year-old son.

'Since graduating, he's changed, he is all quiet, all the time, and besides, is hardly ever home,' Auntie Evette stopped mid-sentence, shone her light across the street and said, 'The old boy going to fall mighty badly one day.' She referred to Baba Harjit Singh, who lived directly opposite us and was about to step onto the pavement. 'He was the oldest on our street, and whenever I saw him wobbling about with his walking stick, I was convinced he would fall, but he never did.' Mum walked over to him. Chilli and I followed her.

'My hearing is not what it used to be. What are they saying, daughter?' Baba Harjit asked Mum in a Punjabi accented English.

'It's too far can't hear it clearly, Uncleji,' Mum replied.

'Whatever it is, it is more dangerous than the darkness of this night,' Baba Harjit said, giving Chilli a biscuit. 'God knows where that no-good son of mine spends his time. He is never at home when I need him.

He was talking about Balbir, his 20-year-old lecherous son. I never told Mum, but he flirted with me and even promised to convert to a Muslim if he could get into my pants. I told him where to go each time.

The announcement was clearer now. A man's voice led a chant, 'The Second Coming is Nigh,' but the reply was too far away and came across as muffled noise.

Chilli turned towards the direction of the noise and barked.

'I think you should go inside and shut the door, Babaji,' Mum warned Harjit Singh.

He nodded and turned around. I grabbed Chilli by the collar, and we crossed over the road to our house, made Chilli go into the house and shut the door, but Mum and I remained outside.

The chants were clearer now. Each time the speaker called out *The Second Coming is Nigh*, a load of voices chanted Bloods' Ten Commandments, one after the other:

Thou shall show no mercy to the enemies of the Second Messiah.
Thou shall show no mercy to the enemies of the Second Messiah.
Thou shall destroy the false prophets of the Satanic Verses
Thou Shall endure all pain in the name of the Lord.
There is no Sabbath in the Holy War.
There is no Honour greater than the Second Messiah and the Blessed Virgin Birth.
Thou shall not sheathe your swords whilst false beliefs roam free.
Thou shall protect the chastity of Christian womanhood.
All Wealth belongs to the followers of the Lord.

Thou shall not allow false witness against the Second Coming.
Thou shall strike those who covet your rights.

Then, around 200 of them came onto our street. The front two had fluorescent flamed upside-down crucifixes in their hands. All of them wore black hoods and black clothes. None of them looked at any of us as they marched past us, chanting one commandment after the other.

Another chanting group came past our street at the other end. This one was going in the direction of Cricklewood Broadway.

The next day, Mum pinned a map of the United Kingdom to the door of her office, placing thick crosses across Northern Ireland and Scotland.

She had a mug of tea in one hand and a marker pen in the other.

'London is lost,' Mum said to me as I walked past, but she grabbed my hand.

'I got a headache from last night, Mum,' I protested.

She pulled me closer, kissed me on the forehead and said, touching Wales, 'The Welsh will huff and puff, but at the end of the day, they will side with the English, like they always do.'

'Your mum has lost her marbles,' Dad shouted from the front living room, 'She's been on the phone to every Tom, Dick and Patel since she woke up.'

Mum clenched her hand around my wrist and continued, 'There is still resistance in London, and things can change, but at present the best hope lies in Manchester, where there is intense resistance to the Bloods, and in Yorkshire, there is from what I hear a pro-independence movement.'

'She thinks breaking England to pieces is the way to stop the Bloods,' Dad shouted again.

'Shut up, Pervaiz,' Mum snapped back, 'or should I call you Peter?'

Mum touched Hertfordshire, clenched her fist with the marker in it and said, 'But there is hope much closer here as well – and all hope lies in fighting back against these monsters.'

I twisted my wrist, trying to free it but Mum held on and said without looking away from the map, 'And London will fight back, you mark my words, it will not let it go.'

'I'm hungry, Mum,' I protested, looking into her eyes. They were on fire.

She released me.

'I made you a stuffed paratha, buttered fried bread,' Dad shouted. 'They're on the table.

My dad is the stuffed paratha-making champion of the world, I thought, walking into the kitchen. He had made a pile of them, each one a perfect golden-brown square shape made from wholemeal flour, packed with a thick layer of crushed potatoes with green chillies and fresh coriander, and all of it dripping in butter, of course, Dad style. I broke a corner off, wrapped it around some stuffing and put it into my mouth. It was crispy, crunchy, heavenly.

'I told him to use olive oil,' Mum said, coming into the kitchen. She sat down opposite me.

'But butter is butter,' I said, chewing another piece.

'Too much cholesterol is not good for you,' Mum said.

'But it's OK in hell, Mum,' I replied.

'It is so unhealthy,' Mum said, breaking a big piece of my paratha. She put it in her mouth and said, 'But by God, it is hellishly tasty.'

She smiled and nodded and said, breaking another piece, 'Zainab phoned on the landline this morning?'

'Why didn't she ring me?' I asked.

'She did,' Mum said, chewing.

I checked my phone. It was silent.

After wiping grease off my hands, I sent Zainab a text:

What's up?

Zainab replied before I broke the next piece of paratha:

Fancy going to Friday prayers tomorrow?
Me: No.
Zainab: What you doing in the morning?
Me: When?
Zainab: 8
Me: Sleeping, why
Zainab: I'm helping in the mosque's kitchen. Join me, earn some swabs, and earn brownie points with Almighty.
Me: Get a life, Zainab!
Zainab: We all need God.

Me: Oh, God, enough!

Zainab: Haha, OK. OK. So, what you doing after I finish prayers?

Me: Surviving Mum and Dad.

Zainab: Poetry?

Me: Yes, what you got in mind.

Zainab: *Banished Dreams*, by Ahmad Faraz.

Me: No.

Zainab: Why not?

Me: Dreams can't be banished.

Zainab: Your place is better than mine.

Me: Mine.

Zainab: Dad calls Faraz a kafir.

Me: Swap dads?

Zainab: And Mums.

I looked at Mum. She'd tied her hair up at the back of her head and was wearing a stripy work shirt. She smiled at me but was lost in thought, still trying to work out how long before the Bloods came knocking on our door, I guessed.

I text Zainab: I'll keep my mad mum.

Zainab: Haha. Your place, then.

Me: Don't be late.

Zainab: Cross my heart and hope to die.

DAY OF THE SWINE

The next morning, Tats burst into my room shouting, 'Something's happening at the mosque!'

He drew the curtains back, flooding my room with light. Chilli was next to him, standing on my jeans, looking worried.

My mobile showed it was 9.25 am.

'Something is always happening there. Why do I care?' I moaned, putting the mobile under my quilt.

I hadn't managed to go to sleep till 4 am, and even after that was slipping in and out of nightmares: sometimes I was being cut up, sometimes my house was on fire, sometimes I was just running and running, but couldn't work out from what, and now the last thing I wanted was to be woken up by this headache.

'They are attacking it,' Tats said and turned around.

Chilli barked and followed Tats down.

I shot out of bed, jumped into my trousers, grabbed my mobile and went down. Mum and Tats were leaving the house, with Chilli barking from the living room where he had been locked up. Many of our neighbours were also out, all walking in the direction of the mosque.

Two police motorcycle officers stopped us at the end of the street. No one protested as behind them someone was being loaded into an ambulance, but even after the ambulance left, we were still not allowed to go through.

Mum stepped forward, walked straight towards the policemen and said, 'Lay a hand on me and see what happens to you.'

'Yeh, you dare touch her,' Dad said as he ran past me towards Mum. He was still in his pyjamas.

The policemen didn't move for a moment, then they got an order on their radios and rode away.

People stopped in stunned silence when we got to the mosque. A huge pig's head, covered in blood, had been placed on the spikes of the mosque's railings. Blood dripped down its sides and down the railings. The door of the mosque had been splashed with a load of blood as well.

I texted Zainab:

You heard what happened?

I'd forgotten she was already in the mosque.

She didn't reply.

And then I found out it was Zainab who had beentaken away in the ambulance. She had been inside the mosque with her dad when they came with the pig's head. She had tried to stop the attackers, and one of them had stabbed her.

Mum drove me to the Royal Free Hospital, where they had taken Zainab. She had been stabbed multiple times, including through the heart.

There were lots of people from the mosque in the hospital's car park. All silent. The corridor leading to the ICU was full of whispers. Zainab was dead. She died on the spot. She died in the ambulance. She died in the ICU. Zainab was with Allah.

We waited around for a while. Mum held my hand and spoke to someone. I heard nothing. We stood silently for a while longer, and then Mum let go of my hand and hugged me, trembling. And then, after how long, I don't know, we padded out of the hospital.

'We were going to read some poetry,' I said as we drove back home.

Mum pressed on my hand.

There must have been traffic, but I don't remember seeing it.

When I got home, I ran up to my room and sat on the bed. Chilli followed me and slumped down by my feet.

How cold and selfish of me, I thought. I should have gone to the mosque in the morning. Maybe I could have saved her.

Chilli looked up at me, questioning, and I said, 'How could I have told Zainab, *Get a life*, to her Chilli? How could I?'

He wagged his tail and placed his head next to my feet.

A week went by in the blink of a nightmare. I felt all cold inside but could find no tears. I wanted the world to stop and just go away. I picked up my notebook, which I hadn't touched for how long I no longer knew and wrote,

I can't think of you,
In the past tense,
Come back as a poem
At least.

All of a sudden, my eyes blurred, and tears fell on the page, and I cried a volcano. Mum ran up. I hugged her and cried and told her, 'I was going to read a poem with her.'

Tats came up and held my hand, and I cried, 'I used to make her call me Baji.'

'I'll call you Baji,' he said.

I cried and cried until my eyes could shed no more tears.

And in the days that followed, I could feel my insides burning up. I could not stop the nightmares. The food had no taste. I felt nothing. I could not sit anywhere for more than a few minutes. If I saw anyone, I wanted to get away from them and be alone, and when I was alone, I could not bear being on my own.

I didn't realise how much I would miss Zainab, and then one night, when I was lost in one of my nightmares, I heard her say, 'Ya Ali, Maddad, Oh Ali, help me.' Then, in another nightmare she said, 'Pray for me, Marah, and you will find peace for yourself.'

I told my mum I wanted to go to the Mosque and pray.

I was expecting her to ridicule me, but she said, 'That's good, dear.'

I didn't know how to pray and just followed what the other women did. When I touched the ground with my forehead, I felt I belonged. When I lifted it off the floor, I felt Zainab beside me.

They would not release Zainab's body for two long months. For the first few days after Zainab's death, Leena came to see me and just sat near me for hours and then went home. Sometimes, I would mumble unintelligibly and, even then, Leena would just sit quietly.

Ash came to see me a few times, but I told him to leave me alone until after Zainab's funeral. He did, but phoned and sent me a message or two each day, with lots of kisses, but I rarely replied, and never with a kiss.

Finally, the day of Zainab's funeral arrived. Mum taught me how to wash myself, according to Islam, and I did my Ghusl before going to the mosque. Mum and I both dressed in traditional white clothes.

There were so many solemn people out on the roads leading to the mosque that it was hard to imagine that they were all neighbours. I covered my head with my dupatta just like Mum, and silently walked into the mosque. I had never seen so many shoes in the women's section of the mosque. All the cubicles for shoes were full and there were so many on the floor, some slippers stuffed into each other, others haphazardly strewn about. I stepped on a few before going into the women's hall. A woman sprinkled me with some rosewater as I stood in the last line.

'Zainab is in the front, sweetheart, let's go say our farewells,' Mum said to me.

I trembled all over. I was not ready to say farewell.

I didn't know what to do until Mum held my hand and led me to the front. We manoeuvred our way to the front, stepping silently through lines of women on the blue-tiled carpeted floor. Each tile was spaced from the next so that one person could prostrate in prayer.

Zainab's family were sitting around her brown carved wooden coffin. It was placed on a trolley. Her mother had one of her hands on the coffin, and with the other, she held her forehead. She lifted her head as I got closer, looked at me with blood-tired eyes and nodded. The top of the coffin had a small piece of glass through which I could see Zainab. But for her eyes, Zainab's face was covered in the white cloth of her coffin.

It was then that it hit me that I was never, ever going to see Zainab again. I wanted to open the coffin and kiss her one final goodbye.

'They stabbed her in the face, but she went with both her eyes,' her mother said in a broken voice.

'Can I stay with her a little while, Auntie,' I cried.

'Only prayers will help your Zainab now, Marah,' Zainab's mother said.

Two women in the first line moved, making space for us. I kissed the coffin and stayed leaning for a little while until Mum got me to sit next to her. I hugged her, and we wept.

Some of the women next to Zainab's coffin started reading from the Quran. I lost track of the time during which Leena came and sat next to me. She had a black and white hijab on, and like me and Mum, she was wearing white clothes.

I realised Zainab was about to leave me forever when some men came and started to take her to the main hall, where the men's funeral prayers were held.

I stood up and shouted, 'Zainab!'

Leena held my hand and tugged it for me to sit down. Mum shook her head.

'I'm not ready to leave her,' I cried, looking over my shoulder as Zainab's body left the women's hall.

Leena held me even tighter.

'I want to pray for her,' I said.

'We can. Later,' Mum said, 'if that's what you want.'

'I want to read at her funeral,' I said. 'Behind her coffin.'

Leena patted me on the back. 'It's men who do it, that's not our role.'

I was about to sit down next to Leena when a ray of sun suddenly shot through the mosque's side windows and lit up large words painted in green on the other side of the wall: *I bear witness that (there is) no god except Allah; One is He, no partner hath He, and I bear witness that Muhammad is His Servant and Messenger.*

I pulled Leena up and said, 'I want to pray for my friend now, and I'm going to.'

Leena was nervous, walking behind me, giving me little tugs to slow me down. But I wasn't really thinking about what I was doing; I just strode towards the men's hall. We were stopped at the big double doors by a bearded man. He had a rose water spray bottle in his hand. He shook his head at me. 'No women allowed.'

'I want to pray for her,' I said.

Leena dug her nails into my hand, but I pushed past the man, pulling Leena along. He blocked her.

Leena let go of my hand, stepped forward towards him and pulled the niqab off her face. The man stepped back. We were in the hall.

My dad came rushing from among the crowd, grabbed me by the arm, and said, 'No, Marah!'

We compromised. Leena and I stood at the back of the hall, and I covered my head with my headscarf. While the Imam gave a speech, lads in ones and twos came and stood next to Leena and me, and by the time the funeral prayers started, some girls had joined us as well.

After the prayers ended, the Imam said through the mosque's speakers, 'I know there is a lot of anger, especially among young people, but we must let the authorities do what needs to be done. We will take the body of Zainab Ali to her final resting place in Watford. And the family of Zainab Ali requests that all those who have come here from outside Cricklewood please stay and have some food.'

I walked out of the mosque hall. Leena was whispering, 'You've got balls!'

I pinched her arm. 'How could you say such a thing at this time, Leena?'

'Sorry.'

I took the headscarf off, tied it around my waist and said, 'Come on, Leena.'

Me and Leena ran down a corridor at the rear of the mosque. It was a narrow corridor, with lines of pipes running along one side of the wall and some panels missing from its ceiling. Paint flaked off its walls. We continue past the kitchen through a cloud of steaming spice from the food being prepared for funeral attendees. To get to where the coffins were loaded onto hearses, we had to get out of the building and back in through another entrance. I opened the fire exit with a push of both hands, and we rushed out into the back, and startled a white man, who threw his cigarette onto the ground and quickly stubbed it under his shiny black shoes, put his black bowler hat on his head and stood soberly to attention. He wore the black uniform of a funeral company. I apologised to him, and we went into the other side entrance, stepped over a pile of men's shoes and came out in the side extension of the mosque where Zainab was being loaded into the hearse. Waiting.

I don't know where Mum came from, but she had a bunch of flowers in her hand. She gave me these, and I walked around the hearse and placed them on the coffin. The top of the hearse was decorated by multi-coloured Lilies, Zainab's favourite flower. In the side glass of the vehicle, it said, in words made out of flowers, *Farewell, Zainab*, and at the back of the coffin, it said, *Daughter*.

Oh God, Zainab, come back, please, I thought.

We waited in silence for a while and waited for the rear door of the hearse to shut. People surrounded the hearse, many from our college. The engine started. The people from the front moved to the sides. A ripple pushed through the people on the sides until someone from one side knocked into me and from the other into Leena.

Leena and I held hands. We were the closest to the hearse. I touched its shining black body with the palm of my hand. It was cold. I could smell the scent of lilies; they reminded me of Zainab's voice when she used to recite poems to me. I felt a bittersweet taste on my tongue. A woman wailed inside the mosque as the hearse drove through the gate. Two mosque stewards with fluorescent waste coats stood in the middle of the road, stopping oncoming traffic.

The hearse turned right towards the High Road. More and more people joined us. Some came out of the mosque, others from the side streets. A moving mass of us crossed both sides of the pavement, silently following the coffin.

On the other side of the road, a woman in green lycra jogging clothes stared at us. She pulled one knee after the other to her chest. An old white man with a shopping trolley stopped, took his hat off and stood still for a moment.

As we got to the top of the road, I heard voices singing. It was somewhere in the distance on one of the side streets.

The hearse turned left as it approached the high street. Some lads ran from the sides and stood in front of it, and then it stopped.

'What's happening,' A woman with bright red lipstick and a black sleeveless tee shirt asked the man next to her.

'Trouble!' the man replied. He, too, was wearing a sleeveless black tee shirt and black trousers.

One of the mosque stewards I had seen early tapped me on the shoulder, pushed past me, and weaved through the crowd towards the front of the hearse, shouting, 'Move out of the way of the hearse.'

The singing became a bit clearer, but the words were still unintelligible. It sounded like a football chant.

More and more people pushed past me and Leena. The front became invisible behind a wall of backs. For a moment, I was squashed between a wall of people, but slowly, it thinned until I felt fresh wind on my face. Leena and I started walking again. We continued to march even after the hearse sped off.

We continued to walk in the direction of the hearse even though it sped north towards the M1 on its way to Watford.

The singing got louder and louder. A horde of English flag-carrying Bloods supporters marched out of one of the side streets. Some of them had baseball bats in their hands. Some wore balaclavas. They clapped and sang, 'Hey-Ho, one down, a million to go.'

We stood still and watched the hearse go. There were hundreds of us now.

I became so angry, raising my hand in the air and shouted, 'Racist scum out of the way – We shall fight and win the day.'

A roar went up from our side, and then everyone started chanting my words.

I joined an angry wave of people, gushing past me towards the Bloods supporters. They fled.

We stopped at the roundabout at the end of the High Road. A long line of police, some on horseback, blocked our path. The Bloods supporters were behind that line.

A helicopter turned up and, through its speaker, ordered us to disperse or be arrested.

The Bloods supporters started clapping and chanting even louder, 'One dead, a million to go,'

Everyone looked at me to say something like I knew what we should do. Someone shouted, 'They're going to be back tonight!'

In that second, I remembered Mum telling me about the times when she'd lived in East London, and skinhead gangs roamed the streets, attacking black people, and how she'd been part of a youth group that patrolled their streets at night. She said the power of numbers was what enabled them to protect themselves without any recourse to violence.

'If they are back, then so will we be,' I said. 'But we don't have to reduce ourselves to their level. We will defend ourselves peacefully but unyieldingly!'

The cheers rang out. The gathering broke up with a great buzz.

' "Unyieldingly". You haven't half got a vocabulary,' Leena said, putting her hand in mine. For someone so tall and big, Leena had skinny fingers.

That evening, when I got home, Dad was glued to the television. There was a breaking news headline: *Muslims Riot in London.*

The news was about us. There were pictures of burning cars and masked kids throwing petrol bombs at the police.

'This didn't happen here, Dad.'

He carried on staring at the television.

Leena rounded up six kids from the neighbourhood, and we met in our kitchen. We made calls. Thirty people were up for patrolling the neighbourhood. We divided them into six groups of five. One group went around in a car, the others stood at strategic entry points. Me and Leena stayed behind, in a sort of a control room, looking at a large map on my computer screen in my bedroom. Someone had recorded our meeting and put out some audio of me speaking in a video and shared this on Instagram. By the end of the night, they'd added shots of our patrols and images of the earlier events. It had gone viral by the morning.

The next evening, when Mum came home from work, Dad had a big fight with her over me: he was ashamed of me for what I had done; she was proud of me and how I had upheld the principle of non-violent resistance. Dad opened a bottle of wine. Mum said he was drinking too much and, besides, what was the point of all the prayers when afterwards, each night, he knocked back his homebrew cider topped up with red wine? He called her a liar, boasting that he never drank more than one bottle of wine, and the cider didn't count as it was homebrew, so the alcohol content was unverified. Then they fought over who drank too much, and Mum finished a bottle off during this scrap – just another cracking night in Cricklewood.

That evening, Ash sent me a message with a link to some breaking news: *Regents Park Mosque Burning.*

I clicked the link. It was dead. I searched on the news sites. Nothing.

THE EXODUS

I finally answered one of Ash's calls. I'd been ignoring him, and he was all grumpy. I said yes to a meet and told him where to pick me up because I wanted to walk a bit first to clear my head.

The air was crisp, and few cars were on the road, making London feel eerie. He rode up, honked, and I asked him to take me to Regent Park Mosque.

My mind was still busy trying to hold on to things as everything fell apart, but my hands fitted snugly around Ash's, and he drove slowly, putting in little dips and leans for me to enjoy as I hung on.

'This it?' he asked when he pulled up. He was checking his phone's satnav, glancing from it to the pile of builder's debris before us.

He kicked the bike stand down, and we looked around a bit. He stopped talking. I could see from his eyes that he'd gone into engineer mode.

'This was a professional job,' he concluded, contemplating the smouldering rubble heaps and twisted steel beams. 'To reduce a building to rubble like this requires a lot more than a bit of petrol. A blast force was required. You can see the pattern of the blast centre, then the blast wave and the reflected pressure. Peak pressure combined with a suction force toppled it and created these neat piles.'

I thought, 'How can Ash reduce everything down to an engineering analysis?' What am I doing with someone who can't think people once came here for peace of mind, a connection with their friends and themselves, with God, and it doesn't matter if you believe or not? They did.

'Enough. Let's go sit in the park,' I said.

He bumped his bike through the broken bike trap at the gate and drove us right into the centre. We sat down on a lake bench. I stared at ducks gliding along the oil-slicked waters of the lake. Ash picked a twig up and flicked it. In the distance, a car alarm stopped pulsing.

The ducks had all disappeared.

'I think you did the right thing, Marah,' Ash said.

I gave a puzzled grin.

'Going to Zainab's funeral, fighting back against the gangs.

And not converting,' he said.

'I don't know what to think any more, Ash.' I leaned into him and sniffed him. Brazenly.

He tossed his sixth twig into the lake and put his arm around me. 'If we love each other and never stop loving each other, that is all we can do. Keep each other going, whichever way we can. Maybe we could just get to Scotland and build a house there.'

'Instead of watching them burn, here,' I added for him.

Then Mum phoned. Cricklewood mosque was burning. Ash jumped up, and we headed back.

There was no traffic as we approached Willesden High Road. It was eerily quiet. Shops were closed. Apart from a few people, the road was all but deserted. Those who were out stared at us as we drove past. We stopped at some traffic lights. I adjusted my helmet and heard some shouting. It sounded as though it was coming from the direction of the Willesden Green tube station. A little while later, I saw the reason.

The tube station was on our left. A Bloods' van parked in the middle blocked the road.

Armed Bloods in crisp new uniforms stood outside the tube station. They all wore dark shades. A large loudspeaker was placed on either side of the Bloods. Beyond the station, shops were being ransacked, and across the road from the Bloods, a load of people on the opposite side of the road were chanting:

England O England
You shall rise and fly,
We shall cleanse you of sin.
The Second Coming is nigh.

Something hit me in the back. A moment later, a bottle hit Ash's helmet. I looked across in the direction from where the bottle had been thrown. A chill ran down my back as I recognised Mohammad Karim chanting with the mob. He had gone to my school and lived in the last house on my street.

I took off my helmet and shouted, 'Karim!'

He had a beer can in his hand. He was dressed in black with a white shirt and a red tie. He used to be a teetotaler. Our neighbours Marcus and Balbir from across the road were next to Karim and were dressed just like him.

'Karim is dead. I am Kevin,' Karim shouted, stepping forward. A chill ran down my back when he said this. How could he be on that side of the road? How could Baba Harjit Singh look Balbir in the face without wanting to slap it?

The masked Bloods on our left stood to attention suddenly and raised their hands. Karim, Balbir and Marcus raised their right hands in the air like everyone else around them. Everything silent.

A pungent burning smell wafted in from behind the mob, and a siren wailed somewhere in the distance. The silence became even thicker. The terror of the silence sent a cold shiver down my spine. I felt my ears burn from its heat.

'Let's move,' I whispered into Ash's ear.

A soldier close to us pointed his gun at us. It was obvious we were to stay where we were. A few moments later, the Bloods lowered their hands. This was followed by the mob on the other side of the road, doing the same, but the silence continued. The Bloods moved away from the front of the station, and a few moments later, seven blond-haired men and seven women marched out of the station. The women were dressed in black skirts and black tops, with long flowing black cloaks, and the men in black suits, with white shirts and red ties. One of the men stepped past the rest and spoke into a microphone. His voice boomed out of the loudspeakers, 'Today, every tube station in London, like Willesden Junction, is being blessed right now.' He stepped back.

The women stepped forward, and orchestral music burst out of the speakers.

It was the tune of *Jerusalem* by William Blake.

The blond Bloods choir burst into song, but they had changed Blake's words:

And will these feet in time to come
Walk upon England's mountains green?
And was the Holy Lamb of God
On our pastures seen?
And did the Countenance Divine
Shine forth upon our clouded hills?
Amongst these dark satanic ills?

Bring me my bow of burning gold
Bring me my arrows of desire

Bring me my spear: O clouds unfold!
Bring me my Chariot of Fire
I will not cease from mental fight
Nor shall my sword sleep in my hand
Till we conquer Jerusalem
Our Lord's pleasant land.

Thick smoke from what must be a momentous fire somewhere wafted up towards us.

The mob let out a joyous roar and split into two. One group ran down Willesden High Road, and the other crossed the road and ransacked a shop.

The Bloods van, which had blocked the road, moved off down the hill.

A Bloods soldier pointed his gun at us and indicated for us to move.

As we approached my street, the sky was not blood red, as I had half expected. No close sirens and big fire engines running. Mister Jones from Number One was washing his car; Mister and Missos Gupta walked their white poodles proudly down the street, and Baba Harjit Singh watered his plants. Everything looked horribly normal. Did he even know what his son had become? I wondered.

Ash wanted to go home, but I dragged him into our house.

'They're looting and burning, Dad,' I said, throwing my coat on the back of a chair in the kitchen.

Dad nodded to Ash and gestured to a chair, and he sat.

Chilli ran in from the garden, looked at me worriedly, did a quick growl at Ash till I shushed him, and then he went back out again. Dad was making parathas. He smiled and said without looking at me, 'Extra virgin olive oil in your paratha, Marah.'

'Did you hear what I said, Dad?'

'Olive oil is good for you,' Dad continued, placing a paratha on a hot tava, a pan. It sizzled away. 'Much healthier than butter.'

Mum came into the kitchen, looking for scissors, nodded to Ash, and rushed out again.

Then there was a crash in the kitchen. Glass everywhere. A rock bounced onto the kitchen table and thudded into the wall where Mum had stood only two seconds before. Dad spun around. He was about to speak when I saw behind him a ball of orange getting larger and larger, spreading to a sheet. Then more glass burst and the kitchen was on fire, and the stench of petrol was everywhere. I screamed. Dad dropped. Then he was scrabbling on the floor tiles, pulling me down with him. We were crawling for the kitchen door.

Ash grabbed Dad by the shoulders and pulled him away faster than he could crawl. The kitchen table was on fire. Flames quickly ran up the walls. Mum yelled at us to move from the doorway. We ran. Our front door was open. We tumbled out. Dad's trousers were burnt at the hems. Ash's face had cuts.

'Take it off,' he told me. 'Take it off!'

Glass shards rained down on the pavement as he shook my jacket. Behind him, people were running up the street towards us. Ash took Dad by the hand and pulled him further from the house.

Mum had gone to the car. She'd returned with a fire extinguisher.

'No. Mum!' She didn't listen.

She was back in there.

Aunty Evette turned up with a giant, hulking extinguisher. And I remembered everyone on our street had bought extinguishers after the fire brigade stopped. Baba Harjit was wobbling towards us.

They killed the fire. Mum emerged, smoky-faced but triumphant with an equally darkened neighbour.

'It's out,' she said. Then, she thanked Aunty Evette as if she'd just brought around some fresh samosas.

'Oh, Lordy, it's like the end of days,' Aunty Evette said, shaking her head.

Aunty Evette hugged me, and then Mum and I went back inside.

That evening, Mum grabbed the large, packed rucksack, put it on her back, pointed to the living room door and said, 'Grab the pram and anything else you can carry. We're leaving.'

For once, Dad didn't argue.

I rushed upstairs and picked up my red notebook and my emergency rucksack. I found Mum's book and shoved it in among the ramen noodles, dried vegan sausage, emergency flare, wind-up torch, glucose tablets, Ordnance Survey official compass and a five-square-centimetre outdoor travel towel. I swung my rucksack onto my back and ran down. I put the big tennis bag with my college books in the pram and pushed it into the corridor.

Tats was ready and packed. Dad sat on his travel bag, trying to squeeze the air out so he could do the zip.

'Ready?' Mum said. She led us out.

We were not the only ones leaving. Some neighbours were hammering up wooden boards across window and door frames, toting bags into cars, loading up white vans, shoving bags onto barrows and lashing them onto bikes. Some looked to be going to other parts of London. Others looked like they were heading for the airport to try to catch a flight. Scotland was the place for all travelling. Babies crying and adults wailing punctured the air, joining the thud thud thud of hammers hitting anvils, wood hitting metal, hopes hitting fears.

Tats, Ash, Chilli and I sat in the back. Ash left his bike behind.

We were lucky. We had a big car which had a full tank of petrol and space for us all.

We got going. I stared from the back seat at the view rushing towards us. Behind the rows of cedars and oaks stood the Bloods Militia. And behind them, unknown packs of hungry wolves.

We did OK and made good time before the first block. On the last stretch of High Road, we were stopped at a checkpoint.

We all had to get out.

The guards forced Tats and Ash to one side.

'How old are you?' a soldier asked Tats.

Mum rushed past me, hugged my brother, and said, 'He's just a child.'

'Looks much older to me,' the soldier said. 'He's got a bigger moustache than mine.'

Mum showed the soldier my brother's passport. He took it from her, scrutinised it, then laughed at Tats, 'You need to shave that stubble, kid!'

He ripped up the passport, causing the torn pages to fall onto the road, and gave the shell back to Mum, saying, 'Not much good any more!'

Ash was being questioned by two soldiers.

'He's with us,' I said, refusing to budge.

'I'll be fine,' Ash shouted over to me. 'Go ahead.'

'You sure?'

'They just want some details about my course. Go. I'll catch up.'

Mum came over and tugged me. 'He'll be fine,' she said. 'Get back in the car.'

I did. I glanced back. I couldn't help it. Ash did a friendly wave that rippled in the lines of the car's rear window glass.

We chugged forward. A little further up the road, a fire was raging in a derelict plot. Militiamen were throwing stuff from a pile into the flames of the fire. They stopped us and forced us out again.

They questioned us. They went through our bags. One of them opened my rucksack and saw my books.

Chilli barked at the soldier. One of them was about to shoot him, but I ran and stood in between the soldier and Chilli and got Chilli quiet.

'They are my daughter's books,' Mum said imperiously.

The soldier looked back at Mum, his eyes cold, then briefly looked up at one of his colleagues and continued rummaging.

'Here, take this. It's my jewellery. Please let her keep the books,' Mum said, holding her purse out towards another militiaman. Judging by the way he stood, with his arms folded across his chest, he looked like an officer.

He whistled at the man with my books, and he stopped rummaging. The officer took Mum's purse, looked into it, and passed it on to another soldier. Within seconds, my rucksack and all its books were on fire.

A soldier pointed his gun at Chilli. Then Ash came running towards us, with soldiers chasing.

''I'll find you, and I love you,' Ash said breathlessly. Then, the soldiers cannoned into him and pushed him to the ground.

I turned to Chilli. 'Please run, Chilli, please. Run. Run.' He lowered his head and ran off in the direction of what he knew as home.

The soldiers had tied Ash's hands with a plastic strip and led him off. They took our car but let us keep the pram. For the next few miles of walking, Dad mouthed obscenities to himself in a rat-a-tat style. Mum was silent. Me and Tats walked two steps behind them. The road to the M1 was one vast sprawl of bowed heads. There were people from everywhere in the world. It seemed like the United Nations was on the march. Me and Tats took turns pushing the pram. Dad kept on about his paratha.

I was numb with thinking. Where was Ash? What were they doing to him?

The road to the M1 was one vast sprawl of bowed heads. There were people from everywhere in the world. It seemed like the United

Nations was on the march. The motorway was the same, coaches, vans, buses in the outside lane, people in the other. Me and Tats took turns pushing the pram. Dad kept on about his paratha. Mum wouldn't stop crying which made Tats cry worse. I was numb with thinking. Where was Ash? What were they doing to him?

Some trains were still running. Mum managed to bribe our way onto one of them at a makeshift station close to the motorway.

We squeezed into a carriage. I looked around. London was my heart, my home. Nobody had planned to leave London like this: wearing shirts inside out, with faces pricked by blood, wet, hungry babies on their arms, shopping bags of mantelpiece ornaments on tables, kids crammed under tables and into the overhead luggage rails, cursing into phones and chomping on cold rice.

I was in a forward-facing seat and, as the train pulled away, I looked back and saw smoke rising all over London – my London. I bid her goodbye. Au revoir, not adieu.

The train sped on for an hour or so and then slowed down. Mega-factories flitted past the windows on either side. On my left, I recognised the Amazon super-warehouse. It was a blue multi-story building that went on for at least a mile. Tanks were guarding its entrances, and drones flew above in the colours of the Bloods flag. After Amazon came a field of grazing cows. Then horses. Then, the Taiping Industrial Concession also guarded by tanks. I had visited Taiping base on a school trip. It had four floors below ground and four above. There were assembly lines for cars. There was a Textiles Zone where machines cut and stitched cloth. There was a 3D Print Light Arms Unit in there. Plus, swimming pools and gyms for the top bosses. When I visited it, I saw armies of workers in winding, transparent tubular corridors, coming and going to work. They moved like zombies.

THE DESTITUTION

Mum and Tats were silent the entire journey to Birmingham. Dad stared out of the train window and muttered to himself. A kind aunty with a sulking teen and a mewling baby offered us daal, lentils and rice. Mum declined politely.

When we got off the train, the station platform was a heaving mass of messy, bedraggled humanity. Lines of people snaked in opposite directions along the platforms. Children bawled and flopped and refused to move. Elders staggered. The young and healthy pushed hard. Elbows and knees became weapons. People called out names beseechingly. God was invoked.

Somehow we managed to stay together and got out of the station. We stopped under a great big broken hoarding with the words "Bull Ring" in blue dangling off it.

'Where do we go now, Dad?' I asked.

He used to be a regular visitor to Birmingham to see Uncle Melvin.

'The paratha would have completely burnt by now,' he replied.

'Thanks, Dad,' I said.

I saw three men with long beards and sky-blue turbans handing out bottles of water. It took me a few moments to realise they were Sikhs, not Muslims. I grabbed Tats' hand and tugged. Where Tats went, Mum automatically followed, and Dad followed Mum. In this way, I shepherded my family to the water distributors.

We got a bottle each and drank.

'Uncle, we have nowhere to go,' I said to the oldest one.

'Are you one family?' he asked.

'Yes,' I said.

The old man smiled and said, 'You can spend a night or so at the Gurdwara.'

That was how we ended up in the Handsworth Temple. We slept on mats in the hall with lots of other displaced people. Everyone had a toilet rota, and we all helped to keep the place as clean as we could. The temple's kitchen was in the cellar and was busy 24-7.

In the sanctuary of the Gurdwara, I became desperate to contact Ash and Leena. I sent messages to them, but our mobiles were not working any more. The Bloods had shut down all the internet. But it was Mum and Dad who I was really worried about. Dad had become a complete mumbling zombie with tired eyes; Mum stared at motes in the Gurdwara air. Tats was terrified of every loud noise, and I became the unsleeping adult of the family.

We were among the lucky few to be given space in a corner, away from any door, in a long annexe to the side of the temple. It was a white-walled army barrack-type building with white-painted interiors and naked bulbs that dangled down from its ceiling. A row of small windows ran along its entire outer structure, behind which was a high barbed-wire-topped wall.

We hung up a few sheets and made a room of sorts. The temple team gave us rubber camping mattresses and a few beat-up pillows, but no one complained, as these were luxuries now.

We waited patiently in lines for food and ate quietly in the din of the silence of the sorrow of the never-ending stream of others like us. The hall hummed with prayers.

For the first two days, Mum did a lot of crying. Dad whispered unintelligible words. Tats became agitated even when Mum went to the toilets. I passed the hours thinking about Leena and Ash: was Leena alive? Would I ever see her again? Was I the twig Ash twirled in his hand and then discarded, or was I a treasure for him, something he would seek to the end of the earth to recover? Was I ever going to find a way of flying back to my dreams of going to med school? Sometimes, Zainab flashed through my mind, and I hoped she was in a better place than where I was, wherever that was now.

On the third morning, Mum woke before dawn. Dad snored on as ever. I was already awake, looking for faces in the shadows on the ceiling. Mum sat up, pressed her back against the wall, put her arms around her knees and looked blankly through me. Tats woke and rubbed his eyes. When he saw the cold look on Mum's face, he stared at me with a pleading gaze. I hugged him. 'Don't worry, we'll get through,' I told him.

Whatever getting through meant.

'Promise?' he asked.

'Yeh, I promise, everything will be alright,' I said and kissed him on the head.

'You're not lying like you used to in London, are you?' he asked.

'No, of course not.'

'I believe you.'

'That's good, dear.'

'Now I know you're lying!'

'Why do you say that?'

'Because you sounded just like Mum,' he said, 'and she always lies.'

I gave him a gentle clout around his head. 'Go clean your teeth. Your breath stinks.'

'Now you really sound like her.'

Dad lifted the blanket off his head, looked at Tats and then at me with his bloodshot eyes, rolled out from under the sheets of our 'room' and went off to the bathroom. Tats followed him. I slid closer to Mum and wiped her forehead with the palm of my hand. 'Where have you gone, Mum?' I asked her.

Not a flicker interrupted her gaze. She continued staring blankly ahead.

I remember what Mum used to say to me about life and living: *The difference between life and death is but a breath, my child. We are born alone, for no one can take our first breath, and we must die alone, for no one can take our last breath, but we can only live together.*

I recited this. Mum made no response.

I put my head on her shoulder and said, 'I'm too young to be the mother, Mum. We need you. We can't pull through this unless we're together.'

Finally, she spoke. 'I know,' she said.

I moved away from her in case she realised I was trembling. I bit back tears.

'I just can't take it any more, Marah,' Mum said, wiping her own tears from her face.

I composed myself the best I could. 'Do you remember what you used to say to me about the strength of women who had to carry on, no matter what?'

'Nothing is stronger than the women who plough the earth with their bare hands...'

I finished off her sentence, '...and grow life.'

She smiled.

'I want my mum back,' I said.

She continued gazing at motes for a moment. Then, by some strange alchemy of the mind, my mum returned with a vengeance.

She raised herself, brushed her hair and tied it up into a French bun, got into her old tracksuit and began doing stretches. Tats and Dad stumbled back under the sheets into our 'room.' Dad didn't seem to notice anything out of the ordinary, but Tats gaped open-mouthed at Mum, then me, then back at Mum again. I shrugged my shoulders.

'Big Mama is back,' I said.

'You betcha!' Mum said, starting star jumps.

Me and my brother followed our crazy Mum as she jogged out of the hall and to the temple gate. We squeezed past a hungry morning queue of refugees. It took us a second to locate her. There she was, sprinting down the Soho Road past an oncoming horde of broken souls. We had to laugh.

Forty minutes later, Mum returned. Her face was flushed, and the freckles on her upper cheeks shone under droplets of sweat.

'You missed your shower turn, Mum,' I said as she flopped down.

'I'll wait,' she said and then asked, 'Have you had anything to eat?'

'Yes, Mum.' I replied.

'What did you have?'

'Today, it was daal-roti,' I said.

'Oh, that's good to know, dear.'

'It's always the same, Mum,' Tats moaned.

With Tats and me on either side of her, Mum unzipped her big rucksack, rummaged around and pulled out a small cloth bag. With a finger to her lips, she indicated for us to keep quiet. Mum emptied the bag's contents. Small things that were individually wrapped in strips of bandage cloth which Mum delicately unwound. A glint of sun. A clink. A gold chain emerged. A few golden nose cloves. Then emerald earrings. A set of gold bangles inlaid with silver. Gold nose rings. A shimmering silver necklace dripping with rubies. I held my breath at the beauty.

'We will make whatever we can of whatever is left of life,' Mum said. 'These are our rainy-day fund. And that rainy day is now. We'll sell them off. She turned and stroked Tats' face, then mine. 'I'm so proud of you for being strong. Marah, I love it when you smile through your tears. Never lose that. It is the sign of a strong warrior.'

I didn't tell her that I didn't think there was anything strong about me. I just wanted to go back to being a little girl and not having to worry about the family being shot and our house burning down. And I wanted Chilli back, and I wanted to tell her I can see beyond the kind strokes of your hands, and I know how much this jewellery means to you, how you had boasted about it coming to you down the generations. I wanted to say I don't want you to sell it all off.

And yet I said nothing. Above all that, I wanted her to help me contact Ash, but I was scared to ask in case she thought I was selfish, especially after what she said about me being strong. So, I smiled and let the tears drop into my lap.

I wiped my eyes and picked up the small nose clove, held it in my hand and remembered how Mum had told me her grandmother had worn it. Mum told me how many a Punjabi song had been sung about the glint of the clove, how it had stopped farmers from tilling their land. I put it gently down and picked up the nose ring, and Mum said, 'That one comes from Kabul in Afghanistan and had belonged to your father's great-grandmother.'

'Is Dad part Afghan?' I asked.

'All I know is she got these in Kabul, but not who she was,' and then added quickly, 'Come on, we're going for a walk.'

So, I went with Mum, and we sold the jewellery at a pawnbroker on the Rookery Road, not far from where we were. She took what she could haggle out of him, called him a thief and put the money into two plastic bags. She gave me one and put the other in the inside pocket of her long coat. I stuffed mine in a coat pocket and zipped it up. Then we left the shop.

When we got to the temple, Mum dropped me back with Dad and Tats and went off somewhere. She didn't get back till late at night, right when Tats was going full-on with one of his where-is-mum anxiety attacks. The next few days were the same, Mum went off somewhere, came back late, gave us big hugs and told us everything was going to be fine and that we were going to change our lives. Dad grunted an assent to these statements of Mum. But I could tell he had no idea what she was plotting.

One evening, she came back just as we were sitting on the ground in the middle of a long line of people having our dinner. 'What's the menu?' she asked. She had one of the biggest smiles I had ever seen.

The man next to me moved away a little, just enough for Mum to squeeze in.

'Today we have roti and daal,' I said, 'and gobi alu, cauliflower and potatoes.'

'Again!' Tats moaned.

Mum rubbed his head as a temple volunteer placed a three-sectioned plastic tray in front of her. A second volunteer poured lentils and vegetables into each section of the tray, while a third placed a handful of rotis in the remaining space.

'So, what's the good news?' I asked.

'We've got a place to live,' Mum boasted.

Mum broke a piece of the roti, dipped it in the lentils, and replied, 'It needs a bit of work, but we can turn it into a home.'

'How, Mum?'

She cleared her throat and looked at me with her younger eyes. She's back alright, I thought, getting ready for one of her rants.

'You see, dear,' she began, 'Capitalism is like a living organism, always evolving, full of parasites that know how to fatten, no matter what the environment. This war, this racism, this life is misery for us all, but it's a great fattening opportunity for some.'

She took a deep breath and smiled. I felt relieved – at least the rant was over.

Mum went on, 'You see, no one really knows who owns what any more, or even if the owner is alive or dead. My women friends told me there was a house up for rent, and the landlord was looking for someone to renovate it for him in exchange for rent for a while. I met him and paid him a deposit.'

'Who is he?' I asked.

'He is a horrible fat man with an ugly smile and stinks of tobacco.'

By the time I woke up the next day, Mum had made a long list of everything that needed to be done. She tapped me on the shoulder. We left Dad and Tats in the Temple and went off to see our new home. It was just over a mile from the away, down the Lozells Road, on what was left of one side of the terraced streets.

'Now, before we turn the corner, I must warn you,' said Mum. 'Mere mortals will think it looks like a burnt-out wreck. But us poets, we can see the beauty in everything. Right?'

We turned the corner.

It was a burnt-out wreck.

I didn't know whether to laugh or cry, so I did both.

Arm in arm, we walked up and inspected the outside. We ignored the tyres, rubbish bags, beer cans, and rusty old front bonnet of a car in the garden. There was a mature birch tree in the front garden with burnt-off and twisted branches. It would recover and provide shelter if summer got hot. The thick front door looked like it was made from some heavy hardwood. The house was technically semi-detached since one of the houses next to ours had been blown away, and the other was all boarded up and even had spiked metal grills all around the doors and windows.

We went inside easy since there was no front door. It didn't have internal doors or any intact windows, but the walls were all solid and without cracks. The roof was in no danger of collapsing on us if we moved in and provided peepholes into the sky, which might be atmospheric, especially if it was a starry night.

We shook on it, Mum pretending to be the estate agent.

'I think you've grabbed yourself a bargain here, Marah Sultana.'

We got back to the temple and took Tats and Dad and all our bags along with us to the house.

When Tats turned the corner, he looked at me with eyes that wanted to know if Mum really wanted us to live in a ruin.

'Appearances can be deceptive, Tats,' Mum said smoothly. 'It's definitely safe.'

While I was gawping at the sight, a white van pulled up close to Mum. She clapped her hands and said, 'Bang on time!' Four men in blue overalls came out of the back of another van and, under Mum's instructions, began to gut the house. They brought more and more rubbish out into the garden, dumped it in a pile, and went back in.

She went to the back of the van, came back a moment later with heavy cloth gloves, gave me and Tats a pair, and put a pair on herself. Dad was having one of his moments and rested on a wall. Me and my brother went to work, clearing the front of the house. Just as I was about to protest that me and Tats couldn't shift and sort it out on our own, when three women turned up and helped. Mum talked to them as though she had known them all her life. One of them, a chubby little one who wore a short-sleeved purple flowery top and dark blue jeans, looked at the pile of rubbish, put her hands on her hips, nodded towards the boarded-up house and said, 'That house is owned by Githu, the little worm, as well, and if he had a heart, he would let youse live there,' turning to me and Tats and smirked, 'With these two strong young 'uns, your mum didn't really need us.'

Then she winked at us and laughed. The flab on her dark-skinned arms and neck wobbled. We named her Aunty Paratha-fit. The one next to her was tall, with a sullen face and fierce eyes. She wore a blue tracksuit top and bottom and tied her hair in a bun at the back of her head. We named her Aunty Don't-Mess-With. The third one was shorter than me. She looked so fragile, with sad eyes, I was worried she would break a bone whilst helping us out. She wore a scarf around her head and a long brown overcoat. She had a large toolbox in her hand. We named her Aunty Sad-Eyes.

Aunty Paratha-fit got the men to make different piles: one for plastics, one for metals and one for general waste. So now we had four piles, one the men had already built and three new ones.

Rummaging through the first pile, Aunty Don't Mess-With carefully dug out a large piece of plastic. Shaking dust off it, she said, 'This is till we get some windows in.'

Aunty Sad-Eyes brought a door out. Tats ran up to help her, and she said softly, 'You don't need strength to move things.' She walked the door to the furthest end of the garden and leaned it against the tree. It had a few bullet holes in it, and some parts of it were burnt.

She went into the house and, a little while later, with the help of one of the workers, came out with a broken three-seater settee. She placed it at the furthest end of the garden near the tree, close to the door.

'Be kind enough to get the other settees, and please put them over there, by the tree as well,' Aunty Sad-Eyes said to the workman.

As he went back in, she collected her toolbox and began to fix the door. She filled in the holes with wood filler and planed the sides. She chiselled out the burnt bits from the door, sawed pieces of wood from the rubbish pile, slotted those into the chiselled-out sections and, before you knew it, the door began to look like a very healthy door. She waved for me and Tats to join her. We did.

Giving us a block of wood and some sandpaper each, she said, 'Scrub, and scrub a little more, the hard work is always in the prep.'

While we scrubbed and sanded, she began to fix the three-piece, and it started to look like something you could sit on once you had some cushions.

When I got her on her own, I asked Mum, 'How do you know them?'

'In war, friends come ready-made,' Mum said.

Mum's new friends were amazing. Aunty Sad-Eyes was, like us, a refugee from the South, the others were local. Mum's little group seemed to know where the new free hospital was being set up and which new charity had set up shop in Birmingham. They had even managed to connect with some of their relatives. The news of the war was always up to date, and sometimes their predictions too: the news was that the Bloods would, for the time being, not invade Birmingham as they were more interested in taking the North, especially Manchester and Liverpool, as these places had declared their intention of joining Scotland. Yorkshire was due a particular blast of Bloods hellfire because it wanted independence from everyone. But no one could tell me what had happened to Leena or Ash or Chilli.

Dad was shutting down. We took him with us a few times to our building site. He tried to help, but he kept dropping things and managed to cut his arm twice. Mum told him to sit by the tree and keep a note of what we needed to do next. Of course, he couldn't keep track of anything. Mum did this just to make him feel involved.

The day arrived when our house was good enough for us to move in. It had doors, windows, beds, water, and even erratic electricity. There were meant to be three bedrooms on the first floor and a bathroom, but parts of the floorboards of the small room were so severely damaged that Mum decided to board it up for now.

Mum's women's brigade managed to get us pots, pans and enough crockery to get us up and running as a house, and through her new network, Mum found a charity that provided us with bedding materials and even a dining table with chairs. Me and Tats rescued a swish, three-seater settee by a skip in Handsworth Wood. Then, an antique, two-bulb post-lamp was standing all alone in the middle of an overgrown park. Before we knew it, our living room felt quite homely. Mum even managed to sew some curtains.

When we first came to Birmingham, I didn't really believe we would be here for long, but that was before the weddings. Before more militias began to be formed and before babies being born, and then I stopped thinking about Zainab, Leena, and Ash, and the life I wanted got lost in nightmares. Everything from the Free Northern Army, the English

National Liberation Army, Anarchists and even some Muslim, Sikh and Jewish militias was on offer. At first, they united and fought the Bloods to a standstill just outside Potters Bar to the south, but sometimes they turned on each other, and I lost track of who was fighting whom or where.

I started sneaking out and going to a pub called The Grove, which was by a small roundabout, a few miles away from our house, and one of the places that was guaranteed not to be bombed, as everyone drank there. It was where I flirted with militia boys, prick-teased the older ones, and promised more to the younger ones. They were all just thick nob-heads, but they did teach me that the safest place to hang out was in the cemetery as they all needed to be buried somewhere, so they treated it as a sort of a holy place, a living deadman's land.

I made some money whichever way I could and gave it all to Mum, but there never was very much. She didn't ask how I got it, and I never told her. Tats somehow managed to find out what I was up to, called me a slut, and complained to Mum, but I gave him a hard one around the ears, and that put a stop to that for a while. Mum, of course, didn't believe him.

THE NEW DAWN

One of the militiamen, a short, ugly creature whose body odour was worse than his looks, was called Shorty. He thought he was the best thing since circumcised naans, as he used to boast about himself. He was always trying new ways of getting into my pants: it was my Islamic duty to let him when he was pissed, and when he was sober, he was head-over-heels in love with me, he would insist. It didn't matter if I slapped him, swore at him, or spat at him, he always had a disgusting grin on his face. When he was particularly horny, he had this smile where he showed all his teeth, and it was difficult not to see the glint of his gold-filled molars, and if I hate anything, it's men with gold teeth. He boasted about how many houses he owned in Birmingham and even offered me a place if I did his bidding. It was then that I connected what Aunty Paratha-Fit had said. She had mentioned the boarded-up house next to ours belonged to a man called Githu, which means Shorty in Punjabi, and therefore, it had to be this sad story of a human being. This was confirmed one day when I was looking out of my bedroom window. I saw Shorty in the house next door and quickly hid. He surveyed the place for a while, looked at ours and left.

Time goes fast and then stops if you are a refugee. That's what I've concluded. It goes fast because new horrors can arrive quicker than the terrors of yesterday, and sometimes, the future just stops and lets the present wounds fester on and on.

Just when I was beginning to enjoy my new house and my new degrading life, the war started across the midlands. A rumour had it that the Bloods would seize Birmingham. Another went around that they were too busy in the South and that the attack on Birmingham was a deflection. Mum got into packing bags all over again; Dad hardly got out of bed; Tats walked about like a scared pup; and I felt the tension in my chest all day, made all the worse by the constant sound of new drones flying above. The fighting lasted a few days and died down, but the drones were always in the air, buzzing away. Their noise made me cringe like it did when I heard someone scratching their fingernails on a blackboard. I began to hear drones in my sleep, even when they were not there.

The front lines didn't change, but the sounds of war did. Sometimes, when a massive bomb dropped somewhere beyond the front lines, an echo would shake through everything, and terrified birds shot up all around; and sometimes, when it was close, bullets would ping by, followed by them hitting a wall somewhere, All the while more and more refugees started coming from the North.

A couple moved into the empty, burnt-out space next door to us. They must have come during the night. The next day, I saw their tent. It was a large blue thing with a door in the middle and lots of poles and strings keeping it taught all around it.

In the morning, Mum and I took them some toast, boiled eggs, and tea. I carried these on a tray covered with a small white towel.

The air was filled with the stench of rotting rubbish and dampness.

A bald man with a grey beard was brushing his teeth outside the tent when we got there. It had rained last night, and even though it was a bit chilly, he only had a white vest and stripy pyjamas on. He looked at us apprehensively, spat some toothpaste on the ground behind the tent, and nodded. The woman sat on an upturned crate with her head bowed. Her reddish-brown hair fell out of the hood of the green anorak covering her face. She wore a long black skirt and held her knees with her hands.

'We don't mean no trouble. Me daughter and I will be on our way as soon as we can,' the man said.

'We thought you might like some breakfast,' Mum said.

He looked away from us, saying, 'We have had our breakfast, but thank you.'

The woman looked up at me. She had tired, hungry eyes. She was around my age. I smiled at her. She lowered her head again.

"My name is Harry, and that is Shyla,' he said, looking at Mum.

I stepped forward, squatted next to Shyla and said, 'I used to live in London and dream dreams once.'

She ignored me, and I said, 'My name is Marah, this is my Mum, Parveen Sultana, and my Dad is lost somewhere inside his head, and I got an arsehole of a brother called Tats, and if he ever annoys you, kick him in the nuts.'

She lifted her head and smiled.

'You're not the only white people in this area,' I said.

'How do you know I'm white?' Shyla asked. 'I've not washed my face for a week.'

I liked her.

Putting the tray down next to her, I said, 'I know you already had your breakfast, but why don't you have some more?'

'Thank you, Marah,' Shyla said.

I went to see Shyla over the next few days. She was always polite but kept herself locked up inside. I invited her home, but she refused. I would be with her for a while, and she would just sit there silently. I didn't see her dad much; if I did, he would nod and go into the tent. Though I waved at her if ever I saw Shyla outside her tent, I left her alone; that was clearly what she wanted.

Three girls were kidnapped in Sparkbrook in the middle of the night. That's what everyone said. They all lived on the same street. Masked men had raided all the girls' houses at the same time, bundled them into vans, and took them away. A week later, two girls were taken from Handsworth by masked men. These, too, were in the middle of the day. A rumour had it that they were being auctioned at the Spaghetti Junction.

Strange as it may sound, up until now, the King Edward VI school for girls in Handsworth, a mile and a half from our house, was the only school still open, but this suddenly shut down as well.

I feared a car's screeching tyres or even a car coming towards me. I would hide if I saw militiamen, and Mum could no longer bear me being out of her sight. Each time we sat down for dinner, she would say, 'Shyla is so vulnerable out there. Go ask her to come and live with us.'

'They want their privacy, Mum,' I said, and usually, this was the end of the conversation, but a mini storm was predicted for tonight.

'It's going to rain badly tonight. They only have a tent,' Mum said but stopped midsentence. Someone laughed on the road.

Mum got up, grabbed a knife, and went outside. I followed her.

Four men, perhaps late teens, were eyeing Shyla. She sat quietly where she always did on her upturned crate outside her tent.

Mum went up to the men and said, waving the knife, 'Fuck off home to your mothers and sisters. You don't want to know what I will do to you if I see you here again.'

They were clearly terrified by Mum and stepped onto the road off the pavement.

'I am coming to your house to see your mum,' Mum pointed the knife at the one closest to her.

All of them ran off.

'Do you know his mum,' I asked.

'No, but he doesn't know that' she replied.

Shyla had eyes on us all the time. Mum and I went to her, and she smiled at us, nodded, stood up, pointed to the crate and said to Mum, 'Please, Aunty, take a seat.'

'So many young women are being kidnapped, Shyla,' Mum said.

'I was ready for them.' Shyla pulled a large army knife out of her anorak.

'These were just boys,' Mum said. 'What good is a knife against militias?'

'Come stay with us, Shyla, at least tonight?' I asked.

'You are so kind and have such big hearts, but Dad and I are fine here,' Shyla said. 'He will be home soon; he has a little job now.'

It rained cats and dogs that night, all mixed up with fierce winds, thunder, lightning and gunfire. By the morning, but for the birds partying in our birch tree, it was magically silent. The sun was even out. Gone was the stench of rubbish. The air was as fresh as it could be, without any trace of war.

The first thing Mum did was rush.

She left a note on the kitchen table: *Shyla can't live like this, back soon*, and was gone before I woke up.

By the late afternoon, Mum turned up with the aunties who'd helped us. I was lying on the three-seater, dangling my feet over its edge, and musing whether to go to The Grove or not, as I hadn't been there for a while, when Mum burst in, grabbed me by the wrist and commanded, 'Come.'

'Where?' I protested, but mum tugged me. I got up, put some slippers on and followed her.

Harry and Shyla sat quietly outside their tent, each on an upturned crate.

The Aunties were looking at the boarded house.

'Why should the house next door be empty when people need a place to live?' Mum said.

'Wow, Mum, we are moving there?'

I'd always imagined it as a house where everything worked, including the toilet flush, not like ours where you had to lift the lid of the cistern and pull it to get the water to release, which miraculously continued to flow.

'We already have a lovely home,' Mum said.

'Ah huh, it's a home. Let's not go over the top, Mum,' I said.

She ignored me, went to Harry and Shyla and said, 'You're moving next door to us.'

'We are fine, don't want trouble, Love,' Harry said.

'Just pack your things, leave the rest to us,' Mum said.

Off came the boards, and Aunty Sad-Eyes opened the door.

'Mum, we could have real trouble here. Do you know who this belongs to?'

'If that Githu so much as lifts a finger, I will cut his tatty, his bollocks off,' Aunty Paratha-Fit said.

The women laughed.

When I entered the house, it was in better condition than I'd imagined. Everything, even the carpet, had dust covers on it.

We took off the dust covers and wiped the surfaces. Someone opened all the doors and windows, and I went to the toilet to see if the flush really did work. The pot had a black film in it, but it worked. I had washed my hands and shaken a dusty towel when I heard Aunty Paratha-fit shouting in the front garden. I rushed out, towel in hand. Shorty was there. I quickly stepped back inside, threw the towel over my head and wrapped it around my face, niqab-like.

'Now listen carefully, Githu. That family over there in that tent, is going to live in this house, till we can find them somewhere else for them. You so much as look at them in a bad way, and I will crush your balls, and those of your shit-faced father, and tell the whole world what your mother was up to when she was young, and I might even tell the world who your real father is,' Aunty Paratha-fit said poking Shorty in the chest.

'They can stay, they can stay,' Shorty said, stepping back. 'For a little while.'

'I'll tell you when they are ready to move,' Aunty Paratha-fit said.

'Yes, Aunty,' Shorty said, walking away.

After he left, Aunty Paratha-fit asked me, 'What's with the niqab, Marah?'

'He is not a nice man,' I said.

'No, he isn't,' Aunty Paratha-fit said, 'if he ever looks at you in a bad way, tell the lech, you know me.'

'I will,' I said.

Harry and Shyla moved in next door to us. Ever so slowly, Shyla began to open up to me.

THE TESTIMONY

12

She looked like a different person after she moved in next door and started showering, and, unlike me, she was really pretty. Her nose was perfectly shaped, so delicate, so beautiful, unlike my round, blobby thing. Her bum and boobs seemed to have been carved by an artist. Even in rags, she looked like a fashion model and, were it not for the dark rings under her green eyes, she could have been a beauty queen. She said she was 23 but looked much younger.

She started telling me her story one sunny day as we sat in my front garden, looking out at some boys kicking a tin can around. The clouds played hide-and-seek with the sun. A drone flew somewhere above. It was one of the nosiest I had heard for a long time.

'My world changed so fast, faster than it changes in the fastest nightmare,' Shyla said when the drone's noise began to die down. 'I lived in Prestwich, and unlike other areas of Manchester, where lots of Muslims lived, like Cheetham Hill, Longsight, Rusholme, Hulme Chorlton and Trafford, ours was safe. We had our Jewish Defence League, or JDL as it was called, and everyone apart from my dad was part of it. It had been around long before I was born and was forever hosting Love Israel Days, but when Israel began to collapse, and a Red Heifer was born...'

'What's a Red Heifer?' I asked.

'It's a cow?' Shyla replied, 'and my mum joined the Red Heifer Brigade. When this happened, Mum and Dad fought so much, I was terrified they would get divorced.'

'They fought over a cow?' I asked.

'Sort of,' Shyla smirked. 'Mum said that with the birth of the Red Heifer in Israel, it was proof that the prophecy had come true.'

'Dad laughed his head off at her, saying, "You couldn't save Israel slaughtering Palestinians, and now you think slaughtering a cow will do the trick."

'"I want to go back to Israel," Mum would say when they fought, and they fought all the time.

' "You can't go back to a place that's no more and should never have been,"' Dad would say.

' "My God-given right,"' Mum would insist.

' "God doesn't exist," Dad would retort. ' "God doesn't exist, how can he give you a fucking right!" '

'I thought mine were bad,' I said.

'Maybe, but did your dad ever get thrown out of a mosque?' Shyla asked.

'I don't think so,' I replied

'Mine got thrown out of the Synagogue,' Shyla laughed. 'It was around the time when the mosques of Cheetham Hill began to be torched, that's when my dad stood up in our Synagogue and read out that, *First they came for the Communists*, but his version:

First, they came for the Communists
And I did not speak out
Because I was not a Communist
Then they came for the Socialists
And I did not speak out
Because I was not a Socialist
Then they came for the trade unionists
And I did not speak out
Because I was not a trade unionist
Then they came for the Muslims
And I did not speak out
Because I was not a Muslim
Then they came for me
And there was no one left
To speak out for me.

'Hard to forget,' I replied. It had been mandatory at school. But my mum used to say, when we learn of only one pain only, this is at the expense of other pains and adds to historical injustice.'

'As I was saying, even though people were shouting at him to stop,' Shyla interrupted me. 'He didn't, he ignored them and carried on. There were lots of people there at the time, loads from the local churches, but because dad had changed the word *Jew* to *Muslim*, this caused such an uproar in the place, and they threw him out,' she sighed and added, 'I don't know why they ever got married.'

'How did they get married?' I asked.

'I think Mum and Dad had it off one dark stormy night and she got in the club (that's pregnant for you Londoners), and what was the poor unmarried girl to do? So they got married. And I turned up,'

She took a deep breath and continued, 'And when Muslims were forced out of Manchester, it was then that the Bloods made a mad rush to capture the North, and before we knew, they'd got halfway down Bury New Road but then were beaten back by the Free Northern Army, and then the Jewish Defence League, went over to the Bloods, but they too were pushed all the way up to the M60, which became no-man's-land.

'One day, a JDL man came with a letter for me to go to London for a test for the Bloods. He stood by the door, insisting I go with him. Mum said I should go, Dad said no, and I was terrified. I'd heard of some girls going for this test, but I hated the idea of it. Dad went to the door to have a chat with the JDL man. When he opened the door, there were loads of them. Dad said, "She will be along in a little while," and before I could protest, he whispered, "Get what you can fit into a rucksack quickly, I'll get the tent."'

'That night, Dad and I left, and here we are.'

I gave her a big hug and went home to sleep.

The next morning, Mum woke me up with a scream, 'They've kidnapped Shyla.'

Everyone in the street searched for her everywhere, but we couldn't find her. I went to The Grove and asked Shorty, but he and all the other men swore they knew nothing. Harry borrowed a motorbike and would not give up looking for her. We managed to get him to eat once or twice. He didn't sleep at night or in the day, and then, one day, he turned up with her. Her clothes were ripped. Her hair was matted. Her arms and legs were covered in cuts and bruises.

Shyla stopped talking. Sometimes, she mumbled to herself. Other times, she laughed madly, but mostly, she sat quietly in her room, door closed.

I went to see her every other day, but I don't think she saw me. Once, when I was leaving, she said, 'They took me to the Spaghetti Junction.'

I didn't know what to say.

THE TOUCH DIVINE

13

One night, after Tats went to sleep, Mum insisted I go for a walk with her. Before we left, she asked me, 'Has your mobile got a charge in it?'

'A bit, but you know there's no reception any more.'

'Bring it with you,' she said.

'What for?' I protested.

'Bring it!' she insisted.

On the way out, I felt all angry inside. Maybe she wanted to sell it. If she did, how would I ever contact Ash and Leena? The networks were all off now, but deep down, I believed that sooner or later, we would be able to connect. Then, I felt angry at myself for being so selfish. After all, Mum had sold all her wedding jewellery for us. Who was I to hang on to the past?

The Lozells Road was a slow-moving snake with all manner of vehicles vainly vying with each other. The church on Hamstead Road, near the Villa Road junction, had a powerful spotlight shining on it. It had been converted to a mosque, but someone burnt it down, and it was now being renovated by an international charity. We walked past the junction up the Villa Road. The King Edward VI girls' school on our right had armed checkpoints at both ends. The men looked like Sikhs. The whole side of the road had multi-colour fairy lights that lit up the buildings behind it. When we got close to Soho Road, I realised that the Gurdwara, where we had first lived when we came to Birmingham, had taken over the girls' school as well as all the roads in between.

Mum looked at the temple dome for a few moments and said, 'Give me your mobile.'

I felt my precious oblong pressing hot into my thigh. It didn't want me to give it up.

The sky above us was cold and dark. Some of the streetlights flickered on and off. Then a flare. And a convoy of cars with masked men flew past us, honking their horns. Mum watched the convoy, stone-faced. Once the last car passed, she unfolded her arms, and I said, 'Please don't sell my phone, I'll get a job.'

'I'm not selling your mobile,' Mum said, holding her hand out. She had the attitude of a military commander who Must Be Unquestioningly Obeyed. I gave it to her, and she swung left towards Hockley and stopped in front of a derelict building with a white sign written in flaking blue paint that said Destiny International Christian Assembly. All the streetlights went off suddenly. We looked up. Clouds shrouded the stars. Tracer rounds shot up from around the city Centre somewhere. Flares exploded to the West, above the Hockley Roundabout. A drone zigged and zagged half a mile to the East, then dropped something.

We crossed the road towards St Michael's Parish. Mum stopped holding my hand as we neared a small van-car with a rolled-down roof. A hooded man lit a cigarette and stared at us.

'You're late,' he told Mum rudely.

'You've come to meet him?' I asked Mum.

'Turn your mobile on,' Mum commanded.

'Why?'

'Just do it!' she insisted. 'And get Ash's number.'

As I turned my mobile on, Mum gave the man some money. My eyes filled with tears. Mum had set this up so I could talk to Ash. I wish she'd told me beforehand so I could have composed myself. I wanted to say so much to him, to tell him so much, and wanted to say it in a voice that was meant only for him. And I wanted to hear from him that he missed me. I wanted him to tell me he had been to our street, seen our house, been inside it, and fed Chilli.

I pulled myself together. All this was possible. I would tell him where we lived.

The hooded man went into his car, took out a box with an old television antenna-like extension, placed it on top of the car, looked at my mobile number and then dialed it on his phone.

'You will give no address or location over the phone. They will track the location and trace the call back to me, and you have three minutes only. It will automatically disconnect after that,' he said quickly after he finished dialling the number.

Mum nodded and stepped a bit away.

Before I could protest about the three minutes, the man pressed the call button and passed it to me. It rang only once, and Ash answered.

'Ash!' I cried. I was lost for words.

'Marah. Where are you?'

The hooded man's voice interrupted the call, 'No addresses, or I disconnect the phone now.'

'Who's that, Marah?'

'Ash, just someone making money out of misery.' Ash. I'd said his name again.

'How are you?' he asked.

I laughed, 'Everything's hunky-dory.'

'I miss you so much,' he said.

'Can you see the sky?' I asked.

'Yes.'

'Look up. We're connected now. We're seeing the same sky.' I didn't care that the creep was listening in. 'I never thought a night could be so long, and it's longer without you.'

'I've come looking for you every day I could. How are you all? How's Tats? Where can I find you?'

The man's voice cut in again, 'Right, call over.'

'She still has time,' Mum protested.

He snatched his mobile out of my hand, jumped in his car and screeched away into the darkness.

Mum gave me a great big hug.

'I didn't ask how he was,' my voice broke.

Mum stroked my head. 'You did.'

'I didn't say what I wanted to.'

'You said everything and more.'

'I didn't hear what I needed to,' I cried.

'You did and much more,' Mum said, holding back her tears.

'Will we ever meet again?' I cried a bit more.

'Yes. You will.'

'Mum. I'm meant to be crying, not you,' I said.

'I know.'

Mum had spent some of our precious jewellery money on that phone call.

The days dragged on. Wave after wave of people arrived. All manner of charities sprang up and set up stalls. Giving out food. Reuniting families. Patching up houses. Supplying tents. Distributing water. Some made us feel like beggars, having us stand strictly in line and keeping records of how much food we were given, for how many mouths and of what age. The best-paid work was with the big charities, but all those jobs were sewn up before they were even advertised. Mum managed to land a job with a small charity called Mending Minds. It lasted two months then one of the local mosques accused it of spreading un-Islamic propaganda and forced it to shut down.

The last of our money was spent on minced meat. Mum made kebabs, and me and Tats tried to sell them on Lozells Road, but a passing gang of armed men forced us to give everything to them. One of them even tried to drag me into their car, but Tats bit his arm, and I wrenched myself free.

When I got home, Dad looked at me, not in his usual zombie-like gaze, but almost like my old dad. I lost it and said to him, 'We can't cope, Dad. Look at us. What little food we have won't last. We are broke. Mum lost her job. We need you. Please get it together. Please find Uncle Melvin. Please, please, please.'

The glimmer in Dad's eyes died.

'He'll just tell you, "My paratha will burn,"' Tats said bitterly. We both stared at the lump of despondency that was our dad.

I put my hand around my little brother's shoulders. We left Dad as he started muttering.

Then, the next day, a small miracle.

Dad looked up from his morning tea-stare-a-thon and said, 'You were right last night, Marah. I'm going to find Melvin. He'll help us. He's my friend. He won't let me down.'

Mum crunched her empty white plastic teacup and tossed it in our cardboard box bin. 'Do you know his address?'

'No, but I know where he lives,' Dad boasted.

'Do you know what day it is, Dad?' I asked.

'Why?' Dad laughed.

'Oh, Marah means you might be worried about burning the paratha,' Mum said.

He went silent for a few moments and then asked, 'What paratha?' Turning to Mum, he said, 'Let's go.' Mum killed that idea fast.

'I'm not leaving the kids. It's too dangerous,' she said. 'You go.' She handed him some money, which she must have had hidden, and added, 'Come back quickly.'

Dad got up.

'Wait,' Mum commanded. She ripped a piece of cardboard off the bin, scribbled our address on it and stuffed it in his pocket. She kissed him on the cheek. 'Be careful.'

Dad sailed out merrily, walking like his old self.

Getting Dad back was one of the most joyous moments of our time here. Even Tats started cleaning up after him.

After lunch, me and Tats went outside. The birch tree had spread its branches, big style, reaching out joyously to the sky. We'd found an old blue twisted tow rope and unknotted it, slung it over a branch of the blasted tree and took turns pushing and swinging. Mum even tried to join in but fell on her arse.

As the sun began setting and Dad still hadn't returned, we were all under the birch tree, and I asked Mum, 'Do you have any idea where Uncle Melvin lives?'

'Somewhere on the outskirts of Birmingham,' Mum said.

Tats kept going to the end of the street every five minutes to check to see if he could see Dad.

'He should have been back by now,' I said when Tats returned, glum-faced, for the fifth time.

'He's probably getting pissed with Melvin,' Mum said.

'He wouldn't do that!' I protested. 'And I shouldn't have asked him to go alone, I should have gone with him. He's not been well.'

When it got full-on dark, Mum went silent.

We got Dad's body delivered to our door the next day. He was brought in an open-backed van. He had been shot in the head near Redditch, inside no-man's-land. The van driver gave Mum the card on which she had written our address and put it in Dad's pocket.

Mum went back into herself. Her silence stretched and stretched. She communicated in gestures. The van aunties came, wailing into our house, and Dad's body was soon whisked away to the mosque. All this time, Mum just sat there, under the birch tree, mute. I had to get blankets and drape them over her because she wouldn't get up. Two van aunties sat there all night with her. Tats crept into my room and slept by my bed on the floor. I woke up, and my face was streaming with tears. Tats was crying in a corner. 'I hate this world,' he told me when I tried to comfort him.

'Me, too,' I said. I let him cry on my shoulder until the shuddering stopped. Then we went down to find Mum. The aunties had laid her out on the sofa, and she was sleeping there. They told us not to disturb her; she needed the rest, and they fed us.

Harry came a few times and brought us some food. Shyla came just once, looked at me, screamed, bent over, put her hands on her knees and cried and then just left. She came back an hour or so later, hugged me, cried a bit more and left.

We buried Dad in the Muslim graveyard in Handsworth. I don't remember much about the ceremony. Only the sound of soil on shovels, the creak of branches in the cemetery trees, and Mum's nails driving into my shoulder as she gripped me, trying not to fall.

I went to visit him every day. Tats only came if Mum came with me, and she came once a week, on the same day he left us.

I didn't cry. I don't know where my tears went. I guess they dried up. All I kept thinking was, why had I asked him to go? It was my fault he was dead. I had no energy or desire left to do anything. I stopped washing and shaving and doing my hair. I had to be forced to eat. I had nothing to say to anyone in the family or any of the van aunties buzzing around like flies and overstaying their welcome. Who asked them anyway?

The day dawned when I'd had enough. I wanted to end it all.

I went down and searched the kitchen for the carving knife but couldn't find it.

Maybe I made a bit of noise because Mum ran in and I asked her, 'Where is the knife? The big, long one?'

'It's gone.'

'Where?'

'I put it away, dear,' Mum said.

'Where?'

'Somewhere safe...'

'Give it to me!'

I pushed her in the chest.

Tats charged into the room and stood between Mum and me, and said, 'Don't you dare touch my mum.'

I was stunned. I had never pushed Mum in my life. I collapsed at the table and buried my head. 'I'm sorry, Mum,' I mumbled through my arms.

Then Mum smothered me in a hug. 'It's OK, sweetheart. We're all suffering.'

'He's dead because of me,' I mumbled.

'Don't blame yourself. He wouldn't want that.'

'Me and my big ugly mouth.'

I slid off the chair onto the kitchen floorboards, and Mum lay down there with me. I could feel her stroking my face. 'This day will pass,' she whispered, 'this day will pass. As all others.' Tats came down and joined us too, and cried as Mum told us again and again, 'This day will pass.' Then the van auntie barged in with food and hot tea and they were dragging us all up off the floor and wiping our faces with wet cloths and pushing food in our mouths. We gave in.

Later, when we had stopped crying, Mum said, 'Let's go visit your dad. Can't keep him waiting.'

Tats went around the graveyard collecting wildflowers as me and Mum pulled tiny weeds out of Dad's grave. And I thought nature, like the van aunties, was also unrelenting. We were spreading wildflowers over Dad when I heard a voice which I thought I would never hear again. I turned. Uncle Melvin.

'Oh, dear God, I'm so sorry,' he said.

We all stood up. Mum let out a scream so loud it shook my sternum. Then she threw herself into Melvin's arms.

For the first two weeks after that encounter at the graveside, Uncle Melvin came daily and made sure we had everything we needed. The van aunties gave him their official stamp of approval by complimenting his red lentil soup, which he insisted on making for us ('a bit bland but very nice gora, white, consistency' was their precise verdict). Then, his visits tapered off. He had a business to run. On his last day, as he sat in the house with us, he unpacked a hi-tech speaker system for Tats. Then, three old laptops – one for each of us. 'Stay in touch if you can,' were his last words.

THE REUNION 14

W e moved around the house like aching spirits, each shedding their pains in unintelligible words that came groaning out of nightmares. Tats couldn't bear to be away from Mum, even when she was in another room. Mum was constantly checking to see if I was alive or had acquired any knives. I couldn't stand being in the house for long, it felt empty since Dad was no longer there. When the feeling became too intense, even in the dead of night, I went to the graveyard and sat with Dad. I felt strangely alive there. The graveyard too, was alive, growing every day. I walked about reading gravestones and tried to work out how many of the residents, especially the newcomers, were younger than me. A new, small grave had been added during the night. It was covered in red rose petals and was close to Dad's. A handwritten note, wrapped in clear plastic, was pinned to a piece of wood at the head of the grave. The note read: *I was only five, I just wanted to play.*

With my index finger, I wrote in the sand among the flowers, *Oh God, come see what is done in your name.*

As I was leaving the little child's grave, my mobile suddenly connected to the network for the first time since we'd left London. I caught my breath. It downloaded so many messages so fast I thought it might melt. Among them were two large streams of texts from Ash and Leena. I flicked through them fast.

Ash had been to Birmingham many times searching for me, like he said on the phone. Leena was in Handsworth, on the other side of Soho Road, a few miles from me. Immediately, I texted her that I'd just got her messages, and I was in the graveyard visiting my dad.

Fifteen minutes later, she was striding through the graves towards me. She hugged me tightly, lifted me off the ground, spun me around, and placed a great big kiss on my cheek. And she cried, laughed, and smiled – a smile brighter than a neon advertisement.

I showed her dad. She told me all on her mum's side lived around Birmingham. Her eyes were bloodshot, and she had heavy rings under them that she was covering up with concealer. She wore a pillbox red padded coat and black distressed jeans. She had short home-cut hair, dry lips, and sleep rings around her eyes. We were talking so excitedly that I didn't notice Shyla until she stopped a short distance away from us.

'My dad said you would be here,' she said. Her eyes lowered. She carried a plastic bag with her, and for the first time I saw her wearing jeans and a top.

'That's my lovely neighbour, Shyla,' I said, introducing her, 'and this unfaithful creature is my cousin Leena.'

'Love your Mancunian accent,' Leena said and then asked, 'And what brought you to this lovely place?'

'War,' Shyla said, looking up.

'Ouch, so much pain in your eyes, girl, so much,' Leena said.

'They took me to the Spaghetti junction…' Shyla said slowly.

I held Shyla's trembling hand.

She snatched it free and said, 'And they sold me.'

She stepped back and said, 'And they laughed.'

We hugged.

We cried.

We cried.

We hugged.

'Let's find the bastards who did this,' I said eventually.

'They were men,' Shyla said, pulling a bottle out of her bag. She unscrewed it, and placed it on a grave nearby, pulled a half-drunk bottle of coke out as well.

'Let's shoot anyone with balls,' Leena said.

'Let's,' I agreed. Shyla poured the vodka into the Coke bottle and held it out to me.

'She is a teetotaler,' Leena said, 'but it is my favourite drink.'

'Only the dead don't drink nowadays,' I said.

'Are we living?' said Shyla, and she took a mouthful.

'If you drink, you don't think,' Leena replied.

I took a big swig and felt my throat catch fire.

We took a few more swigs from the bottle, and Leena pulled out a joint.

'Where you got money to buy this?' I asked her.

'I still have my hijab, you know,' said Leena, passing the joint to Shyla. 'My air of mystery is still worth investing in, even if my looks aren't.'

I laughed and offered the bottle to Shyla, who shook her head.

'Are you a poet?' Shyla looked at me. She had bewitching hazel eyes, which I hadn't noticed before.

'Used to be. I hate words now; they've caused so much pain in the world. I'll never write another poem.'

'You just did,' Shyla said, passing the joint to me.

I took a long drag. My lungs burnt, and I coughed the top half of my lungs out, which amused Leena.

I got my breath back and asked Shyla, 'How come in this garden of the dead, you have become such a vibrant flower?'

'She really can't help but speak poetry, can she?' Leena said to Shyla, giggling and passed some tobacco and dope to Shyla, who began rolling another joint.

I got pissed and stoned and told the world of the living and the dead, with all its armies and wars and lies and foolish desires, to go and get fucked.

I think I was carried home.

Mum was furious with me when I saw her face and tea-potting arms in the shadow of the birch tree. I told her to fuck off as well.

'Fuck off, teapot!'

Mum droned through the haze. It was a long-ass speech. I caught the end of it.

'…I can live without your dad, I can live without food, but I can't live watching you dying each day.'

'Why is everything about you and what you want?' I wailed back.

'What sort of an example are you setting for your brother?'

I tried to spit on the floor but only managed to hit myself. 'I don't give a tiddily shit for him.'

'What would your father say if he…'

'Oh, please, Mum, just fuck off,' I pushed my way into the house, dragged myself up the stairs and collapsed on my bed.

Each time the three of us met in the graveyard, we got pissed and stoned if Leena had managed to get some gear. It was one of these days when she turned up with just a few bottles of coke but no booze. After we finished the cokes, we left and were walking along Oxhill Road when Leena said she couldn't wait and needed to piss. It was quiet, and no one was around. Leena squatted, and I moved away from Shyla so that

I could keep a proper eye out for Leena. We were both hiding behind the mauled metal carcass of a minibus. Shyla was a few steps away from me, closer to the road. Then real shit happened.

A military-camouflaged van screeched to a halt near Shyla.

She screamed. Two masked men in blue-grey camo jackets rushed out from the back of the van.

One of them flung a black sack over Shyla's head. The other grabbed her by the arms and pushed her towards the van. Its sliding side door swept back. They were bundling her in.

'Fuck you!' I yelled.

I rushed at the men and swung at the one who had Shyla by the arms. My fists missed, but I smashed my skull down on his nose. Blood spurted. He screamed. Now, the driver opened his door and made to step out. Just then, Leena came charging towards us, pants dragging.

'There's 20 of us, let's do them, let's show these bastards,' she shouted.

The driver leapt back into his seat and slammed his door. The man who had put the hood over Shyla's head pushed her away. Leena landed a kick in the other one's groin. His legs were still kicking away, half in, half out of the van as it screeched off.

I took the hood off Shyla, and we pulled her to the pavement. Her brown trouser legs were wet. She trembled, held her hands open like claws in front of her, and stared.

'It's OK, it's over now, Shyla,' I said.

Shyla shook her shoulders. A distant explosion went off – tank fire. We didn't normally notice these when we were together, but today, they were coming from lots of different directions.

Leena massaged Shyla's hands.

'What was that about twenty of us?' Leena asked me.

'Bullshit frightens cowards, Mum used to say,' I replied. 'And where'd you learn to kick like that?'

'A bit of training … got to be part of the resistance, you know,' she put a finger to her lips when she said this.

'How many times must I die?' Shyla asked in laboured breaths. She looked like she was entering into a spasm. She hyper-ventilated. Then she screamed so loudly she drowned out the sound of the bombs.

People looked out of their windows at us. Others drew their curtains.

After a while, Shyla stood up, and Leena and I put our arms under her shoulders, took her home and put her to bed. She trembled all the way into her sleep.

Shyla wouldn't come out of her house for weeks after that. During that time, new militias popped up all over Birmingham. Women and even girls started getting kidnapped in broad daylight. Some of the taken were never seen again, others didn't want to be seen again, and some couldn't find themselves again.

Enough was enough, I thought, and decided to get some girls together. At first, we called ourselves the Deadz, but one day Leena turned up with a crate of Gin, and when she was pissed, she insisted she had a vision of a Jinn, and he told her that if men didn't have a hole in their dicks, no oxygen would get to their brains, and because of this, we ended up being called the Ginnz. It wasn't really meant to be a gang, just a group of us who walked with each other for protection so we could get out of the house. At first, there were just two steadies, me and Leena, and whoever we walked with. After a few weeks, Shyla joined us. Though she rarely spoke, she walked with us, her face furious and determined, scared and angry. Before long we numbered fifteen and had worked out walk routes, zones and our Three Commitments. Solidarity. Female Power. Parties. Leena even recruited a hairdresser, who did our members' eyebrows for free.

BELIEVERS

One day, no one had heard of the Believers, and then next, they were everywhere. They wore crisp blue khaki uniforms, topped at one end with a grey beret worn to one side and at the other end by bottle green paratrooper boots. They never took a bribe. They didn't smoke joints while on duty. They cleaned the streets. They repaired old cables and laid new ones so that Birmingham had its own television network and telephone system. They fixed the water treatment plants and the water pumping system so everyone had clean, drinkable water. And they imposed order. Some of them didn't even speak English. Everyone welcomed them at first, even me.

Their world was just one country, one ruler, at present, some dude called Emad Al-Englandi. They condemned everyone except themselves as an enemy of God but didn't mention the Bloods. Some said rich people in the Middle East were funding them. Others said they were a Bloods front, disguised as Muslims. Then, they banned drinking. Men had to grow beards. Women were ordered to go under the burqa.

While the Believers crushed all the rag-tag Muslim gangs ruthlessly, they settled into an alliance with a Sikh militia called the Khalis, who ran the city north of the Muslim zones and banned beef and tobacco in their area. This gave me an idea, which I put to the Ginnz, which I thought Dad would have loved.

We were sitting in the graveyard. It was a lovely summer night. The leaves in the trees sang louder than the birds.

'We should smuggle cigs to the Khalis and Booze to the Believers,' I said.

'But Sikhs don't smoke,' Leena said when I explained my idea to the gang.

'Yeh,' Shyla laughed. 'Like Muslims don't drink.'

Sharp girl, I thought. She was back to the old Shyla.

I dug my dagger in as well. 'And like the Niqabi Leena doesn't shag.'

Leena sputtered, 'Where are we going to get the initial investment from? There are too many hijabis in Birmingham, and no one wants a lanky piece like me any more.'

'That's a big problem,' Shyla agreed. 'No money, no honey.'

I hesitated. 'I dunno. The guards are all men. Maybe we tart our-selves up, flash a bit of skirt and ask for an advance.'

'Skirts are banned!' Leena said dismissively.

'That's where you come in,' I replied. 'You have to dress niqab, gloves, everything...'

'I'll do the same, get me the gear,' Shyla said.

'It's a Muslim thing,' Leena said.

Shyla looked at me, and we both burst out laughing.

Leena looked confused for a moment and then laughed, realising the absurdity of her words.

After a long silence, Leena said, 'When you wear a niqab, it's not your bum you wiggle. You have to start with your eyebrows. You bite your finger through your niqab, and then you lower your eyes and check their pants.'

The hoots and cries of the other Ginnz sailed through the graveyard air.

By the time we'd finalised the finer details, the whole gang was together. We went into the graveyard's main flower patch, held our hands up in our salute, and took our oath. It was something I'd writ-tenone doped-up night in the cemetery, and everyone loved it. Shyla said the first line and the rest of us repeated it:

We, the Ginnz,
Believe in no men's lies,
Not in their gods,
Or their paradise skies.
Boys can fuck their toys,
We will stand upright.
This world's full of shite,
we girls will unite.

And so, it came to pass. We sold booze to Muslims and cigs to Sikhs. Some Sikhs would only eat non-halal meat, so we sold them the halal meat and told them it was not halal, and they bought it. We told the Muslims the meat was halal, even if it wasn't. We weren't scared of any godly wrath, we had too much earthly crap to be worrying about that, with all the guns around us. Our gang grew. Girls came to us from all over the place and all creeds, zones and dance styles. Hindus, Christians, non-religious. White, African, Asian, Arab. Bhangra wavers, shufflers, hip shakers and shankers. Everyone popped in and out of the graveyard, smoked and danced with us.

We did our thing, and nobody bothered us in the graveyard. Nobody except one man. He was from the Muslim Burial Council of Birmingham. He was an emaciated corpse of a man with dyed jet-black beard and hair, and if you saw him in shadow, you sometimes thought maybe he was a dead body that had dug itself up. He patrolled the cemetery and was always telling us how Muslim girls should dress properly, stay at home and respect our parents. But one day he became a bit lecherous, and Leena went off to his cabin with him and he got more than he bargained for. After that, he accepted us as a normal part of the dancing fields of the dead.

Shyla was a key Ginnz member. She never missed a meeting, though she fluctuated between shivering from bad trips, where she went into herself and didn't say a word, to being a ponytailed, loud-mouthed Rottweiler. Leena had now re-joined the English Socialist Republican Party. She took me and Shyla to some of her meetings. At one of them, they were talking about Psychological Warfare and how to keep hold of memory. I was surprised to see Leena leading this one. She talked like such an expert. She told us about how the Bloods are using a combination of mind-changing drugs, sims and drones, about a camp called ERAC, but most of the meetings were dreadful events, people arguing over where to put a Comma, or about something some dead communist had said, and then got drunk. In the graveyard, she trained newcomers on how to kick, punch and elbow men who harassed them. Her favourite technique was what Shyla had named the goolie-twister, where you grabbed their balls and yanked as you turned your shoulder quickly into them, so you got high rip potential and inflicted maximum pain. Leena had us all rehearse this and a series of basic takedowns. We went through the moves with serious dedication for thirty minutes, Leena barking orders, till we were well drilled and ready.

Then, we hit the entertainment. Booze. Joints. Dance. Sometimes, just before getting completely smashed – which meant well after most of the living had left the dead for the night – Leena would sing for us. One evening, she brought along a copy of one of my old poems and sang it.

On the aches of a forgotten melody
I found the banished poet
Imprisoned in the sighs of a nightingale.
Holding the shattered branch
Of a leafless tree
She asked the sweet bird,
Why dance in the mouth of death?
It spread its broken wings and sang.
And as the moonlight shimmered
The poet wrote:
The melody is free.

Everyone clapped. They begged her for another song. Leena said she was going to sing a *hmd* (a religious hymn) in Punjabi for her next song, and nobody was to snigger if she pronounced a word or two wrong. She closed her eyes and sang so sweetly that the old caretaker came out of his shed, sat by a grave a safe distance away from us and dropped his head. I thought he was enthralled by the singing. But, after Leena stopped, he said, 'You should not raise the name of the Almighty in the breath of inebriation!'

His finger wagged at Leena, then at us all.

'It is only that love, which inebriates, as they say, for if it was the bottle, then it would dance,' I replied, remembering a line from a song Mum had told me once.

'Oh, Uncle?' Leena asked.

'Yes, daughter?' the old man said.

Leena lifted her hand towards him, opened and closed her fist, and reminded him of what could happen to his testicles again.

He snorted and left.

From that day, even the cemetery caretaker stopped giving us good-Muslim-girl-behaviour lessons. He walked in the opposite direction, especially when Leena was with us, which was not half as much as I wanted her to be. She'd started disappearing here and there 'on some personal business,' she said. Applying my Leena Translator App, this probably meant she was shagging some militiaman and was too embarrassed to admit to it.

Banning booze was one thing, but when the Believers issued a decree banning dancing, the Ginnz buzzed with rebellion. There were ten of us in the graveyard that day. We got stoned, danced in lanes between the graves and decided we, the mashed-up gang of girls, were going to hold the mother of all dances and to hell with the Believers.

As we were leaving the graveyard, Shyla placed her head on my shoulder, turned her imploring eyes up to me and said, 'Oh poetess of the graves, recite us a line.'

I couldn't think of a poem but raised my hand in the air and shouted, 'Up their decree! We're dancing free!'

And there and then, we started dancing to the chant. It was around 6 pm. The dance turned into a parade around the graveyard. The air was damp, and the light fading. Birds of the graveyard were jostling for position in the trees. Shyla, Leena and I took to the front of the parade. In two blinks, we'd left the graveyard and were dancing on the streets. We were all dressed in flowing Ginnz black.

Leena found a rusty dustbin lid and played a Bhangra beat all the way up Oxhill Road. A woman with a proper Dhol turned up, and we screamed at the top of our lungs as we danced. More and more girls and women joined us the further into Handsworth we went.

Along the way, people shook their heads in disbelief from their windows. Others honked their car horns. Some came out onto the sides of the road and clapped us on. A few overweight aunties joined in as well. I was so happy I didn't realise we had danced our way to the junction of Rossells Rd and Bromwich Lane. There, two lines of masked militiamen blocked our path. We were now hundreds of women bopping to a deafening cacophony of clapping and beats.

'Dancing in public is prohibited,' a militiaman announced through a megaphone.

We ignored him.

'Sisters, your actions are immoral,' the loudspeaker wielder proclaimed.

We danced.

'This is your final warning,' he said.

We danced.

Then, a shot made everyone duck. A militiaman had fired into the air.

'You are ordered to disperse,' the militiaman said. 'Who is your leader?' His words echoed in the sudden silence.

'I am,' I said, standing up. 'Our streets, our day!'

'I am,' Shyla said, standing up. 'Our bodies, our way!'

'I am,' Leena said, joining us. She repeated Shyla's chant.

Before long, everyone stood up, and we were all chanting, 'Our bodies, our way!'

'Let's have a rave of raves, Shyla, the mother of all dances, a dance to shake heaven!' I shouted at her over the noise.

'Where?' Shyla asked.

'Spaghetti Junction,' I said instinctively. 'Where else?'

Shyla hugged me and trembled. How could you be so insensitive, Marah? I thought. I felt her lungs stop heaving, and she settled in my arms. I could feel her tears falling onto my neck. I felt all sick inside for what I'd just proposed. How can you be so insensitive, Marah, given what had happened to Shyla there? You're a bitch. A complete bitch.

She squeezed my hands.

'The bastards, Marah, how could they do what they did to me?'

'I'm sorry, Shyla. Maybe not there, I wasn't thinking.'

Shyla lifted her head., 'Let's go there. I'm tired of the nightmares. That's where we'll dance.'

Shyla held my hand as Leena ducked down, and I wriggled onto her shoulders. She lifted me up. The Dhol player came closer to me, beating a fast rhythm. I signalled to her, and she stopped. Everyone went quiet. What was I going to say? I had no idea. I just spoke.

'Sisters, St Valentine's Day is coming, and even though we should not celebrate a lecherous pig like St Valentine, we could dance. Let's have a Mother of Dances, a Rave of Raves. On February 14th. Come alone or bring a friend, bring two, bring three!'

Everyone clapped and shouted.

'Where?' someone asked.

'Spaghetti Junction.'

There was almost complete silence when I mentioned this. The silence cursed what happened there.

'Sisters, we know what happens there. This no-man's-land is a land of no humanity. We can't live in the fear of shadows or men!' I spoke.

Women clapped, and Leena let me down. She and Shyla were both crying. I kissed Leena on her teary face and smeared her tears with the palm of my hand. I pressed Shyla's shoulder, and the three of us marched arm-in-arm towards the soldiers. They raised their guns at us. We kept on chanting, walking towards them. They fired into the air.

We marched on. They aimed their guns at us, but we marched on until they lowered their guns and withdrew to the sides of the road.

Then we stopped.

'Until February 14!' I cried.

Cheers rang round. The crowd dispersed after a finale of a dance., with harms flying, hips swinging, and shouting and laughing.

We had two weeks before the dance. In that time, Leena organised the Rave of Raves like a military operation. She had an extensive list and project management software running on the old laptop Uncle Melvin had given me. An appropriate safe section of the Spaghetti Junction had to be identified: a generator, speaker system, lights, platform, and, of course, booze. While Leena took care of logistics, Shyla and I took charge of spreading the word.

With a couple of days to go, it was all looking good. The only thing I was nervous about was security. We'd announced our plans in public. Which meant the militias knew and might do something about it. When I mentioned this to Leena, she dismissed it. 'No one comes to no-man's-land,' she said. 'And the Believers are too busy pestering every one with their Convert programs, believing in fuck knows what, to bother with little little us.'

THE CUPIDITY 16

Ever since our brief chat on the mobile, Ash had always been in my thoughts. A dropping leaf became the touch of his hand on mine, a cold breeze, his war kiss.

Even when I was with the Ginnz in the cemetery, he was there, a heavy longing at the core of my being, a loving pain which killed me and kept me alive.

I'm sure Leena knew where I went when I sat on the grass distracted, but she didn't probe. We'd said so many times that we would never rely on any man or be defined by our relationship with any man. Or, I'd add, in her case, any two or three men.

Ash finally roared into Birmingham early one morning and pulled up outside our house. I used to sleep waiting for the sound of his motorbike. I even heard it in my pissed-up dreams. Now, it was real. I was sure. I laughed and didn't bother even pulling on a dressing gown, I just whipped the front door open to the murky dawn light and crushed myself into his arms.

He laughed. I laughed, and Mum made him a cup of tea while he waited for me to dress. They talked ten to the dozen. I could hear his muffled voice through the floorboards in my bedroom. He'd come at the right time for a chat with Mum. She was holding real conversations again.

I scoffed a toast, all the while keeping an eye on Ash's adorable face, doing a quick inventory. The lips were plump and moist. Definitely kissable. The brow was thicker. He'd put on muscle around the neck. A barber had trimmed his eyebrows so they were perfectly symmetrical. And yes, my eyes did stray lower. It had been a long, long, long time.

For all that, he'd chosen a shit morning to arrive. I had a terrible hangover. I lied that it was just a headache. He must have been able to smell the booze and stale tobacco on me, but he didn't complain.

As soon as we stepped out of the house, I couldn't help but cry.

He got on the bike and wrapped his blue silk scarf around my neck. 'It'll be cold on the bike,' he said. 'The morning sun's not yet warmed the air.'

The scarf was so soft. I held it in both my hands and took in a big breath full of lavender. 'You still use the same aftershave.'

'It's by Izzy. I love it so much I bought a box back when money was cheap.'

He pulled his helmet on and handed me mine. 'Where would you like to go?'

'Paradise!' I said.

'Do you know the direction?'

'Sure. Up Lozells Road, down Hamstead Road and keep going till we get there!'

He looked at the map on his mobile for a few moments. Then we rode off. We rode past a steady stream of refugees, and for a second my mind blanked, remembering that had once been us, carting shopping bags, shoes all busted, heads dropping. I wanted to help. And yet, I didn't, I wanted Ash, and I wanted him all to myself. Ash drove on until we arrived at the gates of Shugsborough Park. I had been expecting the trees to have long since burnt out and the buildings razed, but there were no signs of war – just a great big park occupied by ordinary people who looked like nobody had told them there was a civil war going on. There were joggers, dog walkers, love-struck couples, and even an ice cream van.

We found a bench and cuddled. 'OK, spill the beans, then. What happened to you?' I quizzed him as I stroked his chin, his moustache, his eyelashes.

He told me that the day we'd been expelled from London, the Bloods kept him overnight until his ID was verified. His mum and dad were much the same as they had ever been, at home bickering. His university was open again, though there was no guarantee any of the teachers would turn up or that it would not be shut down mid-session. There were power blackouts at his Uni, which lasted for hours. The Bloods were doing presentations for all engineering students.

I told him about how my dad had died. I told him about how I missed my dad's silly sayings about England. Ash said he knew. I was about to ask him if he'd found Chilli when he said, 'I went to your former house...'

'Former?' I interrupted him. He had either gone well posh, or something was wrong.

He ignored me. 'I went round all the streets. No one had seen

Chilli since the day we left.'

Former. If someone was living in it, he could tell me who it was. It was my house; I was born in it. If it was burnt down, then we'd build it again. He stroked my hair, and I decided I didn't want to know about our house, former or not and certainly not right now.

He held my face with a hand and kissed me, then asked me to talk to him about anything and nothing, he'd missed hearing my voice, and he just wanted to be lulled by its cadences again. I bit my tongue and smiled. I loved it. I loved him.

'Go on, then, say something, don't just paw my face.'

I told him I was no longer the same person. I told him I hated this world, this war and all its soldier whores. I told him I tried not to listen to the wind because when it howled, it told me things that were not meant to be heard, horrors that were meant to stay unspeakable. And I told him I no longer had dreams, only nightmares in different shades of scream.

He said he loved me, and I had to keep dreaming. And soon, we would go to Scotland and make our own world, and it would be beautiful and I would start my studies again because I could do medicine there. I listened and loved everything he said, but I didn't tell him I no longer believed in fairy tales. I had wanted him for so long and I could feel he felt the same way. He sped into a grove at the back of a completely unmarked stately home, and I gave myself to him again and again, then I straddled him until his hips stopped bucking, and I collapsed on top of him. We giggled. 'Why did sex always seem a sin?' he said.

I agreed. 'Let's sin again soon.'

Then we dressed and stopped for a post-coital chicken sandwich each on the way back home before nightfall.

'Did you fall off your bike?' Mum asked when we burst into the kitchen.

I looked. We were covered in debris from the grove.

Ash reacted fastest. He said, 'No, we were just lying in the park.'

Mum took his sheepishness to be his usual shyness.

Mum checked the lids of pans and said she had made some special food for us. Even so, Ash made his excuses.

I gave him back his scarf as he got on his bike to go back to London.

'Have I changed then?' he asked. I was scrutinising his face again.

I kissed him. 'War changes us all. Some become monsters and kill, others are killed by the monstrosity.'

'So, you look at me, and you see monsters?' he teased.

There was an explosion in the sky to the West behind him. It had the beauty of fireworks.

'But I get what you mean,' he said, 'Maybe only poets can express what happens during these times.'

'There's no place for poetry in hell,' I said.

I stepped forward and let him kiss me on the lips.

As he revved off, a line of words began repeating themselves in my mind: *May this night be a day without sight*, and I began to sing them all the way up the steps in a happy delirium,

'At least you came home sober for once,' Mum said as soon as I pushed in the door.

'Why do you have to wreck everything?' I snapped. 'Why ruin the end of day like this?'

Mum stepped away, shocked as I yelled at her, 'Who puts food on the table? You? Your son? It's me! Me, me, me! Don't forget it!'

I stomped out of the hallway and up to my room, slumped on the bed, and was sickened with myself for what I had just done. How could you say what you just did, Marah? What are you becoming? What have you become?

I lay in bed for a while, trying to hide in the memories of the day with Ash, but they were chased further and further away by the sound of Mum fidgeting about in the kitchen.

More than two hours passed, and she still hadn't gone to bed. I felt all sick inside. I went downstairs. She was standing where I'd left her, her face to the kitchen window, fidgeting with a spoon on a plate.

'Mum!' I called her.

She turned her head around and looked blankly at me with tired eyes. Her cheeks twitched. She looked frail. I hadn't noticed how she'd aged.

I burst out a torrent of words. 'I'm sorry Mum. I'm sorry for being so bad. This world is no longer one of our dreams.'

Mum nodded. We hugged and made up. We held hands and walked up the stairs together. Mum tucked me into bed and whispered, 'What is this Rave of Raves, Marah?'

'Did that little shit of a son of yours tell you?' I said sleepily.

'Don't be rude about your brother,' Mum said, kissing me on my head. 'And don't go anywhere you shouldn't be.'

I sighed. 'OK, Mum.'

I was a child again. Safe again, with my mummy tucking me in bed.

She kissed me on the head again, and I fell asleep.

THE DEFIANCE

17

We were going to set the bombed-out ribcage of Birmingham's Spaghetti Junction ablaze with life.

We'd defy them.

We'd drink.

We'd dance.

But first, I had to get past Mum. She smoothed her hair, and the tiredness in her eyes shifted for a moment.

We stood not speaking in the living room, both of us bewildered.

'Mum, she's got your perfume on!' my brother said.

'Shut it, Tats,' I snapped at him.

Tats lives in a permanent state of anxiety: I'll get kidnapped by a militiaman; I am becoming a slut; and Mum'll get shot dead. A bomb will land on the roof. He had a frown on his stubbly face, and now it was in Extra mode. I could see his little negative thoughts jumping around like beans in a hot pan.

Mum leaned in, and I let her sniff me. She smiled. Something that was rare.

'She's going to see that boy again,' Tats said.

I stuck my middle finger up to my brother.

I turned to Mum with that tell-your-sexist-little-shit-of-a-son-off stare, but she didn't even bother to look at him, let alone reprimand him.

I smiled, a smile that usually digs right into her motherly heart.

'You can't go. It's banned, sweetheart. It's illegal,' Mum said.

'Like, the Believers are legal, themselves!' I said, drawing a quotation mark in the air in front of her with my fingers. 'Where's that woman who said the laws of male Gods are the shackles of women?'

She raised her eyebrows and said, 'You are getting so scrawny, you've not eaten anything. And I made a special paratha for you.' She held her index finger close to her thumb up for me to see the thickness. 'And I put a lot of butter on it and made you some chicken kebabs, just as you like.'

I stretched my arms in front of me, pulled the sleeves of my black sweatshirt back, showed Mum my hands, and then pinched my stomach and laughed, 'Just the same old bionic me.'

'Must you go?'

'Mum.'

Mum sighed. 'At least put something warm on. If your dad was still here, he would never let you go out on a night like this, let alone the way you are dressed now.'

'I love you, Mum,' I said and shot an I'll-kill-you-later look at my little brother.

'But how can you go out into this?' Mum blurted out.

This was the rapid succession of thud sounds that meant distant guns.

Mum's glasses were off again. I refused to yield to her tears and turned my back on her.

She knew I knew I couldn't leave her like this, and yet that if I didn't leave now, I wouldn't be leaving.

'Bye, Mum. I'll be fine. Don't wait up,' I said, giving her an extra tight hug, but I didn't look back when I walked down the garden path.

Phew. And don't you just hate it when Mum's always right?

It was a cold, cold night. The city lights were beautiful. Wasn't that completely nuts? The reflections in the road from oil spills were like running rainbows. And the rain streamed in neat crisscross patterns off side-on cars. The ginger cat, resting on a dead dog's big, gas-swollen belly, licked its paws. A cat made anything it sat on prettier. The whole thing, cat, dog, the licking, the beautiful rainbow lights all around, looked like a strange nursery rhyme.

The cracked window glass on the bus dinged back my reflection. I liked what I saw. I'd done my Goth makeup well, my Kohl was Goddess-like, and my punk hair was a riot of purple bangs and pink Mohican crown. Marah was a girl not to mess with.

Even though he was a completely devoted atheist for most of his life, I recalled how Dad often said, my success is by Allah, and today, even thunder repeated his praises. On cue, some lightning flashed, though it could have been a distant bomb going off because I waited for the thunder that always follows lightning, and none came.

There were five other people riding the unlicensed Hail bus service, and none of them looked halal. Shifty-eyed, camouflage-ka-gooled men and skimpy-clothed women with hard-bitten faces and furtive glances. And these insides were the tame ones. The wilder ones were out there, beyond the glass, on the broken streets. In fact, out there were all of Mum's fears. And mine, though I'd never admit it to her. In the blink of an eye, I could be raped, shot, kidnapped. Even an adrenaline junkie might look out of this bus window, see the daredevil drivers, the carcasses of cars, the caved-in buildings and say, please, God, too much excitement, turn it down.

I thought about Tats. It was a pity that boys didn't become men the way pupae became butterflies. If only they just hatched out into fully formed, hunky men. Instead, Tats was in that grumpy, grubby, shitty, snivelling, you-broke-Mum's-rules phase!

I was heading for the no-man's-land, for the Rave of Raves. Even though the internet was intermittent at best of times, we'd managed to get messages out on WhatsApp, Snapchat, Instagram, Chichi, TikTok, Telegram, and God knows what else. I'd even managed to get a text to Ash.

My heart beat faster as the bus pulled into the wrecked depot. Once upon a war, it had taken a direct hit and looked like a crushed Chinese fortune cookie, and the Hail buses that still used it were centipedes. I waited until everyone else had gotten off the bus so I could keep them all in plain sight, then I stepped out and leapt over the sandbags, ducked under broken masonry, and avoided getting caught in piles of discarded barbed wire.

I was late to the party and was going to be even later when I met Ash.

He must be either really stupid, or stupidly in love with me, I thought, and how lucky am I to have him dangling around in my life. How I loved that he would come all the way from London, past who knows how many roadblocks to get here, but come he had, and was waiting for me, where we'd arranged, just by the edge of the Jesus slabs. They were large bits of the road that'd been blown up but somehow had fallen together in a gigantic Crucifix, with five iron bars that resembled fingers, and nicely rounded up with a hole through two hand shapes as well. We'd made the slabs into an authentic shrine for youth, of sorts.

Ash. He was dressed in his super smarts: a thick brown leather jacket, dark blue chino trousers and a black woolly scarf around his neck. And his lovely curly hair dangled just above his shoulders. And his eyebrows. His eyes. I didn't want him to know how much I adored him. He wasn't getting that. Not tonight. So, I gave him a quick hug and allowed him only a peck before we broke the hug.

'Any news of Chilli?' I asked.

He shook his head and pursed his lips. Those lips. Damn.

I kissed those lips, and my tongue found its way into his mouth.

When the kiss broke, he laughed.

I pulled him closer and whispered, 'I missed you.'

'Have you seen the time?' he said, pushing me back.

I pulled him again.

He lifted my chin up with his finger. 'You're my dream come true. But so many people are waiting for you?'

I hated it when he did this, his finger on my chin, his voice in my ears, and his face in my eyes. It turned me into needy mush.

'Just stop being so Mister Right all the time, will you,' I said, giving his finger a little peck.

'OK, princess,' he laughed.

'Yes, my prince.'

It started out corny, but now I loved it, this Princess-Prince stuff.

The noise around us got louder and louder. Running feet, yelling. Gales of laughter. I could hear the throb of a bass line. The party was starting. Colour was starting to lick the Jesus Slabs.

'Come on,' he said. He grabbed me by the waist and pushed me up the slope. We scrambled up. Close to the top, the unmistakable silhouette of Leena appeared. She was staring down at us. She stretched out an arm for me to grab.

'You're pissed already, Marah,' she said.

I was pressed close to Leena. I opened my mouth and blew some bad breath at her.

My breath got her nod of approval.

'I'm only drunk on love tonight.'

'Him?'

Ash clambered up behind us.

'Who else?'

'Wow. All the way from London, he must really like you.' She gave me an up-and-down look and said, 'You look so pretty.'

'Love your brows,' I said. 'The Cleopatra wings. Where did you get them done?'

'Ah, you'll never know,' she said with a mysterious wave of her hand.

Ash had scrabbled up the last bit of the slope.

'You're late, again,' Leena said to us both, but looking at Ash. 'Come on, let's go.'

Ash squeezed my hand.

'See you in a bit,' I said and blew him a kiss.

Leena was in a sparkly silver one piece and glitterball earrings. She was the Queen of all the road parties. She passed me a bottle with cola and vodka in it. We shared a spliff, drank, laughed, and joked.

In only three weeks, we'd turned the Spaghetti Junction into the best concert arena on this side of hell. We'd put flaming torches all around, stuck them in holes, and wired them into broken railings, and we'd decorated the sides of the walls with multi-coloured rags, many of which had the Ginnz salute on them. The greatest help we'd had was from the bomb that blew up Junction 6. It must have been the smartest bomb in the world as the outer lanes had collapsed inwards, and the central twisting snake-like ones had tilted outwards when they'd crashed down and had stacked up on top of each other, creating a ribcage of mangled wires under which we could dance. The bomb had even created a perfect stage – a big slab of the road.

And the place was rocking.

'Wow. Just wow,' I shouted over the bass and beats.

'Hurry,' cried Leena. She grabbed me, and we met all the others. We drank. We danced. We doped. The music and multi-coloured strobe lights burst into life. I flicked my high heels off and kicked them to the edge of the stage. The band was going off the scale with guitar riffs. The base line was slaying. We waved our hands in the air and jacked. It was all girls together, and we were all loved up in our dance group, the Ginnz, our girl gang. My life.

'Everyone's here Muslims, Muslim lookalikes, Sikh, Hindus, Jews, white and Asian, African, communists and even kafirs,' Leena shouted over the wall of sound. 'Are you going to take the mic later, drop some poems?'

'Maybe, maybe,' I hollered back. 'If the mood grabs me!'

I was swaying away when a hand dropped on my shoulder, and a dull voice said, 'Don't be stupid, Marah!'

I turned quickly. It was Tats. He must have sneaked out of the house to 'mind' me.

'Don't fret, Twatsi,' I said, shaking him off. He hated being called Twatsi. I waited for an outburst, but it didn't come. I loved seeing him all vexed, he looked so cute when he was like that. I kissed him on his cheek. He let out a loud 'Ugh', wiped his face and pushed me away. Then I saw his eyes caught by Shyla's wavy hair and low-cut dress. And I laughed. Finally, the hormones hit little brother!

I was loving the feel of sweat streaming down my back and feeling all kinds of fire when Leena nudged me and pointed to the stage mic. I shook my head at her. I was blessed out. And anyway, how could a poem compete with a live band? Leena kept on and on with her ear-wigging, and so in the end, I said yes, I'd do my turn before the band did their finale.

There was no cool way to get on the stage. I grabbed the top of an old wooden pallet that we'd hammered into the sides of the ladder as a sort of bannister, and Leena shoved at my bum. In this way, the tanked-up loved-up Marah Sultana managed to topple onto the stage.

Brushing myself down, I stepped forward towards the centre stage light, crossing my feet as I walked like models do on a catwalk. Leena winked at me and clapped her big, beautiful hands. She looked deadishly divine. I winked back at her and then raised my hands in Ginnz' Salute: right fist clenched by the left hand, with its first two fingers raised in V, for victory. I bathed in rapturous applause. I tapped the microphone with a finger and said, 'Happy Valentine's Day! Ready for some lyrics?'

Everyone cheered. There were hundreds and hundreds of people. Right at the front, near the stage, there were dozens of women wearing tee shirts with Ginnz salutes on them.

The cold disappeared, and my nerves dropped away.

'We showed them, didn't we? We can rave and just have fun,' I said. 'Can't we?'

There were bursts of yelling in response.

'Read your poem!' someone shouted.

'We want the band!' someone else called.

'Now for my poem, folks,' I said. I delivered it fast, a tumble of words and rhymes:

> *We can't be written, rewritten or smitten,*
> *Not by the Bloods or preening studs.*
> *Not by Believers, or true love cleavers,*
> *Not by dreamers, schemers or seamers,*
> *We are the triangles of audacity,*

Not the ghost ships of Woke,
We are tailors of new states,
We are the hope!

Alright, not the best poem ever written, but that's what this angry, stoned universe wanted to hear. Or at least most of them. I milked the applause. Yes, I was a shameless, ego-driven artist like that. My hook line had got the biggest cheer and now everyone was shouting it. 'We are the hope!'

The band was waiting at the edges, ready to plug their guitars back in.

Suddenly, the strobes went out. The stage and crowd space went pitch black. Then, flashes in the darkness. Shadows stretched towards me. In the strobes of light, it looked like a giant hand was coming towards me. A thud-thump and echo of what could only be bullets fired into the air cut through the fading chants and joined a whine of drones above.

A flare screeched skywards, exploded, and caught everything in a yellow glow. Five masked militiamen leapt onto the stage; I hadn't seen them coming. They were Bloods. A red cross ran down the centre of their masks. Even though a cold shiver ran down my back, I raised my hands above my head, clapped and chanted:

We can't be written,
Re-written or smitten

Leena ran and stood next to me.

Spaghetti Junction was meant to be no-man's-land, but Bloods were everywhere now, batons drawn. I pointed at the militiamen on the stage and spoke into the mic.

'This mangled shite is ours tonight. Now piss off!'

Throbs of darkness got punched by my words. I saw them hesitate.

'Yeh, piss off!' Leena shouted.

She whispered into my ear, 'Let's go. There's more and more of them. I'm scared.'

I placed my hand on the microphone, 'Stand our ground. We'll be OK.'

More soldiers came up behind us. Two of them rushed and grabbed me by the shoulders. I ducked down – as we'd trained to do – and the soldiers careened into each other. The bass guitarist crossed the stage, and they grabbed her instead, flattened her and stamped on her guitar.

Others were going for Leena. She ducked the first one and tripped him, but the second and third shoulder-charged her down and pinned her to the stage boards.

It was mayhem all around.

I lost it and jumped on the back of one of the soldiers and slapped him in the face. Slapped him. Slapped him. He swore as he tried to swing me off him, 'Get the fuck off of me!'

I saw my chance. I jumped off his back and ran for centre stage. I raised my hands in our salute again and chanted into the mic, 'We're grooving – not moving!'

The crowd took it up, and the words roared up like angry waves from below the stage and raged on. The militiamen released Leena. Still, the words got louder and louder. More soldiers flooded the stage. Leena waved at me to go forward towards the sea of fists and open hands that were raised in the air below the stage.

'What?' I gesticulated to her.

'Dive!' Leena said with her arms.

Then she did. She swan-dived right into the crowd at our feet and disappeared into those hands.

Shit. I hated swimming. I never dived. A slow paddle into the shallowest end of the pool was the most I did.

I saw Ash looking up at me. Fear in his eyes. Calling to me. Everyone screamed at me. 'Go! Do it! Now!

'Dive!' Ash shouted.

Then, the soldiers on the stage rushed at me; I had no choice: I forgot fear and accepted my fate. I flew to the loudest roar you will ever hear. I felt like I was in the air for an eternity, with only the sound of my blood pumping and thumping around my ears.

Hands caught me, and surfed me away from the stage, and my hearing came back, and I was stunned again by a deafening whistling and clapping.

The arms holding me buckled, and I landed on top of people. I slid off some sweaty heads and stood on the cold ground.

'Nice one, my girl.'

It was Leena. Standing next to me. The cheers around us were totes mad.

But our victory didn't last long. Shots rang out. Screams. More shots and more screams. Then everyone was running helter-skelter. I joined the headless chicken-crazed zig-zagging for a bit, then saw Ash waving. He was near the stage. I was caught in a human column being propelled in the opposite direction. I steadied myself and ducked down to get out of the flow. I saw Leena duck, too. We kept low and pushed our way back to the stage.

Then all I saw were knees and ankle chains and painted toes and blood.

When I got back up, Ash's hand was stretched out to me. I grasped it.

A huge flash blinded everyone. Then the bang. And the post-blast silence that rang in your ears like a tuning fork.

Ash still had my hand. He pulled me into him. My brother was stood there, next to him, standing straight as everyone else cowered, like he was auditioning for Bambi or tallest poppy.

'The bastards!' I said to Ash. I called out, 'Leena!'

No reply. The smell of burnt flesh drifted across us. Howls and mewling. Dogs snarling.

Then a voice. Close. Leena's. 'I'm alright!'

She raised herself up behind me. Coughed. A cloud of dust and smoke billowed behind her. She'd lost one of her two glitterball earrings. Her face was cut below her nose on the lip. But she was OK.

'You're leaving now!' Tats ordered.

We just looked at him blankly. Since when did Bambi give orders? That was the patriarchy speaking.

Bloods soldiers were still smashing their way through people all over, their bloodlust running free.

'This way!' I called. We ran to the back of the stage.

'We've got to find Shyla. The Ginnz,'

'Everyone's safe, I saw them leaving,'

'OK, it's breakout time then.'

We had to get out of the cordon the soldiers had put in place all around the stage. They were closing in, boot by boot. Baton blow by baton blow.

Leena spat on the ground.

I nodded to a buckled, metal crowd control fence in the ground by our feet. Leena grabbed one side; I grabbed the other.

'Don't just stand there, Tats!' I said.

Ash could see what I was planning and shook his head but grabbed an end, too.

Tats rushed forward and put the center pole of it by his ribs.

'Ready?'

Leena nodded. The two dudes, Ash and Tats.

'One! Two! And three!' We ran with it as hard as we could towards the soldiers in the cordon. In the smoke and mayhem, they didn't see it coming till too late. We bowled two of them clean over. Rammed the thing into their knees. One of them fell, screaming in pain. His gun discharged as he fell. The bullets traced over our heads. But we were through.

Searchlights from up high swept across. We were in the shadows by the Jesus slabs. The slopes were full, but the arena itself was empty now that we could see.

The strap of one of my shoes was broken. I pulled off a sock and lashed the shoe to my foot that way.

'Let's head for my bike,' said Ash. He was clenching and unclenching his hands like he was ready to strangle someone.

'Take off with him, Marah,' Leena urged.

'The bike can can fit three,' I said, 'Can't it, Ash?'

He didn't answer.

'I'm a big girl,' Leena said. And she disappeared into the slope crowds.

'You reek,' Tats said.

'The bike can't take three,' I said to him. 'Sorry.'

He walked off in a strop.

'You should really go with your brother,' Ash said, 'It's dangerous here.'

I held his hand. 'Where's your bike?'

'Down there, in bushes,' he said, nodding into the shadows.

We went a short distance down the slopes. They changed to greenery, the edge of an abandoned patch of mini-park. He'd found a perfect little hideout where two fallen concrete slabs overlapped with each other and had been covered in bramble bushes.

'In there?' I said, pointing to the hideout.

'Yup.' He crawled in, and I followed. The brambles snagged at my clothes. It was semi-dark inside the little hollow, with only enough room for the bike and the two of us. A sheet of plastic had either blown in or been placed there, enough to lie on. Despite the mayhem, despite the bullets and the now distant shouts. Despite the fear. Or maybe because of all that, somehow, we ended up doing it there. And even though it was cold, it was divine.

When we finished, I pulled a spliff out, lit it and inhaled deeply as ever. Ash shook his head. 'That stuff is so bad for you, and really, the smell is disgusting.'

He said it, but sleepily, with no conviction.

'We could die any minute in this fucked up world, and you go on about keeping healthy?' I replied, blowing smoke out of my mouth and nostrils.

He turned to me, his eyes were full of guilt and sin. I could see the post-coital drowsiness sneaking up on him.

We had the conversation anyway. We always did. It was our ritual.

'Where's that girl who wanted a safe life?'

'She's moved on into the future.'

'Maybe we can save her from smoking herself to death.'

'Come here.'

I kissed him on the mouth again, enough to numb his tongue, then let him go.

He began combing my hair with his fingers. Usually, I would lean my head back a little as he did this and drift away on the magic of his touch, but only before we fucked. After fucking, I just stayed statue still and let him stroke.

'Marah, come out now!'

What the fuck. It was my brother.

I popped my head out. 'You been spying on me?'

Tats was leaning against the side of a slab, staring in my direction. He looked so tiny beside the shattered concrete limbs of the old junction.

'Mum'll be worried to death,' he murmured, rubbing his foot on the ground.

I felt all protective about him, knowing that he really wasn't talking about Mum but himself. I got up and out and went to him, and tried to brush his hair off his forehead, but he stepped back.

'You go now and be careful,' I said to Ash as he crawled out of the hideout.

'I'll text you,' he said, getting to his feet and kissing me on my forehead. He went back and dragged his bike out. Then the engine flared to life, and he was gone into the swirl of concrete and crowd and soldiers and smoke.

Tats turned and walked quickly away from me.

'Slow down,' I protested.

I followed him the best I could. He didn't look back.

He turned into the shadow of another arch and said, 'Bike's here.' He nodded towards a tree-lined field.

Some bullet tracer fire flew about our shoulders.

I fell to the ground. I looked back.

There was no one around. It had to be snipers or stray fire.

'Run, Tats!' I called out.

He did. He scrambled back up and ran.

I stepped out of my shoes and ran with him.

The field, which had seemed so close, kept moving further and further away. Finally, we tumbled through the hedgerow.

'Where is it?'

'Where d'you think?'

'No time for games, little brother.'

It was in a water trough, under the carcass of a dead pony. He hauled it out. It stank. He pushed it out of the field, then kick-started it. It fired the first time. I got on, put my ass down into the dead pony slime and my raw feet onto the maggot-ridden pedals.

I shivered. Tats took his denim jacket off and, without turning around, held it out for me. I put it on and kissed him on the back of the head.

'Why do you call me Twatsi when I do so much for you?' he asked.

'Not now, little brother,' I protested. I hugged him tightly as the motorbike roared away down a slope.

'Fall off the bike, and I'm going to leave you in the gutter where you fall, I swear on Allah, I will!'

All this shouted at 90 decibels into the rushing wind.

We had no helmets, and I stayed quiet, just held onto him. We sped down a stretch of cracked slabs of the old M6. The bike juddered and jerked. I felt sick from all the jolts but hung on. Tats slowed. When we finally joined the A38, he must have felt safe at this point because he slowed to a stop. He looked back. I followed his eyes. Our arena had gone up in flames.

In the early hours of that night, I got a text from Leena:

Leena: 6 dead. Sixty injured. 20+ girls detained. But Ginnz are safe. Oh God, what have we done?

Me: Dancing is no crime in the eyes of God.

Leena: No.

Me: We didn't kill.

Leena: No.

AFTER CONCEPTION

AC – AFTER CONCEPTION

Morning came. Mum was in the kitchen below my bedroom, blasting music out of a Bluetooth speaker in the kitchen. Tats had rescued it from a skip a few days earlier. She was playing one of her favourite singers, singing a poem written 500 years ago. She did this when she was distressed about something and couldn't get it out of her mind.

Sometimes, listening to it, Mum would shed a tear, other times just hugged me and drifted off into her melancholy. When she was down, she became a little girl and thought of her own mother, who had died before I was born and who was buried in Sabz Kot, a little village on the edges of Kashmir, in a grave near the barbed wire that separated India and Pakistan.

Shall I open my eyes? Did I get out of bed now and get the night-after reprimand? These were the big decisions.

I peered out from under my quilt. There was a glass of water on the little food drum that was my bedside cabinet. I drank half the glass of water and then downed the rest with the two paracetamol tablets that had been lined up at exactly three centimetres each from the base of the glass. Mum's signature. She must have left them during the night. I rolled over, farted a great fart, placed my face into the pillow, held the back of my head with my hands and waited for the headache to go. This took around half an hour, during which time Mum kept playing the same song over again. I quite enjoyed listening to it and waited until the song finished before going downstairs.

Mum was dressed in a blue tracksuit-bottom and a black T-shirt. Her hair was tied into a knot at the back of her head. She was pacing the kitchen. I relaxed as this version of Mum usually meant business and was not one of those who would give me a telling-off for last night.

As soon as she saw me, she blinked a few times before giving me a fleeting smile, she unfolded the paper. As soon as I saw it, I hissed a curse.

'We've got this letter from the Royal Medical Research Council....'

'You know that's a Bloods outfit,' I interrupted Mum. 'Correct me if I'm wrong. Everyone knows these loonies are waiting for their Messiah and their Second Coming. You know full well they want to take a syringe full of my blood and test it to see if my DNA most closely matches the DNA of the House of David, of a two-thousand-year dead woman from Syria whose bones they've ground up and tested. Who they say was the Virgin Mary,'

Rant finished, I said, 'Maybe you need a stiff drink, Mum?'

Mum was untroubled. 'It's all nonsense, like I told you, but one thousand pounds, that's a lot of money. We could leave this place and get to Scotland with that and pay someone to drive us all the way there. Maybe you could try med school there. One thousand is a lot of road-blocks we'd get through.'

I'd stopped thinking of med school, or any school, or any future. I unplugged the speakers and went to the sofa. A child cried inconsolably somewhere outside.

I slumped into the foam and nylon and put my hands over my ears. Still, I heard Mum filling a glass of water from the tap. Then she was kneeling close to me, holding a glass and saying the worst thing she could have.

'You would have made a great doctor, Marah.'

'Never say that again, Mum, never,' I whispered.

Tats slammed a door. He was back doing that now we had doors. He whipped the letter from Mum's hands and looked at it. 'There's no way she's the Virgin Mary, Mum,' Tats said. 'Look at her. She didn't even wear knickers last night.'

'Marah!' Mum put her hand to her mouth in shock.

'My knickers are not his business.' I shot up from the sofa and hissed at Tats, 'Perv!'

Tats threw a toast at me. I caught it. It was well-buttered. I scoffed it down.

'Anyway,' Mum said. Her fingers fluttering on her arms. 'You're right. We are not Syrian. We have no Syrian roots whatsoever, so you'll be fine. It's just a quick trip to the clinic.'

'Easy money,' said Tats.

I snatched the letter from Tats, ripped it up, threw it at Mum and said, 'I want that feminist mother of mine back. The one who used to say, *We women must be in control of our own bodies.* She died with Dad, didn't she?'

Mum bent her head and leaked tears onto the sofa arm.

Me and my nasty mouth. Why was I always putting my foot straight into my mum's feelings like that?

'Now look what you've done,' Tats said, putting his arm around Mum.

'Sorry, Mum,' I muttered half-heartedly. 'I shouldn't have said that.'

'I don't know where you get such cruelty from,' she sniffed. 'Not from me. Not from your father, that's for sure. So, just go and be your selfish self and do whatever it is you do. Just leave us alone.'

'I'll get out of your life forever,' I replied, walking out of the kitchen. I pulled my trainers on, grabbed my coat and hat, opened the front door and shouted back, 'Forever!'

'Marah!' Mum called after me. I slammed the door.

I got as far as the doorstep. I was hurting having hurt Mum. I was about to knock on the door when my mobile phone buzzed inside my trouser pocket. It was a text from Leena:

Shorty's funeral!

I smiled, remembering.

Leena texted again:

where z fk r u

Mum opened the door. 'Please come back and have some dinner,' she said softly.

'Dinner?' I asked, 'What time is it?'

I'd slept through the day again.

'Just after 6 pm.'

'I'm so late,' I replied.

Today was meant to be the day we managed to lay our hands on a bit of real gold. I couldn't help laughing.

'What's so funny, you crazy girl?' Mum asked.

'It's payback time!' I said and ran off to meet Ginnz and get our hands on some gold.

I was panting madly by the time I reached the graveyard. Leena glared at me, her arms folded in front. Shyla gave me an extra dirty look.

'At least I made it on time,' I said, nodding toward the funeral procession of a few cars following the hearse. They were heading towards a tall black poplar, the largest tree in the graveyard, and as per season, it had begun shedding white fluff, which fell on the procession like snowflakes.

I raised our salute. The girls hesitated and then returned it.

'That's your landlord going down to hell,' Leena said, nudging Shyla with her shoulder.

'Mum used to say, 'Landlordism doesn't die with the death of a landlord,' I said.

'At least let us enjoy a bit of death in a fucking graveyard, Marah,' Leena protested.

Shorty's body was being lifted for the grave. His wife, a big white woman with flaming blond hair, was dressed in her funeral best. She wiped her eyes on a little white handkerchief when they lowered his body into the grave. We sat in pretend solemnity, a safe distance away.

I couldn't help remembering Shorty's ugly face with his disgusting smile. He'd changed from one militia to another so many times we didn't know which one he had died for or which one had killed him. One thing that never changed in him was his filthy habit of always trying to grope us girls. He even tried it with Leena. That was when the Ginnz carried out their first real deed. I kicked him in the groin. Leena followed with a knee of her own. His open-mouthed screams planted the germ of the idea that we were here to execute today. After he'd hobbled away, clutching his vitals, I'd suggested to the girls that if ever he died and got buried here, we should dig the bastard up and pull his gold teeth out. And lo, he got killed, and Operation Shorty was born.

Over time, we'd become more like a militia than a group of bad-arsed girls with attitude. Leena's military background came of use as she gave us a bit of training with actual guns.

About a month back, she managed to borrow an Automatic and taught us all to shoot. We did the practice on the days when there was a lot of fighting as then no one bothered about a few gunshot sounds coming from the vague direction of the cemetery.

There were no guns involved in the Shorty business, but we'd planned it like pros: spades, ropes, wrenches, hammer, pliers, water and clean clothes; exit strategy, as well as covering tracks all planned, Plan B, C and D in place.

It was a cloudless winter's evening, with the light gently fading. The last speech was made, the flowers were thrown, the soil started slamming down, and the funeral wrapped up. The mourners left dabbing their eyes, and we heard a bunch of them asking if the reception was professionally catered. We stayed until we were sure we were alone, and it was dark. Then we went to work. We took turns to dig the pig up.

In the movies, they make digging the dead out of graves look so easy. It wasn't. You had to dig and dig and keep moving the earth away from the edge or else it kept falling back in. When we finally got to the coffin, we broke into it with a pickaxe. I struck the first blow, and splinters flew. We thought it would take five strikes, but the wood was the cheapest wood ever and just fell away, first blow. The hole reeked. In death, he stank as much as he did when he was alive. I held my breath and nose. It was time to clear the splinters, find that face, open the big gob in it, apply the pliers and start tugging. I'd agreed to do it, but when it came to it, I just couldn't.

Leena jumped into the grave with me and scattered the wood off Shorty's face with the edge of her spade. His mouth was already slightly open. In fact, it looked like the bastard was grinning.

'Do you want me to do the honours?' Leena asked, looking up at me.

I shook my head, took the spade from Leena and said, 'The bastard doesn't own us.'

I pushed the edge of the spade into Shorty's mouth and opened it a bit more, then sat on her knees and pulled his gold teeth out. I had only seen two, but there were four.

We jumped out, filled the grave in quickly and did our best to make it look as it had been. We even remembered to put the flowers back.

We had just finished when we heard a car pulling up into the cemetery parking zone. We scarpered to the far end of the plot and hid behind gravestones.

We watched. The old caretaker got out of the car with Shorty's wife and two other men. Both of these men had a spade. Freelance grave-diggers. We would have run away, but the scene was too good to miss.

We watched Shorty get dug up twice.

Not only did we make a load of money, thanks to Shorty, but the story of his wife kicking his grave, cursing him for being 'a show-off and swallowing his gold teeth or maybe it was those robbing funeral directors, let's go find them!' which became a Ginnz legend. We had more than enough money for each of us, and we even managed to share some of our money with those who had nothing. I bought Ash a teal chiffon scarf.

Mum was happy because I found a bag of quality Basmati rice and a fully working rape alarm in a roadside market. Tats even managed to get some money from me for a pair of trainers.

There was so much happiness in the house for a while, flowing everywhere, I all but forgot about the river of pain that constantly flooded its banks. It was a precious moment in time and space. I had my little family. I had my little life. I had my great big love.

Ash owned my dreams. He never left them. He would text me whenever he could. He sent texts from different numbers for security reasons, and they were often delayed. When we could, we met on Saturday mornings. Plus, he would just turn up, some weekdays, unannounced, and that was fine with me.

The last time we met, I asked him how his mum and dad were, and he looked at me as though I had asked him to solve the Hodge Conjecture or Magic Square puzzle or some other big riddle. He thought for a while, then said, 'What did you say?'

'Is everything OK at home?' I repeated.

'Oh, that, yes, fine, honestly.'

'Why are you so distracted?'

'Am I?'

'What are you not telling me?'

'Nothing?' He avoided eye contact.

'Nothing!'

'Nope,' he lied again. I was sure.

'So. You've been cheating on me?' I asked.

He took my hand and kissed it, and said, 'There is only you for me.'

'A lie hidden behind a lie, implanted in a kiss, can never hide the truth,' I said.

'Ouch!' he said.

'Look at me.'

He looked right into my eyes. He gazed and smiled, lifted his eyebrows and smiled. Either he was a top liar, or it was something else. I hit his chest with my fist. I knew he was hiding something.

THE COVENANT

19

There was a knock on my door. It had to be Mum. Tats would have just stormed in. During the last few days, she had been giving me one of those looks, which meant I had a lecture coming.

'Go away,' I moaned.

She came in, holding something behind her back.

'Well?' she asked.

'What?'

'It's about you and Ash,' she said after a pause.

'What about us?'

'I think it's time to talk, mother-daughter, you know?'

'You've already told me about the birds and bees, Mum,' I said, putting my head under my quilt.

'Why would he send you these?' Mum said.

I threw the quilt off my face. She had a big bunch of lilies in her hand.

'How did they arrive?' I asked.

Mum said, 'Special delivery.'

Yup, even in war, flowers could be delivered across frontlines.

I leaned across and read the small card dangling off the bunch, *Ash. XX*

'I don't want you hurt, there is always so much pain…'

'Love doesn't hurt, Mum,' I said.

'There is no greater pain than the pain of the thought of losing love,' she said. 'But I know it's good to hold on to it, even in a dream.'

'What are you on about?' I asked. 'He sent flowers.'

'Lilies, though,' she said. 'Not roses.'

'You're such an old cliché, Mum.'

She turned and left.

The following week, to the delight of my sweet-toothed, bad-breathed brother, Ash sent a box of chocolates, and exactly three weeks, two days and two hours later, he turned up himself. Mum was out at the time. Tats was in his room, no doubt glued to a video game, but when he heard the motorbike, he stomped downstairs and opened the front door before me.

Ash was dressed in a brown, tassel-sleeved leather biker jacket, high cowboy boots and stonewashed jeans. Was he a walking selfie or what?

He had a shopping bag that he was half-hiding with one hand. I played along and didn't notice it.

'Thanks for the chocs, Ash,' Tats said, shaking Ash's hand.

'Glad you liked them.' Ash stepped into the living room. Tats followed us. There was an awkward silence. Then Ash said, 'I'd like to have a private moment with Marah, if that's OK, Tats.'

Tats threw me a puzzled look.

'And this is for you,' Ash said. He pulled a box out of his jacket pocket and gave it to Tats.

Tats ripped the wrapping paper off, burst open the box and popped a mobile phone out of the inner plastic casing.

'Woah, a Zeexi 5KD. Thanks, Ash!'

New toy in hand, little brother promptly left.

Ash brought the 'hidden' bag into view, pulled a parcel out from it and held it out for me.

'What's happened?'

'A celebration.'

'What of?' I shook the package.

It was soft. Probably clothes. A jumper, winter was coming.

'You won the lottery?' I asked.

'Open it,' he said, nodding to the present.

I did. With the last tear, out spilt a beautiful, fold-over, off-shoulder split-thigh red dress.

'Do you like it?'

'It's so soft, so sumptuous, so graceful,' I said, rubbing it against my face, 'maybe unbefitting this world of ours. Which red carpet would I be walking down in this? Out there, there are only carpets of blood.'

Ash looked away from me.

'Sorry. Maybe that was heavy,' I said. 'It's just, it's lovely, but what on earth will the Ginnz make of it?'

I held the dress against my front and looked at myself in the living room mirror and tried to think when I last wore a dress like this but couldn't remember.

When I turned around, Ash was on one knee on the floor, holding a small box in front of me. 'Marah, will you marry me? I'll leave my Uni, and we can head to Scotland.'

I gasped. I took the box from Ash and opened it. Inside, a small golden ring sat on a plump cushion, with a tiny little diamond for company.

I was dumbstruck.

'Well?' he asked. 'Do you like the ring?'

'It's lovely, it's so bling, so adorable, really, Ash.'

'Can I stand up?'

'No,' I laughed.

'So, what do you think?' he asked standing up.

I paused.

'Well?' His brow clouded.

My words stumbled over each other. 'Look. The gorgeous dress and the ring, and you are beautiful beyond words, and I am lucky to have you in my life. You can have any girl you want. Why me? Why throw your career away for someone like me?'

'Because I love you more than anything in this world. And you love me, don't you?' he asked hesitantly.

There was a burst of automatic gunfire. It was answered by multiple guns.

'Everything inside me is so burnt up, and this life, this unfaithful life, has just taken away all my dreams, and I don't know what will happen tomorrow,' I said quickly.

We stopped talking and listened to the war. The shooting seemed to be concentrated around the Spaghetti Junction. It intensified for a moment and then died down.

'I am scared of moving again,' I said over the dying echo of the gunfire.

'The Bloods are not going to attack Birmingham,' Ash said confidently. 'They are too busy in Manchester and Yorkshire, and besides, Hertfordshire has slipped out of their control.'

'I mean, if they ever do,' I said.

There was a strange silence, one of those where even the birds held their breath and then a loud explosion. This time, it was the other end of the city, but I couldn't work out where.

'We got each other. We can be with each other. There's no hurry,' Ash said when the ceasefire returned, and then quickly added, 'but I don't want to rush you. Whenever you're ready. If you decide "yes," then you can wear the dress and the ring and send me a photograph, and I'll come to you there and then, wherever I might be and whatever time it might be. OK?'

'OK.'

We hugged each other tightly, silently and after a magical lifetime, he whispered, 'We could make it to Scotland, just you and me.'

'Could we?' I wanted to stay in this lovely dream.

'We would have to go along the 'A' roads all the way to Leeds,' he said.

'Would we?' I asked.

'We could stop in Bradford and have curry,' he said.

'We could,' I agreed.

A child's laughter outside brought me out of my dream, and I laughed, 'How would all my family fit on your bike?' He went silent.

'No one believes the Bloods won't take Birmingham. Every day, someone from our neighbourhood leaves the area. Everyone is heading north.'

'It's a mess up there, really, I can tell you,' Ash said.

'How can you be so sure?' I asked.

He looked away from me and replied, 'I just know.'

'But it was nice,' I said, squeezing his hand.

'What was?' he asked.

'Me and you, on your bike, going to Scotland on the 'A' roads and stopping for a meal in Bradford.' I laughed.

He didn't.

Later that night, after Ash went back to London, I got smashed, tiptoed into my bedroom and just as I got into bed, Mum came in.

'And fairy tales are just that – fairy tales,' Mum said.

Tats, you absolute swine, I thought. He'd clearly told Mum. I was too stoned to argue with her and let her words wash over me, I just replied, 'Okay, Mum,' to whatever she said.

'...and if your dad were alive, he would really want you to have a traditional wedding.'

I had the ring Ash had given me in the palm of my hand under the quilt.

'Like you had a traditional wedding, Mum,' I said.

She laughed, 'He wouldn't mind who you married, really, I know he wouldn't. But I mean he would really have liked to be able to have a great big party, at which he could invite everyone, and pretend there was no alcohol, and get that special wedding food...'

'You mean that greasy, oily, stomach-churning wedding food he always complained about?'

The two of us hadn't laughed together for so long, I'd forgotten how musical her voice could be and how so quickly she could lose her years.

'Shall we leave this place and go to Scotland, Mum' I asked when she stopped laughing.

'I've been looking into this,' she replied, 'but this Scotland is not the Scotland of the Bruce, fighting against the murderous English armies of the South. Some of the Scots of today are just like the English, a bunch of racist bastards.'

My old Mum really was back with a bang, I thought, and put my head in her lap, and she continued, 'I heard mosques in Glasgow are being torched, and they've built camps on uninhabited islands, that's where they hold refugees, awaiting processing, but maybe that is still not that bad a place for you to go...'

'I wouldn't go anywhere without you,' I interrupted her. I was a little girl again.

'Of course not,' Mum said. 'But we could never make it by walking, we got no money to pay our way, and so many women are getting kidnapped by gangs and militias,' she stopped and sighed, 'At least we would be safe on the islands, and If only we had enough money to pay someone to drive us all the way there.'

'And I would even take Tats with us,' I said.

'And Tats,' Mum said.

'And my girl gang,' I said.

'Of course, dear, even the Ginnz.'

Mum stroked my hair, and all of a sudden I feared nothing, not the gangs, not the Bloods chasing us out; Shorty was not coming back, and Shyla was safe. I dozed off and drifted back to the time when Mum would go for a jog first thing in the morning, the dog by her side, and come back all flushed, then sing in the shower and come out in three towels and smelling of antique roses. Those were the days when we lived. Once in those times, we went to buy a new television. Tats was asleep in the pram. It was a lovely warm summer, and Dad had insisted on wearing green shorts and blue trainers. So, there was my hairy-legged dad, pushing the pram, my super-fit mum, with her thick curly hair, and me, holding her finger. Mum and Dad couldn't agree on which television to buy, and then the salesman pointed at Mum and said to Dad, 'Why don't you let your daughter choose?'

'She is my wife,' Dad said.

Mum and I laughed. We got the television Mum wanted, which we would have done anyway.

I went even deeper back to the days when I wanted to fulfil the dreams Mum had lost. Mum went to a school in Bradford. She wanted to become a doctor, but her teachers thought she wasn't good enough. She often told me that it took her nearly two decades to realise that the reason her teachers had said what they said was because of their racism. I promised Mum I would achieve her dream. Then my brother was born, and she had no time for me. The only way I could really be with her was when she was reading her poems or listening to them in her music. Mum didn't care that I didn't understand what she was saying when she quoted lines like, *I wrote on the clouds, 'Down with censorship'. They confiscated the sky.*

When Tats grew up, she recited the same poems to him as well.

'How can you write on the clouds, Mummy,' he'd asked her the first time she had recited these words to him.

'The clouds of the poet are not really clouds, dear,' Mum said, 'it's a metaphor. He means he will fight on, by any means, even if he has to write on the clouds.'

'What is "confiscate", Mummy?'

'It's like taking something away.'

'How can you take the sky away? You'd have to be gigantic, powerful monsters to do that.'

'That is so true, my little pumpkin. Now eat another bean.'

As my brother chewed and spat out beans, I imagined monsters with enormous hands. Normal kids fell asleep to bedtime stories, I had to drift away on metaphors. I loved it when she quoted Rumi. She put on a deep, manly voice to do it and say, 'You are not a drop in the ocean, but the ocean in a drop.' It conjured up visions of mountains and clouds all melting into a drop sitting in the palm of my hand. When she was upset with Dad, she would recite Khusrau. *The river of Love flows in strange directions, who steps in drowns, who drowns crosses.*

'...but Marah, listen, do you love Ash?' Mum asked, washing my memories away.

'I do,' I said dreamily.

'I mean, like, really, really love him?' Mum said, 'So that you think you could spend the rest of your life happily together?'

'Can you ever know that?'

'You can dream,' Mum said.

'I dream,' I replied.

THE BETRAYAL

I hadn't told my closest friends about Ash's proposal. How could I, after what all these men and their wars had taught us? 'I wish I was born a cow,' Leena had once said on the subject of wedding rings, 'I would have been spared the bullshit of dates and wedding rings.'

'Yeh, the only good ring is one that goes through the nose of a man, with a long chain on it,' Shyla had concurred.

'Their romance with the rings is just another weapon in their armoury,' I'd agreed.

We had taken a vow that if we got through this hell, we would not swap one bondage for another and end up bound to a man.

And then I showed my friends my engagement ring.

'We knew you'd been keeping a secret from us,' Shyla said, all excited. She held the ring in the palm of her hand as though it was something so fragile it might break.

'We just didn't know what it was,' Leena said, touching the diamond with the tip of her index finger, 'It's beautiful, even though it's only a piece of very hard stone.'

And so, I wore the red dress and took a selfie
And sent it to him.
And he didn't reply.
And I wore the ring and took a selfie
And sent it to him.
And he didn't reply.
And I sent a voice message.
And he didn't reply.
And I concluded that maybe he had just been a highly fragrant lie.

Within days, I started having panic attacks: maybe he was dead or had been kidnapped. Maybe I was right all along and had just been a fool and he had left me for someone better.

Nobody laughed at me. Nobody said, 'We told you so'. Leena got me a stolen mobile, and I rang his house. His mum answered. She recognised my voice and went silent for a moment, then said, 'I'm sorry, I can't talk to you,' and hung up.

Each morning, I woke up, hauled myself out of bed and looked out of my window, searching for a sight of Ash. I lost track of how many mornings went by. I got to know the moment every other curtain on the street twitched, which trees the birds sang from, which they raided for berries. I knew every dog walker's routine and the hiding places of every street cat. And I hated it all. Then, on one of these misty mornings, I saw Leena and Shyla coming towards our house, carrying a bunch of flowers. I waved to them. They waved back.

'Don't be shocked, they're just flowers,' Leena said, walking into the house.

'You didn't need to spend it on me,' I said. 'Your faces are enough.'

'Who said we paid for them?' Shyla replied.

'And we didn't bring these from the graveyard, in case you are wondering,' Leena said. Her voice had filled with sadness.

'What's up?'

'I chose the flowers, actually,' Shyla said.

'Where's Hostess Marah?' Leena asked.

'I'm sorry,' I said and turned towards the kitchen. They followed me, and as I made the tea, Leena found a jug, put some water in it, plonked the flowers in and asked, 'Who's at home?'

'Just my brother. But he's on his computer, so as good as not here.'

'You not having a drink?' Leena asked.

'Come on then, girls, what's the breaking news,' I asked, shaking my head. 'Someone getting married to a corpse from the cemetery?'

'Sit down Marah,' Leena commanded.

I pulled up a chair and sat down.

'You know Marah, I love you,' Leena said.

'And I love you, we all love you...'

'Cut to the point, will you, Leena,' I said.

'We heard some rumours, which we think you ought to be told about,' Leena said after a long pause. 'But they could just be rumours.'

'I'll get a drink as well,' I said.

It can only be one thing, I thought, filling a glass of water at the sink. I steeled myself and sat back down with them.'So, shall I guess or you going to tell me?'

'I don't think you want to guess this one,' Leena said.

'You found Chilli!' I said.

'It's not about that dog,' Shyla said.

'I've heard some bad rumours about Ash,' Leena said. 'If they are true, he's not the old Ash we knew.'

Of course not, I thought, how could he be? He's probably running around making arrangements and getting things sorted out for our future.

'Yeh, it's a bit strange, him not responding to me for a while. I got upset with him, but hey, these things happen. After all, it's a big decision, and maybe he's having trouble with his family. But you know Ash, he'll come through, all fine.'

'It's not about his family, Marah,' Leena said.

'Don't tell me you heard he's cheating on me?'

'Ash has signed up with the Bloods, Marah,' Leena said.

THE SOLICITUDES

How could this have happened? Ash hated all things religious, and above all, he hated the Bloods. He despised them for their claims about the second coming, where no other Christians were good enough for their new Christ; Muslims needed wiping out, and every other religion was just a doormat; they could murder, and their god protected them; they could rape, and their god would save them; they could pillage, and it was all in His name. They took my dream of ever going to med school. They chased me out of my house in London and made us all refugees. They took my dad and extinguished the fire in my mum, and maybe they will once again make me a refugee. And maybe all my hunches were right. I really didn't know Ash, the man, or understand men at all. I thought I loved him, but maybe love was just a joyride for him. If I could go back in time, I told myself, I would never trust love, never let a man into my heart, he will only break it and, with it, destroy the world in which it beats. Ash, the engineer. He'd blown my heart.

I stopped going to the graveyard and told everyone to leave me alone. Everyone did, apart from Leena. She messaged me three times a day. Once when she woke up, once when she was in the graveyard, and then just before she went to sleep if she was alone. I only choked, trying to type words that ran like scalpels across my heart, so we never really talked for long.

If this was love-sickness, I didn't know it could be so deeply vengeful. I could taste its anger in my mouth and smell its rage on my breath. I was about to delete his number from my mobile. Instead, I sent him a text: Why? Why? Why? And then I spent the whole night waiting for a reply.

I waited and waited.

He was no longer the Ash I knew, so why would I get a response? He could join the Bloods or the army of the devil for all I cared. I just wanted him to answer my question. Why?

I thought I was dreaming when I felt my mobile vibrate on the table next to me. It was past midnight. Post-midnight calls usually meant Leena had just returned home from a manhunt. Go on, Marah,

I thought, you've got to stop sulking one day. Without opening my eyes, I stretched my hand out, grabbed the phone, brought it under the quilt and grunted, 'What?'

I could hear breathing on the other line. I looked at the number. It was unknown.

'Whoever you are, just fuck off,' I said. Before I could click the disconnect button, a voice said, 'Hi, Marah.'

It was him.

I hated the sound of my name on his tongue. My chest tightened.

'How the fuck could you join the Bloods? Sign up with those who chased me out of my house? Those who stole our dreams? Or were they ever really *our* dreams? Tell me what you thought I was thinking when I sent you a picture of the ring on my finger. Why did you play with my heart and then crush it?'

'I'm sorry, I don't have much time...'

'You don't have time?' I shouted into the phone. 'You selfish bastard, don't you dare ever phone again.' I stabbed the red End Call button.

I took a deep breath. Then I called Leena.

'Marah!' she answered. 'You, Ok?'

'He called.'

'Who?' Leena asked.

'The dick on a bike,' I said.

'What did he say?'

'He had no time,' I said.

'Lol'

'Innit!' I said.

'I'm a bit pissed at the mo,' Leena said, 'you going to turn up tomorrow? The Ginnz miss you.'

'Don't know,' I said.

'Hang in there, Marah. Love you.'

She sounded sleepy. 'Love you too,' I said and ended the call.

My door opened. Mum came in.

'What are you doing up at this time?' I protested. 'Go back to sleep.'

She sat on the end of my bed.

'Were you spying on me?'

'No, dear.' Mum yawned and smiled. 'You were shouting. I

thought you were having a nightmare. We all need to talk about things that upset us.'

'I'm not upset.'

'We need each other, especially at times like this,' she said.

'I don't need you.'

I was melting inside.

She leaned over, stroked my face, and said, 'It'll work out, don't worry. These are difficult times. They will pass.'

'What will work out, Mum?'

'Between you and Ash. But you have to give him some time.'

'Give him time! Are you for real, Mum? He's joined the Bloods. The ones who chased us out of London, remember! The ones who might chase us away from this house as well if they come here. The ones looking for the fucking Messiah!'

'Lower your voice. Tats is sleeping. Things aren't always black and white, especially in times like this.'

'So, you think it's OK for him to join the Bloods?'

'That's not what I said.'

There was something about the way Mum was talking to me that unnerved me. Her voice remained so unnaturally even.

'Has he been in contact with you?' I asked.

She looked away from me.

I got out of bed, got the box with the ring, opened my window and threw it out. Then I said to Mum, 'Get out. Get out. Get out now!'

I sulked around the house for a month, or was it ten? I didn't care much about Mum constantly saying Uncle Melvin had not sent any money again and we had nothing left, or Leena and Shyla telling me that the Ginnz were going downhill without me. One of these sick days, when I was tossing and turning in bed, I heard a motorbike outside. It was well before dawn. Maybe it was Ash? I thought. I jumped up and looked out of my bedroom window. I cursed myself for thinking it could have been him. But for a small streak of smoke and the fading noise of a motorbike engine, all else was the fucked up normal. I went back to bed, pulled the sheet over my face and cursed the world and all the motorbike riders in it when Mum came into my room.

'You've got another letter for the test,' she said.

'Send it to the devil, I don't give a shit,' I replied from under my sheets. 'How is it that the only thing that works in this war is the post?'

Then I realised that it was too early for the postman. I threw the sheet off my face. My heart began to pound. I hadn't been dreaming. There was a motorbike.

'It must have been him,' I said. I found it impossible to mention Ash's name. 'But he wouldn't do this. Would he?'

Mum looked at me guiltily.

'So, it was him, wasn't it?'

Mum nodded after a bit and gave me the letter.

I read it. It was another letter inviting me to go for a test at a Bloods clinic. This one had a big "By No Later Than 27th February 20:30" printed in red across it. I checked the wording. 'You must... blah blah blah.'

The Believers, who are at war with the Bloods, were telling me I had to attend the clinic for the Bloods DNA test, and Ash had delivered the letter. How fucked up is all this?

How could Ash do this to me? I thought, looking over the letter. He must have come and hand-delivered it. Not even a 'how are you?' Maybe he was just a cold-blooded bastard who took my heart for an old Bhangra drum to be kicked around and pounded whenever the mood grabbed him.

'So, you really want me to go for this test, Mum?' I said.

She didn't say no.

'Go look at yourself in the mirror and tell yourself, "The Bloods and Believers might be slaughtering each other, but they are OK". Go do it. And if the woman who was my mother looks back at you, she will say, "As both of them start with a letter B, it means only that they both believe in Bullshit!'

Tats sniggered by the doorway. Mum kept eerily composed.

'I know so many friends whose daughters have been,' Mum said calmly.

All my clean tops hung in the tall wardrobe as neatly ever. Thanks, Mum. Apart from a half-sleeved silky red one, all the rest were black, as were my tee shirts. She'd folded all my Tees and placed them on a shelf above the tops. Each week, I promised myself to throw the red one away, but I kept it because it reminded me of Ash's red dress that I'd ripped up but still kept in a black plastic bag under the bed, like a red sail from a ship called Misery. The pain the dress caused me made me feel alive, and I was going to find a way to get my own back on Ash and make him pay dearly.

I stood in the window, thinking. Some onion smell came through from a neighbour's cooking.

I was not a superstitious girl, but when I was quietly concentrating on simple things, say peeling some garlic, I often felt my dad was looking over me and would send me a sign for when I had peeled enough. It could be a clove just flying out of my hand. Mind you, sometimes, I just outright ignored my dad.

I left the window and sat on my bed, trying to convince myself that maybe the best course of action would be just to leave this fucked up family of mine, yes, just get a gun, go blow Ash's nuts off and disappear in one of the refugee columns trying to make it to Scotland.

Dad was useless today. His lazy ghost didn't visit me. Even though I was scared of the idea of walking out on Mum and Tats, and being all alone among all those lost hordes, still, no sign from Dad, saying don't do it. But then, he never liked Ash, and maybe he would be quite happy with me shooting that treacherous bastard's balls off, and that was why I was getting no signs.

Don't get me wrong, it's not that I believe in any religion thing. I think it's all bullshit, just someone's delusions which have ended up getting a lot of followers. But still, I did think there was something or someone out there looking after me. I liked to think it was Dad's spirit. Even though I thought it was all rubbish, at the same time, it helped me get through. Or maybe all this was just stupid old me, Dad's little girl who just couldn't get over the fact that he was dead. A little girl holding a wall of tears behind her smiling eyes each time she smelt karahi chicken that reminded her of her dad or saw some bloke with an oversized belly.

I took a deep breath, pushed Dad to the back of my mind, and went and looked out of the window again. It was so dark now it looked like the middle of the night and not the middle of the day. I smiled at the thought that Dad would always have a dig at Allah on days like this and remind Him that only in England could he forget where night ended.

All of a sudden, the sun streamed into my room. The rain

stopped. Pigeons began to coo on my window ledge. Some kids ran around laughing.

This was my sign. I jumped up, opened my closet, got a clean bra and a pair of knickers from the top drawer, shut it with the side of my hip, took a blueish vest from the bottom of the middle drawer, closed it with my left foot, grabbed a pair of odd socks from the third one. This one was easy to open but often took a big bum push to close. After shutting the drawer, I changed into clean clothes, closed the cupboard door and looked at myself. I bared my teeth, pushing my face towards the mirror, as I did every morning.

I pulled the red top off its hanger, grabbed a pair of black trousers, got dressed as quickly as I could and ran downstairs. I pulled Tats' denim jacket off the hook, just to wind him up, and left the house before I had time to change my mind again.

The sun might have been out, but it was cold enough to numb my fingers. I tightened my scarf and buttoned up the jacket. I thought of heading back home and getting my thicker coat but gave up on the idea in case I met Mum and ended up in another intergalactic battle. I blew breath into my hands, rubbed them, then stuck my hands down my trouser pockets the way boys do and set off towards Soho Road in Handsworth. According to the letter, this was where the Bloods would have someone pick me up and take me to their clinic for the test to see if I could be the one to deliver the virgin birth. Me. Haha.

A 12-seater van with blackened windows was parked at the top of Villa Road, close to Soho Road. Its engine was running. A man in a black waistcoat, ridiculous posh hotel porter's hat, bling white shirt, done-up, thin black tie and polished black brogues paced to and fro in front of it, lit cigarette in hand.

When I got closer, he smiled at me, tugged his ginger beard, touched his cap, opened the sliding side door, and stepped aside. Some girls were singing inside the van. The girls, mostly my age, waved at me and carried on singing in a mixture of English, Punjabi, and Arabic. I got in. It was drowsy and warm inside and smelt of twelve girls' morning perfumes. I didn't recognise anyone, sat down in an empty seat behind the driver and put my head against the glass as the interior lights flickered and the van drove off.

The driver called back, 'Seat belts, please, ladies!'

I clicked mine in.

The road to Birmingham city centre was adorned with huge black-and-white banners strung up by the Believers. Drinking is Haram! Women, Dress Modestly!

I drifted back to the time when we sang non-stop on school trips when wars were only distant events on the news, somewhere out there beyond England's shores.

It was 7 am on a Friday, and we were off on a school coach trip to Paris. It was my birthday, yet there were no celebrations – no cards, no kisses, no nothing. I'd just been woken in the small hours, dressed and packed off to school, then ushered onto this coach. I didn't get it. They wouldn't answer any questions. I couldn't understand why there were no birthday celebrations and why they were behaving the way they were, what it was that Mum and Dad were hiding from me. I ended up believing my little brother, who told me the day before that his lips were sealed, but wait and see, Mum and Dad had finally found a way of getting rid of me, and it began with the coach trip. Even Chilli, our black Alsatian puppy, kept away from me that morning. No one spoke. Everyone looked at me as though they knew I was unwanted. I pulled myself on a seat and refused to wave at Mum and Dad as the coach went past them. We'd only just turned round the corner when the coach stopped. There was pin-drop silence inside. The door of the coach hissed open. My brother stepped in. I stood up in my seat and was about to laugh at him and tell him that, hahaha, our evil Mum and Dad have got rid of you as well, when the entire coach suddenly burst out singing Happy Birthday to me. I blushed to heaven and back. Then Mum and Dad boarded the coach with a giant birthday cake that had a great big torch for a candle stuck in the middle of it. The driver banned the torch but allowed the cake and we all ate it and got sick and had a great time in Paris. Happy days.

I woke up when we stopped at a checkpoint somewhere outside Birmingham. The driver opened the door. A blast of air gushed into the van. A bushy-bearded soldier in the black uniform of the Believers stepped up. He went to the back and then walked slowly backwards and stopped just as he went past me. He looked me in the eye and then looked down at my breasts and held his gaze there for a moment.

I placed my left hand on my jacket.

His eyes followed my hand.

I cupped my hand and raised it slowly. His eyes followed my hand.

When it got to the top of the headrest of the seat, I stuck my middle finger up at him. The girls at the back clapped and whistled.

He smirked, turned around, nodded at the driver, and got out of the van.

I felt so good that I stood up to go to the back of the van and join the girls there, but the road was so bumpy that I fell back into my seat. A short while later, we stopped at another checkpoint, this time full of strutting adolescent Bloods. The guards just waved us through.

The van slowed down in front of an 'H' shape of five interconnected Portacabins and stopped under a covered archway. The archway had a flashing neon sign: *Royal Medical Research Council.*

A few girls were waiting outside by the Portacabins and talked excitedly with each other as they waited for us to disembark from the van. We got off, one of the girls who was leaving winked at me and waved a money order as she went past. I nodded to her. Good for her. Maybe I'd made too big a deal of this test business.

The inside of the clinic was pretty much like any clinic: white paint, bored staff, and lots of notices, with a small table in the waiting room filled with old magazines. But you had to laugh at one of the signs that hung above the door. There was a no-smoking poster that had a picture of a cigarette inside a red circle with a red line across it. So far, so boring. But next to it was an equally large poster. This one had a gun inside the red circle with a red line across it. Someone had scrawled underneath, 'Don't pack your guns, girls!' I laughed inside. I'd tell the Ginnz.

A door-shaped, grey-haired nurse with tired eyes did each girl in turn. She took a swab out of their mouth, put the swab into a small tube, and said, 'Thank you, darling'. Then she cut a piece of hair from the girl. Said, 'Thank you, darling' again. Bagged that. Then, pricking the girl's finger and pressing out a sample drop of blood, dabbed the blood and tubed the dab. Said, 'Thank you, darling' again. She took each girl in turn and labelled each sample carefully, going back and forth to the holding tray that held the completed samples. She looked like she must have done a thousand swabs, samples, and dabs already this morning.

My turn came, and she took a swab from my mouth, cut a bit of my hair, did her thank yous in between, and before I could say, 'I'm not a fan of needles!' had pricked my finger and dabbed in a droplet of blood.

'Ouch! ' I hissed snatching my hand free.

'It's just a pin,' the nurse replied. 'Quick pre-test, that's all.'

'You mean there are more?'

'Won't be long now,' the nurse said. She opened a door and signalled we should all come through. We followed her. The new room had a long wooden table with eight chairs around it and a box of tissues in the middle. It was the same shape and size as the other room but windowless. A muted television on the wall played a Bloods' promo film about the Second Coming. I slumped down into a chair at the furthest end of the table from the TV. We were all quiet. I started running my fingers over the table's rough wood grain when my eye caught *Ginnz*, carved into the surface of the table. It had been done by a ballpoint pen. Under it was the letter L, also curlicued and with a flamboyant twist to the long stroke of the L. I rubbed a finger along it. The ink was still fresh. It had to be Leena. The twist of the L was just the way Leena wrote. It could only be her. Leena had been here. She could still be here.

I looked around to see if anyone was watching me. The girls were lost in their own silence. After a little while, the nurse returned. There was a buzz. She had money orders in her hand. She gave each girl a cheque and asked those who received the money to follow her. Everyone got one. Except me. As all the others got up, the nurse looked at me and smiled. I stood to leave, but she waved for me to sit down. I did, and I was glad not to leave because I wanted to find out if Leena was still here.

I was alone for a while. The TV kept looping Bloods adverts. Eventually, a tall blond nurse came in, carrying a tray. Two male nurses were with her. She put the tray on the table and picked up a syringe.

The men stepped forward towards me as the door behind the nurse clicked shut.

THE TRIAL

'My name is Sister Audrey,' the nurse said. 'I read in your notes you like poetry, how sweet.'

I got off the chair, stepped away from her and pressed my back against the cold wall. She didn't move. 'I used to love poetry when I was young,' she said, 'but that was a long time ago, long before the troubles.'

I didn't give a shit about what she knew about me or what she thought about my poetry. I wanted to get as far away from her as possible. I raised my fists in front of my face like a boxer. I must have looked a right sight, 60 kg me, getting ready to fight two professional heavyweight champions of the world.

'Come along, there is no need for this,' the nurse said putting the needle down in the tray.

'What for?' I asked.

'A few further tests,' she replied.

'And then?'

'Once everything is done, we will bring you back here, and you can go, just like all the other girls,' she said.

'And the money?'

'With the money, of course.'

'Am I the only one going for further tests?' I asked.

'Of course not,' she replied, 'this is routine.'

She flicked her eyes at one of the heavies, and he left the room. She threw me a false smile while taking off her surgical gloves. Maybe this is how sheep felt before the butcher went to make them halal meat, I thought.

An hour or an eternity or so later, I was led out of the room and put into an SUV with blackened windows. Two police motor-bikers with their beacons flashing were at the front and the back.

The heavies sat in front, and the nurse sat opposite me, with her back to the driver.

'Where you taking me?' I asked as the van began to speed. Now, I really felt like a sheep being led to the slaughterhouse and thought about jumping out of the van. What's the worst that could happen?

Pretending to lean against the side, I 'accidentally' let my hand press the door handle. It was locked.

Aud shook her head at me. It was obvious she knew what I was doing.

I saw a sign with 'M40' and we drove along the motorway for a long time until we turned off into a small snaking road and eventually ended up somewhere with a massive gate, with armed men in Bloods' uniform, with guard dogs, and a drone flying above.

We drove through a long tree-lined drive towards a massive old-style house with beautiful, manicured gardens and kinds of flowers, like one of the manors which the old rich used to have, and which had been converted into museums. But this one was clearly not a museum. Eventually, the van stopped.

'Will you take me back for dinnertime?' I asked Aud while getting out of the van. She ignored me.

I made what I thought was a funny comment, 'Do you lot really believe in all that Second Coming, all that Virgin birth stuff?'

She didn't find it funny.

Aud stepped out, and I followed her. She stopped in front of a closed door at the end of the corridor. The heavies stood on either side of it. The door had a lock on the outside to ensure it could not be opened from the inside.

Aud unlocked the door and waited for me to go into the room. When I didn't, she nodded at the heaves, who each grabbed me by the arm, lifted me off my feet and took me into a room.

I felt a prick in the side of my left arm, and a moment later saw Aud holding a syringe and shut the door.

My nightmares began.

THE BLESSED

The First Commandment
Thou shall show no mercy to the enemies of the Second Messiah.

THE FIFTH COMMANDMENT

24

There is no Honour greater than the Second Messiah
and the Blessed Virgin Birth

25
LAVENDER

COMETH

COLD

SILENCE

29

GINNZ

CHOSEN

FIRE

32

JESUS

COMETH

THE TESTIMONY

I woke up expecting to hear the music of war, but instead, there was a beautiful silence, free from the whining drones above and the bombs and bullets below.

I felt like I was in someone else's dream. With my eyes still closed, I smiled at the thought that this someone else, an undeserving refugee from Birmingham, had called out to the Lord and offered herself to Him, and He had answered.

For some reason, this thought made me laugh, and then I felt sad for laughing.

Everything was fuzzy inside my head. It was being bombarded with disjointed images and noises. I closed my eyes, and I was in a big white-painted room full of whispers. Some corners of the room were dark, so dark, darker than any place where light could ever reach. Voices chased me around and around swirling waves of my deepest fears. Red-eyed beasts snapped at me, snakes moved around inside my stomach, hissing each time I moved away from them. But then, voices saved me from them by calling on God and chasing my terrors away in the name of the coming Messiah. They cleansed the horrors with burning crucifixes and choirs singing my praises.

Then, there was often a soft hand gently stroking my forehead, easing my pain. 'Blessed Marah. Blessed be the House of David,' said a voice. I opened my eyes. I was in a brightly lit hospital room. A cold shiver ran down my back. This was the room of my nightmares, a big square room with a coffee table and sofas near a sizeable stained-glass window through which sunlight streamed in. It hurt my eyes, and I had a terrible headache. I was tired. My body ached. My throat was parched.

'Good morning, Marah,' a woman said. 'My name is Audrey, but you like calling me Aud.' I knew that was true and that I had seen this woman before, but I had no idea where or when.

'Let's get you up,' she said. She pressed a button on the side of my bed, and as it raised, a giant wooden crucifix came into view, with the crosspiece at the bottom. Below it was a portrait of the smiling King and the words: *Thou shalt show no mercy to the enemies of the Second Messiah.*

I felt a tension in my head, like someone had placed a cold metal band around it, and it was getting tighter all the time. I opened my mouth to complain to the nurse but ended up saying, 'Thou Shall endure all pain in the name of the Lord.'

'Amen,' Aud said, placing my hand gently in between hers, 'There is no Honour greater than to serve the Blessed Virgin.'

When she said that, I felt happy, like a child singing along with its mother. I felt so safe and warm with her being around me. And yet somewhere inside my head, a place I didn't recognise, a little voice spoke.

'Who are you?' the voice asked.

I knew that voice – once, long ago. Whoever it was inside my mind, trapped in a maze, chasing sounds and pictures, memories half-formed, smells, images dissolving, they scared me.

It was forbidden.

'Begone! Leave me alone!' I said aloud.

Aud tilted her head back to look into my face. 'Who are you speaking to, Marah,' she asked.

'I don't know, maybe a demon tempter,' I said.

I was terrified. I shook with fear. I began to sweat. The nurse stroked my head and massaged my shoulders. It calmed me but, all of a sudden, I was really thirsty and asked Aud for some water, who nodded her head and smiled.

I tried to push myself out of bed, but was too exhausted and slumped back.

The nurse left, leaving my door ajar, and a little while later a girl about my age popped her head around it. She looked at me, put her finger to her lips, and disappeared. I had no idea who she was, but somehow I was certain I had known her once. I didn't like her; the sight of her made me nauseous. Later, I told Aud I had aches and pains all over, and she massaged me without complaint. She helped me out of bed and to exercise in the room. I was a bit wobbly at first, but she held on to me all the while and made sure I didn't fall.

But I didn't understand. Something must have happened to me.

'Why am I so weak?' I asked.

'It is His will, Marah. You are from the House of David,' she said, massaging my arms gently with both her hands. 'No harm can come against His will. What He wills will be.'

When I closed my eyes, I saw Aud's words floating above waves of gentle light. The words were echoed by a choir of men and women dressed in long black cloaks, with red crucifixes running down their fronts. A strange sound disturbed these images.

Are you Marah? I heard that little voice asking me from inside.

I opened my eyes, and the singing was not just inside my head after all. The music was coming through some loudspeakers in the room. There was a nurse there. I had forgotten her name. She was singing the words I had heard in my mind, and they were playing over and over again from the ceiling speakers.

'Nurse?' I said, and then I remembered her. I knew her, she cared for me, and I loved her. 'Nurse, have I been poorly?'

'No, Blessed,' she said.

Looking at her, I remembered her name, Aud.

'Am I in danger, Aud?' I asked.

'Oh no. We want to keep you safe,' Aud said. She smiled, pointed upwards to Heaven with her index finger and added, 'He wants us to take care of you!'

'But something's wrong with me.'

'No, my dear. You are healthy. Praise the Lord. You are the Blessed Marah.' She said each word slowly.

I was about to say, Amen, it just came into my mouth without my thinking. But instead, I took a deep breath and found the words I really wanted to say. 'Why am I in hospital?'

'We need to keep you safe and healthy, Blessed Marah,' Aud said. 'It is a great honour for us all. Not everyone gets a chance to serve the House of David, but the reincarnation of the Holy Virgin Mary, Mother of God.'

She looked at me with watery eyes and made a strange sign of the crucifix across her front, going up from the bottom.

Part of me wanted to laugh at being called Blessed Marah, but another part of me was elated. I raised my hand, and Aud suddenly fell to her knees. She bowed her head and said something in Latin. When she'd finished, she looked up at me like I was meant to do something. I felt tense inside, a tension that got stronger and stronger the longer I didn't act. Suddenly, with a jerk, my hand dropped on top of her head, almost of its own will.

'Bless you," I said. At once, I felt relaxed again.

'You are the Holy Destiny, Marah,' Aud intoned.

'Bless you,' I said again. Then I added, 'Aud, my dear, I am hungry.'

'Yes, Blessed,' she said, getting to her feet. "What would you like?' she asked.

'I think I want ...' I paused because no matter how hard I thought about what I wanted to eat, I could not find the words with which to say it.

'How about your favourite dish today?' Aud suggested.

''Yes, that would be lovely,' I said.

She left to get my food, leaving me on my own. My feeling weird began to get worse. Distorted images of burning crucifixes flashed about inside my head, unintelligible voices shouted orders at me. I tried to make sense of this disorder, to remember what had happened to me, how I'd got here – wherever here was in this foggy mind of mine. But my memories were in a mess. There was so much I didn't know. My family. I had no image of a family in my head, and yet everyone had a mother and a father, right? Did I ever have one? Maybe they were all dead. After all, there was a war out there – wasn't there? Was it over?

Or had I just imagined it?

Or perhaps God had invented me upon the earth, like a miracle.

I opened my mouth. 'I am ...' I began. But I could go no further.

I tried again. 'My name is Marah ....' But again, I got stuck. Somewhere along the way, I'd forgotten my own surname. By the time Aud came back with my lunch, I was in a bad state. I was anxious and trembling. I couldn't even remember my own name!

'What's my surname, Aud?' I asked. 'I must know.'

By the way she looked at me, she was clearly surprised by my question, and it took her a few moments to reply, 'The doctor will explain.'

Those words – the Doctor – made me shiver inside. I knew him, but not from here. He frightened me, yet I loved what he said to me.

Aud gave me the tray of food: mashed potatoes, grilled fish, some carrots and mustard.

'But... I don't think this is my favourite food,' I said.

Aud looked closely at me. 'Are you sure, Blessed?' she said.

I took a forkful of fish and put it in my mouth. And yes, it was my favourite food, and I told her so. But at the same time, I knew it wasn't.

Someone was lying to me. But who? The nurse? Me? The demon inside me?

I tried to eat, but my throat was constricted. I wanted to talk to Aud – but although I believed and loved her, I distrusted her.

'I don't know why I say the things I do,' I said.

'Like what, dear?'

Then, I could not think of a single thing to tell her. My mind went blank. With a great effort, I remembered what I wanted to ask her, 'Why don't I know that which I should, and yet know that which I shouldn't?'

'The Doctor will explain, dear,' she said again, and left me to it.

I decided that strange little voice inside of me was a demon, but even so, I decided to let it talk. The odd thing about it was the demon was a girl who knew more about me than I did. She came to me with demands. Don't let go of me! You can never be!

I am, she said over and over again. I am you.

But I couldn't hold her in my mind long enough to answer her the way I wanted.

I didn't know what to make of this other girl who lived inside me. At times, she was angry at me, as if I had betrayed her. Other times, she would float into my thoughts quietly, sneak under the hymns and prayers that were bombarding me and ask, 'Why are you here?'

'Did you love?' she asked. This question made me feel empty inside, from a longing so powerful that I burst into tears. I felt so bad – but my tears were precious to me, they were real, but when I tried to remember my love, I felt so sick it made me literally vomit.

One night in bed, just as I was falling asleep I heard Aud speaking to someone.

'She is being unwritten,' she said. Summing up all the energy I could muster, I opened my eyes. 'I am Marah…!' I wanted to say. But the words died on my lips. I slumped back on the pillow and fell silent, but inside my head, I kept repeating my name, Marah, over and over again, but no matter how hard I tried, I just couldn't remember my surname.

A man with an American accent asked something of Aud. I did not catch what he said, but I knew his voice. Just like Aud, he made me feel calm inside, but at the same time, I hated him for … I did not know what for. But I felt he had done something terrible to me.

'So far, she has not unwritten her name,' Aud said.

Something clamped on my fingers, and then a monitor started bleeping. I felt a sharp prick on my hand and then felt a needle being pushed into it.

'How many times did I warn against using this rewriting technology for the Second Coming, even with the chip?' the man said angrily. 'It might be fine for prisoners in Huntington, but it is not proven enough for our mission. Damn these English buffoons.'

Then I remembered the man's name, Doctor. Yes – this was the Doctor, the one who Aud seemed to think was the fountain of all knowledge.

I lay still, listening. Perhaps they didn't know I could hear them – I might learn something.

There was a brief silence, and then the Doctor said, 'Did we get good recordings of her personality?'

'Yes, sir,' Aud replied.

'Good. Send them to the lab. We need to make duplicates.'

'Yes, sir,' Aud replied.

'Any development problems?'

'No, sir.'

'There is no better match,' the Doctor said. 'Marah is the one, Audrey. We cannot risk her. Remove the implant and begin work with medication and hypnosis. Start her on 10 mg of Sanctadromidex and increase by 5 mg per day until we reach a sub-max of 40 mg. And increase Hypno-sessions to twice a night. Look after her well. She carries the redemption of Mankind within her.'

I wanted to sit up and ask him a hundred questions, but I couldn't move any part of my body. It was like I was glued to the bed.

If there was one thing I could do, it was think. At least, I hoped it was me thinking. I talked to a voice. They opened all sorts of doors inside my mind, sometimes they took me to my childhood, and I could see and smell Mum, and then there was nothing. No scent of her. No image of her. Just a void. They took me to our kitchen back in London, and Dad cooking. Then this, too, would disappear. Occasionally, I smelt lavender, and it made me cry.

THE LIVING

I was so weak I was trapped in bed or a wheelchair for ages, so I was so grateful to Aud for the first time she took me for a walk. It was early evening when I first stepped out of my room into a white T-shaped corridor, with my room at the centre of the top bar of the 'T'.

I paused in the doorway. On my right, someone on a trolley, covered head to toe with a white sheet, was being pushed past by a beefy male nurse. Aud guided me hurriedly left, almost pushing me. We passed a girl I felt I had seen earlier. She had her hands to her face, but she pointed quickly, furtively to the right. I looked. Part of the paint on the wall had been chipped away, the empty space made the letter 'L'. A name came into my mind, Leena. I had known her once. I almost spoke to her, but she shook her head and backed away.

Aud led me out to a garden. It was spring. Flowers were blooming. And that was strange because the last thing I remembered from before when I had had a test of some kind … It had been winter then, but now it was spring.

The girl appeared again at the door to the garden. I went to ask her who she was and if I knew her, but when I opened my mouth, I said, 'Come, you must pray with me.'

The girl winced and quietly hummed a tune. I liked that tune. It was a road to a warm memory I couldn't find.

Abruptly, she leaned towards me and whispered, 'Remember the ones you love.'

I wanted to ask if she knew who I loved, but instead, I said – 'Is there anyone but Him to love?'

At that moment, Aud came to join us.

'Blessed Marah,' said the girl. She knelt, and I put my hand on her head.

'Bless you,' I said. The girl kissed my hand, rose and left. I stood and stared at her. I felt nauseous, and a feeling of panic rose up inside me. Sweat slid down my back.

'Who is that girl?' I asked.

'She should have gone ages ago,' said Aud.

'Gone where?' I asked.

'You know, Blessed, sometimes he just doesn't take my opinion.'

'Who?'

'The Doctor. I told him to let this girl go. But why do you care, you who are so Blessed? Why worry about others?'

'Does she want to go home?' I asked.

Aud didn't reply and took me back to my room and gave me my nightly vitamins.

As I lay in bed that night thinking about these questions, I pulled the sheet over my head to hide my face. My anxiety was terrible. Who was this girl? What was all that about remembering people I loved? I could feel strange dreams reaching out to take me. I had to fight hard to keep my head clear. I could hear the Doctor intoning, cursing my enemies. But who were my enemies? I could see myself standing on a large balcony, waving majestically across at cheering crowds. When I opened my arms and put my hands together, they all knelt, and I led them in prayer.

Every night, it was the same. During the day, odd little pieces of memory would come back to me, snatches of stories, names, ordinary life. But each night, dreams came to take over my mind and in the morning, everything had gone. Even so, each day, I remembered a little more, and with every little bit I remembered, things made less and less sense. I felt it was all bullshit. For instance, all this crap about the second coming? The Virgin Birth? Demons? God! When had I started to believe in that stuff? I was an atheist – wasn't I? When had I converted? Why did I have no memory of it? I tried to speak of it to Aud, but all she said was that only demons pose these questions.

'The Doctor will help you cast them out,' she told me. And sure enough, he would come to me in those strange dreams that would come into my head louder and stronger than ever. Repeatedly, the booming voice of the doctor would scream the Bloods Commandments into my brain.

Thou shalt destroy the false prophets of the Satanic Verses.

Thou Shalt endure all pain in the name of the Lord.

There is no Sabbath in the Holy War.

There is no Honour greater than the Second Messiah and the Blessed Virgin Birth

Thou shalt not sheathe thy sword whilst false beliefs roam free.

But during the day, that other voice, that sweet little voice inside me, kept on and on at me.

'Remember!' she said. 'Remember who you are!'

'But I can't!' I wailed.

'Yes, you can. You will. You must!' it would say.

One thing I did know, if I knew nothing else, I wasn't letting go of myself without a fight.

There was a strong smell of lavender in one of my dreams once. It moved around me, and I could still smell it even after it had left me. Somehow, it helped me hold back the Doctor's voice. Another trick I learned was humming the tune I heard the girl in the garden hum. Somehow, that melody went deep down into my being. It painted fragments of pictures inside my head ... memories of a dark-skinned, potbellied smiling man. But who was he? I loved him, I knew that. And there was a light-skinned woman with dreamy eyes, who I loved as well. And they loved me. And she had freckles across her nose, and I loved them.

Eventually these images brought words into my head, the words Mum and Dad. It took me a little longer to see my little cartoon of a Dad, as *my* dad with his bloated belly and hairy arms, and my beautiful mum and know this was my family – a family that had somehow been stolen from my mind! How I wept that day! And other memories. Scents, the smell of cooking food, of spices. It brought sounds of the wind through tall blades of purple flowers. I wanted those flowers, although I had no idea what they were or where I had seen them. I wanted them so badly, it made me ache. And the melody brought an image of a boy playing with the moon. But how could that be real? I still had no idea of what was real and what was not. Two worlds were fighting for my soul – for my very being.

I kept seeing the girl in the garden or the corridors, but I couldn't get a chance to talk to her. When Aud was near, the girl walked slowly, dragging her feet. Her eyes were dull, she took no notice of anything. But when Aud wasn't near, she changed, she became alert, and she would hum that melody again.

And once she sang.

'Sometimes, I see a poem on the sighs of the storm. Sometimes, I hear a melody in the cries of the storm,' she said. I felt that I had never heard anything so beautiful, and I was struck by the thought that there were other words which followed those the girl had just sung. Sure enough, they flashed suddenly in front of my eyes...

'Sometimes, I taste the tears of a song, dreaming of drowning in the depths of the storm.'

I wanted so badly to tell her that I knew the next line but couldn't. The next time I saw her, I smiled at her. She tossed her head in a way I knew I had seen a hundred times before – and a name flashed into my mind.

'Leena,' I whispered to her as we passed in the corridor. She smiled at me and walked on.

When Aud took me for a walk out in the garden, there was some writing on the wall opposite my room.

On the aches of a forgotten melody
I found the banished poet
Imprisoned in the sighs of a nightingale.

Aud and I both stopped to stare at it.

'It's your handwriting,' Aud said.

'It is, but I don't remember writing it,' I said. 'I like the raining moonlight, though.'

Aud peered at me curiously. 'But it doesn't say that!' she exclaimed.

'No ... but it should do, further down.'

She scowled. 'I'm not sure poetry is good for you,' she said.

'How can something beautiful be bad for anyone?' I asked.

Aud was upset, I could tell.

'Let's go to my office,' she said. 'I think Blessed may be in need of a counselling session, 'The mind, like the body, needs cleaning, but whereas the body can be washed, the mind must be counselled.'

I followed her to her office, a few minutes' walk down one of the corridors. Inside, she drew the curtains and put a lamp in one of the corners. Unlike the whitewashed walls of my room, these were painted in a soothing sky blue.

I sat down on the leather-bound couch near her desk.

'You can talk to me about anything in this room,' Aud said. 'It is a special place, a private place. This is where you can relax and talk about anything that is weighing on your mind. It's just between you and me.'

I loved Aud, but I knew better than to tell her about the secret me, the smaller me inside who was growing bigger every day, lured out by Leena's melody and the smell of lavender. Instead, I told her about the other voice I heard inside me – the loud, booming male voice. The voice that would force me to recite the ten Commandments of the Bloods, which told me that I was the Blessed Marah, Mother of the Christ to come, the Doctor. I told her how loud that voice was and how much it scared me. I wanted to know if I had gone mad and that was why I was here?

'We all hear voices, there is nothing wrong with that. This sounds like a good voice. What we must remember is to have faith in Him, who is Lord of All, for only He can keep the devil at bay. That is the eternal truth,' Aud said.

No, it's not, I thought, but nodded and answered, 'Yes.'

'Good,' Aud said. 'So, tell me. That poem on the wall ... do you really know the rest of it?'

'Yes,'

'How does it go?'

I recited the whole poem.

'What does the poem mean?' she asked.

'It is a metaphor,' I said, 'It doesn't have to have one meaning. It could mean different things to different people, and it could mean different things to them at different times.'

'Do you think the poem is about you?'

'I don't know.'

'Are you the nightingale?

'I don't know.'

'Where did you get the pen to write with?'

'It was on the floor near the wall,' I replied.

'Where is it now?'

'I left it where I found it.'

'You must be careful, Blessed. You must have written this thing in your sleep. It is dangerous. Sick minds conjure up lunatic thoughts.'

Maybe I was just lost in a mad mine of lunacy, I thought. Maybe I need to write.

I asked Aud, 'Can I have a pen and notebook to write in?' I asked at last.

'Why?' Aud asked sharply.

I paused to formulate my thoughts carefully. I wasn't sure why, but I wanted that notebook desperately. 'I feel that God wants me to be ready to write down any message He is going to send me,' I said, pointing skywards with my index finger. Even as I told this lie, I could feel voices and noises fighting against my lie, trying to drown out my thoughts. I bit down on my tongue until I could taste the blood in my effort to keep those other voices inside.

'I'll ask the Doctor, 'said Aud doubtfully.

'The doctor is not mightier than Him,' I said.

I startled Aud with these words. She went into a thoughtful silence for a moment, bit her bottom lip and nodded.

I got my notebook.

That night, after dinner, I managed to stay awake long enough to gather more memories about the poem. Leena used to sing it. I remembered how, even though I felt embarrassed hearing my poem being sung in front of people, I just loved the way she managed to make the melody float around the rhymes and how she could lift the words as if she were singing a eulogy to Allah.

I hummed and let the melody embed in my memory to take me back to myself. I remembered a graveyard somewhere far away. Leena was singing, with me next to her. Someone started drumming a rhythm on an old bucket.

I couldn't hold the memory for long, and soon, I fell back into the strange waking dreams that were trying to turn me into someone else.

The following day, as every morning, Aud gave me my vitamins. As I swallowed the pills, I kept repeating Leena's name inside my head. I picked up the notebook and pen and went to the toilet, humming.

'Why are you taking those with you?' Aud asked.

'I feel I might have a poem coming,' I said.

'In the toilet!' Aud said wryly.

'It comes when it comes,' I said.

In the cubical, after shutting the door, I wrote Leena on the inside of my left arm. When I came out, Aud took the book and pen off me. She flicked through the pages and relaxed.

'What's up?' I asked.

'Oh, I was worried lest you write something inappropriate.'

'Why would I do that?' I asked.

'The Doctor thought you might.'

'This woman is not your friend,' said the little voice in my head. It was louder than ever. And I recognised who it was for the first time.

It was my voice.

Later that day, the pen was fastened to an elasticated chain and fixed to the side of the desk, and placed on top of a new notebook, a dismal-looking, grey-covered thing, with Blood crucifixes on the bottom right-hand corner of every page.

Days passed before I saw Leena again. I smiled at her and mouthed her name, but she didn't react. I couldn't speak out loud as Aud was close to me. It was my first day in what passed in this place for a gym: a small running machine, some mats and a few large balls. Leena was on the machine, walking slowly. She didn't return my smile.

Aud and I waited patiently for Leena to finish so that I could go on. When Leena was done, she walked past us, wiping sweat off her forehead with a small white towel.

I'd love a Chicken Tikka Masala,' she said to Aud in a dull, zombie-like voice.

'It is forbidden,' Aud replied.

But as she spoke, I had a sudden, shocking vision of my father cooking this for me. I could smell frying onions, garlic and ginger, and remembered Dad's voice telling me his recipe, 'When the onions brown, throw in some garlic, and when the garlic browns, throw in some ginger, but don't let the ginger brown. Then throw in a bit of cumin and coriander seeds, wait for them to pop...'

I saw Dad in my mind's eye, crushing coriander seeds in the palms of his hands. I remembered him placing the sizzling dish on plates for me and Leena. It was such a happy memory, but tears sprang into my eyes.

'It is waiting for you,' Aud said. She was pointing at the running machine.

Her words chased memories of Dad out of my mind.
'Why is it forbidden?' I asked, stepping on the machine.
'It is Un-Christian,' she said. 'It is the food of fanatics.'

THE REMEMBRANCE

Even though Leena's name began to fade from my arm, each time I looked at it, it made me remember that I had written it and that she was someone special. Every time I thought of her, more memories rose up from the depths. I saw my dad cooking for me, my brother hovering around, and my mum sitting on a big chair with a laptop. I remembered our dog Chilli. But with these memories came other voices... The Doctor, with his angry booming, warning me of the tricks of the devil. All I could do was curl up on my bed, holding onto the spicy scents inside my head, and cry myself to sleep with the Doctor getting angrier inside me.

I so badly wanted to talk to Leena, but Aud was always shadowing me. When I did see Leena, I smiled at her. She would smile back from time to time, and then she would bow her head and say – 'Blessed am I to be in the company of the Blessed.'

Whilst this cheered Aud up, it depressed me. What was real and what was not real? I could not work it out.

Then, one day, I heard a scraping noise outside my room. Aud had gone to fetch my lunch, and I was trying to write a few words of poetry down but found it hard to think. I put the pen down on the table and opened the door. Leena was on her knees, wiping the floor in front of my door with a cloth. She had a small plastic bucket near her. She was dressed in an orderly blue uniform. Her hand movements were slow but deliberate, as if she was in a trance.

'Honoured am I to be in the company of Blessed Marah,' she said.

'Bless you, Leena!' I replied.

'So, you still remember my name?' she smiled.

'Do you know mine?' I asked, trying to push back a hazy fog inside my head.

She looked around her and said quickly, 'When I say the next word, say the first word that comes to your mind, and say it quickly.'

'OK.'

She pulled on the edges of her gloves, dipped the cloth into the bucket, flicked her eyes at me and went into a thoughtful silence. Her eyes were sharp.

Maybe she has been zombified and is trying to find herself like me, I thought. I became so excited by this idea that the haze inside my mind dissipated, and the nagging voices were silenced. I placed my hand on the wall, and it felt like it should. Cold. I could smell the air. It reeked of disinfectant. The light streaming in through the open window of my room was not being interfered with by the colours in my mind. I really was here.

'Shorty?' Leena said.

I cringed, remembering a man by this name.

'Gold,' I said, recalling his ugly smile and gold teeth.

'Leena,' she said.

'Moo,' I laughed, remembering how I used to call her a cow.

And God, did I laugh!

No zombie could know about Shorty's gold teeth, and only Leena would know how I used to call her a cow, I thought and asked, 'Didn't they try to make you a zombie?'

'They tried. I have to pretend, you see? They thought you were going to die, so they took your SIM out, and they took mine out as well in case they needed a spare part,' Leena said.

'What SIM?'

'They put a SIM in our heads to re-write us. How's your head?' she asked.

'Fucked,' I said.

'No, stupid, does it hurt at the back?' she asked.

I pressed the back of my head, and there was a bump which I didn't know I had. I pressed on it, and it hurt. 'Did they really put a SIM in there? But why am I still hearing voices?'

Leena shrugged. 'Hypnotism, brainwashing. They're using other techniques on you than they did on me. The little I know is that they gave you some sort of memory-changing drugs. You need to focus on strong memories. Do you remember any memories when you were really really scared?' Leena asked.

An image of a hand digging up Dad's grave suddenly appeared in front of me. A demonic face came out of the hand. It changed to the face of a little girl. It was me. The face opened its mouth to scream, but no voice came out of it. Everywhere I looked, there were monsters, some in green, others in red. I trembled. It was cold. My nose felt dry. I fell back against the wall.

Leena put her hand on mine. 'I'm sorry, that was too much. I didn't mean to get you so frightened. Did you have a vision? That was an implanted vision. Don't believe it. They want to scare you away from your real self.'

Leena's voice chased the monsters away, and I realised I was with my friend and not in a nightmare.

I described what I just saw, and she said, 'They really, really fucked with your...' She stopped mid-sentence and asked, 'What's your surname?'

I smiled at the stupidity of the question but became frightened, I couldn't remember it, couldn't find it in the fog inside my mind.

'I don't know,' I whispered.

'Don't worry, Marah Sultana,' Leena said, 'the mist in your brain will clear one day, Insha'Allah.'

'Insha'Allah,' I laughed. Sultana! That was who I was.

'They screwed around with me also and stopped because they think I've been successfully re-written. But I held on to myself. I kept on thinking about the smells I liked, about the tastes that I liked, about the songs I loved to hear. Sometimes I would touch something and press so hard that it hurt me, and that helped to ward off their bullshit.' She looked around to check that no one was listening to us. 'This place is where they put the SIMs in people's heads and are then sent off somewhere to the camp at Huntington – the ERAC.' She paused and said, 'Do you remember going there?'

'No,' I said.

'Do you remember a big fence? Lots and lots of prisoners, mostly black people,' she said.

'No,' I said.

'Do you remember the broken plane in the yard?' Leena asked.

I did and said, 'It had no wings, did it?'

'No,' she laughed.

And then I remembered the prisoners. Yes. There were some black people who thought they were white.

'Why did we go there?' I asked.

'I'm not sure, but they were going test a new drone on you...'

As she spoke voices began gnawing inside my head, drowning her words out.

'Thou shalt protect the chastity of Christian womanhood,'

intoned the Doctor inside me, 'All wealth belongs to the followers of the Lord.'

I bit down on my tongue. 'Silence, I command you to be quiet,' I hissed.

But the voice of the Doctor started shouting louder than ever. I reeled back and clutched my temples.

'Hang on, Marah, we have a plan, we're going to get you out of here,' Leena said. But at that moment, Aud turned the corner and came hurrying up. Leena went back to wiping the floor and her zombie state.

'His blessing upon you, dear child,' I said loudly.

'Blessed am I to be in the company of the Blessed,' Leena replied.

Aud came panting up. 'Are you two having a nice chat?' she said with a forced smile.

'Blessed be you,' said Leena and I, both at the same time.

I woke up the following day with my head clear. I lifted the sheet off my head. I was alone in the hospital room. The door was shut.

I had been dreaming of home. Somewhere behind the smell of disinfectant, spices lingered in the air.

Hold on, Marah, I thought, *they've fucked with your head. This is not you.* And Leena was here! I had an ally.

After a while, I went to the window to look out. Leena was in the garden. I tapped on the window. I'm sure she knew I could see her, but she didn't let on, except that she was holding her hands in an odd way. At first, I didn't know what that meant, but then it came to me in a flash – this was the Ginnz's secret salute.

THE HORROR

I was dreaming of someone I once knew. I could hear them calling my name, but when I opened my eyes, a strange girl stood in the doorway to my room.

'Get your arse out of bed. Hurry up!' she said.

The door to my room was wide open. Aud wasn't there.

'Come on!' said the girl.

'What's happened?' I asked.

'They have a big meeting today, they're all busy for a while,' she said, walking into my room. She pulled the sheets off me and pulled me up by the hand. 'Keep close to the wall and follow me.'

I wrenched my hand free from her and said, 'Who are you?'

The girl started hard at me. 'Have you forgotten already? They've really fucked you up, Marah, haven't they?'

'How do you know my name? Do you know who I am?'

The girl put her hands together in an odd way. I remembered I had seen her do this before. I felt a shiver run right through me, remembering our salute.

'Leena, right?' I said.

She smiled and nodded. 'That's my girl. Remember Tats?' she asked.

I was trying to work out who Tats was when Leena said, 'Your brother?'

A broken image of a stubbly-faced teenager with straight black hair flashed through my mind. I wanted to vomit.

'I don't, I don't know,' I said. I backed away. 'Leave me alone ...'

'Let me help you remember,' Leena said.

A man's voice suddenly started shouting inside my head. 'The God of peace will soon crush Satan under your feet. The grace of our coming Lord be with you!'

'No,' I whispered.

'Let me help you,' Leena said.

'Gravel shall fill their mouths. They shall be washed away in the Blood of the Lamb,' the man said.

'What is it?' Leena asked.

'In my head ....' I moaned. 'So loud ...'

'A voice?'

'Yes,' I said.

'Man or a woman?' Leena asked.

'The true light, which enlightens everyone, is coming into the world,' the voice thundered.

'Why?' I asked the voice and then said to Leena, 'A man, an angry man. He's shouting so loud ... I can't hear ...'

'American accent?' Leena asked.

'Yes.' I replied.

'You've heard him many times, and not always in your head,' Leena told me. 'Is it the Doctor?'

'The Doctor. Yes, that's what they call him,' I said. 'I remember. How could I forget? I've seen him many times. But how has he got inside my head?'

'You'd been rewritten again. They do it to you every night. They are giving you lots of meds. But we've got to hold on.'

'I only take vitamins,' I said.

'Not vitamins, psychotic drugs. Stop taking them.'

'Who's we?' I asked to change the subject.

'Later, later. For now, let's see how much of you is really here. Let's play the word game,' Leena said.

'OK,' I said.

'Dog,' Leena said.

'Chilli,' I said.

'Ah, Marah, you're a fighter! They've spent so much time trying to bury you, but here you still are. Come on now, let's find you and bring you back,' Leena said, pulling me to get out of bed. 'Come on – follow me.'

For a moment, I pulled away. I felt so cold inside, like somebody was rubbing ice inside my throat, inside my head, and inside my back. I heard sounds I didn't recognise, and then silence, and then noisy inhuman screams. I was so scared! So, so scared. But something, or someone, inside me trusted this girl, and it was whispering to me to trust her.

And then, suddenly, the Blessed Marah was gone, and I was back with Leena.

Leena led me along the corridor. Around the back, we found an old door I hadn't seen before, which opened onto a winding stairwell. I followed Leena up the stairs, but soon, we came to a dead end. Our path was bricked up. Leena pushed against the top left-hand corner, and one of the bricks moved. She pushed a few more bricks back until there was enough space for us to crawl through it. Once we were through the hole, Leena put the bricks back as they were, and we carried on. It was dark in there. The air was damp. I kept as closes to Leena as I could.

'How did you find this?' I asked.

'One of the girls told me,' She replied, 'And in case you're wondering what happened to her, she's dead.'

I was overcome with a sudden wave of tiredness. I leaned against the damp wall.

Leena stopped and looked back at me. 'Exhausted?' she asked.

I nodded. 'It keeps happening lately.'

'It always happens.'

Before I could ask what always happens, she started up the stairs again. We stopped when we reached the very top, where Leena opened a trap door and crawled out onto a walled roof. There was a tall chimney in the centre, with all manner of wild plants growing out of its mouth as well as from between its bricks. A wooden bench, broken here and there, ran around the chimney.

You could see for miles around. I had no idea where we were.

'No one comes up here, they don't even know about it.'

'Where are we?'

'Just outside Huntington,' Leena said, stepping towards the bench and sitting down. In the distance, there was a flash of light followed by a thud. 'That's the ERAC, the Evangelical Re-alignment Center, where the Bloods re-write people. There're thousands of them – African people, Asian people, gay people, trans people, dissidents – all being turned into good little Bloods. They implant them with a chip and send drones in at night with Wi-Fi to wipe out their memories and write new ones in.'

A chip. I remembered something about a chip. My hand went up to the back of my head. There was still a little lump of scar tissue there.

'Yes, they tried it with you too.'

It made sense … a kind of sense. I went to sit next to her on the bench.

'They've fucked with my head, haven't they?' I asked.

'Haven't they just!' Leena replied. 'You're a tough cookie, though, Marah, a real tough one. And they haven't cracked you yet.'

'Haven't they?' I asked. I felt so weak.

'If you'd crumbled like they wanted you to, you wouldn't be here with me, would you?' Leena said. 'You've been lucky. They have to use mind games and meds on you – they don't dare re-write you with a SIM. It's dangerous. And you're too valuable for them to let anything go wrong.

'Why?'

Leena didn't reply, she just smiled grimly at me. 'Don't you remember, Blessed Marah? Aren't they telling you what they want you for this time?'

'I'm from the House of David ...'

'Go on.'

I shrugged. 'That's all. Isn't that all?' I added, seeing from her face that there was more.

'Not by a long way. But let's see how much of you we can get back first. Tell me something about your brother or your mum or dad,' she said. 'Something that's nice, just one thing that you remember.'

'Why?'

'Because memory is what makes us. We are because we remember. They can wipe out so much of us, but they can't wipe out love. And Marah – you love so much. Tell me about your dad's parathas.'

'Oh!' Yes, I remembered his parathas! They were the best.'

And somehow, I could smell them right there and then on the roof. And with the smell, my memories came flooding back.

'Tell me!' demanded Leena. So, I did. I told her about the time Mum had banned butter in the house, and Dad pretended to make parathas using olive oil, but the moment Mum went out of the kitchen, he got a bar of butter out and made the most delicious one in the world, crispy and full of mashed spicy potatoes. And then Mum burst in and before she could let rip, he grabbed her, and they both started dancing. And me and Tats stuffed ourselves with the parathas in case Mum took them away from us.'

Once I'd started, the memories came tumbling out of me, slowly at first, then faster and faster. I told Leena about when the neighbour went on holiday. Dad agreed to look after their kitten but vomited each time it did a poo, and how Mum insisted he had to clean it up when

Tats decided to bath the kitten, and nearly drowned the poor thing and my Mum forced all three of them to go and live next door. And then I told Leena the first thing I was going to do when I saw my Dad was to ask him to make me one of his stuffed parathas, crispy and dripping in butter.

And then – something bad. I wasn't sure what it was at first. It was hungry and fearful and terrible – something I never wished to remember. But the memories were unstoppable. I had no choice.

'He's dead. Oh, Leena. My Dad. He's dead …'

'My sweet, sweet sister,' she said. And she took me in her arms, and I wept, and I wept, and I wept until my tears were dry inside me.

THE SLAUGHTERED

We sat quietly for a bit. I was so close to Leena that I could hear her heart beating. Amidst the sound of automatic gunfire, a drone buzzed like a fly trapped behind a curtain. It was slowly getting louder and louder. And then I saw it. It was huge and flew in the distance. 'You've been unwell, right?' Leena asked. 'What do you think that's about?' I tutted, trying to shake off the unease creeping up my spine.

'You might just be the one,' Leena said. But she had a cheeky smile as she said it.

I remembered the voices from my nightmares ringing in my ears: You are the One.

The drone came into view again. It reminded me of a great giant eagle floating in the sky, going higher and higher until it was no more than a dot.

'Are you a mind game?' I asked Leena.

She pinched me.

'That hurt!' I protested.

'Get real,' she laughed, then went all serious. 'Why do you think you're here, Marah?'

'I don't really know, Leena.' A false laugh dropped out of my mouth. My throat dried. 'They kidnapped me and brought me here.'

'Have you been feeling a bit sick lately?'

'A bit sick once or twice,' I replied.

'When? In the morning?' she asked.

I nodded.

'Hyperemesis gravidarum?' Leena placed her hand on top of mine and said softly, 'Morning sickness.'

'No! That's ridiculous. How would that happen?'

Leena laughed. 'You ask that? Of all people!'

I laughed. But inside, I felt terror.

'You are the one,' Leena said again.

'No.' I shook my head. 'Not me. That honour is reserved...'

'What honour?' said Leena quickly.

'... for someone... For someone...' I clutched my head.

'I don't know, I don't know what you're talking about!'

'Marah. You're pregnant, Marah. Get it in your head!' Leena insisted. 'You're three months pregnant. Look.' She rummaged in her pocket and pulled out a sheet of paper. She handed it to me. It had my name and a chart of a baby's growth on it. If it was true, I was carrying a boy.

'But...'

'You keep getting your memories back, so they must knock you out and start again. You're from the House of David, right? That's what they keep telling you. Why do you think they call you Blessed?' She tapped the paper. 'This is your baby. They think this child is going to be the Second Coming. Baby Jesus Mark 2. And you, Marah, are the Holy Virgin reborn.'

I stared at the paper. It made no sense... but at the same time, it made all the sense in the world. All that stuff about the Second Coming... calling me Blessed Marah.

'I thought it was just because I was from the House of David,' I said.

'Oh no. You're the real thing, sweetheart. Every other woman who got pregnant died.'

I went quiet, trying to digest what Leena was telling me. Then I asked, 'There are others like me?'

'There were, but they died,' Leena said.

'Why?' I asked.

'Well, here's where it gets really weird, I mean, more weird than weird,' Leena said, pressing my hand. 'As far as I can understand it, the new baby Jesus they want has got to be of royal blood, a descendant of the King of England. But this old bastard has a genetic mutation – a rare one that makes his sperm toxic. Any woman who gets pregnant by him dies because the baby produces a poison that kills the mother.'

I guess Leena read my face and knew I couldn't get my head round what she was saying. She slapped me on the shoulder and said, 'Let me put it another way, a more poetic way for you. It's quite a big genetic thing, this. We have the King with the killer mutant gene. The King with the poisoned sperm, if you like.'

'Killer gene?' I laughed at the utter absurdity of it all.

Leena bent forward, slapped her knees, and laughed, 'Killer fucking King with a mutant cock.' After a little while, she said, 'And they want the world to think you're the actual, real-life Mother of God.'

'Is that what they've been saying?' I asked.

'Yes and no, because you keep breaking out of the rewriting. They've done everything they can, but they can't turn you into one of their puppets. So, they've given up on you looking after the baby. They won't let you anywhere near it once it's born. You're just a womb, just a carrier for it. As soon as you give birth, they'll take the baby away, and they'll kill you, and they'll kill me too. I'm only alive because I'm your cousin, and I'm a good match in case they need any spare parts for you.'

'But Aud... Aud loves me. She'd never allow...'

'That woman is not your friend. You know that, Marah, don't you? In your heart, you know that every word I'm telling you is true.'

I stared into her eyes. What to believe? How can you ever know what is true and what's not? But there is one thing you can know – your heart. And my heart told me that Leena was my dearest friend. She was real. But what else was?

'If by any chance you are right, Leena, and you're not, then I must have been raped when unconscious,' I said.

Leena went quiet.

'Was I?'

'Do you remember seeing the King visit your room?' Leena asked somberly.

I thought for a while and said, 'I can't remember seeing him, but I am sure I heard him, or heard about him in my dreams.'

'Maybe they aren't dreams, Marah.'

I felt cold all over and trembled. A foul smell went up my nostrils, and I felt sick.

'The King has been here a few times, and when he does, security is so tight...'

'Did he rape you as well?' I asked.

Leena went quiet for a while and said softly, 'I think it was IV.'

Half an hour later, I was back in my room. I paced to and fro. I knew I should stay quiet, but when Aud came, I had to ask her.

'Am I pregnant?' I asked her as soon as she stepped in.

She smiled and replied, 'Blessed Marah...'

'Answer my question?'

'You are the one...'

'Please just answer my question,' I pleaded tearfully.

'You are the one...'

'Answer my question,' I shouted angrily.

'You are the blessed Mother Messiah...'

'Am I pregnant,' I asked.

I was desperate for an answer. To be told, No.

'Of course, Blessed.'

'Get out,' I yelled.

She stood stiffly and didn't.

'Please leave me alone,' I begged.

She unlocked a drawer in my bedside table, took some pills out of a bottle, held them out for me and said, 'You're upset. Here, take these. These will calm you down.'

I took them, put them in my mouth, but hid them under my tongue, and after Aud left me alone, I kicked the toilet door open and spat them out into the pan.

I kicked the walls, the door. I cursed God, and I cursed the sky. I cursed the thing inside me, I cursed the bastards who had put it there.

I wanted to tear it out of me right there and then by the roots.

Me, the Holy Virgin? That was a laugh. Mother of a god I didn't believe in. Leena didn't know if I'd been implanted by a living man or by IV, but it was rape either way as far as I was concerned. And not content with raping me physically, they were raping me mentally as well – stealing my memories from me, stealing my family, myself.

I opened the door and Leena was cleaning on the other side of the corridor. No one else was around. I ran to her and said, 'I'll never give birth to this monster, I'll kill myself first.'

She looked nervously around and tried to shush me.

'I'm going to break out of this place,' I said.

'It's not so easy. We're not ready yet,' she whispered.

'Who's we?' I asked.

'The resistance. You remember I was training with them in Birmingham?'

'What's the plan?'

'We can get you out, but we have to organise what happens once we get outside the compound. We're in enemy territory here.'

We sat quietly for a bit. A crow came through an open door to a courtyard in the middle of the corridor, landed not far from me and looked at me with one eye at a time. For some reason, it reminded me of someone I knew, and then I remembered the name.

'What happened to Shyla?' I asked watching the crow hop away.

'She is going strong, and the Ginnz are her life, but nowadays, they are more underground.'

I couldn't get my head round what the Ginnz being underground meant and asked, 'How can you get me out of here, though?'

'We have a plant inside.'

'Who?'

She paused. 'Before I tell you, it's not like you might think, Marah.'

'Who is it?'

'Ash, Marah. It's Ash. He's one of the Bloods guards. He's our guy on the inside.'

Suddenly I remembered. Ash! The bastard who put me here. She wanted me to trust him. Impossible. He had betrayed me three times already. Once when he dumped me, again when he joined the Bloods, and again when he lured me to the clinic. And this was the man who was going to help me escape?

Perhaps Leena was wrong. Surely, she had been rewritten as well. No one but a fool would trust Ash. There was only one certainty I felt. I was done with this place and was going to get out or die trying. I was not waiting for anyone. What had I to lose? Only my life. Now, that was worth nothing to me.

THE DELIVERANCE

The next morning, I went into the garden and looked carefully around. There was a tall birch tree near the wall. It would be easy for me to climb the tree and get over the wall, but how would I get down on the other side? Then, as though there really was a God, I saw the old gardener walking away from some shrubs near the outer wall. Gardener ... shed. I thought. Shed ... ladders. I had hardly noticed him before. I smiled at him as he got close to me, but he looked right through me as though I wasn't there.

Over the next few days, I kept on smiling at the old man until he finally flicked his bushy eyebrows up in response. I had already found the shed. It stood on the side of the main building, almost completely hidden by some bushes. I'd had a peep inside. No ladders, but there was a bundle of yellow nylon rope piled up by the door.

The gardener was a skinny old man who, in his green overalls, blended so well into the background he was invisible most of the time. Once, when I walked past him, he said nervously, 'I have six grand-children to feed. Whatever you want, I can't help you. Please do not smile at me, or talk to me, or come near me.'

I walked on by without saying anything to him. I was getting no help from him. The shed had a big new padlock on it, but the door itself was old with two rusty rings, one on the door and the other on the side of the frame, through which the padlock went. All I needed was a decent-sized hammer or a stone, and I could try to whack it off the door. It was dangerous, though. There were dogs, there were guards. I doubted if they'd kill the mother Messiah, but there were worse fates than death. I was the living one right then.

I needed to make sure I had as much time as possible before they discovered I was missing. That was going to be hard – I was constantly watched by Aud in the house and outside in the garden by Aud and the guards. But I had one trick up my sleeve to get Aud out of the way. In my room, I had a video link directly to her.

'Marah!' Aud said, surprised, 'Is everything OK?'

'Never better.'

'To what do I owe the pleasure of this call?'

'Could I please have my favourite dinner tonight?'

'Of course, dear, you can have anything you like,' she said.

'And I would like to eat a bit later than I usually do, around 8.30 pm today. Is that OK?'

'Of course it is, dear,' Aud said after a brief pause, 'But why do you want to eat later today?'

'I'm so tired. I was feeling nauseous, but I hope I'm feeling better by then.'

'Poor darling!'

That was Aud out of the way for a while. There was nothing she loved better than getting me those miserable chops. I took my Denim jacket from the back of a chair, got some tissues from the toilet and an old tee shirt, stuffed them into my pocket and calmly set off for a walk in the garden.

There was a slight drizzle, and though the wind had died down, it was cold. I buttoned up my jacket, put my hands in my pockets, and, with my heart pounding inside my chest, set out for the shed. I picked up one of the rocks I'd hidden nearby, waited until the guards had walked past, then I wrapped the T-shirt around the padlock to try to deaden the noise before I smashed at the lock as hard as I could with the rock – once, twice, three times, before the rusty rings broke free of the wood and I could get inside.

The dogs set off barking. I waited, silent and still in the drizzle, but the noise died down, and no one came. I crept inside, grabbed the rope, flung it over my shoulder and hurried across the wet grass to the tree. Under its branches, I paused for a moment to listen. Still nothing, only the rain, which was getting heavier.

I began to climb.

The higher up I went, the windier it became. I was drenched already. I slipped a few times and bruised my hands and face, and once I lost my footing so badly, had it not been for the rope getting hooked onto a branch, I would have crashed to the bottom. As I got close to the top of the wall, I could see razor wire. I hadn't thought of that. I took off my jacket and threw it across the wire – but then, alarms started ringing all around. They were on to me! Torchlights flashed on the ground. Dogs barked. I pulled some branches together and did my best to hide behind them, but of course, the dogs followed my scent. Moments later, they were at the bottom of the tree, looking up. Aud ran up to them.

'Marah, come down now!' she called.

I clung to the trunk of the tree. From further inside the complex, more lights appeared, getting closer and flying above the ground. A drone. In a few moments, it was hovering a few feet from my face, shining a bright light on me. Soldiers came running up below me with ladders.

'Fuck you!' I shouted down. I scrambled up as fast as I could to try to get over the razor wire, but it scared me – it looked so vicious in the bright light with the rain on it. My coat barely covered it. It could cut you to pieces.

'Stop her, she'll hurt herself, 'Aud screamed.

A ladder thudded by on the top of the wall, a soldier running up it. I kicked out at him, but he reached up and grabbed hold of my ankle. I kicked back as hard as I could in his face with my other foot – got him! He let go and slid halfway down the ladder. I caught a glimpse of his surprised face. But almost at once, another grabbed my leg, and one grabbed my hand. I tried to bite him, but someone yanked my head back. I shouted and spat and didn't care if I fell and died, but they quickly put me into a net and lowered me down.

'You could have hurt yourself, Marah,' Aud said when I touched the ground. 'What on earth do you think you were doing? You can't get out. There's a dike beyond the walls of the castle.'

The soldiers picked me up in the net. I hung there like a dead beast.

'You are the herald of the Second Coming. Praise the Lord for protecting you from yourself.'

Masked Templars stood to attention at regular intervals as they carried me back.

'You could have died,' one of them said.

'The Lord will allow no harm to come to Mother Messiah,' Aud said proudly. 'She will never leave us until after she has given birth.'

They took me back to my room, sedated me with an injection and locked the door.

THE SHACKLES

I wept and wept and begged to be allowed in the garden again, but it was made clear to me I would never leave my room again until I gave birth. In other words, never in this life. A guard was placed outside my door 24 hours a day. Closed-circuit TV was in my room, on my bed, in every corner. Only in the toilet could I be truly alone.

I had ruined any chance I ever had of escape.

My mind began to fall to pieces. I stopped sleeping. I had nightmares almost as soon as I closed my eyes. I was going mad, but they didn't seem to care. All they were bothered about was that I gave birth to a healthy baby.

So, then I thought, only in the toilet am I alone. So, in the toilet is the way out.

One night, in between my nightmares, I got up, went to the cupboard, snatched a wire coat hanger off the railing and went into the bathroom. I stood in front of the mirror and took off my top and my knickers. My breasts and stomach were huge – they looked obscene to me. I pointed to the woman in the mirror and laughed at her messed up hair, her swollen eyes, her ugly little nose and her thin lips.

'I want you to fuck off!' I told her.

Her hair covered her face. She brushed it back and laughed back at me, saying, 'Disappear, like?'

'Yeh, just vanish!' I cried.

'Just like that?'

'I'll tell you what,' I said.

'What?' she asked.

'I'll rip the bastard out,' I said, putting a hand in my crutch.

'You can't!' she laughed. 'You can't reach it like that.'

'See this,' I said, showing her the coat hanger. I untwisted the head of the coat hanger, straightened it, held it up for her and said, 'That'll reach it.'

'It might,' she said, 'a knitting needle would be better, just stuff it up and up till you hear it pop.'

'Does it pop?' I asked.

'Don't know,' she said, 'Never done it.'

'So how do you know?' I asked.

'Makes sense,' she said. 'There's something else.'

'What?'

'Don't be a sad bitch,' she said.

'Then do what?'

'Top yourself,' she said.

Then the bathroom door burst open, and Aud charged in with an orderly, who grabbed me by the wrists. Aud covered me with a towel. I didn't resist. I just laughed. They walked me to my bed. I sat down on it and laughed, and the other nurse pulled me up so I could get dressed, and then she helped me get under the sheets, where Aud cuffed my wrist and tied each one to a chain on the side of my bed.

'Mother Messiah will fucking bless you, you bitch,' I told her.

She ignored me.

'I'm hungry,' I said. 'Bring me Chicken Tikka Masala with rice pilau and fresh naans.'

A little while later, pasta and chicken arrived. It smelt delicious. A booming voice inside me told me it was my favourite food, but as soon as I put some in my mouth, I became enraged and threw the tray with everything on it towards the door, shouting, 'Unchain me, you bastards!'

'There is no need for this,' Aud told me. 'It's for your own safety.'

I pulled on the chains, first with one hand, then with the other, and then with both hands, all the while demanding to be released. I wrenched them as hard as I could until my wrists hurt, but they did not give. Throughout it, Aud quietly cleaned up.

Eventually, I gave up and slumped back in bed. Aud washed her hands and then poured some water into a glass. 'You must be thirsty with all this shouting. It is not good for you.'

'When are you going to take these off?' I asked, pulling on the chains.

'Drink some water,' Aud said.

'Tell me this, then. Whose bastard is inside me?'

'God alone decides...'

'Answer me!' I demanded.

Aud stood and looked down coldly at me and said, 'You will give birth, Marah, that is what is ordained.'

THE ESCAPE

As the days and nights passed, I slipped out of dreams and nightmares. I was dreaming of the moon when a loud thud and a flash somewhere beyond the outer walls chased the moon out of me. The ground shook, and the window rattled. I stepped over to look out. Everything was dark. I stood where I was, waiting for the lights to come back on, when my door crashed open.

'Leena!'

'Marah, be quick. We have to go while the generators are down.'

'Go?' I asked, then realised she meant escape.

'The Doctor's gone to the ERAC, the Huntington Loony camp. We must leave now,' Leena said.

I turned to embrace her. Suddenly, a voice bellowed in my head. 'Be sober, be vigilant. Your adversary, the devil, walks like a roaring lion, seeking whom he may devour,' the Doctor thundered.

'What is deception to the fraudster?' I asked aloud. It was the only way to push him away.

'Voices again?' Leena asked.

I didn't have time to answer Leena as Aud was already screaming inside my mind, *Turn away from evil; only a fool and a sinner is reckless and careless.*

'Marah?' Leena said.

I was desperate to find a question to ask the voice, but at the same time, I wasn't sure if Leena herself was real or just a deception.

'Who sings in the voice of fools?' I asked Aud's voice, pressing hard on my ears with my hands to stop the pain.

It worked. The voices didn't stop, but they died away to a dull mutter at the back of my head. I turned to Leena, 'Prove to me you are my friend, no more mind game shit.'

She glared at me and asked, 'Who do you trust then? The Doctor? The nurse? Or us?'

Leena unchained me.

'How did you get the key?' I asked.

'Just move!' she insisted.

Outside, there was a commotion. A scream, something falling

and smashing. Aud charged in, torch in hand. She rushed at me. I grabbed the pen off the table and stabbed her in the face with it. She screamed and fell. Her torch dropped close to her and shone on her bloodied face. I kicked her hard. 'Get out of my head,' I hissed. But someone came out of the darkness behind me and pulled me away.

'Marah,' he said.

I knew that voice. It was Ash. He had a large rucksack on his back and was dressed in the Templar's uniform.

'Bastard!'

'Don't get into a lover's strop now,' Leena shouted at me, and then she added quickly, 'Someone's out there.'

Ash was armed to the teeth. He clipped his gun and ran out. There was a burst of gunfire. Then he called back to us, 'Move. Move!'

I didn't need telling twice. It was death or moving. We raced along the corridors and came out into the garden, where we hid in the shadows. Guards with torches, shouting orders at each other, ran along the top of the walls. Dogs barked nearby and the air was filled with the buzzing of drones.

We set off again, following Ash towards a hedge close to the outer wall a few hundred yards away. He pulled at some branches until there was enough room for us to go through. Hidden by the hedge, we crept along, crouching low, keeping as close to the wall as we could. After another twenty or thirty metres, Ash stopped. Leaving the safety of the hedge, he ran to a large drain and heaved the cover off it. He flashed his torch a few times down into the darkness. A light flashed back. Then he lay flat, lowered his arm and pulled up a rope, which he began to haul up until a rope ladder came out with hooks on the end. Ash pushed these into the ground.

'I go first, then Marah, then Ash,' said Leena.

As she went down, Ash was taking explosives from his rucksack and placed them in the hedges close by. Between the branches and leaves of the hedge, I could see someone shining a powerful torch, moving closer to us.

The barking of the dogs got closer.

'Marah, you have to move quickly,' Ash whispered. He had a rope and tried to loop it over my shoulders, but I cringed at his touch and took the rope off. I'd spent so long hating him, now that he was here in front of me, I couldn't bear him near me.

'In case you slip,' said Ash. He tried to put the rope around me again, but I slapped him off.

'I can do it myself,' I hissed.

'Sorry,' he said, but he let me do it. I climbed onto the ladder and made my way down until I felt a pair of rough hands touch my feet – not Leena's. In a panic I kicked out until I heard a man's voice, 'Marah!'

'Oh my God!' I said. I jumped quickly down and turned to hug him. It was Tats.

'Tats ... Tats ...' I couldn't speak. 'They should have warned me! You sounded just like Dad.' I shone the torch up and down on my brother. He was taller than me and had a big rucksack on his back.

'My God. It's been so long since I saw you!' I said.

'They felt there was a better chance of you trusting us than just a bunch of anonymous fighters,' said Leena.

'Who's they?'

Above me, Ash was swinging down. He dropped the last metre or so and landed by me with a thud.

'ESLA,' he said.

'English Socialist Liberation Army. The resistance, Marah,' Leena said. 'We're all part of it.'

I nodded. It made a kind of sense. I was still suspicious ... even my thoughts weren't mine any more these days. But at least I was out of the Unit and away from that evil Doctor and Aud.

'I'm supposed to trust you all, even this bastard,' I said, poking Ash in the belly.

'Let's go,' he said.

We set off almost at once, Ash leading, Tats at the rear. In about fifty metres or so, Ash stopped and shone his torch into a recess in the wall. 'Wait in here,' he said.

He turned and hurried back the way we had come. We three crouched down and waited. The voices began to come back, whispering crazy poison in my brain. I put my hands to my head.

'Shut up!' I hissed. 'Leave me alone!' Leena and Tats came to hug me. Sitting there with the arms of my brother and my friend around me, just for a second, I felt almost safe.

Ash came running back in a few minutes and crushed us all inside that recess. A moment later, explosions went off above us. A cloud of dust came down along the passage towards us. Something small was running and zigzagging in front of it.

'A rat!' Leena said, shining her light on the terrified creature.

Stepping out of the recess, Ash pointed the light back in the direction from which we had come into the dust. 'That'll buy us some time. But not long.'

We set off again, half bent over, moving as fast as we could. Very soon, I had to lean against a wall and put my hands on my knees to catch my breath.

'Just a little further,' Tats said, putting his arm around me.

'So, what's the plan?' I gasped.

'We have transport,' Tats replied.

'It's not just you three, then?' I asked.

'No! ESLA wants you,' said Leena. 'You're the hottest thing with which to beat the Bloods and their bullshit,' she said.

'It's the baby, though, isn't it, Leena?' said Tats. 'They want the baby. Everyone wants the baby.'

All the time, Ash anxiously shone his torch down the passageway.

'We have to hurry,' he said.

We went on. After a long time of stumbling over fallen rocks, we came out of the tunnel on the other side of the hospital's wall. We were under trees, which was lucky. A drone buzzed above. Behind us, the hospital was aflame.

The barking of the dogs in the distance terrified me. There were lots of them, and they would rip us to bits if they caught our scent.

We followed a footpath uphill, fighting roots and branches, trampling on some, tugging on others. The ground was smoother now, but the way was steep, making it difficult for me to go fast. Tats had to pull me up the last bit of the incline until we reached open space, and I could stop for a breather again.

Below us, I could see the hospital among the trees. There was another explosion. Flames shot into the air.

'You guys did a good job down there,' Tats said.

'We've been planting explosives for over a week,' Ash replied.

'How much further?' I panted.

'Just over there,' said Ash, pointing towards the edge of the field we were in. 'With luck, we'll be long gone by the time they work out what happened.'

Tats put an arm around me and helped me across the uneven grass to the hedge. Behind it was a road with a motorbike parked next to a tree.

'Is that it?' I demanded.

'There's a car, stop worrying,' Tats said. Inside my head, the voices started up again. The Doctor commanded me … *Beware of false friends, beware of the workers of evil, beware of the concision.*

What do you mean by 'concision?' I thought back to the Doctor. He shouted back furiously inside my head, *As a dog returneth to his vomit, a fool returneth to his folly.*

Who created foolishness? I thought back.

I felt sick. I heard whispers telling me I was going to vomit. I bent forward and retched. Leena rushed to me, placed a hand on my forehead and held me.

Are you not just a sick game? I asked quietly. 'Answer me or just shut up,' I said, spitting on the ground.

The whispers went away.

'Marah, we have to hurry,' Tats protested.

'It's OK, Tats,' Just give her a minute,' Leena said. She crouched down by me. 'I know what she's going through. Been there myself. Hang on, Marah. The voices aren't real – they're programs, but for her, this is real,' she went on, putting my hand on the side of her face. 'And this is real,' she added, putting her hand to mine. My hand was cold, but she let her warmth soothe it.

I smiled weakly at her. I'd started shivering. All I had on was a dress. Tats bent to pull something out of his rucksack. Clothes. Jeans and a top, a jumper, a down jacket. A wig.

'Disguise,' he said.

'You really did think of everything, little brother,' I said.

'Hurry,' hissed Ash. 'Get into the new clothes.'

'Look away, you men,' Leena said.

They turned their backs on me.

I undressed and got into the new things. I couldn't help glancing at Ash, but he didn't look in my direction.

Once I had my gear on, Ash stuffed my old clothes in his rucksack and got on the bike.

'I have to go ahead to check it's all clear. I'll see you further down the road. He looked at me then paused a minute – hoping I would say something, perhaps. I felt words forming on my tongue, but before I could speak, he revved the bike.

'What's with my clothes,' I asked.

'To put the dogs off your trail,' Ash said and rode off.

'There is so much that doesn't make sense, Leena. I know you are my friend, and you are saving my life, and then when I think of him, I am all torn inside...'

'He risked his life for you,' she said.

'I know,' I replied meekly, not wanting to believe it, even when it was so obvious.

We walked a short way along the little road. A figure in a dark coat emerged from the hedgerow.

'Marah,' she said.

I knew the voice. I peered closely at her. Where had I seen her before...?

'It's Helen,' said Tats. 'Her and Uncle Melvin ... remember?'

She came to embrace me. I did remember her ... but not well.

'So practically everyone I knew is in the ESLA,' I said.

'Where's the car?' asked Tats.

'This way,' said Helen.

We followed her through some hedges and across a soggy field, which dipped down and then flattened out. In the dip, there was a burnt-out truck and a tank. The words ESLA were graffitied in white paint on the side of the tank.

I leaned against it and looked back towards the hospital. A helicopter hovered over the outer wall. Its powerful beam was shining on some trees about half a mile away.

A man's voice boomed out of the helicopter, 'You are surrounded. Stand up with your hands in the air.'

They were bullshitting. We laughed.

I rested a bit there before we went on towards some trees at the edge of the field. I had imagined them to be a wood, but it was only a line of tall poplars. Behind them, a car and a motorbike were parked. As we got closer, a man came out of the shadows, stared at me for a moment, and then nodded a greeting to Helen. He had an automatic rifle dangling around his back.

Helen got into the driver's side of the car and started it up, Tats in the front and Leena and I in the back. The new man got on the bike and moved forward in the darkness, Helen following close behind, keeping an eye on him as he showed the way. We had no lights on. The road was full of sharp turns and potholes, all of which Helen managed to catch. We had gone a mile or so when the motorbike stopped. The rider ran towards us and said to Helen, 'Message from Ash. Drones ahead! We have to wait here.'

As he spoke, I could hear a drone buzzing around overhead.

'OK, you lead it away from us, we're too exposed.'

He ran back to the motorbike.

'He is so young,' Leena said, referring to the biker.

'Youth dies in war,' I said.

'No sacrifice is too great for the revolution,' Helen said.

We waited silently for a while, with the drone buzzing somewhere above us. As Helen had suggested, it followed the motorbike away from us.

We sat in the darkness, waiting. My heart beat fearfully. I began to remember Helen – Uncle Melvin's new girlfriend on my 18th. It seemed so long ago! Then, she had seemed a lush drunk. Now, she was sharp and quick – a soldier all the time.

After about twenty minutes, the motorbiker came back. He pulled up by the car windows.

'I lost it, but there's a roadblock ahead,' he said. 'Americans, two miles down. Two on duty, at least one in the mounted jeep. There may be others.'

'Status?'

'High,' he said.

'OK,' Helen said. 'We'll go first, you follow. but stay out of sight. Be prepared to disable the jeep gunner when it's time.'

He nodded and left.

Helen stepped out of the car, went to the back and took blankets out of the boot. 'You two hide under these and don't move,' she ordered.

'What's the plan? 'I asked.

'For you to be quiet and for us to carry out our mission to get you to safety,' Helen said, 'Okay, Tats, you drive. Headlights on. We're just off to visit friends, OK?'

Tats got into the driver's side, and Helen took a gun out of the glove compartment. Leena and I got under the blanket, and we drove off.

Shortly, the car slowed and stopped. The window wound down.

'What a miserable night, doesn't know whether to rain or not,' Helen said to someone.

'Where are you coming from?' a man asked in an American accent.

Another voice reported our status over the radio. 'Black Mercedes. Reg. EL3 ELD. Two people. Driver male, Asian. Passenger female, Caucasian.'

'Elderfield house, about four miles down,' Helen answered. 'What happened at the castle?'

'Terrorist attack is all we know, ma'am, and some women fugitives,' he said. 'Do you have proof of address, ma'am?'

'Yes, of course,' Helen said.

The man had no time to reply – gunshots blasted from right next to us. Immediately, there were more gunshots from outside.

I threw the blanket off. Two soldiers were writhing on the ground, and another from the Jeep fell to the ground.

A drone buzzed above.

'Move!' Helen ordered.

We sped away.

The motorbike rider overtook us even as we sped along the deserted country road. The road snaked along for a while and then down towards a crossroad and under a railway tunnel.

'Stop under it and turn off the lights,' Helen said.

Tats drove us into the tunnel and pulled up. She called the motorbike rider over and ordered him to cast his bike on the ground and lie nearby as if he'd had an accident. 'They know this car,' she said. 'We wait here and hope to god someone comes along at this hour. We'll have to steal another one.' She cursed. 'That roadblock was bad luck. They reacted quicker than we thought.'

All we had to do now was wait. And wait and wait. Tats and Helen had started to discuss whether we should drive on in the car we had when headlights lit up a corner at the opposite end of the tunnel.

'See,' Tats said.

I made to get out of the car, but Helen stopped me.

'Sit down,' she told me. Leena pulled my hand. 'Let's make sure it's not Bloods.'

An old Ford stopped close to the motorbike rider who was lying on the ground. There was only one driver in the car, an old man. He came out, and a moment later, a small furry dog jumped out and ran towards us. As he stepped forward into his headlights, Helen got out of the car and pointed the gun at him.

'Don't hurt him,' I told her.

The rider on the ground got up, and Helen told the shocked old man, 'Hands up!'

The man raised his hands in the air.

'Keys!' she demanded.

Leena and I got out. I went to the dog, and I said, 'Don't be frightened, little one.' It looked puzzled for a moment and then wagged its tail. I lowered my hand and let it sniff it. When it finished, it ran back into the car.

'Keys,' Helen repeated.

'The engine's running,' I pointed out.

'Mobile,' Helen said, shaking the gun at the poor old man.

'It's in the car,' the man replied.

Leena opened the rear door of the car. The dog barked at her. I picked it up, put it in my lap and stroked it.

'Please don't hurt my dog,' the man said.

'The dog goes with us. If you report us before 1 pm tomorrow, I will shoot it,' Helen said.

'Take the car, I have food in the back, but please leave Tweety.'

'Do you understand what I just said?' Helen asked.

The man nodded.

We piled into the car. Tats put his rucksack in between Leena and me and got into the driver's seat.

'When did you learn to drive?' I asked.

'Everyone grows up in war,' Tats said.

Meanwhile, Helen was whispering something to the motorbike rider and gave him the keys to our old car. He transferred some bags from it to the Ford, started our old one, turned it around and went right on the fork in the road behind us.

'We'll wait for a moment until the drones lock onto him and then move,' Helen ordered Tats.

'What's he doing?' I asked.

'He is a decoy for the drone,' Helen said.

'But they might kill him,' I said.

She shrugged. 'I hope not ... but ... this is war, my dear.'

'Why is he risking his life? Just for me?' I demanded. 'And what about Ash?' I asked, suddenly scared for him. Helen was ruthless!

'He will be at the meeting place, as arranged,' Leena said.

We drove quietly out of the tunnel and drove along empty lanes in an apprehensive silence.

The dog began to fidget. It had its name and its owner's contact details on a small tag on its collar. The old man's name was Charles Hampton.

'Stop the car,' I said.

'Why?' Helen asked.

'Just stop,' I said, 'I want to let the dog go.'

'We don't have time for this,' said Helen.

'There's no need to be cruel,' I said. 'There's a house – I'll leave him near there.'

Helen rolled her eyes, but Tats stopped. As I put one foot out of the car, Helen said, 'Just let the dog go, and let's move.' I walked up to the gate of the cottage and left the dog behind it. Back in the car, Helen leaned over to speak to me. 'Let's get one thing straight. You're not the Holy Mother of God here. I'm the boss. You do as you're told, same as the others. Right?'

I didn't answer. I wasn't a member of her wretched militia. I hadn't come out of one bunch of bastards to be ordered around by another.

'You need us more than we need you,' she snapped and turned forward. 'Drive!' she ordered Tats, and he did as he was told. I glanced across at Leena; she looked down at my belly. I knew what she was saying. It wasn't me ESLA was interested in. It was the baby.

We drove on. Things felt a lot safer once we got on the main roads and joined other traffic. The hospital was soon long behind us, but a part of it was still with me – inside my head. I could hear the voices of the Doctor and Aud telling me how I would burn in hell for my sins. I fell silent and concentrated on wishing them away.

A thought struck me suddenly. I leaned forward and tapped Tats' shoulder.

'You haven't told me how Mum is,' I said.

My brother didn't answer.

'How's Mum, Tats?' I repeated.

Tats drove silently. I caught his eyes in the mirror.

'Ash came to our house that day after you left for the test centre, Marah – to warn you not to go,' Tats began at last. 'He was sorry he had brought the letter. He found out later that the Bloods were desperate and could not be trusted. He didn't want you to go. I went with him to look for you. Went to the test centre. Stopped the vans to question the drivers. There was nothing – they even denied you'd ever been there. When we couldn't find you, he cried.'

Leena put her hand on my shoulder as Tats talked. My brother kept stopping mid-sentence.

'He went off to London again after that, thinking they might have sent you there. Mum stayed up all night. After a few days, when we still couldn't find any news about you, Mum started mumbling to herself, just like Dad did,' Tats continued. 'She began calling your name at night and cooking food for you, even though you weren't there. Sometimes, she confused Shyla for you. So, one day, there was terrible fighting near our house, and the planes came in – bombs, air-to-ground missiles, everything. I don't know what it was about. I was terrified, but Mum laughed each time a bomb fell. It was so scary, the way she was. The bombs were going off everywhere, they were really flattening our area, and they got very close to us. We tried to get Mum to leave the house, but she kept calling your name and running to your room. We dragged her outside, into the back garden, but she got free and went back to the house, to your room. We ran in after her, but then our house took a direct hit. We got inside and up to the bathroom and kicked the door open, but inside, she was in flames. Burning. We tried everything, but it was too late.'

I should have cried but didn't.

'Guess what the last three words she said were?'

'I love you?' I guessed.

'Find your sister,' Tats said after a long pause.

THE WATER

Some of the bends in the road were so sharp we had to slow right down. At one point, we had to stop at a roadworks' red light. Just as we stopped, a doe jumped in front of our car and looked at us nervously.

Run, you adorable creature, I thought, get away from humans, but the deer stayed. I opened my window, leaned out and let out a loud, 'Shoo!' The doe stared but didn't run off. A moment later, a beautiful fawn came out to join its mother. The mother deer looked at us and then, with her baby, disappeared into the hedge on the other side of the road.

'Did you see the way she looked at us like she was saying, "Thank you for letting my baby pass through safely,' I said.

Leena snorted. 'If that's what pregnancy does to you, I'm gonna pass,' she said.

The lights changed, and we drove off.

We were heading to a rendezvous with Uncle Melvin and another ESLA unit at the Lake House, a property owned by Uncle Melvin, which we used to go to for weekends years ago when Tats and I were kids. It was a long cross-country drive. I fell asleep for a while, and when I woke up, the sun was out, and we were on the M4. This was not the England I knew any more: the motorway was full of cars, lorries, buses and vans going to and fro. There were no roadblocks, no burnt-out buildings, no smell of explosives in the air. Cows grazed carefree in one field, whilst in the next one, a tractor with the Bloods' flags fluttering in the air above it ploughed the land. Facing the motorway was a massive poster of a larger-than-life image of me and the words: *The Second Coming Is Nigh*.

Some vehicles had pictures of me on their sides as well. I looked all holy with dreamy eyes, and my hair was a lighter shade of brown. I had no freckles. I could have been white.

'Shall we give this baby a name?' asked Leena, stroking my tummy.

'Yeh, maybe, but something as un-Messiah-like as possible,' I said.

'Brian!' Leena suggested. 'Or Bob. Bob the Messiah!'

We all cracked up laughing – me, Leena and Tats. Only Helen didn't laugh. Maybe she didn't have a sense of humour. Maybe she was a Christian, who knew?

It was a little after that we hit congestion.

'Not good,' Helen said. 'Looks like a roadblock ahead.'

'And look over there,' said Tats, nodding to our left. Some tanks, followed by soldiers on foot, were cutting across farmland towards the motorway.

'One of the American battalions,' Helen said, nodding towards the tanks, 'They'll go with whoever pays.' She looked over at me. 'It's you they're looking for.'

I looked at myself in the mirror. The girl looking back was an absurd, red-haired me.

'I look stupid,' I said, brushing the wig with both my hands.

'Be grateful, you got it,' Leena said. 'Is there another way round?' She asked Helen.

'We could turn off at the next junction and go along the 'A' roads,' Tats replied. But Helen shook her head.

'We can try, but I suspect whichever way we go there will be roadblocks,' she said.

We turned off on a slip road at the next junction, but Helen was right. There was a roadblock on the exit at the top, by the roundabout. There were cars behind us. We could only go forward.

'Four soldiers, maybe more out of sight,' said Tats. 'An armoured carrier. There'll be more in that.'

The carrier was one of those with multiple rocket launchers at the top and a long automatic barrel in the front. A camouflaged motorbike was parked near it, both partially hidden just to the side of the roadblock.

'They'll know it's a stolen car,' I said.

'Just stay calm,' Helen said.

One by one, the cars ahead of us were checked and left. Finally, it was our turn. Tats wound down his window, and the militiaman looked in. You could see what he was thinking – three Asians and a white woman. Not what the Blood's militia liked to see.

'What Blood is in you?' he asked.

For a moment, I was confused until Tats replied – 'I have one drop of white blood in me, and that is the drop I worship.' Leena repeated it, then me, trying to keep my voice steady. It was the standard response to a Bloods if you weren't white.

The militiaman was looking suspiciously at us. I saw his eyes flick down to my belly. I pulled my coat across it, but it was too big to hide. He stepped back from the car and spoke into a mic attached to his collar.

'Have your weapons ready,' said Helen calmly.

Around me, there was a series of clicks. Leena, Tats and Helen were all armed.

'Hey, what about me?' I asked.

'You're the Holy fucking Mother Messiah,' said Leena. 'You don't get to shoot no one.'

'I've fired a gun,' I protested.

'More to the point, you haven't been trained,' said Helen.

I thought to myself, that's something I would soon fix.

'Shoot to kill,' said Helen gently. 'I'll take the one who spoke to us. Tats, you go for the one by the barrier, then drive. Leena, you take out the girl. Then you and I go for the one remaining.'

'Shouldn't we wait until we see if they know who we are?' I asked.

'Not taking any chances,' said Helen. She leaned out of the window. 'Hey, soldier – one moment,' she called.

The militiaman turned towards us and was in the process of raising his hand to hold her off when she pulled out her gun and fired a rapid burst right into his face. Blood sprayed the car and her. At almost the exact same moment, both Tats and Leena fired. All three went down. I was horrified, I'd not seen any killing like that before. Tats shot off at speed as Leena and Helen opened fire on the remaining soldier, but Tats' rapid start lost them the target. We drove off, engine howling, up the road.

'Allah save us,' I said. Inside me, the baby moved.

'Are we out of it?' I asked.

'Look behind you,' Tats said

I looked in the side mirror. The armoured carrier was after us, and ahead of that a motorbike with two riders was racing towards us, gaining fast.

Helen and Leena leaned out of the back window, aimed their gun at the rider and opened fire. The soldier on the back of the motorbike fired at us, but the bullets hit the ground behind us. The armoured carrier was now close to the motorbike. Helen ran out of bullets, but Leena continued to fire. The motorbike exploded.

Tats pressed down on the gas, and we speeded up. The carrier was a beast, a big heavy thing. It couldn't keep up with us.

There was a plantation of pine trees just a little further down the road. Tats found a dirt track hidden by trees.

We drove on into a future none of us could predict.

THE BOAT

We drove another hour or so without problems until I thought I recognised the farmhouse in the distance.

'Are we close to the Lake House, Tats?' I asked.

'About three miles,' he replied.

After a while, he turned left onto a small tarmacked farm road that ran along the perimeter of the fence. I felt my spirits lift as I recognised where we were. I had happy memories from here, from long ago. But it was tinged with sadness. We hadn't been to visit Uncle Melvin for years. And, of course, when we had, Mum and Dad had both been alive.

'There it is,' Tats said suddenly, pointing to the lake as it emerged between the trees.

We drove for a little while and Tats shouted joyously as he pointed ahead, like a child who is surprised that his prediction has come true. 'There! There's the gate, and there's the road.'

There was indeed the gate to Melvin's land. It had a thick metal grid, one of those used to stop cattle from leaving the field. I recognised it – how, I don't know, as it was just a common road grid. But I did.

Tats parked under a line of birch trees. 'Thank god, I need a number one,' Leena said, getting out of the car.

Leena, Tats and me went behind different bushes. As I crouched down, a soft wind blew across my face and felt so good. The air was so fresh I could almost taste its scent. Overhead, a flock of seagulls flew in a clear blue sky, and a pack of parakeets landed in the same trees. Crows pecked on the ground, and sparrows hopped from branch to branch. Inside my head, the Doctor's voice said, 'The eye that mocks a father and scorns to obey a mother will be picked out by the ravens of the valley and eaten by the vultures.'

'Why? Why? Why?' I said, over and over again, until he fell silent. I was learning – he hated being questioned. But as I came out, there was the sound of a motorbike coming.

'They've found us,' Leena said.

The sound came from round the turn of the road. We all ran to hide. Before us, a pair of partridges shot into the air. It was coming right towards us.

'Don't miss,' Helen said.

Guns aimed.

But the bike stopped before coming any further and misfired again. It was right by the car. For a moment, it seemed like the grass, the trees and the wind all held their breath.

Then ... 'Are you here? It's me!' Ash shouted.

A moment later, he walked round the corner. Tats ran towards him. They high-fived and hugged.

'He made it,' Leena smiled.

'We were doing just fine,' I grumbled.

'Grow up, girl,' Leena scolded. I couldn't help it. I'd spent so long blaming him. But deep inside, I was happy he was alive, and despite my best efforts, I smiled at him when he looked at me.

Once the hellos were over, we set off on foot for the house.

'When you're safely there, I'll come back and get the car and drive it away,' Ash said. 'I can be a decoy.'

'They'll kill you when they catch you,' Tats said.

'Maybe,' Ash replied matter-of-factly.

'Oh, stop being such a hero,' I said. But I felt ashamed for saying it.

The Boathouse was at the bottom of a vast burnt-out mansion that sat along the banks of the Mallards Pike Lake. With a Hawthorn on one side and an old oak on the other, it was built across a tributary of the lake, and like the mansion, it too was gutted. A tattered Gaelic flag drooped off a pole above the main outbuilding of the boathouse. Four teenagers skimmed stones on the surface of the lake. They looked at us for a moment and continued with their game. A few men fished further down.

Ash nodded to the flag above the Boathouse and said, 'After they banned Catholic churches, this is where the Catholic militia made their last stand. The lake ran red when the Boathouse fell.'

'The Templars fought here, right?' I asked. 'You were probably one of the ones who filled it with blood.'

'That's not fair, Marah. You know I was working on the inside. And anyway, I had no choice but to join. I'll tell you when we have time. Right now, we need to find our boat and get you across this lake.'

Ash and Tats ran off behind a building. A few moments later, Tats came back and said, 'It's here.'

We followed Tats to where Ash was waiting, close to a great big, expensive-looking speedboat.

'Wow, that's more like it,' Leena said.

'No,' Tats said, stepping past the big boat. He pointed to one which was hidden behind the big one and said, 'That's it!'

It looked like a long rusty bathtub with two benches across it, an engine at the back, and a pair of oars.

'I thought you were going to take us to a safe house,' Leena told Ash. 'How the hell are you going to do that in this piece of junk?'

But I had seen this junk once or twice before. It was Uncle Melvin's. 'Is Uncle Melvin here?' I asked.

'Can't see him,' Tats replied.

There was a note waiting for us in the boat, on a piece of paper wrapped up in some kitchen foil, which had been pinned to the side. It was in Uncle Melvin's writing:

Sorry for not meeting you here. See you by that place you love, and I know how much you love this boat. Don't wreck it. Haha.

'Oh, Melvin, you are such a stupid jester,' Helen said.

Getting into the boat, my eyes met Ash's for a moment, but I stopped myself from returning his smile.

Apart from the trees on the sides of the lake being decorated by the art of war, nothing much else happened. No drones above. No soldiers lobbing bombs at us.

Ash and Tats were together in the front of the boat, Helen sat on her own behind them, and I sat behind her and watched the ripples in the water, trying to hold back the ghosts pushing up on waves of memories of Mum, and I thought ...

Oh Mother
embroider for this lake,
a necklace of your tears
Come give my lonely breath
An embrace of your sigh.

I thought I saw a smiling image of my Mum in the water, looking up at me. I remembered how Mum really loved Ash, but this thought was attacked by a heavy screeching sound inside my head, like someone scratching their fingernails on a blackboard.

And then I became angry at the thought that my Mum never

said a bad word about Ash, even when he brought the letter for me to go for the test.

I fought back against my own voices, which kept on telling me, 'Look what Ash did to you, not what he did for you. It doesn't matter any more. I don't love him. How could I after he joined the Templars?'

I leaned over and put my hand into the cold waters of the lake and let discarded brown leaves crash against it. The boat rocked a little, and when I turned around, Ash was opposite me. I pulled my legs together and covered my stomach the best I could with my jumper. I felt exposed and ashamed.

'Tats has got the steering,' Ash said, looking at a puddle of water at my feet.

I held my lips tightly shut to stop the words battering me inside from coming out. This should have been our child, not this bastard, I thought, looking at an uprooted tree that had collapsed into the edge of the lake. The baby kicked hard. I remembered Mum once saying to me, 'A baby fills the world with love, it can give no more.'

I stroked my stomach, and the baby stopped kicking.

In front of me, Ash sat silently for a while. He turned round to look at me briefly, and I couldn't help but smile at him. And then I hated myself for smiling at him.

Feelings are ridiculous, right? Sometimes, I almost wish I didn't have them. They're just so stupid!

THE SANCTUARY

44

Uncle Melvin was waiting for us at the other end of the lake, exactly where he said he would be, leaning against the tree I loved where I used to play hide and seek. Helen hugged him. He handed her a mobile phone. She moved away from us and started talking on it.

A car with darkened windows pulled up. Helen put her phone upside down in the palm of her hand and said,' See you soon,' then got into the car and sped away.

I looked at Melvin. 'What is she?'

He shrugged. 'She's very high up in ESLA. She shouldn't have been on the mission to rescue you, she's far too important. But also far too headstrong,' he added ruefully.

I laughed. Uncle Melvin had met his match. 'I don't know about headstrong, pretty cold-hearted though,' I said.

'She has to be,' Uncle Melvin said. 'This is war, Marah.'

But you don't have to be cruel to your own side, I thought. I snatched the wig off my head and threw it on the ground. What a relief!

'It suits you,' Uncle Melvin said.

I was about to kick it into the lake when Tats tutted, 'No, you're making a track. Keep it.' He picked the wig up and put it in his rucksack

'Hey, Tats – can you drive that?' I asked. *That* was Uncle Melvin's big black 4x4 BMW, parked a little further back from the lake.

'Just watch me,' Tats replied.

Ash sat next to Tats in the front, and Uncle Melvin between me and Leena in the back. He smiled at me, raised his eyes to the sky, and talked to my Dad, 'I got the kids safe, now, Pete, matey.' His voice filled with sorrow, and he said, 'No one can hurt them now.' He turned to me and said, 'You're famous, girl.'

'Thanks, Uncle Melvin,' I said and placed my head on his shoulder. He stroked my hair, and I fell quickly asleep.

When I woke up, we'd stopped by the side of the road. Two militiamen had their guns pointed at Ash, who was still in his Bloods' uniform.

'It's OK, he's with us,' Uncle Melvin said. Turning to me, he said, 'ESLA.'

Uncle Melvin lowered his window and handed them his ID. They looked young, even younger than Tats. They had the ESLA insignia of hammer and sickle on their shoulders.

Uncle Melvin lowered his window, 'You know, lads, I can't get used to this badge of yours.' They didn't answer, but their eyes betrayed a smile. 'I mean, who the bloody hell cuts wheat with sickles nowadays, and when did you last see a blacksmith using a hammer?'

'No, comrade Melvin!' one of the soldiers replied, 'Glad you're back and quicker than expected.'

'Comrade Melvin?' I asked.

He grinned.

With a soldier walking on either side of our car, we began to move forward slowly. Uncle Melvin pointed to a small step on the side of the car and said to the soldier near him, 'Why don't you and your mate stand on either side so we can get a move on?'

The soldiers looked across at each other and nodded. They jumped on the car and off we went again. In a few hundred metres we reached a stretch of dual carriageway running parallel to the M1. The militiamen got off. The motorway was deserted, and we sped along. I sat up in alarm and asked, 'Why are we going south?'

'We're going to Watford.'

'But we're miles off course ...' I said.

'Whilst you slept, we took lots of detours,' Uncle Melvin said.

'We should have come along the M25 if anything,' I said.

'That's what they would have expected,' Uncle Melvin replied. 'Who would have thought you would go south, eh?'

We slowed down as we approached a small roundabout. A bullet-riddled sign indicated that the next M1 junction was Junction 5. We turned onto a slip road, away from the motorway, and followed signs to North Watford. An ESLA-flagged convoy was slowly moving towards St Albans. Large photographs of Marx, Engels, Lenin, and Luxembourg hung from the sides of the road. I remembered these; Mum had them up on her wall in her study before she swapped them for poets. A great big piece of cloth, with the words, Religion doesn't have property, property has religion hung across the road. We raced towards the train station and then turned onto lush tree-lined roads, past double-fronted houses untouched by war. Finally, we stopped at a roadblock – the first I'd seen since we set off. Uncle Melvin stepped out of the car and talked to the soldiers. A soldier went inside his sentry box and telephoned. He came out, nodded at Uncle Melvin and as he walked back to us, the barrier was raised.

'How far, Uncle Melvin?' I asked.

'Not far. We're nearly safe, no one will touch you here.'

After going through a few more security checks, we turned up a cul-de-sac and I saw the road markings of Tunnel Wood Road. The top of the road had another security checkpoint with a large barrier. We were there. My safe house.

THE CAPTIVITY

A housing complex became my new prison. I was free to leave if I wanted, but where could I go in my condition? Three months before D-Day – Drop-Day, Leena was calling it – and me with all those admirers after me.

I was given a room in a bungalow, with a lovely view of a small apple tree on a terrace in the centre of a flat section of a sloping garden. It could have passed for a framed painting with robins, magpies, doves, and little sparrows pecking on the ground. My room was in the middle of a series of interconnected bungalows. Beyond them, the garden slowly climbed and then dropped down into some woods.

Over the next few days, as I explored the house and the woods, it was obvious that this was not an ordinary housing complex but the central command base of not just the ESLA but a number of other militias – the Free Northern Army, the Anarchists and even the Great Briton United Front as well, all with their own offices and insignia. The area to the left of a large, three-story house was restricted, as was access to a room marked *Library*.

For the first few days, I mostly ate and slept. I kept dreaming I was in a dream, Aud standing guard over me, burning arrows in hand, and if I woke up, a holograph of her taunted me, but it vanished when I put my foot on the cold tiled floor.

On my first morning in Watford, my brother stood by the side of my bed, looking down at me with his lovely brown eyes. He'd brushed his thick black hair off his forehead. A small, fresh scar above his left eyebrow snaked down his stubbly face. He smiled, and I noticed that his incisor tooth was chipped. Before I could ask him how this had happened, he held my hand, squeezed it, and said, 'I am so proud of you, and I love you. I will never let anyone take you from me again.'

Where is that little brother of mine? I thought, looking at a great big tear forming in his eye. I sat up, wiped his eyes with my hand, and he said, 'I'm not crying 'cos I'm sad, I'm crying because I'm happy with what you did.'

'I didn't do anything, Tats,' I said, brushing his hair with my fingers. 'I just got by and held onto every memory I could, just to be me.'

He blinked his big, beautiful baby eyes and told me of the day I had raised the Ginnz salute on camera, with the Doctor near me and how it went viral. Artists had painted silhouettes of me giving the salute everywhere. They were all over the country, even in London.

'I thought it was just a part of their mind games, an implanted nightmare,' I said.

He smiled, sat on the side of my bed, and told me that apart from Hertfordshire, the Bloods now controlled all of Southern England and were edging towards a victory in the North. That they were really angry with Manchester and Liverpool for their intended merger with Scotland, and to make matters more surreal, Yorkshire independence, but no one took any notice of this. The Bloods fought everyone but the Believers and even treated their injured. The Believers had now gone underground, and they had all but wiped out everyone who wasn't, in one way or another, working with them. Most of my old comrades in Ginnz had been captured by the Believers. Some were forced to marry one militiaman after another as they got killed.

Mum was buried in the same grave as Dad.

'And you know, Marah, you should give Ash a bit of slack,' Tats said after a long, thoughtful silence.

'Don't get involved in things you don't understand,' I said.

'Will you talk to him just once? For me?' Tats asked.

'No!'

'Please?'

He went on and on at me until, at last, I said yes, just to be rid of him.

'He's my comrade now. You don't know how brave he's been,' he told me.

Ash had still broken my heart, and I wasn't ready to give him another chance with it. As Tats was leaving, he reached into his rucksack and took out a beautiful notebook bound in silk and decorated with sequins.

'A present,' he said.

'Thank you for this. It's lovely.' I opened it and looked hungrily at the creamy, soft pages.

I wanted to write, but I wasn't able to. I seemed to be sleeping all the time, and my mind was like a swamp – thoughts just rose and fell and rose again like logs. Helen, who had been a midwife before all this began, told me that it was the pregnancy that did all this – another reason to hate the baby inside me.

'It's all about you, isn't it?' I said to my lump, sitting in a comfy armchair by my window. '… just as if you really were Jesus.'

If it wasn't for the baby, I would never have been kept in the hospital, and ESLA would never have rescued me. But I – Marah Sultana – I hardly counted at all.

'Wars aren't just about front lines. You can control the land, the sea and the air, but if you don't win the battle of ideas to make yours dominant, you can always be defeated,' Helen said.

This was the first time she'd come to see me since I arrived.

We sat outside on the small, paved terrace, having a BBQ, it was a special treat for me. Tats and I had made the spice mix ourselves after Dad's recipe, but I got terrible indigestion just thinking about eating, even though my taste buds were on fire.

'You talk like Mum,' Tats told her, picking with his teeth at a hot kebab.

'Mum used to quote a Chinese writer, something about taking something the enemy wants,' I said, turning a lamb chop over.

'It was Sun Tzu,' Helen said, '"Begin by seizing something which your opponent holds dear; then he will be amenable to your will."'

'Aunty had a quote for every occasion,' Leena said.

'I didn't know she was interested in a military strategist of ancient times,' said Helen.

Inside my head, Aud's faint voice whispered, 'You are Mother Messiah.' I had managed to hold back most of the voices for a while now. An image of Aud sitting in her office flashed in front of my eyes.

'How can you be so certain?' I said aloud.

The image of her faded, her voice disappeared.

"Sorry dear, what do you mean?" Helen asked.

'I was talking to Aud,' I told her.

'They have planted so many voices inside her and some in me,' Leena told Helen. 'These are triggered by words or thoughts. She's talking to them.'

'And sometimes if I ask them a question, they go away,' I said.

'I understand,' Helen said.

'No, you don't,' I said. 'So, tell me, Helen, have you seized me so Bloods are nice to you?'

'We have not seized you, no, we have helped you,' Helen said. 'If you want to know the truth, now listen. First, of course, I am interested in you personally, I have a personal history with you. That goes without saying. I met your parents more than once, not just in your house. I met your mother after your birthday party, and we spent a lot of time talking about this shit world of ours, and about you and your brother, and what the future might hold for you. Although we never really imagined that the world would change so quickly, that I would be doing what I am, or she would be where she is, or you would be where you are,' Helen paused. She took a tissue out of her pocket, blew her nose and continued after a long, thoughtful pause, 'And what doesn't war make us do? It makes monsters out of some, doesn't it?'

'It does,' I said, 'and the monstrosity crushes others under its might.'

Helen sighed and said, 'Do you write this stuff down?'

'She comes out with these all the time,' Leena said.

'But of course, there is politics,' Helen went on. 'We are fighting a war with guns, and the truth is we are outgunned and only just holding out. The Bloods don't know how close our lines are to breaking point. But, like I said, not all battles are won with guns. Birmingham will fall, and Manchester has all but fallen, and if that happens...'

'So, you want the Mother Messiah to show the world what bullshit their whole claims are?' I interrupted.

'Well, in a nutshell, I suppose that's it,' Helen laughed. 'But you could have put it more poetically.'

'She's full of shit, most of the time,' Leena butted in.

'So, and you want me to get up and say, here I am folks, Mother Messiah, and this bastard I am carrying belongs not to God, but some king with the killer cock,' I said bitterly.

Leena put her hand around me and pulled me close to her. 'You are the hottest investment since circumcised naans hit the market, girl. The ultimate destroyer of all this bullshit.'

'You don't have to do anything you don't want, my dear,' Helen added.

'Who said I didn't want to say anything?' I asked.

'That's my sis,' Tats said.

'Then let's expose this evil,' Helen said.

'What do I have to do?' I asked.

'Use your voice,' said Helen. 'Talk. Explain. Write poetry – the poetry of freedom.'

Leena placed one of my hands over the other, adjusted my fingers in the Ginnz salute and held it in front of me.

THE MESSAGE

On my fifteenth day in Watford, Helen and Leena turned up together. Leena was dressed in uniform. Helen patted her on the shoulder.

'For commitment to the cause, comrade Leena has been promoted to the rank of Captain.'

Leena smiled proudly and asked, 'And how are we feeling today?' She looked like a stranger in her crisp new fatigues and with her hair tucked through her cap.

'We are super-duper,' I replied sarcastically.

'Are you good for an interview today?' Helen asked.

At once, the image of the Doctor flashed in front of my eyes, and I heard his piercing voice inside my head: *Put on the full armour of God so that you can take your stand against the devil's schemes.*

'Whose incarnation are you, Doctor?' I fought back.

'We have to expose the Bloods' bullshit to the world,' Leena said. The Doctor vanished.

'We thought it best if Leena interviews you, Marah,' Helen said. 'More like a chat between the two of you.'

I nodded. It wasn't going to be easy with the Doctor and Aud shouting in my inner ear, but I was determined to do it. If nothing else, it would show the voices that I was my own person despite everything they had done to me.

'I'll just go over my notes while the crew set the camera up,' Leena said. She went to the door and opened it. A man with a camera stepped in. 'Excuse me a moment,' Leena added and stepped outside.

Why so formal, Leena? I thought, are we in different hells now?

Helen sat on a chair next to me. 'We thought it would be better if we did it in your own surroundings ...make you feel more comfortable,' she said. I was at a loss why she thought having this lot all over my room would make me feel better, but I kept quiet anyway. 'Don't worry if the voices interrupt and you make a mistake, we will edit them out later,' Helen added.

'If I question them, they go away – they're getting weaker,' I told her. 'I must stop answering them out loud, but it works better like that.

Maybe we should actually put the voices in ... show what it's like ... what do you think?'

'Maybe. But we want to keep things plain – just you telling your story,' she sighed.

'Some people who believe this bullshit will carry on believing it even if God Almighty comes down in person and tells them it's all lies,' I said.

We sat and chatted for a while until the crew was ready and Leena came back.

'Let's get this show on the road,' she said.

'You know Marah, it's hard for everyone. This is a chance to expose the Bloods for the lying, deceiving fascists they are,' Helen said.

Her words dropped out of her mouth like spent bullets.

'We will,' I said, 'And perhaps we can do this like we did when we were the Ginnz, like women, like sisters.'

Leena raised her eyebrows.

Maybe my old Leena is in there somewhere, I thought.

'The most important thing to emphasise is that the birth is not some miraculous conception, but an act of violation of a woman.' Helen stood up and emphasised her words with the shake of an index finger, 'I know exactly how you feel, Marah!'

I felt a sudden wave of anger inside me. 'I didn't know you'd been raped too,' I said coldly.

She turned to Leena and said, 'There is no need to rush the interview, take as much time as you need.'

'Yes, Comrade,' Leena said.

I took a deep breath and sighed out the rage.

The interview was set up with me and Leena sitting close together on two chairs, our knees almost touching. I suppose they were trying to make it cosy, but I didn't feel at all close to this new Leena and her business-like demeanour. Helen stood quietly in a corner of the room.

After we were miked up, Leena asked me, 'Please tell us, who are you?'

I felt so strange having to talk to Leena like this and hesitated. 'How can I tell you of all people who I am?' I said. 'Why can't you just say: my name is Leena, and I am with my cousin Marah Sultana, and we were both kidnapped by the Bloods, and everything you have heard about my cousin is a lie.'

Helen stepped out of the shadows and said, 'She's right, Comrade Leena. Just relax, both of you. Pretend you are talking to your cousin, just the two of you. And Comrade – in between Marah's narrative, you can interject with your own story of what happened as well.'

Leena nodded. We tried again, and this time, she introduced me as I suggested – without consulting her notes.

It took me a while before I started talking, and then I couldn't stop. Together, we went over the whole thing, her story and mine – how I had an unwanted bastard who had been forced on me; this was not the son of God. I talked about my nightmares. We both talked about the voices in our heads, and Leena explained how they had tried to rewrite us with implanted memories.

We relived our lives in front of a camera – but although I shed many tears, and raged and laughed and wept, I felt that Leena and I were in different stories. Everything she said about what happened at the hospital was true, but her words were just sounds, not screams like mine. All the time she was following some party line – not like my cousin, my sister, that I used to know.

The interview took two exhausting days to complete, and then Leena stopped coming to see me. She had been ordered to serve elsewhere, I was told. I didn't see her again for a long time. I bumped into Helen in the garden a few times and asked her when my interview was going to be broadcast, and she replied, 'As soon as the Central Committee approves.'

THE TESTAMENT

I'd agreed to meet Ash because of Tats, not because I wanted to. Sometimes, the thought of lost love made me sad, but mostly, I was still angry with him. Several times, Tats had tried to explain why he had joined the Bloods, but I stopped him. If I was going to hear it, I had to hear it from Ash's own mouth.

I met him next to the chimney of the tunnel. I got there early to give myself time to compose myself. He came soon enough; I could hear him getting closer to me with every step, but I didn't turn around to look at him. The closer he came, the tighter my stomach knotted. He stopped a few feet away from me. I could hear him breathing.

'I never stopped loving you,' Ash said after a while.

'If that's what you came to say, you've said it. Now leave.'

I looked up at him for the first time. He wore a new green ESLA uniform, complete with hammer and sickle.

He glanced at me, but I looked away. Having him near me began to make my stomach churn. He had rescued me, yes. But he had betrayed me, too. Surely, he could have found a way to reply to my messages when I sent him the photo of me in the red dress.

'You broke my heart. Even if I did find it, why would I give it to you?'

He plucked a blade of grass which was sticking out of the wire railings that surrounded the tunnel chimney, twisted it in his trembling hand, and said, 'I was never at peace.'

You were never at peace? I thought. What a selfish pig you are.

'Is this about you? You joined the Bloods. You deserted me. You dropped off the message to get me to be a fucking holy cow for the Bloods with this inside me,' I said, slapping my stomach. I got a painful kick back. I held my breath so Ash wouldn't notice.

'I had no choice,' he said, raising his head for the first time. 'They arrested my mum and dad and refused to give him his insulin unless I turned up for my conscription. You know he's diabetic. He was dying in jail.'

I said the cruelest thing I could, 'He's dead now, anyway, isn't he?' – and hated myself as soon as it was out of the mouth.

'Yes, that old white trash died,' Ash said bitterly, 'Is this what you want to hear? And his white trash of a wife is dead now as well. Are you happy? But they didn't die because I didn't turn up, it was not because of me.'

A London-bound train went by. The ground vibrated. The chimney screamed. A bird shot out of the trees.

'So, because of that, it makes it OK, does it? To join the Bloods, who kidnapped the girl you said you loved and abused the bitch,' I raised my head and faced him. I pointed to my stomach and said, 'And this!'

He threw the blade of grass on the floor and lowered his head.

'Don't think helping me escape makes up for anything. To think I said yes to marrying you.'

'They took my phone off me. I couldn't reply. They monitored us 24/7.'

'You sent me to the Bloods,' I said. 'You brought the letter to my house, telling me to go to be tested.'

'I didn't know it would end like this, I just thought it was a stupid test, and deep inside I hoped I would get a chance to see you, to talk to you,' Ash pleaded, holding out his hands towards me. 'I didn't know, I just thought they were going to do some tests, and you would be able to go back home.'

'I should never have trusted a white man,' I said. I should have listened to Mum. She'd warned me. White men were just after a bit of an exotic treat. Is that all I was to you? A fuckable Paki? An oriental shag?'

I wanted to hurt him like he'd hurt me. It was childish – it was cruel. But I couldn't stop it.

Ash looked stricken. Speechless, he shook his head.

'I bet you would have preferred it if I'd worn a hijab, wouldn't you? Or maybe it would have been even better if I'd worn a niqab.'

Get angry for once, you bastard, I thought. Shout and cry like me.

He didn't. He ripped out another blade of grass and fiddled with it.

'It's OK to hate me for being white if that's what you want, I can't undo this,' he said, looking down. 'Didn't your mum always say that the problem is whiteness, not white people…?'

'Leave Mum out of this.'

Suddenly, I was sick of him, sick of the war, sick of this world. I felt the tears rising up into my face, but I wouldn't let him see me cry.

I flew at him – I didn't know whether I was going to hold him or strike him, but when I got to him, I slapped him round the face as hard as I could, and I fled back to the house.

'I'm sorry,' I cried over my shoulder.

'Marah,' he called. He ran after me. I kept waving my hand behind me, telling him to go back, but I had to stop. He tried to hold me. I pushed him away. I pressed on my back and waited to get my breath. He was crying, too.

'I'm sorry about your parents,' I said at last.

'It's OK,' he said.

'What happened?' I asked.

'Dad couldn't get his meds, they just dried up, and he had a stroke. A week later, Mum overdosed herself.'

'The war took both of our parents,' I said. 'And it's taken our love as well.'

I left him and went back alone to my room.

THE SACRIFICE

It was rare for the Bloods to attack before dawn, but they did. I was woken up by missiles flying overhead and exploding way out in the distance. With each explosion, I wished I were standing under them. To be obliterated. I wanted no more of this life. This war. This baby. This hell.

The first few big heavy missiles, the ones that rattled buildings, landed somewhere on the outer edge of town. Then other smaller ones fell every now and then, all the way around Watford. This went on until well after dawn broke.

The voices came back – the Doctor shouting at me to *cleanse your soul of sin*; Aud hissing that I *must save myself from the serpent of sin and return to the Lamb*. I was too upset to fight back. I sat on the bed, cradling my bump and weeping for what seemed like hours. Eventually, I could take no more of the gnawing and fought them back with questions they couldn't answer.

I was scared. Scared of the bombs, scared of the ESLA, scared of the baby inside ... scared of myself.

Then, the raid was over, and I began to calm down. I went to the kitchen, got myself a bowl of cereal, came back to my bedroom, opened my window, and looked out onto the garden. The birds were back, chirping as though nothing had happened.

Just as I put my empty bowl on the side table, Ash knocked on my door. It was open, but he waited. I could see him clearly in the reflection of the mirror on the wall.

He'd shaved. He was dressed in a neatly pressed shirt and clean black trousers and had polished his black shoes. He'd had a haircut, and his wet hair was combed off his face, falling to the back of his head.

He cleared his throat. 'May I come in, Marah?'

'Let's get this over with, whatever it is that needs to be buried,' I replied. I gave him a quick glance and went back to looking out of the window. The sun was behind some patchy clouds. Two magpies landed near the base of the apple tree and started pecking something in the grass.

'I understand it doesn't matter any more, but I want you to know there's nothing I won't do for you, Marah.'

I turned around slowly and sat down. The frame of the bed groaned under me. Ash held his hands locked together in front of him. The sun had risen, and a beam of light caught him in it.

'What can you do for me now?' I asked.

'I will tell the world this is my child,' he said.

I laughed. 'This is not my child, and you're not a modern-day Joseph, but do you really really want to help me?' I said.

'Don't talk like that, Marah. It isn't the Marah I know and love.'

Words exploded out of my mouth. 'How do you know who I am now? Don't you know, I am the Mother Messiah, remember? The saviour of Christians. Saviour of the white race. The Curse of Muslims. The Sin of Jews. I am the living curse. Repeat after me. You are the living curse. Marah, the whore, the shittiest person on the planet, the reject of humanity. Look at me!'

He was shaking.

'I have never loved anyone but you, and never will,' he said.

'You will do anything for me?' I said, getting off my bed and stepping towards him.

He nodded.

'Then kill this baby for me as soon as it is born,' I jabbed my finger into my stomach.

Ash stepped back against the door.

'Come here,' I said.

He hesitated and then stepped through the beam of light.

'Stop there.'

He was close to my bed.

'Will you kill him for me?'

He shook his head. Tears fell. 'Marah, stop it. Stop,' he begged.

'You've taken life before, haven't you?' I demanded.

He nodded.

'Then save mine and kill him as soon as he is born,' I placed my hand over the baby inside me.

'I've never killed a child.'

I burnt inside, and a cacophony of voices hissed inside my head. I held my face in my hand and cried.

'I can't kill your baby. I won't,' said Ash when I stopped. 'And I don't believe in your heart that you want me to kill your baby.'

'It's not my baby,' I cried. I grabbed the cereal bowl and threw it at his head. It missed him and smashed against the wall behind him.

We stood still for a while, but in this silence, an angry word smashed around inside my head: Why? Why? Why?

He came towards me with his arms open.

'Leave!' I hammered at his face and chest with my fists. 'I never want to see you again. Not in this world or the next.'

I shoved him out of the door. A moment later, I saw him running across the road in front of the house, crying. I slumped on the bed and howled my tears out to the world. I was unfit to live, unfit to breathe. Every second I was here upon the earth, the earth was revolted by me. I wept and wept till my tears burned my eyes and my throat was sore.

Inside me, the baby kicked and moved. I cried aloud, 'Oh Mum, come hold me, even as a ghost.'

The baby stopped kicking but continued to move.

A memory came to me – Mum talking to my brother when he was still inside her. She knew he was a boy from the ultrasound scan.

'My baby feels all that I feel, only he doesn't know he feels it,' she had said, rubbing some oil on her bulge. 'Say hello to your brother.'

'Hello,' I said.

'Tell him you love him,' she'd asked.

'I love you,' I said, then I laughed.

'What are you laughing at?' Mum asked.

'Talking to your tummy is so funny,' I said.

'A baby can hear everything,' she'd said. 'When he comes into this world and hears you, he will know your voice, and he will, deep inside himself, know that you love him.'

'Will he remember what I said?' I asked.

'He will remember how he felt when he heard you speak,' Mum said.

I rubbed my stomach like my mother used to rub hers.

The baby stopped moving.

'Are you feeling better now?' I asked. 'Feel better. Please feel better. Forgive me, baby.'

The days got shorter, the nights colder. The war raged on out beyond the frontlines and in my body. The voices waxed and waned. One frosty

November night, I couldn't sleep at all, and the next night. I paced the shadows, hoping they would give me a place to hide away. In the dying moments of the third day, at last, I felt the slap of sleep. But later in the night, I was woken by terrible indigestion; my throat felt like it was on fire. I sipped milk to ease the pain, but it didn't make any difference.

The boiler in our complex had stopped working, and my room was like a fridge. The cold air clung to my head, even under the woolly hat I was wearing, and my feet felt cold even under a 13-tog duvet. One relief: mercifully, the voices had kept away. I was alone with two heartbeats inside me, one I felt and the other tiny one I kept seeing pulse when I closed my eyes, inside a trembling moon.

I opened my eyes, expecting to wake up with my face inside the moon, but instead, I was under my stuffy duvet. I got out of bed to look out of the window and see if the moon was out tonight. There it was, a beautiful full moon, hanging above the branches of the trees beyond the walls of my prison. A happy memory came over me. It was during my school holidays when we had gone on holiday to the Lake District. Mum woke me up with a kiss. 'Come, my sweet, I want you to see this,' she said.' I liked it when Mum woke me up with a kiss. I was around seven then. And she then kissed my brother and picked him up. He rubbed his eyes, put his head on Mum's shoulder, and went back to sleep. Dad was snoring away, as he always did when we were on holiday. We went outside and sat on a swing chair, Mum in the middle, me on one side and my brother on the other, with his head in Mum's lap. She put her arm around me and rubbed his hair as we swung gently. There was a great big lake in front of us, with a great big reflection of the moon in the gentle ripples of its waters. It was a beautiful, warm summer night, and there was no other light but that of the moon. It was such a beautiful sight, even Tats sat up and looked up at the moon.

'It's raining,' he said.

Of course it wasn't raining rain, but I knew what he meant, it was raining moonlight.

'Mum, can I have it for my birthday?' He asked. He was such a cutie in those days.

'You can have it, my sweet son,' Mum said, 'it's yours.'

He was so happy he sat up and clapped his hands.

'It's the moon, stupid,' I said. 'It won't be there in the morning.'

Tats burst out crying, and I felt horrible for what I'd said.

'It will always be there,' Mum said.

'Always, mum?'

'Always,' Mum replied, 'but tell me what you will do with it.'

'Play with it,' he replied.

I really loved him that day, such a sweetie.

When we got back to London, Mum played a song for me. It was an old song from a long-ago era, before Mum. I'd heard her listening to it before, and this time she played it just for me and told me that it was about a strange little boy who wanted the moon to play with.

A loud thud and a massive flash somewhere beyond the outer walls brought me out of my nostalgia. The ground shook a little, the window vibrated, and then, but for the trembling light of the moon, everything as far as I could see was in the dark.

The cold night dug its claws into my arms and legs. But I wasn't ready to go back to bed. I turned on my reading lamp. Instead of facing down towards the table, it was facing straight ahead of me and shone directly on my stomach. The baby kicked and became restless.

'Oh, you don't like the light?' I said, turning the lamp away from my stomach.

The baby immediately calmed down.

There were still times when I hated the baby inside me – the enemy, the seed of rape, the produce of my abuse. All I wanted then was for it to be gone, to be destroyed.

Sometimes, when I thought about these things, the voices were furious with me. Not only did they shred my thoughts, but they seemed to plant evil feelings inside of me. Sometimes, they floated around in obscene shapes before my eyes. Then it felt like I was dead, made of rotting flesh, and that the baby inside me was more alive than me.

I started writing the next day, but I couldn't remember having written the words. I woke up in the morning and looked at what I had written the night before, scrawled across the page, with some words written half across others and the lines of the sentences wandering across the page. Across two pages, I had written inside a bubble:

whenyouputmeinmycoffindidyounotwonderhowIwouldhavelookedina-babygrow

I turned the page, and I had written:

The most terrifying of the voices is no longer of the beasts that have been implanted in my head but a new one it is humane but not human it doesn't speak to me in words but in feelings and the feelings are painted in wounded echoes this voice is scared so terribly scared it is confused by every new sound it fears anger it fears sorrow and what it feels I feel and what I feel it feels and even though I know what this feeling is, the burden of its pain is too much for me to even capture in my poems or my nightmares or just in the loneliness of the night of this world of killers and monsters and why should you live when life has no meaning and where the cheapest thing is life and so it is better for you to live for I am the creator and I cannot create death but life and when life is created of no worth then death is better for you so it is only right that you should come into the world knowing it is better to die and I want you to know that there you have to be born alone no one can breathe your first breath and you must die alone as no one can breathe your last breath but you and so if there is only loneliness in the life you must live then it is better not to live that lost life and I am sorry I will not see you play with the moon and if I was a different goddess then I would have looked after all that I had created but the world that I own is two thousand light years away and it is nearby and I will go there and no I cannot take you there because you do not belong there, and why should I tell you where you belong for you belong where you belong and it was not I who chose to have you belong where you do and so what if you did not choose to be created and no I do not owe anything to creation for creation committed a crime in conceiving that should not have been conceived and no I am not sorry for I do not have any love left and yes I am sorry for the night is long and it is cold and there are demons and there devils and there is there that which is and which should not be and maybe just maybe the world will see

'Baby, I am so, so sorry for what I have become,' I said to baby after reading my words. My hands were on my stomach, and I could feel him moving under them. And I cried.

The Doctor's voice boomed inside my head, t*here will be signs in the sun, moon and stars. On the earth, nations will be in anguish and per-plexity at the roaring and tossing of the sea.*

'And what happens if I pass the anguish of love into this raging sea?' I asked the Doctor's voice.

It didn't answer.

I turned another page, and I had written,

If you visit my grave
Knock three times
I'll know you forgave

I turned another page, and I had written:

Oh, Mother, who do I tell of this unborn sorrow,
Bread of aches
Soup of bloody thorns
Cooked on the firewood longing
Dancing in the fading scent
Of a discarded moon

I closed my notebook. The baby had begun to kick again. I kissed the tips of my fingers, pressed them onto my stomach, and asked him to forgive me.

'There is nothing to fear from the dark, baby, it is a friend of light,' I said.

I sang in whispers to my baby, songs my mother had sung to me, in languages I didn't understand but whose melodies now took me away, out of this city, beyond its ravages, beyond its hate, above the clouds, past snow-capped mountains into never-ending lush fields, where flowers hummed, and scents danced. I went to a world awash with butterflies, where nights were lit up by fireflies and where my baby could play with the moon.

THE UNION

A sh came to me one morning before I'd had breakfast.

'There will be no clouds today,' he said.

'Is that what you came to tell me?'

'I came to ask if we can have breakfast together,' he said, holding out a bag. 'Parathas.'

'I've already had breakfast,' I said.

'Liar!'

I opened the door and let him in. I put the kettle on, and we sat down at the table together. He didn't give up easily, I'll say that for him. He'd made the parathas, too.

'They're dreadful,' I said. 'But I'm going to eat them anyway, out of respect for Dad.'

Ash bowed his head.

We nibbled in silence for a while before I asked him a question that had been on my mind for the past few days.

'In those days, in the hospital when I was unconscious, when they were rewriting me, did you sneak in to see me?' I asked.

'I did. As often as I could. I got into trouble for it – sneaking into the Mother Messiah. I told them I had come to pray by your side.

I laughed. 'It's a bit stalky,' I said. 'So what did you do?'

'I couldn't do much, they had cameras on you most of the time. I knelt by your bed and whispered that I loved you.'

Tears sprang to my eyes.

'I don't remember it,' I said.

'I didn't know what else to do to help you save your memory. I felt so helpless. But I slapped lots of lavender scent on me. They say smells go very deep – deeper than anything else, into the memory.'

'The lavender. Yes, I remember the lavender. Even though I didn't know where the scent came from, or if it too was a mind game, each time I smelt it an unsheddable tear formed in my eye. But maybe that was one of their implanted memories as well.'

I bent my head.

'Why are you here? What do you want from me, Ash?'

'You,' he said.

'I have nothing left to give.'

'I don't want you to give me anything,' Ash said.

'I have changed from what I was, inside and out, and I don't understand either one of me,' I said.

'I want to understand all of you,' Ash said. 'I want to understand everything there is to understand about you if I can.'

'But why?' I asked.

'Because I love you,' he said.

'I am unworthy of that love,' I said.

'Never. Never,' he replied. Under the table he reached for me, and I let my hand lie limply in his. 'Can you ever love me again?' he asked.

'Can we live in the past of our wrongs?' Ash said, pulling a hot water bottle out of his bag.

'That's deep,' I replied taking the hot water bottle. His hand touched mine. It was hot, but I felt no warmth.

It was a red rubber bottle, bloated like me. I moved it from one hand to another wondering how long it would take for it to flatten if I stuck a knife in it.

The baby twitched, and I felt a pull on my eyelids at the same time. I lifted my quilt and placed the bottle under it, and only then did I realise my quilt had a clean new green cover, with large leaves on it.

'Tell me what can I do?' Ash asked, placing his hand on mine.

'I don't remember when I changed the quilt,' I said, 'but I know I did.'

'Does it matter?' he asked.

'It matters,' I said. 'Everything matters.' Idly, I ran my finger over a leaf printed on my cover. A missile screeched high in the night sky.

'It matters to me to find the way back to you,' he said.

A gust of wind shook the window.

'I've changed forever,' I said.

'Can I wait for you?' he asked, clearing his throat.

'It was not meant to be like this, Ash. What can change me now?' I asked.

'Love,' he said.

I took my hand out of his.

'Tell me what more I can do for you?' he asked.

I didn't like the way he said, for you.

Tell him the truth, he deserves to know, I thought.

He locked his hands together and placed them between his legs and looked down at them. I sat on the edge of my bed. He was on a chair nearby.

With the tips of my fingers, I lifted his head up by the chin, turned his face towards me and said, 'I know you have put your life in great danger for me and I am so grateful to you. I know you care for me but it's not the love of yesterday. Those yesterdays have gone forever and today, I just don't feel the same as then. I can't give you the love you want. I don't have it any more.'

'Shh, Marah,' he said. He closed his eyes and added, "Sometimes, no matter how many times we tie moonlight around our heads, the pain just won't go away.' Isn't that what the lyrics of that song you liked said?'

I didn't reply. Ash put his hands on his knees to rise.

'I didn't say you had to leave.'

'Do you want me to stay?'

'You got the words of the song all wrong, you big oaf. It's "strips of moonlight," you great big Naana. These were soaked in scent, and then tied around his head.'

The wave came so quickly, quicker than it had ever been before. It started in my neck, like a flame and melted down into me as a tingly itch. My throat went dry and the look in his eyes knew why.

He stood up. I held his hand and felt his throbbing blood.

'I thought you didn't love me any more,' he said, putting his fingers in mine.

I tightened my hand around his.

'The light is still on,' he said.

'It is,' I said, turning it off.

'It's dark,' he whispered. He was short of breath.

He ran his fingers up my forehead, through my hair, and held it tightly in his hand. I raised my head backwards, and wondered what my breasts would look like now, if the light came on, but this thought was extinguished by the heat of the wandering fingers of his other hand. My thighs twitched. I wanted to be filled so much, right there. Right then.

Our tongues battled for space. I thought of the tree in the park behind where I'd had sex for the first time, but then our hearts beat together, and there was only now. In the rolling waves of the night, for a while, I was not me, and he not him. There was only one sensual formless being. But this was a different Ash to the one I had known before.

'Gently,' I said.

He was at first, but then he became loud and rough. He was so noisy that an image of a braying donkey flashed through my mind, but it was thrust asunder as quickly as it had come. I dug my nails into his back, and then put a hand across his mouth, lest someone burst into the room, but then I didn't care about the vicissitudes of the impositions of this world, I was riding my own.

I pushed him away from me immediately afterwards.

'Are you OK?' he asked. I said nothing. I felt dirty and I went to shower without saying a word. When I came back, he was gone. I was stricken. Not for the first time, I wished I had a phone that worked, but of course any messages in or out of our enclave had been banned. Suddenly I felt so lonely, going to bed alone after making love, and I cried myself to sleep. But Ash was back in the morning with another bag of parathas. I was furious. I threw my pillow at him.

'You deserted me, like the rat you are,' I told him.

'You rejected me so suddenly after coming. It felt awful. You never used to do that.'

'That's how I felt then,' I said, and I couldn't help laughing, 'And now is now.'

'What is so funny?' he asked.

'Nothing, you stupid donkey,' I said, kissing him on the lips.

It was a bright, sunny day. Ash wore a black and white striped suit. The trousers were above his ankles and the jacket was also too short for him. He waved his arms as he talked to my brother, who, like Ash, wore a suit. They were in the garden.

When Ash realised I was looking at them, he turned his back to me, but after a moment, turned around and waved at me. I became angry at him for wearing a suit, but baby didn't like my anger and wriggled about. I got upset with the thought that they must have had some good news which they hadn't bothered sharing with me. Baby didn't like this and told my ribs. When the pain in my ribs died down, I said to my baby, 'OK, let's make a deal. If you stop being cross with me, I'll stop getting angry.'

The baby didn't move, and I guessed he was happy with the deal. I went to the bathroom and when I returned, there was a knock on the door.

It was Ash.

I opened the door, held it ajar and said, 'So you got a job?'

'Can I come in?' he asked, shaking his head.

'What for?' I asked.

He looked to his right, then left, where he held his gaze for a moment and said, 'I can't tell you, not just now.'

I stepped back. He came into the room.

I shut the door, and with penguin steps, walked back to the bed and sat down. When I turned around, Ash was on one knee, his hand held out towards me, with the same box he had given me the ring in back in Birmingham. It was a little battered now.

'Oh God, not again! It was so corny last time; couldn't you have come up with something original?' I said, 'And you've put weight on!'

'Maybe a little,' he replied.

'The suit's too tight,' I said.

'It's not mine,' he replied.

'Whose is it?' I asked.

'Tats got it from someone,' Ash said.

'Why didn't you buy one for yourself?' I teased.

'I'm broke.'

'Why didn't you sell the ring and get a suit?' I asked.

'Then what would I propose with?' he said.

'Why don't you put it on my finger then?' I said holding my hand out.

He did.

'Congratulations!' Tats said bursting into the room. He had a tray of sweetmeats in his hand and asked, 'So when's the big day then?'

'Let's get our breath back at least,' I said.

'Let's get married today!' exclaimed Ash breathlessly.

'It's Sunday,' I laughed. 'Besides, who is going to conduct the ceremony?'

'I will,' Tats said.

'By God, won't the Bloods be pissed off when we circulate the photos of Mother Messiah getting married,' I said. 'I suppose you do look a bit like Joseph,' I said to Ash.

'Who do you want to invite, apart from me of course?' Ash asked.

'Uncle Melvin. And Leena.' I still hadn't seen Leena – it had been weeks now.

'She's been away on some secret mission the past few days,' Ash answered.

'What's that?' I asked.

'It's secret, we don't know,' Ash said.

'Duh!' Tats said, and then added, 'My sis can't get married without a bridal dress.'

'I'll get one,' Ash said, making for the door.

'No – I should pick my own wedding dress.'

'... can't wait ... you might change your mind ...' Ash was already out of the door.

'And it should be red!' I shouted after him.

'Red?' he asked, popping his head back into my room. 'It's always white.'

'I'm not a virgin,' I said.

'It's red for our brides you know. As Mum would say, she had a word, Boti. That's what Mum would have wanted,' Tats explained.

'That's not what Mum said, dumbo, it was Voti – bride. Boti means a piece of meat.'

'Same thing!'

'Cheeky bastard!'

Tats went off with Ash on the great wedding dress hunt. They returned just before sunset a few hours later, with a bunch of flowers and a bag.

'I hope you like it,' Ash said. 'All the shops were closed, and this is the best we could do.'

He took out a parcel wrapped in newspapers. I opened it carefully. It had a bright red sheet inside. 'It's beautiful,' I said. 'Let me try it on, see what it looks like.

I tried to wrap it around myself like a sari, but it was too small. I threw it over my shoulders and pulled it down, but it only just covered my bulge. I tried to wear it as a skirt, but it kept slipping. Each try was more ridiculous than the last.

'Perfect,' I said.

'Let's get on with it then,' Tats said. He put the bedspread from my bed over his shoulders, arranged Ash and me together, side by side and looked skywards.

'Mum, Dad, and Allah, as you are all my witnesses, I hereby declare ...'

'Hey, I want my Mum and Dad here too,' said Ash.

'OK. Mum, Dad, Ash's mum and dad ... Allah and Jesus and anyone else holy enough to participate as you are my witnesses, I hereby declare my sis and this man, Ash, man and wife. No, wait! First ... Ash Williams, are you fine marrying my sis and promise to put up with her in sickness and in health, even when she's irritating, which is most of the time?'

'Yes,' Ash said.

'Marah Sultana, can you put up with him in sickness and in health?' Tats asked.

I played at being Ash for a moment and went silent, but before I could say yes, Tats said, 'You are now husband and wife. And a middle finger up to the Bloods!'

In the days that followed, I forgot the pains of yesterdays; the voices rarely bothered me, and I forgot that everyone in the world had seen pictures of me. I re-found my heaven in Ash, and I managed to say the three magic words as well.

Ash was so excited about the baby, he read books with me on childbirth, filled a rucksack with everything I would need for the delivery, as backup. He spent hours sitting by my side, talking to the baby, telling him not to worry about anything, that he would let no harm come to him. I didn't stop Ash from promising the heavens to the baby. I just pretended this moment, of waiting, of hope, was a dream, would never end. But as my due date drew closer, there were hard decisions to be made.

He was now spending almost all his time with me in my bungalow. ESLA seemed inclined to let him off his duties if he was spending his time with me. It wasn't long before I found out why. One evening he came home withdrawn and pale.

'What is it, Ash?' I asked. He was looking out of the window into the twilight. The generators were off. We only had an emergency light on in the bedroom.

'I rechecked whose sperm they used,' he said.

'Tell me,' I said.

The baby moved.

The emergency light flickered. The distant sound of guns became louder. Someone walked hurriedly in the corridor past my room.

'Tell me,' I repeated.

'It was definitely the King,' Ash said.

Even though I already knew, still my chest tightened. Blood thumped around my ears. I went back into fragments of memories from hospital: The Doctor; Aud; Blood soldiers; The King. Blood thumped around in my ears as I remembered Mum's words on my 18th birthday. I was just a pawn in a much more sinister game than I thought.

'We will raise him to burn Buckingham Palace, and that bastard of a King in it,' I said.

'Yes,' Ash agreed.

'If he can't, I will do it,' I said.

'The baby is ours,' I said. 'You are the father.'

'It's all I want,' he replied.

'He will forever be ours,' I said. 'And now you must never mention this again.'

We sat silently for a long time and then Ash said, 'It just brings it home to me. They will never let you or our baby live in peace, Marah. They will do anything to get the baby back.'

The generators came back on, and a moment later my room was filled with light.

'We will be OK,' I said, 'I know we will.'

The words *our baby* filled my eyes with bitter tears.

'We'll go and live in Scotland,' I said. 'We will not give up.'

Ash nodded. But he remained silent.

'So, what do you want to do?' I asked.

'We will just be together till the end, whatever that might be,' he said. 'But I have to tell you ... they have asked me to tell you what they want. ESLA. I was in a meeting with Helen. I said no at first, but they will tell you anyway, so I thought ...'

'Tell me what?' I demanded.

'They want you to give the baby up for adoption. To a family somewhere – somewhere anonymous, so no one will know who he is or what he is. You see ...'

'No!' I said coldly. How could he even say those words to me?

'I said I'd tell you what they want. Hear me out. The baby is the Messiah; he's also the future King of England. You see what they want, the Bloods?'

'Yeah. Some plan,' I said, placing my hand on my belly. The baby moved. So many hopes and wishes on one not even born, I thought.

'It sounds so grand, doesn't it?' I said. 'The Messiah – the Second Coming. King. What a lucky boy! But, in fact, they want to turn him into a monster, into a puppet. We can't let that happen.'

'No.' Ash looked at me. 'We must do whatever it takes,' he said. He paused and then added, 'They have put a bounty on your head.'

'How much am I worth?' I asked.

'Twenty million. There are pictures of you all over the place. TV, posters, everywhere. You have been kidnapped by devil worshippers. Helen thinks it's going to go up.'

That night I stayed awake, thinking about the possibilities. No point in pretending. I was too well-known to hide anywhere in England. There was no realistic way of making it out of the country, not even to Scotland. I was worth a fortune to every group in the country, if not for the money, then as a bargaining chip. There would be bounty hunters, individuals, groups, fighters. It would be no better in Scotland. Anyway, ESLA wouldn't countenance ferrying me out – too dangerous, they had told Ash. The bitter truth was there was no realistic choice.

'We must let no harm come to him,' I said to Ash the next day.

'No,' he said.

I could not bear the agony of the words I needed to say and let them drop out of my mouth, 'There must be some caring soul, somewhere who loves the love of innocence. Someone who can keep the baby, and care for him, and keep him till we find a way of getting safely back to him.'

'There must be, 'Ash said.

'But promise me one thing, my love. We hide somewhere, and for one month let me breastfeed my baby,' I cried. 'At least let him have some strength.'

'I will ask,' Ash said. 'I'm sure they will grant us that much. Actually, Marah, they have done so much for us. You know that, really. They helped rescue you, they're hiding you here, they've asked for nothing – perhaps it is enough for them to deny the Bloods their Jesus. But it's not right to expect them to hide us forever.'

'So, we are alone in the world,' I said. 'But, my love, at least we are together.'

That day, I cried the bitterest tears of my life.

And so began a search for a family for my baby.

When I finally met Uncle Melvin again, he came with Helen. She was dressed in new military fatigues and was now the most senior ESLA security commander of the complex. Uncle Melvin had a strange look on his face, a cross between mystery and mischief. I didn't care to know what new scams he was up to, I just wanted some answers from him.

'Thanks for looking after her so well,' Uncle Melvin said, coming into my room.

'All going well?' Helen asked, looking at my bulge.

'Really well,' I said.

'Oh, how lovely,' she replied clearly missing the sarcasm.

'Didn't I tell you, Marah, that Helen would take super good care of you, and how sexy she would look in uniform?' Uncle Melvin said.

He hadn't said anything like this before.

'Stop objectifying women, Comrade Melvin,' Helen snapped.

'I promise,' Uncle Melvin replied, 'cross my heart and hope to die.'

Helen tutted disapprovingly and said to me, 'We have a group for expectant mothers, perhaps you would like to join them. They meet every morning at 10.00 am,' holding me by the hand, she added, 'Come, let me show you the delivery room.'

I followed her, and Uncle Melvin followed me.

My delivery room had a new bed, monitors, oxygen canisters and breathing apparatus, it really looked like a hospital ward. The sliding window had a metal grille on the outside.

'What's happening with my interview, Helen?' I asked.

'The CC will decide on the most appropriate time,' Helen said, 'In war it is not just having the bullet, but when to fire the shot.'

Helen inspected the room quickly, led us back to my room, and left with a look of contentment.

After Helen went, Uncle Melvin sat on the edge of my bed and said, 'You might think I am acting like a monkey, when Helen is around, but she is the one person who can keep both of us safe.'

'Are you in trouble?' I asked.

'Is Helen helping you cos you're her ex, then?' I asked. 'Or is she getting a cut?'

'I help their cause.'

'Their cause?' I asked. 'I thought you were comrade Mister Arms Dealer.'

Melvin shrugged. 'Not always the same quality arms to both sides,' he said, with a wink. 'Helen knows she gets only the best from me.'

I never knew how little I knew of Uncle Melvin.

'I don't like Helen. She reminds me of the nurse at the hospital,' I said.

'Helen is a bit shifty, that's true, but she is very clever as well,' Uncle Melvin said. 'She knows the Bloods want you alive...'

'For now,' I interrupted.

'Yes, for the time being. So, they can't mount an all-out attack on the complex here, or even send in a special mission to get you. You are too well protected, and they know if they try that, then they can kiss their arse to the Messiah!'

The baby moved and I said, 'Baby didn't like what you just said, Uncle Melvin. You mean she's prepared to kill me if they attack, right?'

'No! They suspect ESLA have you, but they don't know where. But it's a threat. They are holding back the big guns on our positions. You mean more to them than anything ... even territory. They're crazy of course – but Marah – you are their biggest weakness.'

'Did you notice anything odd in the delivery room?' I asked.

'No,' he replied, not that I've been to many, mind you.'

'The window in the room has a grille on the outside of it. It's a bit weird, no?'

'It's odd,' he nodded.

'It's a prison cell,' I said.

'Of course it is, sweetheart,' Uncle Melvin said. The way he said it reminded me of the way Mum used to say this when she wanted me to do something I didn't want to do. 'We're all in prison these days. None of us can go where we want. But now let's talk of nicer things.

Today's your birthday, had you forgotten?

He turned around and looked at me. He had the birthday smile on, where I would have to pretend I didn't know he had a surprise for me.

'Please, Uncle Melvin!' I pleaded. 'You know it's not my birthday.'

'I think it is.'

'I know when my birthday is. Dah!'

'Let me see if I can change your mind.' Uncle Melvin turned his head towards the door and shouted, 'OK!'

'What you up to, you crazy old man?' I laughed.

'Wait and see!' He paced the room excitedly until my door slowly began to open. Suddenly, Tats burst in ... with Chilli! I was so astonished all I could do was sit and stare. But as soon as he saw me, Chilli went bonkers. He came rushing over, licking my face and wagging his tail so hard he nearly knocked me out. And I wept and held him and kissed his nose. It was such a glorious moment.

'You don't know how much trouble I went through and how much I spent,' Uncle Melvin said.

I hugged Chilli. He continued licking my hands and face.

'Oh, Chilli! You're worth every penny and much more,' I said.

But even then, at the back of my mind, I was thinking how they had gone to all this trouble to get me back my dog. He was just a dog to them, although he meant the world to me. It showed just how valuable I was to ESLA, as well as the Bloods.

For the next few days, Chilli was my world. He followed me everywhere. For a while, I forgot about the war, and the shitty place I was in, and watched Chilli run around in the garden, full of energy, like he was in the prime of his youth, not the old creature that he was.

Everyone loved him and he loved being loved. He could roam around where he wished. Even the regular bouts of shells stopped falling once Chilli turned up and this turned him into a mascot for everyone. The only person he didn't seem to like was Helen, in whose company he became agitated.

THE PURIFICATION

I was one week away from D-Day, and was getting ready to go to bed, when the drones began overhead, followed by the terrifying boom of the fighter planes. Then came the rockets and the missiles. Some exploded way out around the M1, I guessed, and others streaked above us and went on their journey. The Bloods had started to clean up any resistance down south before they carried on further north.

Then, out of the blue, Leena turned up. I had forgotten when I last talked to her.

A whiff of shampoo drifted into my room with her. She'd just showered. She was wearing a white dressing gown with deep pockets and had tied a bow across her waist. She had something in a plastic bag with her.

'There's nothing like a hot shower when you can hear bombs falling,' Leena said, brushing her hair with her fingers. She looked at me and smiled wryly. 'Have you got a towel? Me hair's still wet,' she asked.

I held angry Marah back, who had so many questions for comrade Captain Leena, but right now, I just need my old Leena back, so I threw her a towel. She caught it and laughed, 'Thanks, I was expecting you to toss a grenade at me!' She lowered her head and dried her hair.

'Would you have blamed me?' I asked.

'I'm sorry, Marah. I'm a soldier. I follow orders,' she said, 'and yesterday I thought, what the fuck have I become? I even missed your wedding.'

'And have they ordered you to be here now?' I asked.

'They don't know,' she said. 'I've not been away because I wanted to be, Marah. You must know that. But this is my leave. I'm here now for as long as I can.'

She sounded like the old Leena.

I nodded.

Somewhere in the distance a series of huge explosions made the building tremble.

'The Bloods must know I'm here,' I said, 'That's why they've started.'

Leena shook her hair off her face. 'They won't dare attack anywhere they think you might be. If comrade Helen had her way, you'd stay pregnant forever.'

'And after I give birth?'

Leena smiled grimly. 'Everyone wants Jesus, don't they?' she said. 'Your own personal Messiah. She'd keep him forever if she could. But there are others higher up than her who just don't want that around. The Bloods would do anything to get him into their hands. And since no one wants to kill a newborn baby ...' she flicked back her long hair, 'you're good to go. But they won't let you keep the baby, Marah, you know that. And they're right. It's too dangerous for you, for him and for us.'

My Leena was definitely back.

'Everyone wants my baby?' I asked sarcastically.

'Which is why we need to give him to someone who doesn't even know who he is.'

A huge explosion somewhere in the north of the town shook the ground. 'Wow! Tomahawk,' Leena said. 'They're not messing.'

One thing this war taught quickly was the names of the bombs that flew above, which you could hear, and those that landed some-where, which you could feel.

There was another explosion, somewhere near the centre of town. '107mm Grad,' we said in unison.

'That one was likely to be one from our side which had misfired,' Leena said.

We sat on the bed and played name-the-missile for a while, with a point going to the one who was first to identify the projectile.

Tats burst into the room. He was out of breath and said quickly, 'Bloods breached Junction 5 for a bit, we got it back, but things up north are really bad. Another massacre in Handsworth and the Bloods have linked up with Nottingham and Leicester. Two new American bri-gades are on their way here from Huntington.'

'Do I have to move?' I asked.

'I don't know, but maybe,' Tats replied. 'Uncle Melvin said be ready.'

'We're not moving, Marah's little brother,' Leena said, picking up the bag she had brought. I don't care which boys are coming with what toys,' she said calmly. 'Your sis can't move.'

Tats started to protest, but Leena ignored him. She put her hand inside the bag she'd brought along and pulled out a pair of large nail clippers.

'You're a darling,' I said to Leena while looking at the clippers.

'I don't like it,' Tats insisted. I kinda felt proud looking at him all grown up, in his blue jeans and black leather jacket.

Leena rummaged about in the bag, as another four rockets landed in quick succession, somewhere in the woods at the bottom of the garden.

'Katushkas. That's 25,' she said.

'Katushkas don't count,' I said, 'Bloods don't use them, probably some new outfit trying to take advantage of the fighting.'

'You have the point. 21 to you then,' Leena said, putting three nail varnish bottles on the floor near her feet.

'Jesus, that was close,' said Tats. 'Leena, we have to move her.'

'Moving your sister in a bumpy car when she's due to drop in a few days is not a good idea,' Leena said calmly, pulling my foot towards her and resting it on her knee. 'Even so, it might be an idea for you to go to HQ and find out exactly why the Bloods are raining hell down on a spot that might well hold the King of Kings, would you?'

Tats dashed out. Leena clipped my toenails one after the other. When she'd done, she said, 'I've got blue, purple and silver.'

A whining projectile flew over our roof; the noise was a bit louder than a firework.

'Black,' I said.

'Nice choice,' Leena said. 'Purple it is. The others are as dry as a bone.' She stood upright a little, flicked my eyebrows with the tips of her fingers and added, 'And when I'm done with the toes, these need sorting out. They're a disgrace.'

Tats came rushing back in, 'Apparently the Bloods think that you can't be here, so they're going to take the complex.' He paused to stare at us. 'What the fuck are you two doing?' he demanded.

'Pass me a mirror, will you Leena?'

She did. I looked at my eyebrows and protested, 'My god, they are bushes!'

'What shall I tell Uncle Mel?' Tats asked. 'He's getting a car ready.'

'Tell him we need some black nail varnish,' I said.

Leena looked Tats up and down, turned back to me, painted another nail and said, 'Doesn't he have lovely big hands, and what long fingers. A girl could die for a set like that.'

Tats blushed and stormed out, slamming the door behind him.

'He was always doing that when he was young,' I said.

'What?'

'Slamming doors.'

'Testosterone.'

We laughed.

After Leena had painted my nails, she sat on my bed, placed her foot on it, and I painted hers. I was so glad I'd found my friend again and asked her, 'I need some books to read Leena, why is the library always locked?'

She stood up and said, with a hint of the old naughty Leena in her voice, 'Books for Marah, right now!'

There were no lights. Leena used a small torch. I followed her quietly down the winding corridor to the door marked Library. It had a digital lock on it. Leena quickly punched some numbers. There was a loud click. I was about to push the door open when she whispered, 'We have to wait 30 seconds, or the alarms will go off.'

Leena put her shoulder against the door and pushed it open. When we got inside, she pushed it slowly shut again and flicked a light on. On the inside, the door was all metal.

The room smelt of dusty old books.

'Won't someone see?' I pointed to the light.

'It is light and soundproof,' Leena said.

There were rows upon rows of long wooden bookshelves, haphazardly stuffed with books. I pulled out one close to me, it was a travelogue. The one next to it was about chemistry.

'Is there a catalogue?' I asked.

Leena laughed, 'At least we saved them.'

I walked around picking up books at random and putting them back again.

When I got to the end of one of the aisles, there were some steps that led down to another room, it was enormous. We went into this room and I rummaged about, but nothing really caught my eye so I kept on walking. There was a break between the aisles, and I noticed a double door at the furthest end of the room.

'More books behind that door?' I asked.

'That leads to a secret tunnel ESLA uses for supplies. Even I need special permission to go there,' Leena said.

'Have you ever been?' I asked.

'I have,' she said. 'Now get a book and let's go back.'

I rummaged through another stack and was about to give up,

when I came across a small book, *Being Me*, by Peter Kalu. I had never heard of him, but I liked the title and decided to take it.

When we got back to my room, I asked Leena, 'Do you think the Bloods will get here, I mean take the place?'

'Nah. She'll stop them, one way or the other.'

I sat on the edge of my bed, placed the book in my lap and asked, 'Helen?'

'Who else?'

So we plucked our eyebrows and painted our nails purple while overhead the missiles whizzed and the rockets crashed, one of them so near the whole building shook. Then, as suddenly as it began, the barrage stopped – abruptly, as if someone had pressed the off button.

'Is that it?' I asked.

'I'd say so,' said Leena. She leaned back and let out a huge sigh – the only way I knew that she'd been as scared as me.

'But why so suddenly?' I asked.

Leena looked at me and pulled a Why-do-you-think face. 'She's told them I'm here, hasn't she?'

'That would be my bet, sweetie.' She sighed again. 'The sooner you give birth and we can whisk the little terror away, the better for us all, I tell you. Tell me, Marah – would you have agreed to kill the baby inside me if I had been in your shoes? If it had been me who got pregnant instead of you?'

I cried.

The book fell on the floor.

Leena picked the novel off the floor, placed it back in my lap and asked again, 'Would you?'

'I could not kill your baby, Leena,' I said, 'or any baby.'

'I thought so, Marah. Who can kill a baby for god's sake? Helen has found a good family who are desperate for a child. Shall we talk to them?' Leena said.

'Would they give my baby back to me when it was safe?'

'You can never know who they are, and they can never know who you are, that is best for baby. As far as you are concerned, the baby died at birth,' Leena said. 'That's how you have to think and let go. There is no other way.'

THE KINSHIP

Over the next few days, I stayed in my room and read *Being Me*. It had been so long since I'd read a novel, since I had been transported into another world, into another story, that I read it twice, wondering how difficult it was to be when the world around us was never going to be, where everything was so fragile, and so much pretence, and where pain was never too far from a naïve dream of happiness.

Leaving the world of stories, I went out into the garden. I was alone. It was so quiet – no drones in the sky, just the autumn leaves falling from the trees. A beautiful red-chested robin landed on an apple tree, twisted its neck and looked at me suspiciously. Two fluffy little nervous birds, with blue and red striped heads and white beaks, goldfinches, eyed me up, flapping their wings. A large blackbird landed at the base of the apple tree, quickly pecked on something, and then hopped away from me.

As I took a step forward, the birds shot out of the tree in terror.

'You don't have to go, little ones,' I called after them.

Then I heard a voice behind me. I turned and saw what had scared them. It was Leena, waving her arms in the air, calling me.

'Are you deaf?' she called. I stopped and waited for her to come to me, but she hung back. 'I have news,' she called. 'They've found a family to take the baby. Isn't that good news, Marah? Well,' she added, seeing my face, 'at least now the waiting is over.'

'But who is it? Where are they?' I asked.

Leena shook her head. 'You know I can't answer that, and I wouldn't tell you even if I knew, and I don't – you don't want to know, Marah, you really don't. But we'll talk later. I'm on duty – Helen's waiting for me.'

She turned and hurried off along the footpath, stumbling briefly on the brambles.

Is that it, Leena? I thought. All you can do is shoot some words at me.

I heard the cry of a child but could not work out whether it was coming from the bungalows, or from somewhere beyond the trees, or if it was real or was just inside my head. I put my hands on my ears, but the child continued to cry. I felt dirty all of a sudden. I turned and hurried back to my room. It was cold. The sun was warm when it was out, but all it took was a cloud across its face and the day was cold.

The cry followed me and echoed on in the shadows.

I hid under my quilt for a while and begged Allah to make it stop. What was it, this crying child? Some voice the Bloods had implanted in me, designed to come out at some trigger or other? I had no idea. I huddled under the bedclothes like a scared child myself, until after a while Tats turned up with Chilli. I heard him calling for me in the hallways and I callout out that I was in bed.

'What's up?' Tats asked.

'Nothing, don't say anything for a while, just stay with me,' I said. Chilli put his head on my legs. 'We never meant to leave you in

London, Chilli,' I told him, stroking his nose.

'You're one of the family, Chilli,' Tats said, smiling at me.

I took my brother's hand and held it in between mine. 'Maybe he came searching for you when he died, Chilli,' I said.

Chilli lifted his head and placed it between Tats and me.

For the first time since they died, Tats and I enjoyed memories of Mum and Dad ... how they argued all the time, and how she would run rings round him, especially when she became all metaphorical and Dad couldn't work out what she was saying, and just ploughed on with his arguments like an old bull.

'I loved it how Dad never stopped trying, one little business idea after another,' Tats said, 'Remember when he became a publisher?'

'Yeh, and we had boxes of books everywhere,' I laughed, 'and Mum cursed him, saying "You turned our money into paper."'

'And remember during the Covid pandemic days, he started a home delivery Lockdown Curry Service, one dish per day?' Tats laughed.

'Which no one bought!'

'And we had lentils every day, even for breakfast,' Tats said.

'And Mum refused to go into the kitchen for a week!'

We both howled with laughter.

'Did Dad ever succeed in anything?' Tats asked.

'He never stopped trying though,' I said.

And then we rode on the loving memory of our Mum.

'I'm so sorry for being so cruel to Mum,' I said.

'Isn't that what kids do?' Tats said.

I leaned over and kissed him on the head for what he had just said.

'They might have always fought,' I said, 'but they loved each other, you know.'

'And you're just like Mum,' Tats said, 'you're strong like her.'

A few tears of fond memories fell out of my eyes. 'She was *sooo* strong, but she became half the woman after Dad died. Maybe I shouldn't have asked Dad to look for Uncle Melvin. Maybe I should have thought about Mum. Oh, Tats, I was so bad to you both after Dad died.'

'Maybes will not get us through the night. Didn't Mum used to say something like that?' Tats asked.

'"Maybes of the day are toys of the night." That's what she said,' I corrected Tats.

Chilli lifted his head and looked up at me with melancholy eyes, and then put his head down again.

After Tats and Chilli left, I slept and the whisper came for me.

THE DEDICATION

'Who am I?' the whisper asked. I ignored it. It became angry ...
'Who am I?'

'This is all wrong. Mum?' I called out, hoping for her to make an appearance. She didn't. The whisper cried. A cry so loud, it brought me out of my dream, but the echo of the words continued to ring in my head.

But for a distant reminder of the war, and the echo of the whisper, it was a quiet night. I was alone.

The voice cried again. I didn't want to hear it any more, but neither did I want to betray it.

I knew the voice. It had implanted itself in the shadows in my room, just as it had implanted itself inside me.

'Tell me what to do, Mum,' I said aloud.

Then I thought, You know what to do, Marah. Stop wasting Mum's time.

I pushed the heavy quilt off me and stepped onto the cold floor, perhaps hoping that this would clear the voice in my head, just like it had of the voices of the Doctor and Aud, but it didn't. The cry lingered on, rolling in and out of the same question.

'You deserve a mother better than me, baby,' I said, stroking my stomach.

The baby gave a butterfly tremble in response.

'You are family. You will not come into this world and be named by anyone other than me. I gave you life, just as my mother gave me life. I will give you a name. I will carry your name with me, inside me, until I come back for you.'

No matter what they say, I thought, I will come back for my baby when I can. They want me to give up everything about it – my own flesh and blood. ESLA. The Bloods – they all want to decide my baby's identity. But I will not let them.

I rushed barefoot out of my room and headed for Ash. He and I shared a bed, but my sleep was bad, I became restless, so he often slept in the bungalow next door, where he shared a bunk with Tats. I barged in and turned the light on. Ash shot up and stared at me.

'What's up?' Tats asked sleepily.

'I have to name the baby,' I said.

'Now, Marah?' Ash asked.

'Can't it wait till tomorrow?' Tats asked.

'No,' I said.

For fuck's sake!' Tats moaned.

'Just get up,' I said.

Ash pulled the blanket off his bed and wrapped it around himself. 'What is the name?' he asked.

'There is only one name my baby can have.'

'Then why wake me up?' Tats protested.

'Sultan,' I said.

'Lovely,' Ash said. 'I will call him Suli.'

Tats groaned. 'You just took the 'a' off your own surname!'

'From Sultana,' Ash said. 'That's cool.'

'Suli baby,' I like that. Or should I say, Baby Suli, and insist that only I can call you this. The world must call you Sultan, and they must know it was I who named you,' I said, stroking my baby. I pressed on my stomach and asked baby, 'So what do you think?'

Sultan kicked.

I shivered. Would the family who was going to take Suli even accept he was called Sultan? And what happens if the Bloods find him? What poison would they fill his head with? And what sort of a wretch of a mother was I, naming my baby only to give him away? Giving him life, only to take it away?

Ash walked me back to my room and lay with me till dawn.

THE REVELATION

Sultan grew more and more agitated the more I thought about losing him. I convinced myself that I had finally understood the many ways he had of letting me know how he felt: kick when he was angry; tremble when he was frightened; and make me shiver by being still when he was upset. But he also knew how to make me happy, or what could pass as joy for me, by doing a sort of a butterfly flutter, and when I felt his heart beat inside me.

I was tired of crying. Now I just felt numb all the time, and time just lingered on from one numbness to another. But I loved the moments when Ash was off duty and could come and see me. If Suli was agitated, he would calm down when he heard Ash's voice. I still wasn't seeing much of Leena, but one day Ash brought me a scribbled note from her. It said, I love you and everything will be fine, and I will see you very soon.

Why do you need to tell me you love me through hand scribbled messages? I thought. If you were the Leena I once knew, you would just turn up.

But what exactly did she mean? She thought everything was fine, didn't she ... the baby going away to the family, the unknown family ESLA had found.

Was there a problem? Didn't they want him after all? As soon as I had that thought, a wave of joy spread through me. How strange I was! Not so long ago I hated Sultan. Now I loved and adored him. All this, even though we had never met. How could we be parted when we have never been apart?

But you don't need to meet someone who lives just under your heart, I thought.

I became so obsessed with trying to decipher Leena's note. I decided that it really meant that the family were ready to take the baby. It could happen any time – the next hour – this hour! Within this very hour they could come to take my Sultan away from me!

Inside me, Sultan was not moving. He was terrifyingly still.

'Don't be mad with me,' I said, pressing on my stomach. 'I was angry at what they did to me, Suli, and now I am scared of what they could do to you.'

Suli was still.

'How would I know when you were ill?' I asked. 'How could mummy kiss your little finger if you hurt it?'

Suli was still.

I couldn't bear it any longer. I called out, 'Ya Allah, protect my baby!'

Allah spoke back to me, I felt it in the wave of Suli's butterflies.

Suli wanted the peace my prayers brought, so I began to pray five times a day again. I didn't know what I was doing, or what was the right or wrong way to pray, but I knew what Mum would have said, 'There is no wrong way to go to Allah for those who believe.' I couldn't touch the ground in prostration, so I sat on the chair and just leaned forward. It still wasn't enough. Ash was a bit puzzled when I told him I wanted a recording of all the verses of the Quran on a USB, but he brought these for me, unbegrudgingly. Suli and I listened to the Arabic recitations of the Quran, but I prayed five times a day in English, quietly inside my head.

The prayers were a secret between me, Suli and Allah. But although the prayers brought me much comfort, I felt alone. Ash wanted to give my baby away, so did Leena, and Helen and Uncle Melvin. With each day that passed the conviction grew inside me that I could not, would not give Suli away. Everyone wanted my baby, and if they didn't want him, then they wanted rid of him.

But Allah answered my prayers. Or was it fortune, or the closeness of good friends? Believe what you will, but one day Ash and Leena burst into my room. Both of them looked upset and furious.

'What's happening?' I demanded, rising from my chair.

'We have been lied to, Marah,' said Ash. "All the time. There is no family to take Suli, it is al l...' He fell silent, tongue tied with upset.

'They are going to trade the baby with the Bloods for ESLA prisoners. I was so naive to believe there was a family who had suddenly been found. Helen's been lying to us all the time,' Leena added.

I turned to Ash. 'I never wanted to give him away,' I said. 'These lies are a blessing.'

Ash burst into tears. 'Neither did I.'

'We don't have time for this,' said Leena. 'The baby ...'

'He has a name,' I said.

'Did you hear what I said?' Leena asked.

'Truth is the still-born child of war, not as they say, its first casualty,' I said.

'Marah, this is not the time for poetry...'

'My son has a name,' I interrupted Leena. 'Sultan. And if he had an aunt, she would call him Suli, just like his mum.'

Leena took a deep breath, straightened up and looked at me the way she used to when she was cross with me.

She raised her eyebrows and a tear dropped out of her eye. 'Like I said, the family I went to see was just a fraud,' she said. 'It was a put-up job. Helen has a direct line to the Bloods' military command and the Doctor. They are going to release over 2000 ESLA prisoners in exchange for...' Leena hesitated before saying, 'Sultan,' and then added quickly, 'the families of the prisoners are campaigning hard for the swap, and the military is fully behind Helen...'

'No one is taking my baby!' I said.

Leena pursed her lips and looked hard at me. 'No,' she said, 'no one takes Suli.'

'You're with us?' I demanded.

'Always, Marah. Even when I wasn't here, I was always working for us.'

'OK.' I folded my hands on my lap. 'So, what's the plan?'

Leena came and put her arm around me and gave me a kiss. 'We can't just leave; they won't let you go. We do have to plan, well sort of, and the most important part of it is for you to act as if you are fully part of the show in this place, and when you meet Helen, just pretend you know nothing.'

'What do I do?' I asked.

'Just do normal things,' Leena said, and looked at my frown and laughed, 'OK, there is nothing normal in this mad place, but you know, don't ask too many questions, just be. We got a plan.'

'For how long,' I asked.

'Well we sort of have a plan,' Leena said.

Suli did a butterfly flip inside me.

'Suli likes you now,' I told her, and she burst out laughing.

'You're the same mad bitch you always were, Marah,' she laughed.

THE MISSION

I had to just act all *normal*, and go along with *The Plan*, and that was the plan! Me, about to give birth, wanted by all the evil bastards on planet earth, I just had to *be normal*. So I made normal tea, took extra-long normal naps, smiled at anyone normal enough to smile at me, and went for normal walks.

It was late afternoon and there was no sound of war. Only birds in the garden and a gentle wind rustling through the trees. Uncle Melvin re-materialised, from somewhere, knocked on my door and stomped in before I'd said anything, with a great big grin.

'You look champion, girl,' he said, handing a small package to me. It was lovingly wrapped up in gift paper.

If this is part of *The Plan*, then he deserves an Oscar, I thought.

I placed the parcel on the side of the bed and before I could tell him to go, he blurted, 'At least look at the present?'

It was a blue baby grow, which I threw in his face and cried.

He caught it, looked at it in silence for a moment, put it on the back of a chair and said, 'What do you want me to say?' and then answered himself, 'Sorry, I suppose.'

Suli kicked.

I blew my nose into a tissue and apologised to my son, 'Mummy shouldn't have done that.'

'Have you noticed how things have changed around here?' he asked.

Like it was difficult to avoid seeing all the new soldiers with their new hardware, I thought, and shrugged my shoulders.

'Let's go out and have a coffee at Watford Central Library, and be all normal like,' he suggested.

'Can I have ice cream instead?' I was a little girl again.

'As much as you can eat, and there's no Mum to say, "Make sure it's sugar free."' He was the old Uncle Melvin again, the one who used to take me and Tats out to Southall for kebabs and ice cream whenever he came to visit us in London.

I got up.

'I'll get the clearance sorted,' he said, and he'd left before I could ask where to meet him.

I got into my padded black coat, draped its belt across my bulge and walked out to find Uncle Melvin. Even though it was a lovely bright day, it was still cold. I blew into my hands and rubbed them and saw Leena talking to a soldier by the main entrance to the complex. She waved at me. A large SUV pulled up near her and out popped Uncle Melvin, who shouted, 'What the hell are you waiting for? Come on!'

He had a smartly dressed ESLA chauffeur, with a cap and dark glasses.

The car had a central armrest. We sat on either side.

'You've made lots of money then, Uncle Melvin?' I asked.

'Can't say I'm doing that bad, and I've bought a great big house in Glasgow,' he said as we drove through the checkpoint.

I waved at Leena. She winked back at me. 'Can I live there, Uncle Melvin?'

'That's why I bought it.' I pressed his hand.

The Watford outside the housing complex was not like the Watford I remembered. I had been to the city many times. Sometimes on Ash's bike, and a few times to weddings that always started late and never seemed to finish. It was easy to tell where Muslims must have once lived. These places were either burnt out, or in the process of being repaired by their new occupants. I couldn't find the Watford of my past.

'Oh, please!' I protested as I noticed Uncle Melvin taking the cigar out of his pocket.

'I'm not going to smoke inside the car,' he laughed, and then said to the driver, pointing to the lawn of the library, 'Pull over and park over there, where other cars are.'

Militiamen and women in different uniforms were milling around. Some people handed leaflets out and others sold magazines.

'I thought you brought me here for ice cream, Uncle Melvin,' I reminded him.

He ignored me, and asked a woman in a multi-coloured hat, 'Comrade, do you have a program?'

'It's in SW,' she said, taking a *Socialist Worker* from her pile and holding it out for Uncle Melvin.

'See how she's cornered me into buying a paper,' Uncle Melvin whispered to me, 'she's a capitalist at heart.' He took the paper, gave her a five-pound note and said, 'Donation.'

'Why don't you check out our meeting in Victoria Hall, comrade?' she said.

'Might do,' Uncle Melvin replied, stepping away from her.

He opened the paper and started looking through the program.

'No meeting!' I moaned. 'Been to enough with Mum.'

'We got to go to at least one, just to be normal like...'

'So this is *The Plan*?' I interrupted.

'How about this?' he said, reading the *SW*, 'Sport and the English Question.'

'When is it?' I asked. 'But just this one.'

'It's taking place right now,' he replied. Turning to the paper seller he asked, 'Where's Victoria Hall?'

She pointed to a building on the right.

'My ice cream?' I demanded.

'I promise,' Uncle Melvin laughed, 'Let's get this over though.'

And so we went to Victoria Hall. It was packed with people. We stood at the back of the hall. Proceedings of the meeting were being projected onto two large screens, one either side of the front of the hall. Helen sat on the stage between the screens. A balding old bespectacled white man next to her spoke passionately into a microphone. Helen shook her head in disagreement to his cockney accented words, which boomed around the hall, 'Cricket is a symbol of English imperialism. To propose holding the English tournament at this historical juncture, in the midst of all this madness, is surely playing into the hands of the forces of reaction. Into the hands of all that is bad. All that is backwards. All that the working masses have fought against for centuries. It would amount to a complete betrayal of the class struggle and here lies the basis of the primary contradiction...'

'How the fuck can you equate a ball and a bat with English Imperialism, Comrade?' a woman heckled from the audience.

'The primary contradiction is easy to identify, as all others revolve around it. The ball represents the colonised, and the bat the coloniser. It is time for us to embrace the movement for decoloniality of cricket.'

A few clapped, others shouted, 'Rubbish!'

'My kids are hungry,' a man shouted from somewhere in the and audience, 'and wet the bed every time there is an explosion, and you rant on about cricket!'

Someone near me whispered, 'Is it her?'

A woman sitting in the last row looked at me all startled.

'It's really her!' a louder whisper said from a different part of the room, and before long all heads were turned in my direction. The whisper quickly spread all the way to Helen. She saw me, smiled and nodded. I pursed my lips and nodded back.

'It really is the amazing Marah Sultana, comrades and friends.' Helen's voice rang through the P.A system. 'We are honoured to have such a courageous young woman in our midst.' Beckoning me towards her with her hand, she said, 'Come to the front, Marah, come say a few words.'

I waved my hands in refusal and shook my head.

'Please pass a microphone to Marah,' Helen asked.

I hadn't seen her come in, but Leena stood close by, near the door.

A man with a beard and round glasses handed me a cordless microphone.

I took the microphone and words just dropped out of my mouth, 'I came here because ...' I stopped, and looked at Uncle Melvin and said, 'he promised to buy me an ice cream.'

I went silent. Everyone clapped. I felt embarrassed at the stupid words that I had uttered. An image of Mum flashed through my mind and said into the microphone, 'My mum used to say, the pain of today, is the unresolved ache of yesterday...'

'I am sorry, Comrade Marah,' Helen interrupted me.

'Let her continue,' Someone interrupted Helen.

'There is an emergency broadcast of the Bloods coming right now,' Helen said authoritatively.

The screens behind her switched to the broadcast. I felt cold all over, seeing the Doctor standing next to the wheelchair bound aging King of England. They were in a great big room, in between two enormous English flags. Black cloaks with Bloods crucifixes draped down from the sides. Hundreds of candles burnt all around the room. Smoke rose from the ground and twisted up in a gentle blue light ground light.

I felt nauseous. I could smell the disinfectant of my hospital incarceration room, the Doctor and a memory of the King passing close to me in there flashed through my mind.

A Bloods choir suddenly erupted into song. *Jerusalem* burst into life on the screens, its sound resonating through the hall.

'I can't bear it, Leena,' I said to her. 'Let's get out.'

'Shhh,' a few whispers reprimanded.

Leena squeezed my hand, leaned towards me and said, 'We will in a minute.'

The choir continued. The King waved his frail hand. The camera zoomed in to his heavily made-up face. His head shook a little, and he smiled. Then waved his hand again.

I felt sick again, thinking that the King had been close to me, and didn't want to think anymore.

The Doctor stepped forward, raised his hands, looked up, and said, 'Lord God, your will is about to be fulfilled. The Lord of the world is coming. The Lord of Greater England is coming. The Second Coming is nigh. With the blessing of his Majesty, the next phase of our battle plans for the liberation of this long-suffering land are going to be declared today,' the doctor paused. There was pin drop silence.

I couldn't take it anymore and spoke into the microphone, 'Ya Allah, banish these bastards to the deepest of your hells!'

'Marah, stop!' Helen thundered.

The man who had given me the microphone stepped towards me and held his hand out.

'Do you want me to stop, Helen?' I said into the microphone, my words cut across those of the Doctor. 'I am a woman. God did not impregnate me. This is not the second fucking coming, but whatever it is, is mine. It is my body. My life. I ask the women in here. If they can do this to me, and claim this is Jesus, by Jesus, what else could they do to you tomorrow?' I took a breather, touched my stomach and said, 'This is my body. My baby, not God's. My baby, not any man's. Mine and mine alone, and let the world know, the world belongs to my baby and the babies yet to be born.' I stopped again and asked Helen. 'And you want me to stop talking? OK. I will.' I stopped, and threw the microphone in her direction as hard as I could and left the meeting.

Uncle Melvin and Leena followed me. When we got out of the building, Uncle Melvin said, 'Well, my girl, at least you were normal, you kept a low profile.'

'And that was one of your best poems,' Leena smirked.

I know you have no bloody plan, Leena,' I said.

'Oh, we do,' she said, 'you are so, so wrong.'

Can I please have my ice cream?' I whimpered.

'The biggest you can eat,' Uncle Melvin replied.

'Thanks, Uncle Melvin,' I said, 'Now what's this plan of yours?'

'To get Helen to trust you, you idiot,' Leena laughed.

THE DELIVERANCE

I was lying on my bed looking out of the window a couple of days later. A big brown leaf twisted and turned in the air, going down towards the ground. I felt very much at peace with the world, strangely, even when I saw Helen marching towards my bungalow. She had a uniformed male ESLA officer on either side of her and a fierce, determined expression on her face.

I adjusted a pillow underneath me for back support. There was a loud, confident knock on my door and Helen walked in alone, leaving the ESLA officers guarding the door.

She picked up a chair, turned it around so the back faced me, planted herself on it, one leg on either side, and gave me a toothy smile.

'Marah,' she said.

'Helen,' I replied.

Helen sighed and looked up at a corner of the room. 'I hope you are not upset with me for what happened at the meeting?'

'No, honestly, Helen,' I lied, 'I am a bit hormonal, you know.'

She nodded and said, 'You know, Marah, I really miss the long chats I used to have with your mum. If she was alive, she would be right here, with us, fighting for the true spirit of England, one that takes its rightful place among the free nations of this world. Don't you agree?'

Suli, your grandma would say, I said to my son inside my head, *The only way to free England is first free it from its Englishness,* but I said to Helen, 'Yeh, Mum had a saying for everything.'

'England has been an important nation in the world, and it will be again, and we will fight for it,' Helen said.

That England, which went on to conquer others, Hath made a shameful conquest of itself, I remembered how my mum told me Shakespeare had said this, and I told my son inside my head.

'Such a small country to have ruled such a big part of the world.' Helen continued.

My son, your grandma would say, *It only takes a few thieves to ruin the peace of the street.*

'Look at how much we've given to the world. What other language has given so much back to the world as English? Sack loads of new words, a universal language. As a poet, don't you agree with me, linguistically speaking, I mean,' Helen said.

I stroked Suli and thought, your grandma would say, *England plundered the world, and English has risen on the carcasses of so many languages,* but I replied, 'Indeed, English has taken a lot from others.'

'Marah, I believe in my heart of hearts England will defeat the Bloods. It is only a matter of time,' Helen said, throwing her words out carefully, one at a time.

I said nothing.

'I know how you feel,' she said, looking at the floor. 'I know how much trauma you have been through and how painful it can be for a woman to lose a child. I am one, after all,' she paused again.

Without looking at her, I nodded and thought, my son, she knows nothing about the pain of a mother.

'When you are better, you can join us as a poet fighter and recite for our troops.'

'Of course, I promise to do all I can,' I played along.

She smiled and declared, 'But I know you must be so anxious and scared. So let me tell you, we have ensured the best possible facilities are made available for your delivery and the family who are going to adopt the baby – I tell you, there could be no one better. They are such dedicated parents and they're desperate for a new baby. Their only child was killed in a bombing raid. I know they will care for and love your child as if he was their own. You do know we're doing all this for you, don't you?'

'I do,' I said, looking her in the face.

She blinked and turned away.

I had a few days left to my due date when Leena turned up late at night. She had a black bag with her.

'They have announced November 9 as the date of the second coming and have declared it a holiday.'

'But mine is November 15,' I said.

Leena shrugged her shoulders.

I rubbed my hands on Suli, just to reassure him, and said, 'No one will violate me again. No, will take my son.'

Leena pressed on my hand and said, 'Fate is on our side. Helen is no longer going to help in the delivery herself. She's appointed a new midwife, but this is all a sham, as they have decided they will do a caesarean. They don't want to take any chances, but our plan is simple really: we are going to fool them.' She looked at me proudly and continued, 'We are going to get the midwife pissed, and I am going to pretend to be you...'

'You're not serious!' I interrupted her.

'Seriously,' Leena said. 'Melvin knows her. He says she is a junky and always off her head...'

'Even pissheads know you have to get pregnant to deliver a baby,' I interrupted Leena again. 'Just a minor detail, is it?'

'Melvin will make sure she is off her head before she gets here, and by the time she arrives, the baby will have been born, and we will tell everyone,' Leena said, rummaging about in her bag, 'and to make it more authentic, we've got a plastic baby.' She waved a doll in front of me, which let out a baby cry and said, 'Wallah.'

I put my hand in front of my face to make sure my disbelieving grin didn't stop Leena from telling me the rest of this ingenious plan.

Leena continued, 'Ash and Tats will take you to the library and drive you through the underground Tunnel,' Leena said confidently. 'And, of course, Chilli will go with you.'

'And what happens to you?' I asked.

'I will knock the midwife out before she knows what is really going on and calmly walk out of the complex and find you before anyone suspects anything,' Leena paused and then added, 'The doll bit was just a bit of entertainment for you.'

'You're such a cow, Leena! This isn't the time for jokes. And the rest of the plan is just as bad.'

Leena laughed, 'If you can make poetry, I can have jokes. But don't worry – it's better than it sounds. We've organised some friendly people on the inside. You're going to have a sudden early delivery tomorrow – by the time the midwife comes, you'll have been whisked away. I promise you – it will work. We just have to get you into that tunnel.'

Typical Leena. She sat on the edge of the bed and held my hand. We talked about the old days and the days to come. Me and Ash living in a little house by the sea with our baby, that was my dream. But how likely was it to come true? We both knew there was a lifetime of hiding ahead until the Bloods were out of the way, at least. I was a woman with a price on my head; they would do anything to get me, to take my baby, and to end my life. But if that was my fate...

We didn't talk about any of that. We played make-believe. Usually, I like to speak about what is real, poetically or not. But I had my baby to think of now, and I wanted him to feel he was coming into a happy world. I would protect him from the horrors of the real world for as long as I could.

The light suddenly went out.

Leena stood up, looked out of the window and said, 'This is all wrong. 'Why are none of the generators working? Not one of them.' She thought for a moment and then said in a soldier's voice, 'We have to get out of here, now!'

Ash and Tats burst into the room, torches in hand.

'It's bad,' Tats said fearfully. I should have been scared, but for some reason I felt completely at ease and calm, as if I was certain that nothing bad could happen. But deep inside, I knew this was an illusion.

'The Bloods have arrived,' said Ash. 'They're not going to hand over the baby after all. They're going to hand over Marah.'

I got up suddenly.

'Where are you going?' demanded Leena. 'The toilet. You'll find out when it's your turn.'

I toddled off to the loo, leaving the three of them arguing furiously. When I came back to the room, I felt exhausted all of a sudden. Tats had run off somewhere, while Ash was on his radio in a corner, talking rapidly to someone. Leena told me what she knew. All fighting between the ESLA and the Bloods had stopped on all fronts, including the skirmishes between the Believers and the ESLA.

'Maybe the war is over?' I said.

'The war is not over. They made a deal,' Leena said. "So why knock the generators out?'

'It's a trick.'

Tats burst into the room and shouted, 'They're coming!'

'Ya, Allah, not now!' I said.

My waters broke.

Tats shone his torch on me.

'Give me some fucking dignity, Tats,' I swore, and he lowered the light.

※⁓⁓

A generator burst into life somewhere in the complex. It evened into a steady splutter and the lights began yellowing, then brightening with the fluctuating voltage. Outside, there was the roar of an engine. We all four ran to see. A wide circle of fairy lights had come on in the garden. They formed a circle around the apple tree. I could see a silhouette. Helen stood close to the edge of the lights, looking up. Then, the sound of the generator was drowned out as a helicopter roared across the sky in a howl of engine noise and hovered metres above the fairy lights. Aud was inside with an eyepatch. The Doctor was next to her.

'Marah, go with Tats!' Leena shouted at me.

They rushed for me in a collision of elbows. I struggled upright and let myself be hauled out of the room. The baby's head rocked into my spine. Corridors twisted, turned, dropped levels and switched surfaces, and I cursed creation.

We got out. Leena whacked a bar on a fire door behind us as we stumbled into the night air – straight into a stretch-skinned, goateed security guard who put his gun to her head, 'Right there. All of you. Freeze!'

The guard held Leena tight in front of him so Ash and Tats would have to shoot her to hit him.

Behind the guard came a streaking shadow that became a leaping blur. Then Chilli had the guard's arm in his fangs and tore at it. Leena slammed into the guard's groin with her knee, and the two of them rolled on the ground. I kicked away at the bundle of two bodies, trying to hit the black uniform of the guard. Both Tats and Ash had their guns out. In the end, it was Tats who bent down, put his gun to the man's head and blew a hole in it as big as my fist.

Leena got up, covered in blood. 'Take Marah, Tats, get to the tunnel.'

'I don't know my way around, you take her,' Tats said.

'He's right, Leena,' Ash said. 'You have to.'

Leena paused. 'You were to be with her. This was not part of the plan, Ash,' she said.

'It is different now. Go! Go and look after my son,' Ash said.

Suddenly, a powerful torchlight shone in our direction. Ash and Tats ducked, but a red dot flashed on Ash's head.

Leena grabbed my hand and yanked me towards a corner. Chilli followed.

'Run!' shouted Tats. Shooting behind us intensified. Leena dragged me into a nearby bungalow. We crashed through doors till we got to a locked one, marked Library. Leena fumbled with the combination and unlocked door, and we pushed our way in.

Behind us, the shooting stopped.

Inside, it was pitch dark. There were no windows – the air smelt of books. Leena put a torch on, and rows of shelves stacked with books spread in all directions. Leena dragged me forward through another door that led down some steps into another room. It, too, was pitch black. She switched on the light. A single naked bulb dangled down from the middle of the ceiling. It was a large workshop-type of a room with a small red car.

She opened the door of the car and said, 'Get in!'

Behind us, voices were shouting. Someone was kicking in a door. Leena ran to the furthest end of the room and opened a sliding door, came quickly back, and with me in the front and Chilli in the back seat, she picked a key up from under the mat.

As we drove off into a dark tunnel, Leena kissed me on the forehead. I put my left hand over my clenched right fist, with a 'V' for victory. The Ginnz salute. Leena did the same, and I said, touching my stomach, 'At least Suli will have an auntie Leena.'

Leena cried.

Chilli barked.

'And you too, Chilli,' I said, holding my salute up for him to see.

-»->-<-←-

Tariq Mehmood is a writer and filmmaker. He has authored several novels, including *Hand on the Sun* (Penguin 1983/Daraja Press 2024), which he wrote awaiting trial as part of the Bradford 12 – a group of young men arrested for organizing armed self-defense to protect their community in Bradford, northern England. Tariq was a leading defendant in the case, which carried the potential of life imprisonment. After a national and international campaign, all defendants were acquitted. The case of the Bradford 12 established the legal right of a community under threat to organize its own self-defense, including armed resistance.

Tariq is currently directing a feature-length documentary about this landmark case, which will be accompanied by a book. He is also the co director of the award-winning film *Injustice*, which exposed the scandal of police impunity in custodial deaths in the UK.

Tariq teaches at the American University of Beirut in Lebanon.

Also by Tariq Mehmood
from Daraja Press

You're Not Here

One brother goes missing in action in Afghanistan, the other falls in love with an Afghan girl in England.

Bitter divisions engulf an English town where young Muslims oppose the British army's presence in Afghanistan.

To the disgust of his white friends, 17-year-old Jake Marlesden, whose brother is missing in Afghanistan, is in love with Leila Khan, an Afghan. When Jake tries to find out what happened to his brother, neighbour turns against neighbour and lover against lover.

ISBN 978-1-988832-07-4 • 239 pages

Hand on the Sun

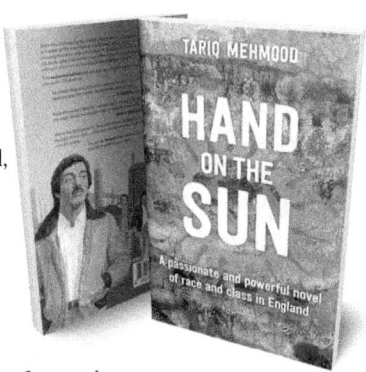

This was Tariq Mehmood's first novel, published by Penguin Books in 1983, charting the experience of second-generation migrants to the UK.

Set in the declining textile industry of the north of England, it is a raw story of pain and anger at the relentlessness of British racism, from the street to the state.

Are the issues of today just the issues of today, or can we learn something from the past?

In this new edition, Mehmood provides a foreword that describes how the novel came to be written and the lives of real people on whom the characters were created. In the Afterword, he revisits some of the characters.   ISBN 978-1-988832-58-6 • 200 pages

--------- **COMING SOON** ---------

Lines Of Fire
Poetry of the Afro-Asian Writers' Movement

This collection of poems features voices that have been persecuted for the power of their words. The poetry cries out against the injustices and brutality of the colonial powers of their time, raging against tyranny and the festering wounds of racism, especially in Palestine. Many writers of the movement faced torture, imprisonment, exile, and even death, but their words continue to call for a just world.

These poets span the length and breadth of Africa and Asia, and their poems speak to all of humanity.

ISBN 978-1-990263-45-3

Daraja Press

Order from **darajapress.com**